MW00761500

Sadie's Secret

A real story

by

Barbara D. Hall

and

Jon C. Hall

AuthorHouse™
1663 Liberty Drive, Suite 200
Bloomington, IN 47403
www.authorhouse.com
Phone: 1-800-839-8640

First published by AuthorHouse 12/17/2007

ISBN: 978-1-4343-3853-2 (sc)

Printed in the United States of America
Bloomington, Indiana

This book is printed on acid-free paper.

SADIE'S SECRET

Dedication

This book is dedicated to our generous ancestors
who had the wisdom to set aside some of
our most beautiful land for public enjoyment
and the preservation of habitats for the
bountiful creatures residing therein.

Of particular appreciation and enjoyment
of the authors are two of Florida's gems:
Myakka River State Park and
Ocala National Forest.

Barbara Hall

December 2006

SADIE'S SECRET

Acknowledgements

I would like to personally thank my sister Barbara D. Hall who continually encouraged me to take a pen in hand and put my stories down on paper. I first told her this story on returning home after my major brain stem stroke in December 2000. Her support included taking me to revisit Myakka River State Park and Ocala National Forest to refresh my memory of the pristine beauty of our natural world. These visits to two of my most favorite places in the world were the final stimulus for me to begin to tell the story on paper. Again, much appreciation and thanks go to my sister, whose untiring efforts and support in being a sounding board assisted in making this book a reality both in the ideas and assistance in writing this manuscript. Without her continued support and belief in my abilities, this book would not have been possible. Her continued guidance, perspective, and editorial assistance in the preparation of the preliminary and editing and writing the final drafts to complete the manuscript were crucial for the completion of this book.

Jon C. Hall

I would like to commend my brother Jon C. Hall for his untiring persistence in working on the preliminary drafts of this manuscript. His natural ability for story telling and unending creativity always held me captivated when he began spinning his tales. Sadly, Jon did not live to see this manuscript completed nor this book published. I am pleased to have the honor of finishing the final manuscript and seeing the book published. Again, I wish to share one more of my brother's tales with the reader.

I thank my father, Russell S. Hall for his unwavering support for both Jon and I in our endeavors to complete this manuscript and our other two works, *Bokuru* and *Adam's Eve*. His objective support is greatly appreciated. Thanks go to the continued support of The Write Group in Montclair, New Jersey. For completion of Sadie, special thanks go to Hannelore Hahn, founder of IWWG for her vision in creation of "the magic" at Skidmore, my spiritual guide Nina Reimer in her workshop, Dolls for the Soul, and to Leiah Bowden who guided me to remember the Indians. Information about the South Florida Indians and restoration of the Florida swamplands was found at the following websites: http://everglades.fiu.edu; www.seminoletribe.com, www.miccosukeeseminolenation.com;. Photographs for the front and back covers were taken by Barbara D. Hall on the visit to Myakka River State Park with her brother Jon.

Barbara Hall

SADIE'S SECRET

Introduction

For many years now, we have been captivated by stories and sightings around the world of a large, hairy humanoid creature known by many names as Bigfoot, Sasquatch, Yeti and other local names. The opinion behind these stories is that this enormous creature is so shy and elusive, no one has ever been able to make direct contact with an individual. But what would happen if such an actual creature lived next door or in your neighborhood? Would anyone believe it? Would people come to accept such a creature as a friend? Would the media make a news spectacle over the discovery of such an individual in our midst?

These are some of the questions the protagonist, Mike Byrne has to resolve in his own mind when confronted with a challenge to meet an alleged such individual. Digging down deep into his natural curiosity, Mike meets and investigates Sadie Sutton's mysterious origins. Will he find the truth? What will he do with it when he uncovers Sadie's Secret? Do others know the truth and what will they do with that knowledge?

The story of *Sadie's Secret* is set in the pristine natural environment surrounding what is now Myakka River State Park. The authors explore how and why these acres of land may have become a public park. Appreciation and respect for the flora and fauna in our Garden of Eden is an underlying theme of the story. How will an aging Sadie protect her heritage and the land after she has passed on, knowing that she has no living heirs to take over when she passes? Who will help her, or will others take advantage of her for their own personal aggrandizement or financial advantage?

Barbara Hall

SADIE'S SECRET

This book is the fictional story of one man's journey from agnostic concerning unusual phenomena into the realm of belief in the existence of humanoids in the swamps of West Florida. Inspired by the natural beauty of present day Myakka River State Park, not far from Sarasota, Florida, the story deals with human vulnerability to belief and how our natural propensity to adopt beliefs without scientific proof of their validity can be manipulated and used by others for their own purposes.

The story is mostly seen through the eyes of Mike Byrne, a member of the local Palmetto County Historical Society, as he volunteers to interview the oldest known citizen of the county, Sadie Sutton. He gradually becomes convinced there is more to her distant past than what she is willing to disclose for the society records. He becomes open to the ideas of the speaker at a presentation sponsored by the local Almas Association where his suspicions quickly evolve into the belief that Sadie carries the blood of the DeBosi in her veins.

As he struggles with his desire to prove his belief is true, Mike is drawn into the carefully structured snare of those who seek to use his belief for their own purposes. In this story, the end justifies the means in the name of a noble cause, and the swamp where Sadie has lived all her life is preserved. However, there is concern that belief, once encouraged and nurtured, may put in motion forces that will destroy the objectives of those who seek to take advantage of others.

Jon C. Hall

Contents

Chapter One

The Historical Society

Mike Byrne was late. By the time he drove into the parking lot of the Banyan Hotel, he knew he had missed most of the meeting. A last minute phone call at his office in downtown Brandon, Florida, had delayed him and had trapped him in the height of the evening rush hour traffic. The six-mile drive out on State Road 744 to the hotel at the intersection with Interstate 275 had taken longer than he had planned.

Wasting no time parking his car, he entered the lobby. Walking briskly down the corridor to the meeting room, Mike did not pause to check the room assignments posted in the lobby. The familiar sign stood on a chrome pedestal outside the third door on his right. The sign announced: Reserved: Palmetto County Historical Society.

Embarrassed by being late, he quietly slipped into a seat in the back row. He recognized the three women seated at the speaker's table. Ms. Abigail Abernathy, president of the society, seated in the middle, was speaking into a microphone. As she spoke, she turned to address Samantha Edgerton, treasurer, sitting on her right.

"Thank you, Samantha, for our comprehensive treasurer's report. We are always comforted to know the society is sound and solvent and our funds are securely invested. Do we have any questions from the floor?" she asked, now turning to face the audience.

Surveying the room, Mike silently counted the attendees. Of the thirty-seven people in the audience, including himself, no one responded to the question.

"Do I have a motion to accept the report as written?" she asked, looking at the attendees.

"I move the report be accepted as written," a bald man in the second row responded. Mike could not identify the man because he could only see the back of the man's head.

"I second the motion," said a woman a couple of rows in front of Mike. He recognized her from prior meetings, but could not recall her name.

"The motion has been moved and seconded," said Ms. Abernathy. "All those in favor, raise your right hand. Remember, guests are not members and do not have the right to vote. Members only, please."

The majority raised their hands.

"Do you have a count of hands, Sandy?" she asked, turning towards Sandra Stillwell, the society secretary, sitting on the opposite end of the speaker's table. Sandy, a thin, plain woman in her mid-twenties, dressed in a gray business suit and steel framed glasses, stood momentarily counting the raised hands.

Mike had missed hearing the report, so he did not vote.

"Twenty-seven," said Sandy, addressing Mrs. Abernathy.

Mike normally didn't like to stereotype people but Sandy matched his mental image of a bank teller, knowing, in fact, she worked as senior teller at First Bank in Brandon. Mrs. Abernathy and Mrs. Edgerton were in their mid-seventies. Both retired widows lived in the Briarwoods subdivision just north of town on U.S. 41. As he chuckle to himself, he remarked how, actually, all three women matched his visions of what officers of an historical society would look like.

"Now, those opposing the motion, raise your hands," Ms. Abernathy requested.

No hands appeared.

"Well," she said looking back at Samantha Edgerton, "I think that says a lot for how you are handling our finances."

The attendees applauded lightly, following her remark. Samantha smiled and nodded appreciatively towards the audience.

"Under the category of old business," continued Ms. Abernathy, "Mr. Hugh Taintor, the architect and one of our members, was scheduled to speak to us this evening about the feasibility of renovating the old Graystone Abstract Building. However, Mr. Taintor called to inform me he had to go out of town and could not make this meeting tonight. He promised to address this project at our meeting next month. Mr. Taintor sends his apologies. We already discussed the potential grant funds for the restoration project if costs for acquisition and restoration are reasonable and fall within the projected budget. The committee plans to meet next Tuesday here at the hotel. Mr. Taintor assured me he will be present. If anyone would like to attend this meeting, please see Sally Bartlow, the committee chairperson, immediately after this meeting."

She paused for a moment before continuing.

A woman in the first row raised her hand. Mike recognized her as Mrs. Bartlow.

"Yes Sally…"

"Mr. Alfred Justin, over there is a guest with us this evening. Please raise your hand. He asked me before we opened the meeting why we have our meetings here and not in the municipal building downtown. He was concerned about the cost, commenting that use of the municipal meeting room is free. He wondered why we pay to rent a room here instead. We have not addressed this topic for some time. I'll answer his question while we're in general session." She glanced around the room before continuing.

"This society is not associated with the state, federal or local government in any way. We are a state chartered not-for-profit corporation. Unfortunately, insurance requirements restrict the use of the room you referred to, Mr. Justin, to government functions. As a result, the general public is prohibited from using the municipal building rooms. A few years ago, we did meet in the public library down the street from the municipal building, but this arrangement didn't work out. The library required us to commit a month in advance to reserve the room so that hampered our need for flexibility. In addition, the town manager added a surcharge for air conditioning since we don't contribute to the town taxes. To use the room, we had to obtain keys in advance to lock up the room when we were finished and return them the next day. Frankly, their requirements were not worth the time and trouble. One month, we forgot to pick up the keys and were locked out, and on another occasion, we had no air conditioning due to a mix up in scheduling. Everyone agreed, the lack of a coffee shop nearby contributed to more dissatisfaction. We enjoyed meeting socially afterwards and the library could not accommodate that activity. Here, the hotel coffee shop operates seven days a week until 11:00 P.M. A good number of us enjoy socializing in the coffee shop after the meeting. So, the library also wasn't convenient and did not accommodate the camaraderie we are used to. The costs here are a bit more, but the hotel can adjust to our meeting times as needed. Since they have several meeting rooms, one is always available. For example, we reserved the Cypress Room down the hall, but earlier today we realized that we wanted a larger room. Moving the meeting into this room took a simple phone call. In addition, attendees coming by the interstate appreciate the advantage of missing rush hour traffic. Now, have I answered everyone's questions?" she asked.

"Yes," a male voice responded from the front of the room. Mike assumed it was Mr. Justin.

"I'd like to know what happened to the free coffee," stated a woman in the second row.

"Some months ago, the hotel management discontinued free coffee with conference room rentals of less than half a day. The coffee shop, as I said, is open so we can get coffee there," said Ms. Abernathy. "Now, does anyone else have a question?"

The room was silent.

"The only other item we did not cover earlier," continued Ms. Abernathy, turning again towards Sandy Stillwell, "is the status of the Sadie Sutton Project. I know Sandy wanted to open the discussion on this project when Mr. Byrne arrived. Now that he has arrived, I pass the chair to Sandy," she said as she slid the microphone across the table to where Sandy could reach it.

"For our guests here this evening," Sandy began, "Sadie Sutton lives alone at Indian Bend. Indian Bend was a turn of the century settlement in the Seminole Indian River Slough. The slough is located about fifteen miles east of here off SR 744 and north on the old shell road about two miles."

"What is a slough?" asked a man in the third row. "You keep using that term and I'm not familiar with it."

"A slough is a swamp, a low wetland area with a shallow stream running through it. Have you ever visited Everglades National Park?" asked Sandy.

"Sure," answered the man, "A couple of times."

"As you pass through the entrance to the park, an overhead culvert crosses the main road beyond the welcome area and before the turnoff to the Anhinga Trail. Right at that point, a sign labeled Taylor Slough marks the beginning of the slough. Taylor Slough spreads across both sides of the road extending down to and including the Anhinga Trail. This particular area provides an excellent example of a slough. Slough is an old term used here in Florida for a large number of swamplands throughout the state. The Seminole Indian River Slough includes an area of about twenty thousand acres, surrounded by large ranches and farms. Because of the farms and ranches, the only way to find it is local knowledge of the access roads. Due to limited access, the natural wetland has remained pristine. This swampland includes the area where the Seminole Indian River makes an interior delta before reforming and resuming its course out to Sawgrass Bay and emptying into the Gulf of Mexico."

"Thank you," said the man who had asked the question.

"A year ago, Ms. Abernathy asked me to see if I could find the site of the original Indian Bend settlement," Sandy continued. "At that time, we were considering working on an article or a small booklet on Indian Bend for the library. The land where Mrs. Sutton lives covers many acres surrounded by farms and cattle ranches. When I first visited there, I found the remains of several structures and one intact cabin that appeared to be occupied. When I knocked on the door, Ms. Sutton invited me in. I learned from talking with her that she was a widow, well over one hundred years old. She was mentally as sharp as someone half her age. Once I told the society about her, we decided to slant the project as a story about the early years of the county from the perspective of a person who had lived without all of our modern conveniences. Ms. Sutton graciously agreed to be interviewed. Mr. Stan Kovolesky, the former editor and owner of The Palmetto County Gazette, volunteered to interview her. As an active member of the society, he was enthusiastic about doing the story for the paper; however, when he suffered a serious stroke, he was not able to start the project. Recently, I talked with Mr. Mike Byrne, one of our newer members, about the project. He is here with us this evening. When asked, he graciously agreed to take Mr. Kovolesky's place on the project."

She paused and looked directly at Mike.

"Mike, would you kindly stand, so everyone can see who you are?" Ms. Abernathy requested.

Mike stood briefly, smiled, and nodded slightly as the attendees turned to see him in the back of the room.

"Sadie was born right here in Palmetto County and she has lived in her cabin at Indian Bend her whole life. Due to her age, we must interview her as soon as possible, while she still has her health. Her age underscores the urgency, as she appears to be somewhere between one hundred eight and one hundred fifteen years old. We believe Sadie Sutton is one of the oldest residents in the county, if not the country. We are deeply indebted to Mr. Byrne. He has scheduled his first interview with Ms. Sutton this weekend," said Sandy, as she passed the microphone back to Ms. Abernathy.

"The Sutton Project committee consists of Ms. Stillwell, Mr. Byrne, Mr. Kovolesky, who is still on our list although inactive, and myself. As a former newspaper reporter, I've volunteered to help put together the final manuscript. We encourage any other interested members to contact Sandy if they would like to work on the project. We have restricted the actual interview process to one person for continuity and to assure Ms. Sutton will be comfortable with that person. Again, I extend many personal thanks to Mr. Byrne for volunteering his time to the project. For those of you who don't know Mike, he works in the County Clerk's office, in Brandon. He's been a member of the historical society for about four years. If I'm not mistaken, he just celebrated his thirty-second birthday last month," said Ms. Abernathy, who paused to smile at Mike momentarily, then continued.

"We are interested in Sadie Sutton because she provides us with a living example of what life was like before the automobile, electricity, air conditioning, television, and all our other modern conveniences. I understand, she reads a lot and is up to date on current events. In spite of help from some of the local ranchers, for years Miss Sutton has lived in her primitive cabin without the modern conveniences we take for granted. Ms. Stillwell has arranged for Ms. Sutton to be added to the county support fund as well. Anyway, I agree with Sandy, that time is of the essence for this project. We appreciate Mike's willingness to give up a few Saturdays to support this project. Again, I thank you Mike, on behalf of the society for contributing your time," she smiled again in Mike's direction.

The attendees applauded.

"Now we can move to our program for this evening. I am pleased to introduce Billie Fleetfoot from the Immokalee Seminole Reservation. He will inform us about the history of the Seminole Tribe of Florida and how they are surviving today. Billie, my pleasure."

Billie Fleetfoot rose from his seat in the first row. His tall, heavy framed figure exhibited the traditional Seminole dress for a male. A colorful plaid, wool turban was wrapped majestically around his head. He sported a full-cut shirt decorated with a colorful patchwork placket stitched down the front, and a leather belt tied loosely at his waist. He joined Mrs. Abernathy at the front of the room, taking the microphone into his hands.

"Good evening ladies and gentlemen of the Palmetto County Historical Society. Thank you for inviting me here this evening to tell you about my people and their history here in southern Florida. The Seminoles have been continuous residents here for many thousands of years. We owe our existence to the land. As Seminoles, we believe the health of the land and our health are inseparable. We as a people cannot be separated from the land. Our oral history tellers recount our belief in maintaining the land. Historically, they have warned us that if the land becomes ill, then we shall soon become ill as well; and if the land dies, the Tribe dies. We are a proud, free people who fought bitter wars in the 1800's with the white man to continue to live here. We were the first inhabitants in Florida, many years before the Spanish found us when they came looking for the Fountain of Youth in the early 1500's.

"Without going too deeply into the dark history beginning with the departure of the Spanish colonization of South Florida, I will summarize our history. Before the Revolutionary War, the Indian tribes from the North were driven southward as the American colonies grew. Constant turmoil with the Spanish, the French and American colonists caused many Indians to flee into the Spanish territories to join the native Seminole in Florida. Prior to their arrival we spoke one language, Mikosuki, even though we were hundreds of different tribes. But, we became a blended culture as the other tribes of Creek, Hitchiti, Apalachee, Mikisuki, Yamassee, Yuchi, Tequesta, Apalachicola, Choctaw and Oconee refused to be dominated by the white man as he pushed the native Indians out of the northern states. With the advent of the Civil War and rebellion of American slaves, many escaped slaves from Virginia, Georgia, Alabama, and the Carolinas joined the Indian settlements throughout the state. All of these peoples shared the same goal, refusal to be dominated or ruled by the white man. These people exhibited steadfast determination to hold onto our homelands, unlike the history of other Indian tribes in the US. As hard as they tried, for nearly forty-five years, the white man failed to remove the Seminole from Florida. Our ancestors resisted relocation and refused to give up their homeland. We fought three wars initiated to dominate and break our spirit. Many lives were lost on both sides, with great expenditures of money by the US government to prevail. However, the US government never signed a peace treaty with the Seminole nation. The Seminoles were so stubborn, the US government finally gave up, lacking money and manpower to continue the dispute in the inhospitable swamps where the Indians retreated. This history is probably one of the blackest for the US government due to their trickery in proposing false truces to Osceola and Billie Bowlegs. These two fearless Seminole leaders were duped by false truce meetings, captured and imprisoned in hopes of ending hostilities and motivating the Indians to move to reservations in Arkansas and Oklahoma. One of the Seminole's greatest leaders, a medicine man named Abiaka led the spirit of the Indians to hold strong in the swamps and the Everglades. He remained one of the strongest forces holding the spirit of the Seminole resistance.

"After the end of the Seminole Indian Wars, slowly the remaining Seminoles began trading with the white man at the edges of civilization beginning in the late 1890's. These Seminoles were hunters, trappers, and fishermen, trading alligator skins and egret feathers for things they needed for survival in the harsh environment. As the white man expanded into the wilds of Florida, they set up farms and cattle ranches.

By the time the Tamiami Trail opened in 1928, many of the Seminoles had developed trades at the edges of the swamp offering Indian baskets, blankets, necklaces, clothing, and wood carvings. Many set up tourist attractions along the roads with alligator wrestling, village tours and boat rides into the swamps. With these attractions, the Indian economy took a new step out of the deep retreat into the swamps. When the government began to drain the swamp in the early 1900's, life in the swamp for the Seminoles collapsed. Those few remaining in the swamps moved to subsistence and tenant farming, beginning the move out of the swamps. By the late 1930's, the US government had set up several large land grants to return land to the Seminoles where now Big Cypress Reserve, Hollywood and Brighton reservations are located. Few Seminoles moved into these lands due to the long-standing distrust of the white man and his politics. Only when threatened to lose the land in 1947, the Indians recapitulated and took interest in accepting management of the government reservations.

"From that time on, the Seminoles learned other trades to develop a successful economy. In 1971 the Tribe began selling tax-free tobacco on the reservations. Taking on new trades caused the change in how the Seminoles viewed themselves. In 1979 the Tribes established Bingo games in Immokalee and Tampa, followed by Hollywood in 1981. With the advent of high stakes bingo in Hollywood, the Tribes moved into running limited casinos. By 1982, gaming had become highly successful in Hollywood, Immokalee and Tampa. In 1996, Fort Pierce was added as a Reservation. Now, we have become a major employer and generate a significant income to become self-supporting of the Seminole Tribes of Florida. Our governing body built its headquarters in Hollywood near the original Oak Council tree where the tribes historically met.

"However, the Tribes have never forgotten their responsibility to the land. Out of concern for the damage done to the swamps and particularly the Everglades when the government started draining the swamps in the early 1900's, we have played a major role in the restoration of the natural environment in Southern Florida. We work closely with the government agencies, universities and environmental groups to manage the watershed, the lifeblood of the Everglades, and to restore the land to its natural state. As a result, there have been many pieces of legislation passed to continue this activity, including the Everglades Forever Act, the Comprehensive Everglades Restoration Plan, the Restudy program, the Everglades Expansion and Protection Act as well as educational programs sponsored by the National Park Service. These projects have brought money, people and programs to turn around the threatened death of the ecosystem.

"Today, the descendents of the original tribes including the Seminole Tribe of Florida, the Miccosukee Indian Tribe of Florida and the unaffiliated Independent or Traditional Seminoles have grown from a few thousand individuals who held fast to the land in the Everglades and swamps of Florida, refusing to be relocated under the direction of the US government. The Tribes now encompass six financially powerful Reservations: Big Cypress, Brighton, Ft. Pierce, Hollywood, Immokalee, and Tampa under the government of the Seminole Tribes of Florida and the Miccosukee Seminole Nation. Believing steadfastly in maintaining the health of the land, we are committed to assure the health and survival of the land in Southern Florida.

"Thank you everyone. I invite you to visit our reservations, villages and museums, including the one nearby here in Immokalee. Thank you Mrs. Abernathy."

"Thank you Billie. If anyone has any questions, Billie has agreed to stay for a few minutes to chat with our members. Now that we have covered all the issues on our agenda this evening and if there is no other business, I will entertain a motion to adjourn. Those wishing to join us for coffee may do so in the café."

Chapter Two

Orientation

The rain drizzled down steadily on Saturday morning when Mike left his apartment complex in downtown Brandon. He drove east on SR 744 towards the interstate on his way to Sandy's designated meeting place, the Lucky Star Diner. The diner was located about a mile short of the intersection of SR 744 with the Interstate. The rain had discouraged the usual morning customers, so he pulled into a nearly empty parking lot.

By the time he parked his car, the rain had diminished to nothing more than a light sprinkle. He decided to leave his umbrella on the front seat. Habitually, he would leave his umbrella in the car whenever possible unless a heavy downpour demanded use of the umbrella. As usual, he chose to brave the rain to avoid forgetting it when he took it with him. Once inside the diner, he found Sandy seated at a booth near the front window reading a newspaper. When she looked up and saw him, she smiled and waved.

"Good morning, Sandy."

"Good morning, Mike. Thanks for coming out in such bad weather," she said putting the newspaper down. "I was worried that you might just roll over and go back to sleep this dismal morning."

"No problem. Remember, I volunteered for this project, rain or shine."

"Here's a menu. All I've had so far is a cup of coffee. Let's order something. I'm starved."

"Sounds good to me. The aromas are firing up my appetite."

"Breakfast is on the society this morning. I recommend the breakfast special. It's the best buy on the menu."

Mike accepted the menu from her. When their waitress arrived, both ordered the breakfast special. Sandy ordered her eggs sunny side up and Mike had his scrambled, "Like my brains in the morning," he grinned.

Mike had first met Sandy at one of the historical society meetings. Several years ago she had introduced herself after the meeting and had invited him to join the usual group at the hotel coffee shop. Mike enjoyed the camaraderie of the group, so after that time, he regularly joined them for coffee. On one of those occasions, Sandy had asked Mike to help her with the Sadie Sutton Project. Intrigued by the information Sandy had told him about Sadie, he readily volunteered. Sitting with Sandy in the diner, he realized that he knew very little about her or her personal life outside the historical society.

"I always start the day with a good breakfast," she said. "For me, breakfast is the most important meal of the day. On Saturdays, if I don't feel like putting something together at home, I like to come here."

"I'm a creature of habit. I usually skimp on breakfast and have a donut or bagel and coffee in the morning at the dashboard cafe. Today's an exception. I'm not used to eating such a big meal so early."

"The health experts say it's best to start the day with something substantial, followed by a light lunch, if you're into healthy eating. Anyway, I appreciate the time you're donating to this project. I need all the help I can find to complete it. You realize you must give up a few Saturdays."

"I don't mind. I have some extra time on my hands right now and interviewing Sadie sounds interesting to me. I'm happy to volunteer."

"Does your wife object to missing you on Saturdays?"

"Oh, I'm not married. In fact, I'm recently detached. My ex-fiancée decided she didn't want to battle the humidity and insects in Florida. She missed her family and friends in Delaware."

"Sorry about your fiancée, but I'm glad you have the time."

"I'm looking forward to this project to fill in some empty time right now. Besides, I'm also interested in the slough. My grandfather used to take me out a lot into the parks and fishing in Delaware when I was a young boy. He wanted me to develop a love and appreciation for nature. I have many fond memories of our times together."

"I'm glad you're interested in the project. Some of the others really didn't want to go out into the slough. I got the feeling they were actually afraid of going out there. The insects and potential of meeting some wild creature of the slough intimidated them. Most people these days aren't the least bit interested in nature or the creatures living there."

"Well, I'm not afraid of nature. Lizards and insects play an important role in our food chain. Most people support the authorities in spraying to kill the mosquitoes. What they don't realize is that the insecticide kills more than the mosquitoes. They forget that all these insects supply food for the birds, fish, frogs and lizards living in the same environment. What ends up happening is the creation of a dead zone where they've sprayed. Spraying affects the whole food chain."

"You're right. No bugs, no birds. You won't have that problem today at Indian Bend. I hope you brought some insect repellant. They can be pretty bad this time of year."

"I'm set. How do I find Sadie's cabin?"

Sandy pulled a folded paper out of her handbag. "I sketched this map to show you where we are and how to get to Sadie's cabin. It's really easy. On your way out of town, stay on SR744 going east, pass under the interstate overpass, then watch your odometer. Your turn off SR744 onto the old shell road is almost exactly fifteen miles past the interstate."

"I see it marked on the map," said Mike.

"Don't lose my directions. Since it's a private road on private property, the shell road doesn't appear on any commercial maps. The tricky part is finding the entrance from SR744 since the turn is easy to miss. If there ever was a county road sign for it, it's long gone. Be careful, the vegetation obscures the opening for the road. You can only turn left and go north. Since the road isn't paved, it blends in with the surrounding area."

"I'll rely on your map."

"Here's the key landmark, right there on the sketch," she continued, pointing to a mark on the map. "I drew the corner of a fence on the edge of the shell road. That fence marks the boundary for the Circle T Cattle Ranch. The ranch property runs on both sides of SR744. The fence on the south side of the state road begins about a half mile closer to town, so when you see a white fence on your right, start looking for the fence to start on your left. That's the exact point where the turn onto the shell road is located. Remember, when the fence begins on your left, turn immediately off SR744, keeping the fence on your right."

"Okay, watching for the fence makes it easy. Thanks for the help."

"If you see white fences on both sides of the highway, you've gone too far. It's that simple."

"From your map, it looks like Sadie's house is located about a mile and a half north on the shell road."

"That's right, watch for the cabin along the road. Only one cabin remains standing out there now, Sadie's cabin. It's set into the vegetation on the left, just before the road swings around in a wide turn to the right to avoid the slough. That curve is called Indian Bend. Years ago, five or six cabins were located at the Bend. When I first went exploring there, I was looking for the settlement. All I found was Sadie's cabin and the remains of the others."

"Isn't Indian Bend one of the former locations of a Seminole settlement?"

"Yes, they set up some tourist traps along the shell road when the relationships with the white man started turning around. That was in the early 1900's, well after the end of the Third Seminole War and the Civil War. The Seminoles began emerging at the edges of the Everglades around the turn of the century. A few of the renegade Seminoles remained at Indian Bend."

"I'm sure the Indians played an important role in Sadie's life while they were there. I've studied the stories of the Seminoles here in Florida and attended many of the lectures we've had about them at the historical society meetings."

"Well, the Indians weren't able to stay there long after the government started to drain the swamps and the hurricanes hit. Sadie will fill in her story. You shouldn't have any difficulty finding her cabin if you follow the map."

"You've been very helpful. This is an adventure for me. I've never driven out SR 744 beyond the interstate. With your map and directions, I don't see how I can miss. Since I only make one turn off SR744 onto the shell road, it's simple. I can handle that. What happens if I miss her place and keep on going?"

"The road only goes around the bend a short distance before it ends, maybe a quarter mile, but that's all. The rest of the road washed out years ago. If you drive around the Bend, you can't go far. You'd have to turn around and come back. The shell road used to be the east-west road across the State, ambling all over the place. The state straightened out all the twists and turns with the paved two-lane highway when they built SR 744. The state abandoned the shell road when it washed out. Just watch for the fence."

"So, tell me about Sadie Sutton. I understand our objective with the society is to write a book about her."

"That depends on how much information you're able to obtain. The outcome of the project lies in your hands. Maybe she'll remember something about the Indian settlement. Ask her about that, too."

"If she's as old as you say, will she understand me? Will I understand her?" asked Mike. "With the elderly, sometimes communication can be an issue."

"Mike, don't be concerned. She's amazing. She's alert beyond the norm for her age. She can hear and understands everything you say and she speaks clearly. Do you have something to write notes on?"

"I brought my briefcase with pens and notebooks. I left them in the car with my tape recorder."

"Good. But don't take anything into the cabin with you that might intimidate or upset her. We don't want anything to inhibit her from talking freely. Leave the tape recorder in the car. I think it might intimidate her. Take notes manually."

"Okay, I can do that."

"Mike, you'll like her. She's a sweetheart, but you'll have to go slowly and listen carefully. Can I offer another suggestion?" she asked.

"Sure."

"Don't even wear your watch. She doesn't have any modern conveniences and she doesn't want them either. We don't want to do anything to create any anxiety. Leave your briefcase and your watch in the car. Let her be able to see what you have openly, so carry your notebook and pens into the cabin in your hands. She's very sensitive and sharp as a whip."

"If I don't have my watch, how will I know when to stop?"

"Don't go beyond a couple of hours, anything longer will tax her physically. She tires easily and then she fades away. Watch her carefully and stop when she gets tired. You'll hear it in her voice. End the session when she tires and excuse yourself. You're set to go back again next Saturday so don't try to do too much in one meeting. Since she's so old, be alert and considerate."

"I've got it."

"Oh, yes. There's one other thing. Occasionally, an old ranch hand stays there and looks out for her. His name is Ivan something. I only know him as Ivan. You probably won't see him, but he'll be around somewhere."

"You're sure I won't see him? Should I interview him, too?"

"No, just Sadie. He's shy and will avoid you. Would you like another cup of coffee?"

"No, thanks. One cup is all I can handle. Is there anything else you can suggest that might help? You've been great so far."

"Oh, now that you ask, check your gas tank."

"My gas tank?"

"Yes, there's nothing on SR 744 past the interstate, Mike, nothing but farms and ranches for miles and miles. You'll see undeveloped woodlands and swamp along the river, but that's all. There isn't another gas station beyond the interstate for over forty miles. To find the nearest one, you'd have to go all the way to Pahokee or down to Immokalee. So, be sure your gas tank is full," warned Sandy.

"I filled up this morning. I should be fine. Thanks for the warning."

"Good. I think you're ready. Remember, we'll meet back here today at two o'clock to debrief and review your notes. Remembering what you didn't write down will be fresh when you get back. We'll tape the debriefing then. I wrote my home phone number on the back of my business card. Keep it with you." Sandy said as she handed Mike her card. "Call if you get back early. I live down the street in the Greenleaf Apartments, the ones you passed on your way here."

"Well, I'm on my way to my first interview with Sadie Sutton."

"Good luck," said Sandy. "I'll take care of the bill. As I promised, today, breakfast is on the historical society."

"Thanks for everything, Sandy. I'll see you at two."

Chapter Three

First Encounter

By the time Mike drove under the overpass for the interstate, the light drizzle had stopped and the hot Florida sun had disbursed the fog and was piercing through lightly scattered clouds.

Sandy's map was accurate and her directions crucial. Without the map and her warnings, Mike realized he would have missed the turn. Exactly as she had described, the entrance to the shell road was hidden by thick, overhanging vegetation where the white fence for the ranch began. The compact concretion of shells, coral and sand kept the weeds from completely taking over the single lane trail.

The narrow road ran north, straight back into the woods beyond the open grasslands and palmettos. The white fence extended parallel to the road for about a quarter of a mile before it turned east into the trees. Spanish moss hung from the live oaks that peppered the open range where cattle grazed behind the fence. Gradually, the open grasslands gave way to a subtropical forest where the sabal palms dominated the oak/palm hammock. Once he passed into the dense forest, the thick canopy of trees blocked out the sun. He found himself surrounded in a land of shadows, broken only by occasional rays of sunlight that filtered through the lush foliage. Here and there, the sun sparkled off raindrops left over from the morning shower. The remaining humidity created a thin, mysterious mist. What a magical place, Mike thought to himself, magical with a feeling of timelessness mixed in.

Birds of all kinds flew amongst the trees. Wildlife scurried through the thick vegetation. The forest teemed with birds, insects, tiny mammals and reptiles scampering through the underbrush. The birds and insects fluttered in the upper levels of the trees. Mike had grown up with an appreciation of the outdoors in his childhood home in Delaware, guided by his grandfather, but looking at the wonderland before him, the woods there did not compare to the richness of the hummock spread out before him. Although it was mid-morning, he recounted the wildlife he had seen already: chipmunks, squirrels, a family of wild boar with piglets scurrying across the road in front of the car, and even an occasional armadillo grazing in the grasses. He turned off the air conditioner and opened his window to hear the chorus of birds. His invasion of the woods along the narrow road had not disrupted the delicate beauty of this natural world. The air smelled of the damp, humid aroma of warm, rotting vegetation from the open wetland. Due to the thick vegetation, he could see no more than a hundred yards to his left. The heat and humidity here was less intense, not like it had been back up on the open grasslands by the highway under the direct rays of the sun. The denser vegetation shielded the lower levels of the forest from the constant barrage of the tropical sun.

He passed a break in the trees on his right where he could see a rich green meadow through the trees and shrubby growth. There, a doe and her fawn stood alert, frozen in place, like plaster statues on an unkempt lawn, looking intently in his direction. Curiously, they appeared to be unafraid, as they did not bolt. Perhaps invaders such as he were so rare the deer needed time to assess the danger before reacting. As he eased his car slowly past the meadow, the deer resumed feeding, unconcerned about the intruder in their domain.

Man, he thought silently to himself, and his contraptions did not belong in this rich wilderness. He felt guilty that his presence could only spoil its natural beauty. Ahead, the road began a gradual curve to the right. He had reached Indian Bend.

Just as Sandy had told him, the cabin was nestled among the palmettos along the turn, exactly where she had marked the map. The road and the cabin broke the density of the trees and vegetation for a brief interlude in nature's prolific growth. To his left, Mike observed a complex strangler fig tree, wrapping its narrow tendrils around a huge cypress tree between the cabin and the shell road. He parked in front of the cabin, partially blocking the road, unconcerned since there would be no traffic there. From the strong smell of tar intensifying as he approached the cabin, Mike could tell the exterior of the logs had recently been coated with creosote to ward of nature's unrelenting assault. The screens in the front porch appeared to have been installed recently. Wood shingles lined the surface of the roof, also appearing almost new. Although, the cabin had obviously been built a long time ago, it emitted an aura of being well maintained. Between the cabin and the fig tree, a walkway made of flat weathered boards ran back about seventy yards through the hummock extending to a dock at the edge of the swamp. Sitting in his car, Mike noted the lack of exterior electric light fixtures, lack of electrical and telephone wires, no mailbox, and no numbers affixed to the cabin, yet the cabin gave him the unmistakable impression of being occupied and cared for.

When he turned off the engine, the tranquility of the forest pleasantly replaced the steady rumble of the engine. Only the sound of the chattering birds and occasional croak of the bullfrogs in the swamp broke the reverie. He gathered a couple of pens and a notebook and stepped out of the car. Once in the warm moist air, he felt as if he were wrapped up in a heavy blanket. Removing his jacket, he silently realized he would have to endure the absence of air conditioning for this interview. As he contemplated the implications of living without modern conveniences in the cabin, he tapped lightly on the screen door.

"Ms. Sutton," Mike said in a soft voice. "Are you home? I'm from the historical society."

"C'mon in Mr. Byrne. I've been expecting you. Sandy told me you were coming. You don't have to knock on no doors here in the slough," came a voice from within. He was at a loss for words. Her voice resonated with a haunting pitch that he could not describe.

"Yes, Ma'am," he said softly, as he opened the screen door. Mike was not prepared for what he encountered when he stepped inside. Perhaps, he thought, she would be an old woman, a grandmotherly type, sitting in a chair, knitting, but no more. The vision he encountered stunned him. The porch was draped with a fine, gauze curtain hanging from the ceiling to the floor and stretching from the front door of the cabin across to the screen door at the front of the porch. He could barely detect the silhouette of a small figure seated in a rocking chair at a distance behind the curtain. A small, square table covered with a clean, white linen tablecloth sat in the open area in front of the gauze curtain. A tall glass of light brown liquid rested in the center of a coaster in the middle of the table. A single wooden chair beside the table faced the curtain and the silhouette behind it.

As Mike gazed at the empty chair, Sadie spoke from behind the curtain. "That chair is for you, and the writing table and a glass of tea to refresh you. You go ahead now and have a seat."

"Thank you," said Mike, trying to adjust to the unusual decor. Nothing in the cabin, including Sadie Sutton, matched what he had expected to find.

"Don't you mind me none," she said. "I'm not up and about as I used to be. I put up this curtain to keep out the no-see-ums. They never used to bother me none, but I'm not so immune in my old age. The no-see-ums never did bother me in the old days, but they sure do now."

"I understand," said Mike, as he settled into the stiff wood chair. "I'm fine." The truth was that he felt uneasy talking to a vague silhouette behind a white curtain. As his eyes adjusted to the lighting, he began to see the outline of her face and body as she rocked back and forth in the chair. Her eyes had a pale red glow that he could detect through the thin curtain. She was staring intently at him. The odd color of her eyes unsettled his nerves.

"You're right on time, Mr. Byrne."

"I try to be prompt."

"Miss Stillwell told me about you, Mr. Byrne. I don't need no long introduction. I promised to do this interview on account of her being so nice to me."

"She told me a little bit about you, too."

"You go ahead and have some tea whenever you want. I want to see that glass empty before you leave."

"Yes, Ma'am." Mike smiled at her motherly concern. Sandy was right; Sadie's voice was sharp and clear.

"Now, that tea there is good for you. I don't boil it. Down here, we put it in jars outside and let the sun heat it real good. It'll still be warm. We don't have refrig'ration, but that tea will quench your thirst better 'n' anything outside the slough. Cold drinks where you come from just make you want more. If it's a hot day, warm tea is what you need. I know that for a fact."

"Thank you," Mike replied as he marked the date at the top of a blank page in his notebook.

"We don't like formalities here in the slough. I don't suppose you go by the name 'Mike' or some short hand version, do you?"

"You can call me Mike."

"Good. Makes things easier. Now you just call me 'Sadie.' I don't need any of that Ms. Sutton stuff. I've always been 'Sadie' and I plan to die plain old Sadie."

"Yes Ma'am," said Mike.

"And I don't need that either. My name isn't 'ma'am,' just, Sadie. I don't call you mister Mike, just Mike. If you go ahead and call me Sadie, we'll get along fine."

"Okay. That's a deal. Sadie it is from now on."

There was an awkward silence while Mike pulled his thoughts together to think of something to say.

"I think I owe you an apology."

"For what? You don't owe me an apology for anything."

"For this curtain. It's their breedin' season. That's when the no-see-ums bother me bad. I used to be immune to all the insects in the slough. Now I have to be careful. It'll pass in another week or so when breedin' season's over. They won't be so bad then." Sadie repeated herself.

"That's nothing to apologize for. I'm all set over here. I don't want you to be uncomfortable just for me. They aren't bothering me over here." Mike was grateful he had taken the time to apply a dose of insect repellant before he left his apartment.

There was another silence.

"You're a young man. Tell my why you want to hear the stories of an old woman like me, out here in the slough. Seems to me that this job fits someone much older."

"Not a problem. I'm curious to hear your story. My grandfather used to take me out into the woods in Delaware. I enjoyed listening to him tell me about his life when he was a boy. He taught me to respect nature, so I wanted to meet you. I believe we need to listen to our elders. They harbor our history. That's why I joined the historical society and how I met Sandy. She probably didn't tell you, but I volunteered to come out here for the historical society. I'm a member."

"Oh, I know all about why you're here. She told me all about that book you're gonna write. I thought this task was much more suitable for someone closer to my age. But then there probably isn't anyone as old as me that can do it."

"Oh, not me. I'm not a writer. Some one else in the society is going to do that part. My job is to be the interviewer and note taker. I believe history can be just as much fun for the young as the old. Anyway, Sandy didn't tell me much about your past. In fact, she didn't tell me what year you were born."

"Don't you know about not asking a lady her age, Mike?"

"Well, yes, but a history book needs all the facts to tell the story. I thought it was appropriate to ask for factual information. But, you don't have to answer if you don't want to."

"That's only a joke, Mike. I don't mind none. You ask me all the questions you want. The problem is, I don't have any papers to tell me when I was born. I know I was born right here in the slough and not in any fancy hospital. No doctor ever came here to the slough that I remember, never did. Maybe only the Indian medicine woman came when the Indians lived nearby. Of course, we never paid no mind to calendars or clocks down here. Time don't mean much here in the slough."

"In the outside world, just about everything is structured around time. You don't have to worry about time, do you?"

"We go by sunrise and sunset, that's all. Time don't have any meaning 'cause you don't know how much time you got. Besides, you can't do nuthin' about it anyway. We never had any spare time anyway back in the old days. Seems like all we did was prepare for the next meal or the one after that. We had no use for new fangled inventions."

"Sandy seemed sure you were born before 1900."

"Oh, I figure I was eight or ten at the turn of the century. I remember people talking about it like it was some big deal, but to us it was just another day. The outsiders carried on so much about it we even knew about it down here in the slough."

"If you were eight in 1900, that would make you one hundred and thirteen years old now."

"I can't do numbers none, but I do remember that year, so I know I wasn't three or four. When you're young, you don't remember things too good. Do you remember your past that far back, Mike?"

"No. I think I remember a few things when I was six or so. I'm not sure of anything earlier."

"Truth is, no one would remember their birth date except that it's on a piece of paper and your parents told you over and over so you would remember. That's all you've got really, a piece of paper and somebody's word…"

"That's true. What do you remember about your parents? Where did they come from?"

"That's too far back. I have no names, Mike, no memories of them. I have no pictures of them either on paper or in my mind. I don't remember having parents. My mind's blank on that."

"You don't remember your parents? That seems strange. How about brothers and sisters? Did you have any?"

"No, I don't remember any and I don't think there were any. What I remember way back is that the Big 'Un took care of me. We lived in a crude shelter made of cypress and palmetto fronds woven together for the roof. We lived along the edge of the slough, a couple of miles from here, near the Indians. That's my earliest recollection."

"*The Big One*? Sandy didn't mention him. What do you remember about him? What was his name?"

"I don't remember much about him. I just remember he was big, hairy, ugly as all get out, and smelly. I don't remember him having a name. I don't think he could speak any, either. He didn't say much to me, but he was kind and gentle. I do remember that much, but I don't remember any name. I just remember him as the Big 'Un, that's all."

"That doesn't help much. What I really need is a name."

"Well, if that's what you want, names, I remember Johnston. Yup, I sure do remember him. He showed up here in the slough from out northwest somewhere, along the Gulf of Mexico. He said he came out of New Orleans but I never believed him."

"Why not?"

"Because he wasn't no city man. I can tell you that. I think Johnston was just a name he used so's everybody else could call him something. I knew he was a swamp man. Anyway, he moved in with us and the three of us lived together until Johnston built me this cabin."

"What else can you tell me about Johnston? What was his first name? Did he have any local family, relatives from around here?"

"I don't recollect any first name. He was just Johnston. Oh, I'm sure he had a first name, Mike. I just don't remember what it was. He showed up when I was about fourteen or so. I'm sure he didn't have no kin around here. We was his kin here. He showed up here all alone."

"That would mean he joined up with you around 1906 or 1907 and when he built this cabin it must have been around 1909," Mike calculated out loud. "If my pencil calculations add up correctly."

"You do the numbers. I jus' know he built the cabin for me a couple years after he showed up. I never did learn writin' or 'rithmetic. I learned to reason myself, an' my specialty, of course, was readin'. I'm real good at that."

"What did the guy you call *The Big One* do for a living? What did Johnston do?" asked Mike.

"Well, I don't remember much about the Big 'Un. He passed most of his time in the slough. He did help Johnston a bit to build this place as I remember, but he didn't stay here in the cabin. He slept sometimes in the woodshed in the back or here on the porch when it rained real heavy. Johnston built a second shed for the firewood. It's still standing out there in back. It's in bad shape now. We don't use it much any more."

"You don't go out for firewood now?"

"Naw. I'm too frail, now. My legs don't hold me up too good anymore. The boys over at the ranch brought us in bottle gas back a bit, so we don't have to spend time out getting wood to burn. Firewood made up a lot of my early life, Mike. To survive here, we had to keep the fire going. That was the hardest part. If the fire went out, it was hard to start again. We didn't have matches in the early days and the flint starters were hard to spark in humid or rainy weather. Getting good wood to burn was hard to do in the rainy season. It's too wet and humid, so now the ranch boys take care of the bottle gas for me."

"I see. What about Johnston? What did he do?"

"Johnston was a good man, a hard worker. He was my husband. Well, I always said he was. An' he told others we was married, too, but that sex stuff, it never worked out none for us. We just told people we was hitched so they wouldn't talk none. We never did have any ceremony or anything. There weren't any kin folk to come anyway and all those trappings others do these days was too fancy for us."

"So, no children?"

"No, thank goodness, too. We didn't have time for that. We got along real good though. This cabin was our home." Sadie stopped talking and became pensive. "If it hadn't happened, Mike, I know he would be here right now."

"If what hadn't happened?" asked Mike. "You've lost me."

"You have to understand how it was here in the slough. Things were hard, real hard. We did everything by hand. Johnston built this cabin with his two hands. Oh, some of the ranch hands around here chipped in but he mostly built it. The Big 'Un helped, too, an' some of the neighbors, but Johnston was the one who did the most of it."

"So this is all his handiwork?" said Mike.

"He built this log cabin with no nails, like the early days. Everything fits together real good, that's all. He chiseled out notches and grooves. The high beams fit together with hand carved wood pegs. They're still there today. He made the original roof from boards cut up at the sawmill, held on with pegs then overlaid with another set of boards set vertical with pegs. Then he sealed the roof boards up with pine pitch. There were no nails up there until recently when they got the shingles. They nailed the new shingles down a few years ago. I don't remember what year that was."

"Boards and pine pitch sounds like a lot of work. I can't picture a world without nails."

"Johnston finished this place for me in about a year, best I can remember. We moved in as soon as the roof was up. That's when we told people we was married. The Big 'Un stayed in the slough. He didn't need much. He kept to himself."

"What happened to Johnston? Sandy told me you're a widow."

"Well, Johnston, he joined up with a partner up the river somewhere above the slough on the high ground. His partner's name was Turner, as I recall, Seth Turner. Funny how I remember his name and not Johnston's. Anyway, he claimed to have come here from up in Tallahassee, best I recall. Well, he brought in a whole wagonload of equipment from Tampa Bay to set up a sawmill and the two of them did real well together. They made all the boards for this cabin up there at the sawmill. They made all the furniture here, too, including the table and chair where you're sittin.'"

"That's impressive," said Mike as he lifted the edge of the tablecloth to examine the table.

"In those days, we didn't have much use for money, Mike, never did. We only used it when we had an uneven trade. Like the Indians back then, we lived by trading. The boys would make a big raft of logs. They made pine barrels, some from oak, but they were a lot of work. The pine barrels didn't last long; they were too soft. At least the barrels stayed together long enough to make a trade trip down river. They shipped wood boards, some furniture, pine pitch, barrels of fish from the slough. They'd salt down sunfish, perch, bass, and soft mud turtles. To preserve the catch, they salted everything."

"Why salt?" asked Mike. "Where did all the salt come from?"

"We used the salt to preserve things. We had to salt 'em or smoke 'em. We didn't have salt, so we had to trade for it. A family down on Sawgrass Bay, right on the Gulf had a bog where they let in the high tide from the Gulf and then dammed it up. The sun baked down on the shallow pond in the mangroves so the water evaporated, leaving salt. Salt was the fastest way to keep things from spoiling. 'Course now if you want to live long, eating salt is no good. We didn't use it none up here in the slough ourselves. We just used the salt for trading. Salt was everything back then. Back in those early days, they sailed loads of ice from frozen lakes way up north, but they would lose half of it from melting before they got anywhere near here in Florida. It took electricity to bring ice here."

"Now we take ice for granted," said Mike.

"Today you take everything for granted," she snapped back. "Well, they floated their loaded raft down the river to the community dock on the Gulf. A whole bunch of the boys built that dock. Before my time a trading company out of Key West ran local schooner barges up and down the coast. We traded for what we needed and brought back salt and whatever else we could trade for. In those days, the tradin' was all done through Tampa Bay."

"What did they look for in trading?"

"Florida never had much for natural resources. Things made up of iron and copper topped the list of what we needed most. Those things had to come from up North. I still remember my first big pot. Utensils, knives, axes, saws, nails, lamps were all important. We also needed sewing needles, hemp rope, metal barrel hoops, cloth, oil for the lamps, too. I could go on, but those were the things we needed the most."

"I'm trying to write all of this down."

"I never had electricity brought down here. 'Course I had the chance to have the poles put in, but I said no. I could see where that was leading."

"You didn't want to depend on the outside world," observed Mike.

"We needed a few things, but we lived close to the land. Like the Indians, we did a lot of hunting and fishing. We was mostly self-sufficient."

"You still didn't tell me what happened to your husband, Johnston," said Mike.

"Oh yes. I do get sidetracked sometimes. Well, you see, when they came back from a trade trip, they had to pole the raft back up river against the current. They took two days to come back up here from the Gulf. They even had to sell off some of the logs to lighten the raft to bring it back. We depended on the water for our living. Water was our only way to go anywhere outside the slough. If you look out back there now, the dock is all rotted out and nearly gone. It's not safe anymore, but it was real important back then."

"You did it all by raft?"

"Yep. Johnston and Seth, both of them did all our tradin'. They'd take our stuff and some from the Indians down to the dock at Sawgrass Bay to trade for things from the North."

"What did they take to trade?"

"They mostly had alligator hides and bird feathers along with fish, turtles and alligator meat. The Indians made duck carvings and palmetto woven baskets and some necklaces. They took things for the Indians to Sawgrass Bay and sometimes to the East. And, well, Johnston was a good man, but his problem was when he finished trading, he filled his jug with whiskey. He felt that was his reward for all his hard work, but in the end it was his undoin.' When he got back here, he'd get stinkin' drunk and he'd stay that way for a day or two. Then he'd settle down and go back to work. I had to stay out of the way when he got out that jug. I saw the big picture. Johnston was a good man, except for that jug."

"What about *The Big One*? You didn't tell me what happened to him either."

"It only happened once," she said. "Johnston shared that jug with the Big 'Un jus' that one time. They both had too much. I jus' stayed in the cabin but I could hear them both letting on real loud into the night. The Big 'Un had never drunk liquor before. It was new to him. Anyway, it was a mistake, a real bad mistake. Sounded like they got to wrestling around and it got out of hand. Johnston was no match for the Big 'Un. He was much smaller so, in the end, Johnston had to shoot him."

"Johnston shot *The Big One*?" gasped Mike.

"Well, let me put it this way, I believed Johnston when he said he had to defend himself. I didn't see what happened. Anyway, when I heard the shot I could hear the Big 'Un howl for some time. Then after a bit, it was quiet, real quiet. I knew it shouldn't have been that quiet, I thought, but I stayed in the cabin. I learned to wait until after Johnston slept off that jug. He was all right once he'd slept it off. Well, that time, 'next day, he told me the Big 'Un died from that shot. Johnston told me not to come out. He said he'd take care of things. Later he told me he'd tried but he couldn't move the Big 'Un cause he was too heavy."

"So what did he do?"

"Johnston buried him right there, right where he was. The next day after that, I came out and there was this mound out back of the cabin, made of sand and mud with rocks on top to keep the swamp critters away. I thought it looked real nice. Anyway, the slough runs along the water so you can't dig a grave. Once you'd start diggin' down, the hole would fill right up with water as you went, so Johnston made the mound. It's still there today. You'd like it now cause it's real pretty, covered with moss and ferns an all. You go see it before you go," she said. "It's out back, behind the cabin. You can't miss it."

"So, you're telling me Johnston buried *The Big One* back behind this cabin?" Mike could hardly contain his excitement.

"Yup, he's buried right where he fell. That's what Johnston did. 'Course the mound is still there, like a memorial, so we can remember him."

"But, you didn't see it happen. You stayed inside, hiding the whole time?"

"You bet. I stayed in the cabin like I always did when Johnston got out that jug. I didn't come out until Johnston told me to come out and look. You can see it, too. Go back down the boardwalk towards the riverbank and you'll see it. Then you'll know what I'm saying is true."

"I'll take a look before I leave. I assume you reported what happened to the authorities."

"This is the slough, Mike. The slough takes care of its own. There are no authorities here, never was. If we stay smart, there never will be. There are things about the slough that we keep to ourselves."

"I see. That's what happened to *The Big One*, but you still haven't told me what happened to Johnston."

"It was that jug, Mike. That jug finally got him, too. The last time I saw him, he left for a trading trip with his partner Seth. What happened was something on the way back. That's what Seth told me when he got back. I'd say it happened three years after he had that business with the mound. He just never came back. Seth made it back alone and told me the whole story. He said they'd stopped on the river bank for the night, and Johnston did what he never did before."

"And what was that?"

"He started drinking out of that jug while they were still way down the river. The next day when his partner 'woke, Johnston was gone. No one ever saw Johnston again."

"Maybe he ran off."

"If you knew Johnston, you wouldn't say that. This was his home. He'd still be here if he could. I'm sure he slipped off that raft and fell into the river and drowned. When Seth brought the raft back up here, he gave me the stuff Johnston traded for. After that, Seth just went on up to the mill. He never did recover. He missed Johnston jus' about as much as I did. When he lost Johnston, he lost his best friend and partner."

"I wouldn't be so sure Johnston fell in the river and drowned."

"Well, I'm sure. I knew Johnston. You see, one of the things his partner, Seth, dropped off was that jug, Mike, and the thing was half full. Now Johnston was not one to waste a drop of whiskey. Maybe he just stood up on the raft's edge to answer nature's call, as men folk are apt to do when they get to drinking, and lost his balance and fell in. It was probably some fool thing that simple, a slip up when he was drunk. I always told him if he was gonna take out that jug, do it at home where he was safe and I could keep an eye on him. I told him I wouldn't say nuthin' to anyone, about that jug, an' I never did."

"But why do you think Johnston drowned?"

"Because he couldn't swim none. He'd be here now if he didn't drown. It's one of those things a body knows. His partner, Seth, stayed with the mill for a while but I guess it wasn't the same without Johnston. Seth couldn't find another partner he could get along with so he moved back up to Tampa Bay. When he left, he told me I could have anything at the mill I wanted. He told me the place was mine."

"That was generous. Sounds like you got the better part of an uneven deal."

"He said he owed Johnston his wages so it was a fair trade. But look at me, what could I do with a sawmill? Everything was too big, too heavy and I was alone for some time after Johnston was gone, so I gave it all away."

"You gave away a sawmill?"

"Yup. What could I do with it? Did you see that fence up by the highway? The white fence?"

"Sure, that was my landmark to turn into the shell road."

"Most all those boards came from the sawmill. After Seth left and I met the old man, the boys at the ranch went up and ran the mill to make the boards to build that fence. I gave the whole mill to the Circle T. 'Course they've probably replaced a lot of those boards by now. They're a lot like me…"

"How's that?"

"They're getting' up in years."

"When you lost Johnston, you lost the only man in your life. How did you survive out here alone?"

"I always did most of the food gathering, anyway, the hunting, and cookin'. Johnston worked up at the mill long hours. When he came home, it was my part to be sure there was always a hot meal for him. He liked that a lot. I know he did. I know he didn't eat so good up at the mill or on trading trips." Sadie paused and looked closely at Mike. "You want to know a secret?" she asked.

"Sure."

"My secret was, I always had a stew cooking in that big kettle. See that big kettle there in the hearth? I'd clean it out every so often, but usually I just added things to keep it going. Nothing kept good here in the slough. We had to cook things as soon as we got them, either in the pot or by smoking them out back. You had to eat meat quick or the other swamp creatures and the bugs would get them first. Johnston would help with a deer or a wild pig, now and then, but I did the cookin'. We did pretty good, but I spent my whole life getting things and fixing them. Nature provides lots of plants out here you can eat, raw or cooked. I could show them to you if I was up and about. I know them all. The Big 'Un and the Indian medicine woman taught me about the plants. He didn't like meat much."

"That sounds like a hard life."

"Yes, it was, but I've always lived the same way, jus' like I do even today."

"I find it hard to believe you didn't adopt at least some of the modern conveniences."

"Them new fangled things take folks away from the land. Up your way, people gave up their knowledge of how to live off the land. They've become dependent on things they don't know anything about. They're trapped into spending time earning money so they can pay for things that come from far away. I don't understand it. I know I'm not saying it right, but you see how I live here."

"The world changed, but you didn't."

"Oh, I know I'm past my time, but I've always lived close to the land. We had to trade for some things, but that was it. I didn't want to be dependent on others. I still live as I always did."

"That's what we want to put in the book."

"There's a danger that threatens us here. You gotta put that in the book, too."

"A danger? What danger?"

"The danger is that people don't want to just get by. They're looking for a lot of money to get ahead. Then they want more and more. They'll kill every last one of a species jus' to make more money. There'll be a day when they'll regret what they did, but I won't live to see it. You getting everything down?"

"I'm trying to keep up. It's hard to keep up with you."

"Want to know a another secret?" she asked.

"Sure."

"I don't want to be part of that new world out there. No way. I live here like the native Indians. I agree with them, the land belongs to nature. This is my home and this is my time. You tell them in that book what it was like, in case they have to come back to the land someday. That's what you can do. All those people out there can't survive without electricity. I always worried, what if someone turned it off for good? You'd be fine for a day or two, but in the end you wouldn't survive 'cause you're too dependent on it. And the worse part is there's nothing you could do if it just stopped."

"But who would turn it off?"

"Same foreigners they bought all those newfangled things from."

"So what you're saying is the world has changed and you refuse to change with it."

"Sure, why should I change now? I don't think anyone can live the old ways anymore. Money has become too important for living today."

"So working to get rich doesn't make much sense to you."

"I don't understand the need to get lots of money and contraptions, Mike. Why this big important need to get rich? We all know we're gonna die and you can't take any of it with you. When you die, the lawyers and the government divide up what you leave, they take out their share, and give what's left to people who may not ever have even liked you. You spend your life chasing after money, and then you're gone forever. It makes no sense down here in the slough."

"You have a point there, Sadie. Tell me more about the old days."

"I remember when sealed jars came out to keep things in. I have some of them jars right here. Now they did help, because I could keep things during times of plenty."

"But this looks like a place of plenty to me."

"That's because the rain is heavy now. We have times down here when there's floods and times it's dry so bad we have lighting fires. 'Course we work to put out what we can, but sometimes the slough burns. Look close at the logs outside the cabin and you'll see where the fire came right up here and burned some of the wood. You can see where the water flooded some, too."

"The cabin looks fine, now."

"That's 'cause the ranch boys have helped me keep it up. They put on a new roof a bit ago and the screens, too. I'm thankful for their help, from the Circle T. As I was saying, sealed jars were important so we could cook and preserve foods. That was important, like the day Johnston brought me my first big iron pot," she beamed.

"That must have been an important day."

"It was. You see we did need some modern things just to survive. You know, I remember picking mushrooms in the spring. They were important because we could keep them without sealed jars and without refrigeration and even without cooking, but it was always a race. We had to be fast to get them."

"A race? With who?"

"Yep, a race with the boars, the wild pigs. They love those mushrooms, too. It was always a race in the spring to see who got to them first, us or them. 'Course we had the advantage."

"The advantage, how so?"

"'Cause we could eat the wild pigs, too. We could put them both in the pot, the pigs and the mushrooms together," she chuckled to herself. "Local folks down on Sawgrass Bay provided fresh food like shell fish and saltwater fish from the Gulf down the end of the commercial dock. Sometimes the boys brought fish up from the bay. Those were mostly mullet and mangrove snapper, some grouper, but none of the real fancy ones like sea turtles or deep-water fish. They were too rich for us. We were jus' simple folk."

"Did you eat alligator meat? There must be an endless supply around here. I've heard people eat them."

"Yep. Sure did, but I can't say much about it because I didn't like 'gator meat. Gator meat's not very tasty. Johnston made a big deal about gator 'cause he had a way to catch 'em real easy. Learned it from the Miccosukee Indians. 'Course he didn't want to hear me none 'cause there was no flavor in it. Gator meat needs seasoning to give it flavor so it worked best when I just put it in the pot and the other things with it. That's how I learned to eat hot meals, even in the summer. They were the best for us. Warm food and drink cures a thirst, too. Don't eat cold foods. Cold's not natural. Cold makes your thirst bigger, an' I think it brings on the cancer, too. Some folks think it stops the heart."

"I'll remember that. I wrote it down."

"Course that's jus' the opinion of one old lady from the slough."

"Well, that's what I'm looking for. I want to hear your opinions and stories."

"In those days, life was simple. If we kept up a regular effort all the time finding things, we did fine, but we couldn't store foods. Nothing ever stored well in the slough. Everything changed when the profit fishermen came and the government started draining the swamp. That's when things started to disappear. When I was a young girl, the mullet filled the streams so thick you could almost walk over them to cross the river. You didn't need a pole or hook to catch 'em. Your bare hands would do, there were so many. I caught plenty with my bare hands. But now, in most places they're gone. The whole stream is fished out for a bunches of different fish."

"That's true nearly everywhere, even for things other than fish." Mike paused to change the subject. "So, you lived mostly on the barter system. Tell me more about that. That would make an interesting topic for my book, the monetary system of the old days."

"Well, no one down here trusted money. They all figured it would be worthless like the confederate currency that everyone had in Florida back at the time of the War Between the States."

"You mean the Civil War?"

"Yep. That was before my time, but everyone around here thought the federal money would be worthless one day, too. They said the cost of that war and the later ones would eventually destroy the currency, so we kept as little of it as possible. 'Course some money was necessary because all trades weren't equal, and they had to make adjustments. So they used the currency to make the trade fair."

"You didn't accumulate money. You only used it to balance a trade?"

"We couldn't eat it. We couldn't use it for anything except in a trade. If we needed something from up north, we depended on the sloop to bring it to the commercial dock where we could work out a trade. If the boat didn't bring something we needed real bad, money meant nothing, Mike. If the boys needed barrel hoops, then they needed barrel hoops. If the boat didn't bring hoops, they couldn't make barrels. It was that simple. Money had no real meaning except in the trades."

"Today people can have anything they want. It's just a matter of money, so money has become the goal," said Mike. "The more you want, the more money you need to get it."

"That's 'cause everything needed to survive is easy today, you don't even have to think about it. That was what we all struggled for back then, our basic needs. Those things were what was important. Money did nothing if we couldn't get the things we needed. Today, everything is right there. All you need is money. Back then it was different. There wasn't any point in getting ahead as there is now."

"We take everything for granted."

"Everything has changed. I'll say it simple, Mike. Today folks look to the future. Future means something to you. Back then, we were focused on today for survival. There was only today. No one thought much about tomorrow or beyond. There was no time for that."

"That's how our culture has changed our times. Life is much easier and we have so much more."

"Those changes in things that made work easier made it possible to get ahead and to have more free time. I saw what was happening, but it wasn't for me. I refused to bring those things down here to the slough. The slough hasn't changed. You write that down, Mike. That was the big difference to me. Working to make a surplus to get ahead is foreign to me. I still don't think much about tomorrow, never have."

"In all these years you lived off the land here in the slough, what was your favorite food? What did you like the best?"

"That's been one of the biggest and best secrets of the slough, Mike. I suppose I can tell you now. It's not legal any more and I understand that, but we ate swamp chicken. That was the best. If Johnston was here, he'd agree."

"Swamp chicken?" asked Mike.

"Swamp chicken. What you folks call white ibis or sometimes egret. The sky was full of them back then. They were the best. They're still around now, but there aren't as many. The law protects them, so if you go out to the open slough beyond the trees, you'll see lots of them today."

"Tell me, what do you think is the secret of your long life? That's the question everyone wants to know the answer to."

"I call it the roll of the dice. Folks is either born with good blood or not. 'Course one can be born with good blood and a bad lifestyle, too many cold drinks. Smokin', drinkin', an carryin' on can shorten it but you can't make it any longer than your original roll of the dice."

"That won't be very reassuring, to the readers of our book. Everyone wants to know some special secrets of how you lived longer."

"Livin' a long life is like living in the slough. You have to deal with what's there. There's a lot of things people don't talk about from the past."

"Such as…?" he asked.

"There are so many changes. It's hard to go back. Today, when folks get old and you can't support or care for them, you put them in a nursing home. You have all kinds of medicine to keep people alive and avoid the pain of being old. In the old days, they didn't have these things. When folks couldn't care for the old people any more, they took them out behind the barn or locked them in their rooms and let 'em starve to death. No one liked it, but that was the way it was back then. Now, you put that in your book."

"Oh," said Mike. "That one's hard. No one likes to hear hard truth. What else can you think of?"

"I can't describe all the changes. Once a thing was discovered, it would change so many other things about your life in little ways you couldn't see. The changes just snuck up on folks and took over. Folks didn't know what happened, so I stayed out here so's I didn't have to deal with the changes."

"When do you want to stop today? Sandy warned me to watch out for you. She said you tire easily. We've been going on for quite a while now."

"Thank you for your courtesy, Mike. I've been running on my emotions. I get all excited talkin' about my life here. I've had it good and I've had good health. I've seen many others come and go, and most aren't with us any more. I'm the only one left down here, now. Even the Indians have all moved to the reservations. There used to be a lot of them living around us here at Indian Bend. That's how it got it's name, but they're all gone now. Just me, Ivan and the swamp critters are left here. Just thinkin' about it, I do feel tired," she said softly.

"Well, then, let's break for today. I'll come back next week, if you like."

"Oh yes. Come back here next week and the week after that. I suppose we can go on and on as long as I can think of something to say and I don't run out of tea for you. I'm looking forward to helping you, too. You will come back now, won't you?"

"Sure. This has been a pleasure, talking with you."

"Now when you go out the door, go around to your right. You'll see the boardwalk I was telling you about. It goes straight back to the slough. Just be careful. Those boards are getting pretty old and some are rotten, so walk real careful. If you go back past the cabin, you can see the mound. It will be right beside you. You can't miss it. Then walk on down to the dock on the edge of the old stream. That's all that's left of the river after it spreads out into the slough."

"I'll do that before I leave."

"Now don't step out on the dock. It may be still standing, but it won't hold you. It's all rotted out. You can see the open slough from the end of the walk. Now don't you try to wade across the stream, either. If you do, you'll sink down into the muck. The river's filled up with thousands of years of rotting plants. 'Course if you jus' stand still and watch, there's more wild life in the slough than anywhere else you'll ever go. So, you walk on down and have a look before you go. It's not far. What's left of the river is good for critters, but it's no good for rafting anymore. The river water's all filled in with years of dead plants. Those days of rafting on the river are all gone."

"Will I see Ivan there?"

"Oh, Sandy told you about him? Well, he's hiding around here somewhere, Mike. As soon as you leave, he'll be back here to help me. He sleeps in the shed out back when he's here, but he likes the slough so he'll stay out there, somewhere, until you go. You won't see him. He's too shy, but he's there. Don't you worry none about him. He takes care of himself. He won't bother you none. He knows you've been with me."

"Then we agree to stop for today? We've covered a lot for one day."

"Don't forget to finish your tea before you go," she reminded him.

Mike put the cap back on his pen and paused to drink down the remaining tea Sadie had prepared for him. He noted the strong and surprisingly refreshing flavor as the tea ran down his throat. The warmth of the tea soothed his nerves as it flowed into his body.

"It's good. Thank you," he said as he rose to leave.

"I'm glad you liked it. I'll have another one for you next week."

"I'm looking forward to seeing you again."

"Don't worry, the slough won't change, it can wait a little bit longer, jus' like me."

Chapter Four

Debriefing

When Mike closed the screen door behind him, he did not go directly to his car. As Sadie suggested, he followed the path down the side of the cabin. He felt uneasy. While she remained sitting on the porch, he walked alone in a strange environment. He could hear the sound of the rocking chair, creaking back and forth on the floorboards on the porch. Then, too, he knew the man called Ivan was somewhere out in the hummock, watching him. The canopy of trees kept him in a world of shadows as he stepped cautiously along the old boards. With each step, the boards eased down into the muck and the water threatened to ooze over the tops of his clean shoes. After he passed the cabin, he could see the two sheds. The one attached to the back of the cabin was in good condition, but the second one, a few feet away, was seriously deteriorated. The roof and outer walls had caved in.

Once he passed the sheds, he saw the mound behind the sabal palms. The mound consisted of a patch of earth elevated roughly two feet high, about eight feet long and two and a half feet wide. The piles of rocks covering it were coated with thick, blue-green and silver-gray moss. The ferns scattered over the floor of the palm hummock thickened around the mound, enveloping the surface so completely he would have missed the area if Sadie had not advised him where to look.

If observed casually, the mound appeared to be nothing more than the remains of long dead, rotting tree trunks.

Mike stopped. He could see the open slough ahead and decided not to go any further. As he stood in the shade of the palms, his uneasiness increased. The only sounds he heard were the continuous chorus of the birds overhead and the frogs in the water. Everything appeared exactly as Sadie had described it. He might have overcome his anxiety and gone out to the edge of the dock, but he was concerned that his feet would slip through the rotting boards and into the muddy ooze of the bog. He decided it was time to leave. He sensed he had seen enough and was not prepared to extend his stay.

He returned to his car parked in front of the cabin and was relieved when it started right away. He wasted no time turning it around and driving back to the highway. He was still awed but intimidated by the lush beauty of the area as he drove out of the protection of the trees and onto the open grasslands. He wondered why he felt this way. The interview had gone well. Sadie was a harmless old lady. Yet coming back up the shell road, he felt more like returning from a journey through time, not distance. He felt as if he was returning from a time warp going back a hundred or perhaps a thousand years into the past, a place where he did not belong.

When he reached the highway, he turned east, away from town. He had never been this far out into mid-Florida, away from the civilized parts he knew. He decided the drive would provide an opportunity to clear his mind and review his conversation with Sadie. He drove easterly for a little over a mile along the highway where the white fences framed in the cattle ranches. Sandy had described how the fences ran along both sides of the road, delineating each ranch from the next. He remembered her comment that it was a long way to the nearest town, so he used the front entrance to Circle T Ranch to turn around. Checking his watch, he noted he was late for his meeting with Sandy back at the diner. He quickened his pace as he drove back along the state road, under the interstate overpass, and continued for another half mile before he turned into the parking lot for the diner. He was relieved to be back where he felt comfortable again.

In contrast with earlier this morning, the diner was busy with a heavy lunchtime crowd. Sandy was sitting at a booth at the back of the diner near the windows, not far from where they had met only a few hours earlier. After his meeting with Sadie, breakfast with Sandy now seemed a long time ago. Sandy was sipping coffee and reading a paperback novel.

As he approached the booth, she looked up.

"I'm sorry I'm late," he apologized as she smiled back at him.

"Have a seat. You're not late, you're right on time. Here's the lunch menu. They're busy, so I suggest we order right away to get our food in line. Your interview worked up an appetite for me while you were gone."

"I didn't realize I was hungry until I walked in the front door and got a whiff of all those tantalizing aromas from the kitchen. Now I'm starving."

As soon as they ordered and the waitress left, Sandy spoke. "How did you do with Sadie? Isn't she charming?"

"Everything went smoothly, as you said it would. I took a lot of notes. She's a treasure. I've never met anyone like her."

"Well, let's start at the beginning. Did Sadie tell you what year she was born?"

"Not exactly. Her memory of the past is sketchy. Although she was sure it was way before 1900, she didn't know the exact year she was born. She was sure she was around eight or ten years old at the turn of the century, so I put down 1892 for her birth date, as a conservative guess."

"That's unfortunate."

"Unfortunate? I think it's a miracle. That means she's around a hundred thirteen years old. I bet neither one of us will last that long."

"That's unfortunate, we need to have an exact date for our book. Estimates don't cut the mustard for an historical work. So that means we don't really know how old she is. You're right, though, she is special, a real character. Someone who has lived as long as she has must have some good genes."

"Sadie would agree. She said that good blood was the key, and poor choices in lifestyle cut short what you're born with. She also said that avoiding cold foods was important in warm weather climates. I wrote that down."

"I'm sure she's right," said Sandy. "She's observant about people."

"You know, I was supposed to be the one asking questions, but I've come away from our meeting with some questions of my own."

"Such as?"

"Such as, who is *The Big One*? She mentioned this guy she called *The Big One*, but she couldn't remember his name. He was the sole contact she remembered from her childhood."

"I haven't a clue. She never mentioned him to me. What did she tell you about him?"

"She said that he was very tall, very big and very ugly. She also remembered him as smelly, which I thought was odd. If she can remember all that, why couldn't she remember his name?"

"That's a reasonable observation. What else did she tell you?"

"She told me he never spoke, so maybe he was deaf or a mute so a name wasn't important. I don't know," puzzled Mike.

"Anything else? That's not much to go on. We need a last name or something to trace. Did she know where he came from? What happened to him? What did he do for a living? Did she remember any of that?"

"No. She only remembered that he was very kind to her. She said he was a 'man of the swamp,' whatever that means. I got the feeling that he was probably a relative or someone close who took care of her as a child."

"Well, we can't trace him from that. I need facts to check historical records, official documents. Who else did she remember? I'm looking for names of people so I can trace them in the official records. We need to put some meat on the bones for the book. That is, if we have enough factual information to write one."

"Well, she mentioned a man named Johnston, the man she said was her husband. At least she said she lived with him, " said Mike, looking at his notes. "Seems she had a common law relationship with him."

"Johnston, now we have a name to work with. I'll do a search on that name."

"I noted that she lived with *The Big One* until she was around age ten. Then she said a couple of years past the turn of the century, this man named Johnston came to the slough and moved in with them. She said that they lived in a crude shelter that was not as nice as her cabin. Johnston built the cabin she lives in now. She said *The Big One* helped, but didn't move in with them. She said she and Johnston told outsiders that they were married. She was about fourteen when they moved into the cabin. That would mean she's lived in that cabin since 1908."

"Did she remember Johnston's first name? Women don't marry men and not remember their names."

"No, nothing. She only remembered his last name, but she said they didn't have a formal wedding, they just moved in together."

"I think Florida recognized common law marriage a long time ago. So much for the official records. No official wedding, no records."

"She also said they didn't have any children either."

"So, no children, again, no records," said Sandy. "What about the names of the other people who built homes at Indian Bend? There were about half a dozen homes there once. Did she talk about her former neighbors or her parents?"

"Nothing. She remembered that other people lived there but they didn't stay long. She had no recollection of a mother or father so I came to the conclusion that something happened to her parents early on. Most likely another family took her in and then left her with *The Big One*, when they moved away. Whoever he was, she didn't explain. Anyway, that's my take on the situation. In reality, she just didn't remember a lot of things."

"Well, you've got to keep pressing her on these issues next week. She's not giving you much to work with for our book. The foundation for our book looks shaky if you can't get more facts."

"Yes, but she told me a lot of details about how they lived, what they ate, and how they bartered to get the things they needed to be able to live in the swamp. I hope I can remember it all."

"That's good. Your memory will be as important as your notes."

"She told me how she refused to change when all the modern conveniences came along. She refused to bring in electricity when the opportunity arose."

"I think that's the core of a book. We can focus on how she saw life change around her while she retained the old ways. We can compare her life with how the neighbors lived, so work on that angle. I'll help you. I'll set up a meeting for you with the manager of the ranch down the road. They must know about Sadie. That fence where you turned to go down the shell road belongs to the big cattle ranch called the Circle T. I'm sure they'll have some information about Sadie. The historical society has discussed plans with them to contribute to a project documenting the history of this area in the future. We've told them that we're working on this project with Sadie and plan to bring them in later."

"Oh, I know where the ranch is. I saw the house when I drove by there on my way back. I wanted to get a flavor of the area. You're right. The Circle T is a big spread. I turned around in their driveway."

"Good. If I can set up a meeting with someone there, you already know how to get there."

"Absolutely, no problem. The ranch house is about a mile further east on SR 744. The ranch lands back into the swamp."

"You keep referring to it as the swamp. Everyone here refers to this area as the 'slough.' Technically, the formal name is the Seminole Indian River Slough."

"That's what Sadie called it, too."

"Well, the society needs as many names of those early settlers as possible, if we're going to write a history book. You'll have to get better information about the other people who lived there to get the whole picture. Let's hope her memory will be better next week. I don't expect to be able to trace her back to a specific slave boat, but she has to have a family connection somewhere. Maybe all we'll find is information about the people she knew, the other families that were there. Right now, all we have is her name and the last name of a common law husband."

"I'm sorry. I haven't been very helpful. I'll prod her more next week. I just let her talk about what she wanted to this week. I want her to be comfortable with me and establish a good rapport with her. Of course, she's no youngster. Maybe her memory of earlier times isn't there any more. Oh, I almost forgot…"

"What?"

"There's something really interesting she told me. She said the remains of the one she referred to as *The Big One* are buried behind the cabin in a burial mound. When I checked her story on the way out, it was there, just like she said."

"Was there a grave marker?"

"No, nothing. Just natural vegetation on a big dirt mound."

"Well, we can't trace him without a name. Mike, I need names to research if I'm going to be able to trace historical data and tie it to official records for the book." Sandy sounded frustrated.

"I'm sorry. She couldn't remember names of any friends or neighbors and from what I can tell there are no relatives, no family, no parents, siblings or children either. The only one she mentioned by name was this guy Johnston and his partner Seth."

"So far there's nowhere to look if we don't have names. Mike, I've already researched the name Sutton and it doesn't even begin to appear in the local telephone book until recently. I've called every one of the Sutton listings and none of them know anything about her. No long lost relatives there either."

"Check out this guy Johnston. She called him her husband."

"Yes, but without a first name, there's an abundance of people with the last name Johnston. I'm afraid that won't help us. I need a first name. Now, since I have to go out there this week, what else can you tell me? What else do you think I should know?"

"Go out there? You? Are you going by yourself? Is that safe?" he asked, not sure he understood what she had said.

"Yes, I'm going out to see her. Ms. Tucker from the County Aid Society collected boxes of clothing, fabric, reading materials even some medicine she wants Sadie to try. Ms. Tucker planned to go out there Tuesday or Wednesday, but she had a family crisis so she called me to sub in for her. She called after you left this morning and asked if I would make the trip for her. I have to pick everything up this afternoon so I can make the trip tomorrow morning. You look concerned. I'm just going to drop some things off."

"I didn't know you were planning to go out there," said Mike, surprised that Sandy was going out to see Sadie also.

"Didn't she tell you about the dolls?"

"Dolls? No, she didn't mention dolls. What dolls?"

"Didn't you see some of them in the cabin when you were there? She's working on a few right now."

"Oh, we stayed on the porch for the interview so I didn't see the inside of her cabin."

"I'm surprised she didn't mention the dolls. Sadie spent time with the Miccosukee Indians and learned their ancient art of doll making. From what she told me, the process becomes a spiritual experience. During the creation process, she conducts a special ritual and prays to what she calls the universal spirit to guide her hands during the creation of each doll."

"Sounds a little bit like voodoo to me."

"Well, it's not quite like that. She doesn't make dolls to stick pins in them or send bad spells to other people. If you think about it from an historical perspective, doll making has been around for years in most human cultures. Dolls play a role even in our culture, maybe not so much for adults anymore, but they are important for both sexes."

"Boys don't play with dolls." Mike scoffed.

"Sure they do. Males just don't call them dolls. They have action figures and other figures representing different forms for play. Remember transformers? Even video games have all kinds of fantastic figures that boys as well as girls play with. How different is that from the Egyptian hieroglyphics and carvings?"

"Oh, you're right. I never thought about it like that. I did play with action figures. I just didn't think of them as dolls."

"I bet you had a teddy bear or a favorite stuffed animal that gave you comfort as a child."

"Wow. You're right. I can't think of anyone who didn't have a favorite doll or stuffed animal."

"Well, Sadie believes humans never outgrow the need for dolls, even as adults. She says the doll fills a different need for the adult. Adults don't really play with them like children do. The dolls she makes serve a different purpose. She calls them medicine dolls for the spirit."

"As I think about it, many cultures did make dolls or carved figures out of natural materials as wood, stone, bone or even vegetable material. My grand father took me to a pioneer village where they had a workshop on making cornhusk dolls. That's a lost art. We don't make dolls or carve images like primitive cultures did, we have a new commercial variation."

"Well, the historical society found out about her doll making and Mrs. Tucker and her women's group support Sadie's efforts by collecting fabric, ribbons and lace, dried flowers, and any other materials she may use to make a doll. They drop off what they have collected periodically. Sadie says that the dolls become more powerful in their healing when the materials used to make them have been donated. She says the dolls collect the spirit of the people who have donated to its creation."

"How did she get involved with doll making?"

"She told me she learned how to make them from the Indians when she was a young girl. Years ago, there used to be an Indian village near Indian Bend before the government drained the swamps. Apparently the Indian medicine woman there took a liking to Sadie and taught her the rituals and craft of her people. The Indians were very serious about their dolls. They felt that each doll had a spirit of its own drawn from the energy in the universe to provide special healing for the recipient. The recipient could make the doll or be gifted the doll by someone else. Sadie has made dolls for years. Her craft has evolved beyond what she was taught by the medicine woman. Sadie has become a medicine woman of her own style."

"That's very interesting. I've never heard of medicine dolls. I gather these dolls are for adults, not children. Have you seen any of these dolls?"

"Yes, a few of them. For the most part she creates dolls for adults. She makes the dolls for someone who needs one, including an occasional young child. In fact, Sadie told me a few weeks ago she sensed that I needed a medicine doll and she had started making one for me. I'm rather skeptical, but she told me it would be ready soon for me to pick up. I'm anxious to see if she finished it yet and what it looks like. I'll see tomorrow when I drop off the box of donations from Mrs. Tucker."

"Be sure you go early. Since she doesn't have electricity, she lives by the sun. I know I'd be nervous going out there in the dark. The slough seems a bit mysterious to me."

"I'll be alright. I've been there many times."

"You were telling me about the dolls, what do they look like?"

"Oh, yes. The few I've seen are magnificent creations. I've also heard that the recipients have had some unusual experiences around the dolls, special spiritual experiences."

"I'm surprised. She didn't mention a word to me about making dolls."

"Maybe she feels it is a personal, spiritual process and she wasn't sure how receptive you would be about her craft. Maybe she wanted to keep it a secret."

Mike chuckled. "Sadie seems to like secrets. She talked about several in our discussion. She told me about her perpetual kettle of porridge, her philosophy of life, and, oh, I almost forgot the biggest one." Mike became very serious.

"What's that?"

"Oh, I just remembered there's something else about *The Big One*."

"A secret?"

"Sadie said that *The Big One* died of a gunshot wound."

"What? He was murdered?"

"Well, sort of. She claimed it was an accident. She said Johnston pulled the trigger."

"Johnston killed *The Big One*?"

"She said it was an accident. They were drinking and wrestling around and somehow Johnston shot *The Big One*."

"Finally, that's our best lead. There must be a police file or newspaper article about it and an investigation. Great, there should be records about that."

"No, Sandy. You don't understand. I doubt it. Remember, *The Big One* didn't have a name and no relatives to check up on him. Sadie said she and Johnston made a pact to tell no one about the incident. I think I'm the first one she's ever told the story to."

"What? They did what?"

"She said *The Big One* was too heavy for Johnston to move, so he buried him there where he fell. Sadie also said something important. She said that 'the slough takes care of its own.' I don't think anyone knew about it or even missed him. Sadie and Johnston were his family."

"Wow. No investigation, no records, again. She never mentioned anything about *The Big One* to me. What about Ivan? You didn't mention Ivan. Did you meet Ivan?"

"No, I didn't even see Ivan. She told me he was there but I wouldn't see him, either. She didn't talk much about him. Like everyone else, I don't have a full name for Ivan, either. She told me Ivan was born mentally retarded and lives with her in the slough. Apparently he's sharp enough to take care of her, but she said he's so shy he hides in the slough."

"What did you think of it?"

"The slough? It's beautiful, but mysterious. I don't know how to describe it. If you like nature, the slough is different, special."

"I've been there. Remember, I'm the one who found Sadie."

"Of course. I forgot. How did you find her?"

"I love nature and the outdoors so I frequently look for new places to explore, places I've never been before. One weekend I picked the slough to explore and study the natural vegetation and wildlife. Somehow I stumbled onto the shell road. When I found her alone in the cabin, I informed some of the other members of the historical society."

"So that's how the society became interested in her."

"Yes," Sandy paused for a bite of her sandwich and a sip of iced tea. Then she continued. "I thought you could tape your notes about your meetings with her right here at the diner while we reviewed your meetings, but it's too noisy. You'd better do it at home when there's no one around."

"I agree. I'd be uncomfortable taping our meetings here."

"When you get them done, I'll help transcribe the tapes if you speak clearly and slowly. I can type, but I'm no wiz. You should probably do it today while your memory is fresh. In a couple of days from now, you may have forgotten something."

"You're right. I'll do it this afternoon," Mike paused. "Do you get the feeling there's more to the relationship between Sadie and Ivan than she's telling us?"

"Yes, that's why I've encouraged you to be patient with her. I'm uneasy about them but I don't know exactly why. Woman's intuition?"

"Perhaps you have an overactive imagination. Seriously, though, I've never met a woman who tells all her secrets to a man she just met."

"You bet. You are a wise man."

"You know, someone needs to save the slough before some big developer comes in and drains it for farms or a big housing project."

"See, didn't I just say you're a wise man? I agree, but I must get going so I can pick up those packages for Sadie from Mrs. Tucker. Remember, you're on for next Saturday. I'll meet you right here, same time, same place for breakfast."

"I'll be here," said Mike. "I'll buy lunch today, since you picked up the breakfast tab this morning."

"Okay, as long as I treat breakfast next week."

"You have a deal."

Chapter Five

Second Encounter

The second Saturday morning scheduled for Mike to meet with Sadie was bright and sunny. As he drove down the narrow shell road, the shady canopy of trees protected the dark color of his car from the intensity of the summer sun. He parked in front of the cabin like he had the week before. Everything was more familiar this week. Most of the anxiety he had experienced the first week had worn off. When he knocked on the screen door, Sadie welcomed him in. Once inside the cabin, he noted that his chair and the small writing table were arranged exactly the same as the week before. Again, a fresh glass of tea rested neatly on a coaster on the clean, white tablecloth. His initial reaction was that everything was the same until he turned to greet her. Immediately he realized everything was different.

The gauze curtain was gone. Sadie sat in her rocking chair facing him; however, he was no longer looking at a silhouette behind a gauze curtain. This week nothing shielded her from his direct view. Her appearance riveted his attention. She wore a dark green print dress with a brown blanket draped over her lap. Looking directly at her face, he was stunned.

Her eyes, which had shown a hint of red through the curtain last week, now burned openly like red-hot coals. There was no soft white at the edges of her pupils like he expected in the normal human eye with a blue, brown or hazel pupil at the center. Her skin, while black, as he had expected as Sandy had told him that Sadie was African American, rippled with the wrinkled texture of a chimpanzee or gorilla, nothing like the smooth skin of a normal human. Mike believed most Caucasians held some unconscious prejudices that were often hard to overcome or even detect, but still he did not think he was dealing with the usual African American with pigmented skin. Sadie appeared to be something more, something different, something he could not describe. He had read enough to know that human beings of African heritage developed the darker pigmentation, giving them greater natural protection from the intensity of the strong ultraviolet rays found near the equator. He also knew that lighter skin color evolved as man began to live further north, away from the intensity of the ultraviolet radiation found at the equator. Still, he thought, Sadie was different. The issue here presented a question greater than one of skin color. Her face, her eyes, and her skin presented characteristics markedly different from Caucasians or Africans, not like anything or anyone he had ever seen or heard about.

"You gonna stand all day, or sit down?" she asked.

Embarrassed, he sat down quickly, avoiding her eyes as he fumbled for his pen and notebook. The one thing he did not want to do was to stare at her and upset her. He had started this visit badly. The open exposure to her unusual appearance had upset the casual approach he had intended to convey.

"I'm all set," he said, regaining his composure.

"Seems we let things get away from us last week. You'd ask me some simple question and I would take off jabbering like a wild turkey."

"That's fine, I learned a lot listening to you. After reviewing my notes, I wrote that I wanted to ask you more about the plants you used for food and medicine. I think the reader of a book about this area would want to know what you ate and how you used the plants for your survival."

"I know 'em if I see 'em, Mike. I don't know any of those fancy scientific names. I just know which ones are good for you to eat and which ones you have to boil first, and which ones you have to leave alone. 'Course you don't need me to learn about plants. Ask any of the native Indians like the Seminole or the Miccosukee that live around here. They know the same plants as me, maybe more. That's where we learned about the plants, from the Indians."

"I'm sure I can get a list from a book in the library. I can look up the Latin names there, too. I'll bring a book out here with photographs so you can identify them visually for me. That way you won't have to go anywhere to look for them."

"Yes, you bring your picture books here. I'll check your list. I can help you with that. Jus' remember there's good ones and bad ones and it's important to know the difference. Some are used for food and some can be used for medicines when folks get monkey sickness or have bad dreams or a speeding heart. The Indians taught me how to use the plants but they wouldn't teach me the healing songs. Those were sacred to the medicine woman. Some plants are used to make the medicine dolls and depending on the sickness, we would add certain plants in the stuffing."

"You didn't mention them last week. Sandy told me you make medicine dolls."

"I learned how to make them as a young girl, from the Indians who lived here. The old Miccosukee medicine woman taught me how to collect the mud and clay on the banks of the Seminole River and mix it to match the skin color. She showed me how to bake the molded head in the sun and sculpt the hands and feet and attach them to the body. She used fronds from the palmetto to weave the body together. The Indians traded for fabric from the early settlers because they mostly used animal hide for clothing until the white man arrived. I use herbs and other plants for filling and decorating the dolls."

"You still make dolls from what Sandy told me. Will you show some of them to me? I'm curious about them."

"Sure. The historical society invited me to demonstrate how I make them. That was many years ago. The women in the historical society support me now by sending discarded clothing and items they can't use at home anymore. Some other women from the local churches bring me donations to make the dolls, too. Making the dolls helped me adjust to missing Johnston and the Big 'Un once they were gone. Making the dolls builds a healing spirit for me. Sharing that healing spirit helps others when they have lost someone close or are sick. The

Indians knew the power of that healing spirit and transferred the spirit to the dolls with rituals and special plants."

"Last week we were talking about how you got along after Johnston disappeared. So you found the doll making helped you while you helped others."

"I was used to being on my own most of the time anyway. Johnston was a busy man, so I had to have something of my own to work on. He spent most of his time up at the sawmill, so I was mostly by myself even before he was gone. I made do for about a year on my own while I learned about healing plants from the medicine woman."

"So, if you were eight in 1900 and Johnston showed up four years later, then you met him when you were twelve in 1904. If he built the cabin when you were thirteen and you moved in at age fourteen, then that would have been about 1906," Mike calculated. "Does that sound right?"

"That sounds about right. Jus' remember, I didn't learn no 'rithmetic an' we didn't keep no calendars here. Time wasn't important in the slough. Don't forget radios didn't exist then either. I'll leave the calculating to you."

"If all that fits together, you lost *The Big One* two years later. That would have been about 1908. So how much later was it that you lost Johnston?"

"I think I was nineteen or twenty, but that's just a guess."

"So when you were nineteen, I estimate the year would have been 1911, if the math stands up. That's when you lost Johnston."

"We can use your numbers. I'm lookin' to you to do that math calculating."

"Last week, all you could remember about the guy who took care of you when you were a youngster was that you called him *The Big One*. Did you remember any other name for him during the week? Was he a relative?" asked Mike. "Sandy thought he might have been your father. I had the impression he must have been a close relative."

"Naw. He was jus' the Big 'Un to me. He didn't speak, so I never called him a name," said Sadie.

"What about Johnston's first name? All I wrote down in my notes was his last name. Did you remember anything more about his name?"

"Well, I thought about it some. I think they called him Jake up at the sawmill."

"Like in Jacob?" asked Mike. "Jake can be short for Jacob."

"No. Just Jake. All's I remember is Jake. When I talked about him, he was jus' Johnston, now I remember he said his name was Jake. But he didn't use it much, an' I never did. Folks 'round here got used to callin' him Johnston. That's what I called him, too, Johnston. I never did call him Jake."

"See you are remembering things. Didn't you say he came from New Orleans?"

"That was the name of the place he used to talk about some, but I know he lived out in the bayous. He told me the bayous're a lot like the slough."

"In Louisiana, they use 'parish' instead of county, from the French who settled there. Did he ever mention a particular parish?"

"Naw, nothing like that. He just talked a little about New Orleans, but a lot more about the bayous. I got the feelin' that's where he came from because he was right at home here in the slough. He was no city man, that's for sure."

"I guess he had no relatives around here?"

"I never saw any of his relatives. He was a stranger here. He came here by himself. I know he was a long way from home."

"You said you were alone for a year. What happened then?"

"One day I saw that the ranch hands were makin' those fences from old boards. They had to cut the boards themselves. I made friends with them and told them I had some wood they could use, so they introduced me to the old man."

"The old man? Who was he?"

"Oh, old man Williams. He owned the ranch, the Circle T. When his wife fell ill during one of her pregnancies, he came down here for a healing doll. I made one special for her and she came through her troubles okay. I made teas from the plants to help her, too. When any of the ranchers got bit by a snake or an alligator, they came to me for potions to treat them. After that, we got along real good, so when Johnston disappeared, I gave the old man the whole sawmill that Seth gave me. It wasn't doin' me any good and there wasn't anything I could do with all those big boards and logs. I figured he knew what to do with it and put it all to good use at the ranch. From then on, we was like family."

"I'm sure they appreciated the boards. Did you say the Circle T Ranch?"

"Yep. They're not far from here. I could walk there with no problem as long as I went through the woods, over there," Sadie said as she pointed in the direction of the Circle T. "The road's longer. The Circle T's my closest neighbor."

"I drove by there last week on my way out. I turned around in their driveway."

"You been to the ranch?"

"Yes, it's a really big spread. I didn't meet or see anyone. I turned around in the entrance and then drove home."

"They're real nice up there at the Circle T. You should meet them. Closest I ever had to family besides the Big 'Un and the medicine woman. I did real good from then on, after me and the old man got to be friends. He made sure I had bread and eggs and milk and all sorts of what I call luxuries. The old man liked me so I worked for the ranch for four years part time then I stayed on in the kitchen for over 30 years full time. When I was there during the week, I had my own room. It's the pantry behind the kitchen now, but it was my home at the ranch all those years. The old man adopted me."

"But you kept this place up, too?" asked Mike.

"I came down here on weekends. 'Course I had no time to hunt and trap after that. I spent all my time working. That worked out 'cause by that time all the Indians had to move out of the slough, too. The living conditions had become too difficult to survive here so some moved to the ranches and later onto the reservations. Over the years, the government stopped hostilities so that the white man and the Indians worked better with each other."

"You didn't bring any of the modern conveniences down here. What did you do at the ranch?"

"The ranch folks were always up on things. They always had the new inventions as soon as they were available in Tampa Bay. I mostly worked in the kitchen so I was first to use a lot of those things. I remember the electric stove, the washer, and the electric mixer the most. All those things helped 'cause we had so many mouths to feed up there. That new fangled stuff made sense there."

"So you remember when the telephone came in, electricity, refrigeration and all the appliances?"

"I saw them all. Using them made sense at the ranch. That's a big place, and they could use all the help they could get. I remember the steam tractor engine and the gasoline car and trucks. I think refrig'ration was the most important one for the ranch 'cause it meant they could plan meals ahead and adjust to what the markets had available at reasonable prices. Refrig'ration allowed them to plan ahead a week at a time for meals."

"Do you remember when you started working at the ranch?" asked Mike.

"I remember, about a year after Johnston was gone. That's all. I remember that real well."

"Some of the modern conveniences could have helped you here. Why didn't you bring in electricity and some of the appliances down here in your cabin?"

"I was careful. I could see what was happening. The more they brought things in, the further they got from the land and the more they became dependent on others far away. When they had a horse it was there at the ranch, they had to feed it and take care of it there. When they switched to the tractor engine, it ran on steam, which meant they fed it with wood that they had but they didn't have parts to fix it when it broke down. The parts came from far away. So they had to send away and wait for the replacement parts. Then the gasoline engine came in and that meant they had to bring in fuel from very far away plus parts from far away. When they switched over to the new contraptions, they became totally depended on others, things, and people far away. They didn't even notice what was happening. But I did, I saw what was happening. Most things were simple at first and could be fixed locally, but even that changed. I didn't like that. Most things I have we fix them. I don't want anything that when it breaks, I gotta find someone to find the parts and then someone to fix it. Today fuel comes from half way around the world from people who aren't always our friends. I saw that as dangerous to be dependent on things and people you don't know and can't control. Today everybody is dependent on someone else. Me, I never even had a horse. I couldn't keep one down here in the slough, so I simply traded my time for the things I needed."

"I'm sure those new things made work more efficient."

"Sometimes. Most things were simple at first and were fixed locally, but that changed too. As time went on, they had to send things out or bring someone in from the outside. I didn't trust that. You couldn't see what they were doin' and they charged a lot of money."

"I can see you have brought some of those things down here to the cabin. They make your life a little bit better."

"Well, yes, the most important change for the cabin I agreed to was the windows. I wanted to have glass windows and screening. I had a hard time getting those things for a long time. The ranch helped me get both the glass and screens. They went to Tampa Bay by train from up north someplace to get the glass and screens. When Johnston built this cabin, he wanted the windows and screens, but I didn't get them until after he was gone. We didn't have the money to buy them and have them put in. To me, it was the screens that was most important. The bugs bothered us all the time and I wanted to keep the bugs out. We didn't need to close the place up like windows do, so the screens were important to me to keep the bugs away."

"I'll bet it was hard to get a lot of things out here. Trading through the ranch must have made a real difference for you."

"After Johnston and the Indians were gone, everything I needed I got from them, through the ranch. I traded my time for essentials but I thought a lot of things they gave me were extras. They got things for me in town and then brought them down to the slough by wagon or later by truck. They brought me cloth and sewing needles and fishhooks and candles and oil for my lamps, and pots and pans. I know I spent most of my time at the ranch where they had all the modern conveniences, but my life here was much easier. I know they didn't pay me much of a wage, but I didn't need money. I thought I was rich. Can I tell you a little secret?" she asked leaning toward him quietly with an air of conspiracy about her.

"Sure," he said.

"I have a couple of old cigar boxes full of money hidden under the floor boards right now, in case I have an uneven exchange."

"Well, out here that's probably as good as any place to keep it."

"I think so. It's safe there and I'll know where it is when I might need it."

"So the big change in your life was the ranch. Maybe even more than losing Johnston."

"I guess I told you last week, I think Johnston got drunk from that jug and drowned. He couldn't swim a lick when he was sober. That was sad. In a way, he lived most of his life right on the river, rafting up and down tradin'. For him to drown was the real tragedy. I still blame that jug."

"You're convinced he didn't run off. Did he ever tell you why he left Louisiana?"

"No. It wasn't any of my business. The way I see it, everyone's entitled to a few private secrets they keep to themselves. 'Course I always knew he ran from something to come all the way down here. He never did say what it was, and I knew better and didn't ask. But I can tell you this, the slough and this cabin was his home. The one problem he had was with that jug, whenever he came back from a river trip, but I could tell this was home for him. He was comfortable here. I suppose he was unusual for his time."

"Unusual. How?"

"I read about it. Most people in those days never did go far from where they were born. Look at me. I've never been further out of the slough than the ranch, and I never wanted to either. But to me, Johnston, he was a real traveler. He came here from somewhere else."

"It's very different now. Everyone travels, and some go great distances."

"Some do," she nodded. "I told you last week, me and Johnston was best friends and after that mound thing, we made a truce. As long as he left that jug alone, we got along real good; otherwise I left him alone. We was home to each other, that's all. I know if he could have come home, he would have. Sometimes I think I'm still waiting for him to come back, even after all these years. He was a good, hard worker and good company for me. He treated me real good, especially after the Big 'Un was gone. I think he felt guilty about that mound and all. This cabin was a special place where we were safe together from whatever was out there. That's all I can say about it."

"I think you were lucky he found you. What do you remember about *The Big One*? How long was he with you before Johnston came around?"

"I was lucky that Johnston came around and the Big 'Un, too. Yes, my early memory is that there was a bunch of people around here. I was living with some folks right here at the Bend. Some was white folks, colored folks and some Indians. The Indians built their settlement nearby. Their houses differed from the log cabins built here. They used cypress frames and covered them with palmetto thatches. They called their houses chickees. I spent most of my time with the medicine woman. The folks here, I'm pretty sure they weren't my 'kin or parents. I vaguely remember them. When they left, I just remember the Big 'Un. That was a long time ago, Mike. He took care of me for some time. Then Johnston came along and they both got along good except for that one time when they both got into that jug together. That was bad, Mike. It still hurts me today because he was big and ugly and all those things, but he was kind, a gentle giant to me. He made me feel safe." She sighed, remembering.

"Then he was your only family."

"Well, yes. But the mound is still there, and the sheds. I go out there and visit the mound sometimes and think about the Big 'Un."

"I saw the mound last week. I did what you told me. I went around back and looked at it before I left."

"I'm glad you did. That's how we remember him…" Sadie spoke softly. Mike could hear the affection in her voice, mixed with a trace of loss. "I remember how he taught me about dry oak bein' the best firewood. It makes good, hot coals, but oak is heavy and hard to work with. I learned early on that I can heat the big pot with a small fire, so I could save firewood."

"How did you learn to read? Sandy told me you love to read. She said she brings you books and newspapers to keep up with the news of the world."

"Old man Williams up at the ranch had me sit in with his two kids when they had a tutor come in. The school was too far away. He's the one that got me started reading. Once he knew I could read, the old man gave me books. Of course, he gave me lots of books to read. One year back then, he gave me a dictionary. That dictionary was my favorite and what got me serious about readin'. I could look up words on my own and find out what they meant. I used to sit by the fire at night reading and flip through the pages of the dictionary reading about all those words, what they meant and where they came from. Did you ever read the dictionary, Mike?"

"No, never thought of it. I guess you're right, the dictionary has a lot of valuable information."

"Well, when his son Richard had his own kids, I was the one who ran the nursery as a teacher for them before they went on to the county school over by Arcadia. Richard had three girls and a boy and all went on to college. I was real proud of that. There was something wrong though, Mike."

"Something wrong? What was that?"

"I don't know what it was. Elizabeth, Richard's wife, she died young. I don't know what it was because they had her in some place up in Tampa Bay. Richard also died before his time from the cancer. The old man lived on beyond them. He outlived his children and died in his eighties jus' like his wife, but his son Richard and Richard's wife, they both had short lives. The old man had a daughter, too."

"A daughter? What happened to her?"

"She ran off with some fancy guy from up New York way. The old man didn't like the guy, so after that he had nothing more to do with her. She died in some accident without any kids, so the old man gave the ranch to Richard. Richard's four kids now own the place. Mostly his son Doug runs it. He's the only one in the family living there on the ranch now. We get along real good. He watches out for us. He stops by regular or sends one of the ranch hands several times a week to be sure we're okay, just like the old man did. He's a skip generation, a chip off the old man."

"What did you do with the extra money you earned at the ranch, besides hiding it in the floor boards?" asked Mike, grinning.

"My wages were never great but, as I told you, I still have some saved in cigar boxes. The real thing was that I traded with them at the ranch. 'Course I had free room and board and food when I worked there during the week. I would tell them what I needed for this place and they would add my things on the list when they went to town for supplies. I never went to town or anything. I wouldn't go. They'd always ask if I wanted to go, but I refused. I knew it would change me. No one gets rich working on a ranch, but it's a good life, Mike. I wouldn't change my life for anything. If I could do things all over, I'd do it all the same."

"Most people wouldn't say that. They have a lot of desires and a lot of regrets. You're fortunate."

"My life was just fine because I lived so close to the ranch. The ranch saved me when life collapsed in the swamp. The Indians moved to the ranches as farmers and workers. A lot of them went to the Circle T. Even though I worked, I had my freedom. I could come back here anytime I wanted. Life up there at the ranch changed everything. They brought me flour, cooking oil, all the utensils I needed, cloth, candles, lamp oil. Anything extra I needed came through the ranch."

"Sadie, some of the biggest changes in our civilization all took place during your lifetime. Do you realize that? You saw them all, cars, telephones, computers and even a man walking on the moon."

"Things is always changing, Mike. That's life, always something new, something different. Change just keeps happening. The biggest change for the ranch was refrig'ration, though it didn't mean much to me down here. I still did without, just like today. See, my tea? It's probably still warm from sitting in the sun to brew."

"Do you think all modern technology is bad?"

"Some things are good for some folks, but all these modern things take you away from the land. If you do too many of these new fangled things, you're gonna be in real trouble sooner or later."

"What about the man you call Ivan? Is he the 'we' you keep referring to? I understand he helps you a lot."

"I couldn't keep on living down here now without Ivan. He stays out in the shed at night. He says he's more comfortable out there. I met him up at the ranch. He's mentally retarded, you know, but I think of him as limited, that's all. The ranch hired him as a regular employee years ago, but he's a problem for some. We have to treat him like a child. They weren't set up to do that forever, so I brought him down here after a time. He still works for them checking the fences, rounding up strays and acting like a night watchman. In exchange, they bring us food and things we need 'cause I don't work any more. He's the one of us that works so he watches out for me."

"I didn't see him last week, and he's hiding this week, too."

"You won't see him, but he's around. He's real shy. He likes it here in the slough. I understand him and he understands me. We just adopted each other. The ranch doesn't pay him a salary anymore, but they give us supplies in exchange for what he does. We don't need money. They know someone is watching out for them and they appreciate that. 'Course he keeps helping on his schedule. He's good around here, too. I'm all he's got in the world."

"That's good. You really need to have someone watch out for you now."

"The years have gone by fast. Seems like they just slipped away, but they've been good years. I don't regret living here, Mike. I like my privacy and I don't miss all those new fangled things you have. I just don't need 'em, that's all. I like my simple life down here with Ivan."

"Isn't the key to your getting along, the things you did bring down here are simple items that don't require fuel or repairs?"

"If something breaks, we can fix it. The real secret is that there isn't much to break down. In your world, life is tied up with things you don't understand and you can't fix. That's bad. If you had no electricity or gasoline your whole world would stop. If you take care of the land, it will take care of you. Do you know what I think?" she asked leaning towards Mike.

"No, tell me. I'm all ears."

"One day it's all going to collapse."

"What is? Our society, our civilization? Business? The whole modern world?"

"One day it's just going to collapse. When it does, they'll all want the land back, and it will be gone. They'll have to start over. It'll happen, you wait and see."

"You might be right, Sadie. I don't know what to do to stop it."

"People will change. They can change, Mike, but not until something really bad happens. All they can do now is protect what's left. The slough is good for some folks, like me and Ivan. There are things that live here and you don't know anything about them, but you should know they are there, Mike. We need the wild places and the wild things that live in them, like the slough. Go put that in your book," said Sadie.

"Sure, I promise to do that. What else can you tell me?"

"I never did have much spare time, but if I did, I'd spent it out in the slough watching the natural world. Mostly, though, I spent every minute working on just surviving. I had to make all my meals, find the food, and cook it. Surviving took all my time. In your world, most folks really have very little to do. They don't even know about the world here in the slough nor do they want to. When they see the natural world, they destroy it. I think nature scares them. They don't see the beauty in it. They don't realize how much their lives depend on nature. Some day it will be painfully apparent."

"You sound like a philosopher," Mike chuckled to himself.

"You're here to listen, so I might as well tell you a thing or two. Besides, I don't have anyone else to talk much to. Ivan doesn't really understand about these things. They confuse him. He's lived out here too long, like me. He had trouble getting along with folks. They'd make fun of him and tease him 'cause he's slow. If I talk, he listens but he doesn't understand a lot of what I'm saying, and he doesn't talk much. Now I have you to talk to and you can tell my story. I want others to know what's going wrong in the world and how important it is to be close to the land before it's too late. You getting this all down?"

"Sure. How are you holding up?" asked Mike. "We're supposed to only go on for so long, remember?"

"I am getting tired. I do get so worked up when I talk about my life here. I didn't used to tire this easy."

"Then let's quit for today. We can talk again next week," said Mike, closing the yellow notebook. "There's always next week..."

"I'm looking forward to it. You better finish your tea. I made it special for you."

Mike picked up the glass of tea and drank it all down.

Chapter Six

An Invitation

The following Wednesday at 3:00 P.M., the phone rang in Mike's office.

"Hi, Mike. It's Sandy. I hate to bother you at work, but couldn't find your home phone number. Sorry."

"That's okay. You can call me here at the office or at home anytime. I told my boss I'm working on a project for the historical society. He knows I might get some calls about the project from time to time. He has no idea what it's all about, but he thinks it's great that I've volunteered to help you. I won't get a raise or anything for doing this, but the brownie points help."

"That's great you have his support, Mike. The historical society also appreciates that you're giving up your Saturday mornings to interview Sadie."

"Oh, that's nothing. I'm glad to help. Besides, not only do I enjoy talking with Sadie but I'm beginning to grow fond of her."

"That's the reason I'm calling you. They just told me they have a little reward for us," said Sandy.

"A reward? For us?"

"As a not-for-profit organization, the historical society gets a lot of invitations to attend other events, including those sponsored by other not-for-profits. The society received two tickets to a lecture sponsored by a paranormal group here in town. The speaker is coming in from Oregon and is supposed to be really good. They're expecting a big turn out. Anyway, the lecture is tomorrow night at the Banyan Inn on the Interstate."

"Isn't that the same Banyan Inn where we meet for the historical society?"

"Same place. Mrs. Abernathy thought you and I were due for a perk for working so hard on the Sutton Project, so she gave me two tickets. Would you like to go?"

"Tomorrow is Thursday. I work on Thursdays."

"It's an evening event and doesn't start until 7:30 P.M. We would have time to grab a bite at the restaurant right there at the hotel before the lecture if we could meet around 5:30. The timing will be close."

"Oh, an evening engagement should be okay. Did you say it was a paranormal organization? I like history, but I don't believe it's haunted. What sort of topic is it anyway?"

"I'm not sure, but I think we should accept their generous offer."

"Well, all I had planned was a microwave dinner and a baseball game on TV. I can tape the game so I really won't miss it."

"I promised to get you a copy of that book on Old St. Augustine. I'll bring it with me tomorrow night. It has a couple of good chapters on early Florida history that might help with your meetings with Sadie."

"That would be fine. I don't know a thing about that paranormal stuff, nor do I follow the subject much."

"Neither do I, but it might be interesting. A change of pace might be good for both of us."

"For your information, I don't believe in reincarnation either. That stuff about coming back as a butterfly doesn't turn me on and I don't really want to sit on a cloud strumming a harp for eternity."

"You don't? A lot of people do. They just don't think about it now. Mike, everyone has beliefs. You must believe in something."

"Well, I know what I don't believe in, like guardian angels, and crop circles created by aliens. I think it's people seeking public attention for their works of art, not little green men in flying saucers. Oh yes, and the Bermuda Triangle was created by someone who wanted to sell a lot of books. I understand the author's found another triangle, the Dragon Triangle, in the Pacific Ocean and is selling more books."

"My, you are the skeptic, aren't you? But, actually, I agree with you for the most part. Personally, I'm a religious person and go to church regularly. But, to be honest, I'm not sure I buy into a lot of the stories. To me, they provide exemplary parables for teaching lessons for living. So I guess I'm a fence sitter. I do believe there's something out there, I just don't claim to know what it is."

"Sure. But do you believe in the Loch Ness monster? Or little green men with big eyes crashing on the desert, or creatures landing in Puerto Rico? Or unidentified objects flying into and out of the ocean? I'm just a major cynic about a lot of this paranormal propaganda."

"Okay, I don't believe in most of those things either. I guess I'm more spiritual than anything else. Anyway, the speaker's topic is perception so that's a different twist on the subject. He's supposed to be educational and he comes highly recommended by friends of mine from Jacksonville. They heard him and strongly suggested I check him out when he came here."

"Ok, so we don't know what he's really going to talk about but it might be entertaining. Since I'm not really doing anything important tomorrow night, I'll go to keep you company. How about I pick you up?"

"That would be great, but it will be easier for me if I meet you in the hotel lobby. I'm scheduled to train a new teller for the bank's North Port office. It's just a few miles up the interstate, at the next exit. I can come straight down the interstate and meet you at the hotel. That will be more convenient for me. The evening will cost you nothing but time and dinner with me."

"I've got the message. I'll meet you there. There's nothing lost since it's free."

"By the way, I heard the speaker was written up in the newspaper a couple of months ago. Apparently he's known internationally and has a large following."

"Okay, but I've got to get back to work now so I'll see you in the lobby at the hotel tomorrow at 5:30. If I'm late, blame it on rush hour traffic."

On Thursday, Mike met Sandy in the hotel lobby as promised. Traffic was not bad, so he was only a few minutes late. The restaurant was busy. By the time they ate, they were just in time to make the presentation. The marquee in the lobby listed the presentation in Conference Room A, a room with a stage and seating for three hundred people. The speaker's name was listed as Kenneth Tomlinson of the Northwest Paranormal Research Institute in Corvallis, Oregon. The Almas Association of Palmetto County was sponsoring the presentation. A line of people had already formed at the entrance to the conference room where they were purchasing tickets from an older woman seated at a table outside the door.

"What is the Almas Association?" asked Mike as he passed the tickets to the usher inside the door.

Sandy looked at him, smiled and shrugged. As they entered the dimly lit room and took seats near the back, Mike noticed that there were only a few vacant seats scattered throughout the room. Sandy seemed to know a good number of people in attendance who she cheerfully smiled and waved to as they settled into their seats.

"Bank customers," she whispered defensively in Mike's ear.

Slowly the lights in the house dimmed, leaving one spotlight on the dais. The audience responded to the dimmed lights by quieting down for the beginning of the program. Now, he would find out what this paranormal stuff was all about.

Chapter Seven

The Australopithicine

Once the lights had dimmed and a single spotlight remained on the dais, the audience was silent. A short, partially bald man in his sixties approached the dais. In contrast with the casual dress of the attendees, he was formally dressed in a black suit and tie. He adjusted the microphone to his short stature and glanced around the room before he began addressing the audience.

"Good evening, ladies and gentlemen. My name is Harry Friedman, president of the Almas Association of Palmetto County. Welcome members, associates and especially our guests this evening. For those of you who are not familiar with the Almas Association, we are a Florida not-for-profit corporation. For your information, we have also printed contact information on the back of your program. Tonight's program is divided into two parts. Our guest speaker will entertain you during the first half and the second half will be our regular monthly meeting, which, of course, all are welcome to attend.

"During the intermission, please feel free to introduce yourselves to us. We would like to get to know you better and share our mission. We set up a table in the hallway with information about the association and membership staffed by our membership chair, Ms. Geraldine Small. Complimentary coffee will be available in the lobby during the intermission.

"Tonight, I am proud to announce our guest speaker, Mr. Kenneth Tomlinson. Ken is president of the Northwest Paranormal Research Institute of Corvalis, Oregon. As most of you know, our organization recently joined the Institute as an associate member. For those of you who are not familiar with the Institute, only local field organizations may join as associate members. Ken has asked me to remind you that while you as individuals cannot join; they do accept individual contributions to support the cost and maintenance of their database and research efforts. Our speaker will provide more information for us about all of this in the program tonight.

"Before our association became affiliated with the Institute, we actively sought to find the best research base around. Being keenly aware of our own limitations, we sought to expand our knowledge by aligning with a larger, broader based association. We found four possible affiliations, each of which was developing a national database. None of the other groups were even close in size or scope with what Ken and the Institute have put together. While we have had to overcome a number of stumbling blocks to become affiliated, we have done so enthusiastically. In chatting with Mr. Tomlinson this evening, he informed me he has also divided his lecture into two parts. First, he will discuss the science of the projects, and second, an analysis of the database itself through an overview of their interview form. Mr. Tomlinson graduated from the University of North Dakota in business and went on to establish the Institute. I could go on for a long time listing Mr. Tomlinson's accomplishments, of course, but we summarized his credentials in the program. Last month, I attended Mr. Tomlinson's presentation in North Carolina and was awed by the nature and extent of the information he has compiled. I doubt you will be disappointed this evening."

Although Mike was impressed by the man's ability to capture the audience's attention, he still had no idea what the speaker was going to talk about.

"Without further comment, I present to you this evening, our guest speaker, Mr. Kenneth Tomlinson." As he finished, a tall thin man wearing a dark suit emerged from backstage, shook hands briefly with Harry Friedman, then took his place at the microphone. He spent a moment readjusting the microphone to his six-foot height.

"Thank you, Harry. Good evening, ladies and gentlemen," he said as Harry Friedman left the podium. "I told Harry earlier how pleased I am at the attendance here this evening. Harry told me that many of you have traveled from all over the state to be here, and, as I have recently experienced while driving here, this is a big state. I plan to stay on schedule in consideration of those who live at a great distance. My goal here tonight is not to convert the non-believer or even the rail-splitter. My purpose is to provide you, the members of a local support association, with the knowledge that is available through science and our database. We want to help you become a better field collector for the data that is so crucial to our efforts. I hope to inspire and better educate you to be informed observers and able interviewers. Our long-term success is dependent on obtaining the highest quality fieldwork possible. In addition, the quality of our efforts is crucial to our short-term goal of gaining acceptance of our projects by mainstream scientists and our long-term goal, of course, species preservation.

"My comments will be technical. Feel free to take notes, if you so choose. The venue this evening is superb for this type of presentation except that it is not set up in a classroom style. I will try to be as entertaining as possible so please sit back and absorb as much as you can. If you do not take notes, a summary of my presentation will be available from your local association after this evening.

"Let's see," he said, almost to himself as he looked down at the control board on the podium. "To control the visual aids, press the buttons on the remote. Hmm…I'm not familiar with this one. So, there we go." The spotlight on the dais dimmed as a second one came on and the curtains behind him opened.

The audience gasped as they adjusted to the appearance of a wooden carving of a tall, grizzly bear standing behind and to the left of the speaker. The closer Mike looked at the figure, the more he realized that it was not a bear at all but a tall, upright apelike figure. Mike's only exposure to such a creature was on a late night cable program titled: "Mysteries of the Planet Earth." The seven-foot carving on the stage was riveting.

"The Institute acquired this exhibit here with us this evening as a representation of a full size adult male carved in pine two years ago by Inooki Uyri, an Eskimo Indian from outside Calgary, Canada. The background story giving impetus to this work comes from the artist who became so annoyed at being asked the same questions about his sighting that he took out a chain saw, an axe, and a chisel, and created this life-sized carving. We purchased this model at great expense because it closely matches what our database supports as the typical adult male's appearance. I don't want to plant any preconceived notions in anyone's mind because it's important to do the homework for each and every sighting. Nor do I want this exhibit to bias your observations. We brought this exhibit here tonight to serve as an appropriate visual aid of the subject. This exhibit represents only one person's representation of his encounter. As such, it provides no real value to us. However, this particular rendition correlates remarkably with the statistical norm in our database. Because of that striking resemblance, we decided to share it with you tonight.

"This fellow usually stands in the lobby of our headquarters in Corvalis, Oregon, when he's not traveling with us. I will talk in depth about the database later. First, let's make this exhibit real by calling it by its true identity, the Latin, or scientific name, *Australopithecus DeBosi*. This creature is not related to the one often referred to as Gigantopithicus, whose fossilized bones have been found in China. For simplicity, I will refer to our subject this evening as DeBosi. I recommend dropping all the old Indian and slang names and references used in the past, and start using the proper scientific name. Using the proper name will go a long way to professionalize our efforts. So, meet our subject tonight, DeBosi." Ken Tomlinson gestured for the audience to meet the creature behind him on the stage.

"At this point, I will clarify what we refer to as the 'one million year gap.' The mainstream scientific community agrees with this part of the program. They differ in opinion from us, believing that DeBosi became extinct one million years ago; whereas our database and all who contribute to it tell us that DeBosi walks on this earth today.

"Because scientists only deal with cold, hard facts, they have adopted their belief simply because they have found no fossils of DeBosi since one million years ago. Such an absence of scientific data justifies their conclusion that DeBosi must be extinct. This belief causes them to categorically dismiss all observations and encounters since then, producing what we call the 'one million year gap.'"

He pressed a button on the console and a slide appeared on a large screen suspended from the ceiling above and behind him. "The slide above shows the African continent divided in half by a line drawn across the continent horizontally from east to west.

"Modern anthropologists and archaeologists in Africa agree with us in that a common ancestor lived in southern Africa roughly five million years ago. Please note when I refer to southern Africa, I mean the southern half of the continent as shown on the slide and not the political demarcation or specific country. Scientists have no name for this ancestor nor have they found any bones for this individual to add to the fossil records. However, they know this ancestor was comfortable in both trees and on the ground. A species event occurred about five million years ago, and the common ancestor yielded two evolutionary lines, the *robust* australopithecines and the *gracile* australopithecines. Of the *graciles*, *Australopithecus africanus*, became the ancestor to *Homo erectus*, the direct ancestor to *Homo sapiens*, or modern man. The best scientific theory projects that modern man originated about one hundred eighty thousand years ago along the southeastern coast of Africa. All *Homo sapiens* descended from this core group of humanoids originating in that area.

"Our exhibit here this evening, DeBosi represents one of three primary species of *robust* australopithecines that also arose out of southern Africa at about the same time as the *gracile* australopithecines. However, DeBosi has remained the same without further evolutionary change to this day, except for the spin off of Gigantopithicus in our evolutionary chain. Comments in the popular press that DeBosi is somehow a missing link are simply incorrect.

"Anthropologists work hard to find good fossils, and rarely find DeBosi fossils. Fossilization progresses slowly, requiring special conditions. Especially for creatures living in the forests, skeletal remains decompose quickly due to acid soil conditions. If we had to use the argument proposed by mainstream scientists for extinction, half of the known creatures living in the forest today would be classified as extinct. Visual sightings provide the only evidence available to bear up their existence, the exact situation that exists for DeBosi."

He clicked the button again and a new slide showing the skeletal remains of two lower jaws appeared on the screen.

"Most importantly, our fossil records tell us a lot about DeBosi. Starting with the teeth and jaws, which are well represented in the fossil record, we learn much about DeBosi's eating habits. Notice the two representative jaws on the screen above. The image on your left comes from a fossilized jaw of DeBosi found in southern Africa. The image on the right was taken from the jawbone of a contemporary adult male *Homo sapiens*. First, compare the differences in both size and structure. The massive jaw of DeBosi makes that of *Homo sapiens* appear almost fragile in comparison. Observe the second difference in tooth structure between the two examples. DeBosi exhibits much larger, thicker grinding molars."

He paused and pushed the button again. The picture on the screen changed.

"This slide shows a larger picture of the DeBosi lower jaw bone. Dentition reveals a great deal about the life style of the species." Using the pointer, Tomlinson pointed to the molars on the jawbone and continued, "These large molars belong to a creature that spends a lot of time chewing. You may not have noticed the lack of eyeteeth or canines. The lack of canines signifies the most important difference between the two species. As a result of this trait, DeBosi cannot be a great carnivore and cannot be responsible for cattle mutilations or attacks on herds of wild herbivores. Due to the lack of canines, DeBosi becomes primarily a vegetarian, and as such is much more likely to be seen in the blueberry patch than out on the range attacking wild animals, or your neighbor's dog, or the farmer's cattle."

He pressed the button and the screen changed again.

"Note how this slide more clearly shows the upper and lower jaws of DeBosi, again found in southern Africa. The extent of the development of large molars for chewing and the absence of canines in both the upper and lower jaws is readily apparent. Without canines, DeBosi is relegated to the role of a vegetarian, not a carnivore. Without canines for ripping and tearing flesh, DeBosi could not penetrate the thick hides of even a mid-sized herd animal. If you find a DeBosi in your back yard, don't worry about your dog or cat. Look for DeBosi in your vegetable garden.

"Excuse my melodrama. The scientists at the Institute say we should classify DeBosi as an omnivore, which means he also, eats meat.

However, due to his dentition, the meat must come from small rodents such as mice, rats, chipmunks, and other small animals. Simply stated, if DeBosi picked up small creatures to eat, he would have to pop them into his mouth and grind them up using those giant molars. He would not have been able to rip into the flesh as most meat eaters do using their canines. We at the institute agree that the occasional use of grinding molars to chew up small animals does not justify separate classification."

He pressed the button and again the slide changed.

"Now, this slide compares the reconstructed skull of an adult DeBosi on the left with that of modern man on the right. The differences are extensive. Notice the ridge line running from front to back along the top of the DeBosi skull. Please feel free to correct our friends in the modern press. A missing link, DeBosi is not. The comparison here represents a million and a half years of widely divergent lines of evolution."

He tapped the button. The slide changed.

"This close up of the same DeBosi skull clearly shows the ridge line. This bone structure, unique to the *robust* australopithicines, evolved to anchor the large jaw muscles that made a life of endless chewing possible. This unusual skull also reveals more about DeBosi. Anthropologists focus on the issue of brain size and the implications of brain size, whether small or large when studying specimens. They conduct their research simply by taking the empty skull and filling it with sand. Then they measure the volume of sand that it took to fill the cranium. The volume of sand substitutes the volume of brain matter for the living subject. In summary then, the volume of sand correlates scientifically with the volume of brain matter for that individual. For example, on average, *Homo sapiens* yields a volume average skull capacity of 1400 cubic centimeters of sand.

"DeBosi skulls, on the other hand, average a capacity of around 600 cubic centimeters volume of sand. They infer that with the smaller brain, DeBosi is not capable of speech. Anthropologists expect communication for the DeBosi to be restricted to grunts, yells, and howls. Due to the small capacity of the skull, DeBosi does not demonstrate a structure for sophisticated methods of communication beyond primitive methods of vocalization. The fossil findings of pieces of the larynx, thyroid cartilage and hyoid bones or throat bones substantiate this theory. The hyoid bone and the thyroid cartilage, both crucial to speech, are poorly defined in DeBosi, although the pieces of fossilized bone from this area of the skeleton are still extremely rare. Skull size is not the total determining factor, but the scientists who study these structures and functions universally believe the brain of DeBosi is well below the threshold required for even rudimentary speech. In addition, anthropologists hypothesize that the shortened neck also impacts the poor development of the skeletal requirements for speech in DeBosi."

He pressed the button once again and a new slide appeared.

"Here we see a comparison of foot prints of DeBosi with modern man. While the differences in size are obvious, the average length of a human footprint measures less than ten inches and that of DeBosi measures well over thirteen inches. However, the shape of the imprint demonstrates a more striking difference between DeBosi and modern man."

The slide changed.

"This slide shows a close up of the best example we have found of a DeBosi foot print. The DeBosi foot lands flat as opposed to the human print that lands on its toes and heel with a distinct arch in the middle. The intersection of the leg bones with the foot falls further forward on DeBosi, placing the body weight substantially closer to the center of the foot, differing significantly from *Homo sapiens*. Also, note the difference in the bone and muscle structure in this foot cast. They differ dramatically when compared to *Homo sapiens*. This DeBosi footprint comes from a collection found in Washington State."

He changed the slide again.

"Now on the screen we see the fossilized bone structure of a DeBosi foot compared to that of *Homo sapiens*. The differences in structure are better shown here than in the footprint. Our foot print came from Washington State, but these fossilized foot bones come from southern Africa."

The picture on the screen changed again, showing only the enlarged bone structure of the DeBosi.

"This structure shows that DeBosi must walk in a manner quite different from that of modern man. We extrapolate that from the way

DeBosi leg bones are joined so far forward on the foot, the structure would cause the individual to walk with an awkward gait. Scientists speak of the correlation between foot size and height for humans. We can transfer this correlation to the DeBosi model. In addition, scientists extrapolate weight of the individual to some degree, although not with as much accuracy. Scientists project for the sample human footprint, the individual represented would be five feet seven with a body weight of 175 pounds. The foot for DeBosi on the screen, using the same extrapolation, would be representative for an individual seven feet tall and weighing at least 340 pounds."

He changed the slide again.

"This slide shows *Homo sapiens* man striding in a normal fashion. Stride length or distance between the left foot when it touches the ground and the next right foot impact is known as stride length. For *Homo sapiens*, the stride length spans about 30 inches as compared to an estimated 50 inches for DeBosi. Such a significant difference in stride length makes it impossible for *Homo sapiens* to physically fake a sequence of footprints of DeBosi. To be able to repeat the more flat equal weight distribution of the foot of DeBosi and then reach the second imprint of a stride would be difficult at best for a modern man to emulate.

"To summarize the scientific information here, we will revisit the slide of the upper and lower jaws of DeBosi."

He moved the slides through the carrousel to the earlier example.

"Anthropologists decipher much information about the life of the individual from dentition. Tooth enamel preserves well, providing excellent study material. Tooth development in infants and juveniles can be detected from enamel and yields clear indications of age. More importantly, a life of endless chewing means that the regular ingestion of sandy or other grainy material wears down the teeth. The resulting steady deterioration of the teeth reaches such a critical point that the individual can no longer gain the minimum caloric intake required for survival, causing the individual to slowly die of starvation.

"Scientists estimate that this process limits the life span of DeBosi to about 50 years. In the example before you, we have a young male estimated to be in his mid-twenties because the teeth are fully developed and have little evidence of wear except for a small chip off one front tooth.

"While we are still on the topic of age, I'm sure many of you have visited an elderly friend or relative in a nursing home. There we find examples of the one most powerful forces of nature, gravity. Slowly gravity wins over the lifetime struggle for the individual to walk upright. We ultimately lose to the unyielding power of this physical force, as the individual is pulled slowly and inevitably downward. Even our feeble attempt to fight back through the use of canes, walkers, and crutches and other devices cannot ultimately avoid the wheel chair as a means of temporary mobility. Finally, if we live long enough, gravity becomes a horizontal trap from which we never rise again. Since DeBosi has no nursing homes and no dentists, we estimated the fifty-year life span from the decay of the molar teeth. The inevitable power of gravity on the functionality of the spine, weighing more heavily in the larger Debosi, reinforces this theory."

The screen went dark and disappeared as the side curtains drew closed across the stage behind the speaker. High ceiling lights flooded the interior of the theatre.

"While my assistants pass out some blank interview forms to everyone, let me summarize this part of our program. The fossil records of the past remain sparse for the DeBosi. In the future, we expect to find more and expand our knowledge significantly over the next few years. We are now beginning to experience greater political stability in the southern half of the African continent and, as a result, we are able to expand the archaeological fieldwork in a non-threatening atmosphere. We do not know enough about the DeBosi as an individual or social creature to know where and how they bury their dead. Until we discover more information or find the historical links across the 'million year gap,' we have to continue to rely on information collected in sightings. However, without more dramatic discoveries today and in the future, the one million year gap will be addressed by our own efforts to develop and maintain our database. Every one here this evening may play a critical role in this effort."

Chapter Eight

The Database

"Now, each of you have received a copy of Report Form 1001. Check the lower right corner of page one where the letter 'R' appears followed by the current month and year. Our goal to bridge that one million year gap begins here.

"While I'm not going to go through this new version of the form line by line, I will provide an overview of what the form does, how it works, and some insight about what our database shows after having processed over eight thousand reports.

"If the information memorialized in our database says anything about the future by looking at the past, we might be able to guess where the next encounter or observation will occur.

"I predict from the database information, the next report will be an observation by a person who is neither affiliated with the Institute nor a member of any local support organization. Further, this observer will not be a 'believer,' as we currently use the term. In addition, the duration of the observation will not last more than one minute. The observer's only interest will be to report the sighting to a source where their report will be treated seriously. The observer will most likely want their report to be used for the advancement of knowledge. The observer will never have a repeat event in their lifetime and they will continue to live a normal life after making the report. Keep this prediction in mind as you read the form.

"Be careful in collecting the data and filling in the form. The report must be an accurate record of exactly what the observer has experienced. Avoid leading the observer or including your own preconceptions or beliefs in the report. Occasional inaccurate observations as well as most fraudulent reports will be handled within the database system. If you feel it would help us, add a supplemental page with your comments. As a field representative, we welcome your comments. If you do add a comment, include your name, local association, and membership number so we know who you are. Any report submitted by an associate member must be counter signed by a full member.

"Now I will explain how the evaluation system works. Internally, we selected fifteen key identification characteristics for each category. If a report does not show that category to be representative in a high percentage of cases, we rate that item with a negative mark. For example. on the form, find the category heading for TEETH. The item asks only for evidence of long canines. Reports rarely include observations of long canines in DeBosi. If the observation includes having canines, we rate the entry with a negative mark. Of course, if the observer indicates that no observation could be made on teeth, the report is not given a negative mark.

"If, out of the fifteen characteristic items we monitor, a particular report shows five or more negative marks, the report registers with less than full weight in the system. We reject reports with ten or more marks. For example, we selected CORNEA EYE COLOR as an evaluator item. Since DeBosi is an animal, the database shows we should anticipate red corneas, not white corneas like those of *Homo sapiens*. For the evaluator item, HAIR COLOR, we anticipate the color of our exhibit here.

"Remember, we recognize observers may not be able to answer all the questions completely. A sighting of a silhouette in the dark at night on a distant ridge yields little data. In such instances, mark the box labeled 'unknown.' Notice, we collect data for time of day, weather conditions such as fog, rain, moonlight, and whether the event occurred in the deep forest or an open field. All these details represent important information addressed on the form.

"Go to the section on TOOLS. Examples of tool use include a rock used as a hammer or a stick used to dig for insects. The use of a club as a weapon does not rate as a significant characteristic in our database, so it receives a negative mark. The fossil record for DeBosi fails to show use of stone or bone implements even as basic as Chilean I level. Thus, we define the use of tools simply as the use of natural objects to aid in the accomplishment of the individual's goals.

"On the top of the second page, we provided space for the interviewer to write a summary of the observer's sighting. Complete this section by asking the observer detailed questions. We have found that everyone who has experienced an encounter or an observation anxiously wants to tell his or her story to an interested party. Telling the story becomes the highest priority in their minds, so address it as quickly as possible. Human nature presses the observer to relieve the anxiety of holding the story inside. Human beings need to tell their story to someone else as soon as possible.

"The characteristic of SMELL indicator says the observer should detect a strong repulsive odor generally described as skunklike. The database marks the lack of odor in the report with a negative mark, but only where the encounter lasts over one minute and the distance between the observer and the subject is estimated at less than 150 yards. We do not discount any other factual variation. Wind direction, if the observation is upwind of the subject, will obviously negate an odor component. The database program takes all of these observation characteristics into account.

"Our results show that domesticated animals as dogs and cats, fear DeBosi, engaging in avoidance behavior if confronted by the subject. Domestic animals characteristically retreat during an encounter, our expected result. Report all other exhibited behavior for domesticated animals in the remarks section. These alternate reactions rate a mark.

"The database clearly demonstrates on the characteristic of SKIN TEXTURE the anticipate black skin color, with a texture like that of an adult chimpanzee. Skin texture for DeBosi differs from the thin or smooth characteristic found in *Homo sapiens*. Thus, skin texture provides another evaluator characteristic for the DeBosi.

"NECK anatomy provides another unusual evaluator characteristic. We expect the observer to report a short or lack of a visible neck. The DeBosi head appears to rest almost directly on the shoulders with an extensive hair mat at the back of the neck. If the observer reports seeing a long neck, the database adds a mark for this report.

"For example, if the observer reports red hair color, not brown, and there are no other marks on the report, the color remains in the report and receives full weight. Only reports with five or more marks rate less than full weight in the database. As I said before, the interviewer may also submit a supplemental statement to the report. Use common sense. Don't waste any time on obviously fraudulent reports. If common sense tells you the observer's story appears fraudulent, or will accumulate more than ten marks, or the observation seems too outlandish, do not submit it. If the observer insists on the validity of their report, seek confirmation. We designed the database to take into account occasional human frailties in observation and obviously fraudulent submissions. If you need help, consult with the officers of your local association.

"We use specific terminology as it appears on the form. We define *observation* as an incident of less than one minute where the subject has no awareness of the observer and an *encounter* includes incidents of longer duration where the observed becomes aware of the observer. These definitions provide consistency in using the form, so I urge you to understand the differences and apply the terms as we have defined them.

"Previously, we defined representatives as strictly an interviewer. We encouraged the interviewer to remain objective and limit their activities to simply filling in the form. We have changed our position to a new perspective. We now encourage the interviewer to expand their role to be more of an investigator, to be more pro-active.

"Go with the observer to the location of the incident. Act like a detective at a crime scene. Actively look for spoor droppings, hair samples, and footprints. The observer may want to avoid going back to the scene of the observation out of fear. Usually the observer will not look for spoor, hair or footprints. We request that the report be thorough and the interviewer make the effort to find other significant details, including an investigation of the location of the observation.

"For example, we received a report where an observer estimated the height of the subject to be seven feet tall. However, the observer reported that the subject was standing under a tall pine tree where the subject's head came up just under the first branch. After the sighting, the investigator took a tape measure back to the same tree and measured the distance from the ground up to the branch. The investigator added a supplemental note to the report including the true height measurement and how it was obtained. Often our biggest problem remains the lack of witnesses. In this case at least, the tree served as an important witness, providing factual data about the subject, becoming a 'witness tree.'

"Amazingly, at the Institute, we receive many single sample footprints, as are found in other collections around the world. We possess no evidence that DeBosi can fly or hop or appear out of nowhere only to disappear again. In fact, no one has ever reported a subject at a full run. Most observations report the subject moving in a brisk stride, so we have determined that to be the norm for the subject to avoid the encounter. Rationally, the subject must come from somewhere and go to another location after the encounter, but no reports include any indication the observer has tracked the subject.

"The logistics of the encounter and nature of the terrain influence the quantity and quality of footprints. DeBosi can move quickly over a wide area precluding any opportunity for the observer to follow due to its greater stride capability than *Homo sapiens*. Logically, we cannot explain the high percentage of the footprints submitted as one and only one foot. Tracking a subject over a short distance with even minimal skills should yield more than one footprint. We hope to find long sequences to provide the opportunity to measure stride length in the field. For obvious reasons, we don't give full weight to single prints, especially those that are not accompanied with a report of an observation or an encounter. Plaster casts of any single footprint have no significance to us either; however, a series of multiple prints may carry heavier weight.

"So, in summary, be prepared. Keep a still camera or video camera in your car at all times. Avoid locking photographic equipment in the trunk or being without film or batteries, as that serves no purpose. Keep a supply of the report forms with you at all times. Usually, most observers retain detailed recollections of an observation for a short period of time, so write down your observations immediately. If you are not prepared, the opportunity to capture the subject on film slips by quickly as does the opportunity to provide an accurate written report.

"Now, what do we do with all the data we collect? How does the data help us? For all observations entered into our database, ten years ago we found the percentage involving males was seventy-two percent, females yielded nineteen percent, and the percentage of young or juveniles reported was nine percent. In recent reports collected over last ten years, the percentage reporting males was ninety-one percent, the percentage of observed females slid down to seven percent, and the percentage of juveniles and young has dropped to two percent.

"If we extrapolate indicator trends from this data, we face an alarming situation. As far as we know, DeBosi lives and forages alone, and rarely groups socially. The percentage of observations of multiple subjects continues to be small, as it always has been. The dramatic drop in the percentage of females and juveniles concerns us the most.

"Five years ago, we estimated the world population at under five hundred individuals. Now, primarily due to the figures derived from the database, we have adjusted that figure to fewer than three hundred individuals. In response to pressure from both within and outside the Institute, these diminishing numbers spotlight the situation we believe we are facing. All of this is academic. With an estimated lifespan of fifty years and the rapid loss of habitat taking place due to environmental changes, we hypothesize DeBosi as a species pivots precariously on the edge of extinction, no matter what number we use.

"Our goal remains to bring conventional science to our aid. If we succeed to bring them in, what one thing can the membership do to assist this goal? My answer becomes the core reason that has scared mainstream scientists away: Our history of being a bunch of 'believers.' Scientific inquiry and belief are contradictory concepts.

"We often accuse traditional scientists as having adopted the assumption that this species became extinct one million years ago. The basis for this belief rests solely on the lack of any recent fossils younger than that one million year sample. We face the reality of the problem in the mirror every day. In general, cults of believers characteristically shun everyone outside their circle of belief. Cultural, social and political groups usually accept only those who believe the same credo as the majority of the individuals in a close-knit group.

"While scientists avoid us, we actively seek to share our knowledge with them. If we enlist their aid, we must embrace their methodology, their tools, and their techniques. Why believe in something when our actions assist in extinction? We live on planet earth where ninety-nine point nine hundred ninety-nine percent of all the creatures that have ever lived are extinct. Currently, we are experiencing the greatest mass extinction that has ever taken place on earth. The cause primarily falls on humans in their ever-expanding population, squeezing out the vast remains of the undeveloped natural environments around the world. The rainforests are shrinking and the deserts are expanding due to the loss of much of nature's beautiful ecosystems. Society applies a double standard when it convicts a man of murder or rape based on eyewitness testimony, but rejects our reports out of hand because they are only an eyewitness observation. We know science also functions on belief as do we. Sometimes negative beliefs are difficult to resolve.

"To succeed, we must throw away the shackles of belief and embrace the concept of the open mind and scientific endeavor. Our intention, to spread the knowledge of our findings, requires adoption by the general public. Our investigators must adopt our report form and support the local associations now, before DeBosi becomes extinct. Assisting in expanding our knowledge through the database and lectures, as this one tonight will make a difference.

"Oh, I have one final comment before closing. As you know or may have heard, the Institute investigated three reputed instances where DeBosi hair samples were found. We learned for the 'Nepal incident,' the hair sample DNA came from a yak. In the other two instances, both of which occurred in this country, where the samples were allegedly tested by a qualified laboratory, the results reputed to find the hair belonged to no known species of animal. Unfortunately, neither case was based on an Institute report, so we don't know any more. We are unable to establish the veracity of the reputed incidents or the reports. Both remain in the area of hearsay and pure conjecture. Hopefully, we will be able to find more substantial information in the near future.

"In conclusion, thank you for this opportunity to discuss the database and the efforts of the Institute. I hope to have both motivated and informed you this evening. Thank you and good evening.

The audience stood and applauded enthusiastically.

Harry Friedman returned to the microphone, "Thank you, Ken, for such a comprehensive presentation. We will now take a fifteen-minute break. Help yourself to coffee in the lobby. We have handouts and brochures at the information table. The general meeting will start at 8:15."

Sandy leaned over to Mike. "This is our exit call. If we go quickly now, we can beat the traffic."

Mike only nodded. He could find no words.

Chapter Nine

The Believer

Mike had visited Sadie in her cabin twice. Initially, he thought her appearance was simply, strange. When he had first seen her, he did not know how to explain his unsettling feelings about her. To compound his reaction, he realized that Sadie had really not revealed much factual information about her past or *The Big One*. Even Sandy had said nothing about *The Big One* or mentioned Sadie's unusual appearance. Mike could not even imagine what *The Big One* might have looked like. Sadie had only vaguely described his appearance, leaving most to conjecture and imagination. The mental images of this strange man who had taken care of Sadie as a child remained vague and mysterious for Mike. His frustration grew as he faced the absence of documented facts so far: no names, no faces, no traceable personal information. He planned for his future visits to keep pressing Sadie for more details in spite of her poor memory and tendency to spin her story on her terms. No one, including Sandy had opened any of these topics for discussion or dialogue, so, he continued to keep his opinions to himself.

He would have let go of his uneasiness and that would have been the end of it if he had never attended the presentation at the hotel. With this unusual experience, he had abruptly changed his opinion and now put a face on his feelings. Sadie, he convinced himself, was born of mixed blood; she was not a full-blooded human being. He concluded that she possessed the eye color, skin texture, and general appearance of the DeBosi described in Ken Tomlinson's presentation. Yet, in contrast with the model, Sadie stood barely five feet tall and possessed a frail bone structure. She did not present the gross physical stature of the DeBosi or shaggy brown hair in the DeBosi model. No, he thought, her characteristics mixed traits of both human and the DeBosi model.

The one she called *The Big One* had frustrated him initially. Now, his mental image of *The Big One* began to gel into the standard description of the model DeBosi at the presentation. If Mike accepted the model as a real being, then her vague description of *The Big One* matched the standard description of the model proposed by the Institute's database. Recounting Sadie's story, Mike now also believed that the remains of a pure blooded DeBosi were buried in the mound in Sadie's backyard, buried where Sadie said Johnston had buried *The Big One*. Mike convinced himself that he could now put a name on his previous uneasiness and unexplained feelings. The more he thought about it, the more he felt a compulsion to talk with someone about his new theory about Sadie and her heritage. As his impressions strengthened, he began to feel alone and isolated. He sensed that he must be careful about whom he selected to discuss his theories. He needed to avoid any premature, unwanted attention to Sadie or himself, or to be labeled irrational for verbalizing his thoughts.

Mike had kept his thoughts to himself about Sadie for some time. He began to feel as if he had stepped out into a foreign planet and he was the alien. He could not ignore her unusual appearance or her story about the origin of the mound behind her cabin, a part of the remote timeless land of the slough. For Mike, the pressing question became, in whom could he confide? He sensed that he could not confide his theories about Sadie to Sandy. She had intimated nothing unusual about Sadie in any of their conversations. As a result, his inhibitions remained strong, preventing him from disclosing his theories or even allowing an opening to discuss what he had on his mind. He sensed that Sandy would not be receptive to his thoughts or share in his beliefs. Ultimately, his decision was not an easy one. He simply decided to find someone else to talk to about his beliefs. He refused to continue to bottle up his theories about Sadie inside, especially now that he had identified an image for them. His thoughts grew to become an obsession. He had to have answers, to verbalize his theories with someone.

His pressing question continued to be in whom could he confide? Then the answer became obvious to him. At first, he had wanted to call Mr. Tomlinson at the hotel after the presentation, but he remembered that Mr. Tomlinson had left for the west coast immediately after the presentation. Mike reached into his jacket pocket and found the brochure the assistants had passed out at the presentation. The phone number and a post office box address for the local Almas Association in Brandon were printed on the back.

Mike knew his theories were superficially outrageous. Instinctively, he feared a response of ridicule and scorn from other people. He knew he could not handle that kind of reaction from other people for his opinions and beliefs. He did not like to have his opinions judged harshly, either. So, Mike refused to speak them aloud. Finding a truly open-minded person to discuss the subject of Sadie and her heritage presented Mike with a difficult challenge. Since most of the members of the local association would most likely be believers, following a logical assumption, certainly, one of the members could be someone he could talk with. As believers, he felt someone would at least listen to his story and he would not be scorned or judged harshly. Right now, having a sympathetic ear seemed to be what he needed. Feeling confident in his assumption, he settled on finding someone in the association to help him decide what to do.

Mike opened the brochure and located the phone number for the local representative in Brandon. He dialed the number and a man with a deep voice answered the phone.

"Hello, Cole residence. Stanley Cole speaking."

"Hello," said Mike. "My name is Mike Byrne. I found your phone number on the brochure for the Almas Association from the meeting last month at the Banyan Hotel."

"Yes, my wife Margaret and I are field representatives for the association. How can we help you?"

"I'd like to talk to someone about an observation."

"You have the right number. We're trained to handle interviews and prepare reports. You can talk freely with us."

"Okay, I'd like to tell you about my experience."

"That's fine, but we don't discuss this subject over the phone, Mr. Byrne. I prefer to meet with you in person. Are you willing to meet in person?"

"Sure," said Mike. "I work so evenings are more convenient for me."

"We find that time is of the essence, Mr. Byrne. Are you available tonight?"

"Sure, how's seven o'clock?"

"Good. That's fine. If you don't mind, I'd rather you come here. We live in the Kensington Apartments, on US Highway 41, south of town."

"I'm writing this down. Give me your apartment number. I won't have any trouble finding you. I know roughly where the complex is located."

After Stan gave him the apartment number, he asked, "Were there any other witnesses to the observation?"

"No," said Mike. "I was alone. I'll see you at seven."

"I look forward to seeing you later. By the way, we prefer you don't discuss your experience with anyone else until you meet with us."

"I understand," said Mike. "I attended your last meeting so I understand."

Mike's insecurity increased and second thoughts entered his mind as he drove to Stan Cole's apartment. He recognized the desperation he felt to relieve his anxiety by talking to someone about his experience with Sadie. Since Stan Cole belonged to the association, he felt Stan presented his best chance of finding someone sympathetic. Even though he would be talking to complete strangers, a common belief could reduce the chance of ill feelings. Believers would listen to him in a confidential, intelligent manner. Hadn't Stan reassured him that he was making the right decision?

When Mike knocked on the door to the apartment, a short man of about forty-five responded immediately. Mike noted his full head of wavy, brown hair and scruffy beard. Stan had not shaved in several days. His appearance reminded Mike of a lumberjack or woodsman from the Pacific Northwest. Giving credence to his impression, Stan

Cole's faded jeans were topped by a red plaid cotton shirt and Mike could smell the unmistakable aroma of beer as Stan spoke.

"Mr. Byrne," he said, moving to shake Mike's hand. "Stan Cole, here."

"Yes," said Mike, taking his hand. Stan Cole's grip implied the sure grip of a manual laborer, matching his attire. "I just called about the observation."

Stanley looked both ways down the corridor, as if to make sure no one had seen Mike's arrival. "Glad to meet you. May I call you Mike?"

"Sure," said Mike.

"Look, let's not dally out here. Come in and have a seat." He motioned Mike towards the sofa in the small, casually decorated living room. Mike caught the last frames of a basketball game on the TV in the entertainment center as a beer commercial interrupted the action. Stan crossed the room and turned the console off. He turned back to join Mike on the sofa. Four empty beer cans, napkins, and a large, half eaten pizza cluttered the coffee table. Before sitting down, Stan cleared the items off the table and carried them into the kitchen.

"Sorry for the mess." Stan paused, "Hey, are you a beer drinker?"

"Yes, but I'll pass for now. I just ate dinner."

"I'll get you one anyway," said Stan, ignoring Mike's response. Stan went back to the kitchen, and removed two beers from the refrigerator. Juggling them as he returned to the living room, he gently tossed one to Mike and settled down on the sofa popping the opener on the other.

"Go ahead," said Stan, facing Mike with an intense look. "Talking about it'll do you good. My neighbor Bill and I were watching the game when you called, but he's not one of us, if you know what I mean. I told him I had a sudden business problem to go over some change orders for tomorrow's work. He bowed out to let us talk privately. I'll call him back when we finish. He's a good sport, but I don't know where he comes out on these things, you know. Besides, the association trained us never to interview anyone with someone else present. They drilled us to take interviews and reports with only the observer present or any witnesses. Most folks don't want anyone else to know about their encounter. They feel uncomfortable about it."

"Yes, it's a private thing," said Mike as he opened the can out of nervousness and began sipping the cold beer.

"You seem anxious, Mike. Relax. You're among friends. That's what we're all about. If you've had an encounter or just an observation, we support you. We understand, you know. We never ridicule anyone or question their story. I won't interrupt or challenge you. We accept what you tell us about your encounter. I write up what you tell me, nothing more, to send it into the database."

"Sounds fair to me. I remember Mr. Tomlinson's presentation. The database is what's important."

"I'll keep your name confidential, if you want. First, I'd like to show you something." Stan stood up and removed a large book from the entertainment center. As Mike looked it over, Stan removed a large three-ring notebook and a framed picture from one of the shelves above the TV and carried them over to the sofa. "Here, Mike, take a look at this picture."

Mike looked carefully at the picture Stan was showing him. The ebony wood framed a picture of a small group of people on a wintry mountainside. All of them were bundled up in hooded parkas, gloves and scarves. The fresh layer of snow glistened pure white in the sun and white frosted pine trees lined the edge of the forest in the background, like sugar powdered candy.

Stan continued, "This is our group from the association here in Brandon. We all decided to take an expedition to the mountains in Washington State last year, hoping to have an encounter or observation of our own. That's me on the right, and my wife to my left. She's visiting her mother tonight, or you could have met her, too. Maybe another time. That was a special trip. We had a good time, but nothing happened, no observations or encounters. Well, maybe a couple of the women had a fleeting sighting in the dark, one evening, but they never convinced me it was real so we never wrote it up. I thought it was wind in the shadows of the fir trees. Anyway, we met some of the people up there. They showed us a whole collection of plaster casts of footprints. The trip was worth it for that alone. A lot of us around here are believers. We share our experiences within our group and we look out for each other, you know. We're a close knit group."

"I see that." Mike hid his growing concern that the confidentiality he desired might not be as secure as he wanted with Stan. Stan belonged to a clique within the association. Mike was not looking for a group.

"We're all believers through and through. Each one of us will do whatever we can to help you. I know when you called me, you felt isolated. Something happened that you don't understand. You need to talk to someone about it and you need to feel comfortable. Believe me, we know how you feel. All of us have felt that way, one time or another."

"You're right about that," said Mike. "This isn't a topic you can mention to just anyone."

"You got that one right. Bill, next door, is one of my best friends, Mike, but I've never brought up the subject with him. I'm not sure how he'd react if he knew about the association. I don't want to risk my friendship with him. If he found out about my beliefs, who knows what would happen to our friendship if he didn't share my beliefs. Or worse, he might call me a fool or crazy. So, in the group, we depend on others to find us through advertising and meetings. We generally don't try to recruit neighbors or co-workers. We wait for them to find us, as you have. If someone is interested, they'll find us. We prefer for them to find us on their own.

"With something like this, you're right, you don't know how a person will react," said Mike. "Certain issues in this world polarize people. You can easily lose or make friends depending on which side of the fence you're on. You either believe in something, or you don't. When it comes to believing, emotional extremes affect a person's opinion, and even the whole relationship."

"You know, Mike, we share our observations, encounters and beliefs among our own group. That helps all of us alleviate the feeling of being alone. Our group provides the one place where we don't have to feel concerned about our opinions or reactions of others. Knowing the group is behind us helps a lot. You'll see as you get to know us."

"Thanks. I'm comforted to know there are understanding people in the world," said Mike, convinced now that his need for confidentiality was in jeopardy. His discomfort with Stan had escalated as Stan continued to talk about his group of believers. Mike knew Stan would share the story of his encounter with Sadie among the other members of his group. This revelation ran against his concern for Sadie's protection and his own sensitivities, if others knew his opinions.

"You be careful, Mike. When you deal with outsiders, you could lose a job, friends or even family over this sort of thing. As I see it, our only hope is to convert the non-believer. If we're going to get anywhere, we *have* to convert the non-believer. We need to tell the outside world about our observations and beliefs to bring them on board."

"I attended the recent presentation at the hotel," confessed Mike, uncertain how to start and feeling very unsure of himself. "I was a guest."

"That was a good presentation. We were there, too. All the local believers were there. That was the problem," said Stan.

"There was a problem? I thought the association unanimously supported the speaker."

"No, I mean the problem with the general public, you know, the press. No one invited the press. We'll never convert others if we stick together among ourselves. We have to spread the word. I hope we bring Mr. Tomlinson back next year. He's great. Next time, we need to invite the press and do a better job of soliciting the general public."

"So, advertising will help?"

"Sure, others need to see the truth, that we're right. Think about it. Finally someone else will recognize we're right; we have fossil records, proof. We even have an official scientific, Latin name now. They'll have to deal with us now." Stan was getting excited. "Someday, maybe we can come out of the closet. I hope it happens during my lifetime. I want to see it happen while I'm still alive and have something effective done before it's too late."

"I'm astounded about the amount of research involved, the existence of such a large database, the whole thing. I didn't know we knew so much or had so much information about these beings."

"We were all impressed, " said Stan, putting down the picture and lifting up the heavy notebook. "Look. My wife collects newspaper articles from papers from all over the country on sightings. She keeps this up diligently, has for over ten years. Go ahead, leaf through the book. The plastic covers protect the pages. She works hard on this project, a labor of love. Some of those articles are old and the paper is fragile," warned Stan.

Mike carefully turned the pages. "Look at all these articles about sightings. I'm impressed. I didn't know there were so many. Your wife spent a lot of time putting this album together."

"Think about how we can reach the public with our story. We need exposure, Mike. I know who to call locally at the Brandon Times, Dan Meyers. He works as a reporter. He'll get us in the daily paper anytime as long as we have corroboration. For example, I can prepare a report based on our interview, and tell him the story. He'll write up an article that says what happened and to whom. He spells out the facts reported to him. Of course, he has to mention names. It's the best way to convert folks, Mike, exposure, the press, names of local people in print. We haven't talked about your observation yet, but think about it. Or, we can leave your name out if we do it the right way. You know, protect the sources," he said smiling.

Mike was not smiling. He was mortified thinking about Sadie and what her reaction would be if an article appeared in the newspaper about her and his suspected beliefs about her true heritage. Right now, he wanted to keep her story confidential. That much, he was sure of. He only wanted to talk to someone he could trust to air his thoughts and feelings, but it was becoming obvious that Stan and his group of close friends, and maybe even the association were not what he was looking for.

"Collecting data I can understand, Mike, but if we don't share it with the public, what good is it?" asked Stan. "That's where a lot the members differ with that speaker. Of course, we understand the real problem."

"Real problem? What's that?"

"The government."

"The government? What does the government have to do with this?"

"They're from the religious right. They claim to be believers, but they really aren't. They don't know science, only religion. They think of DeBosi as the missing link, a threat to their beliefs, so they diffuse our information. Look what they did with UFO's."

"What was that? What did they do with UFO's?"

"The government's agenda for UFO's discredited the reports and anyone who spoke out in favor of their existence. They don't know what they're dealing with and they don't want the public to know their lack of knowledge on the subject. So they hide what information they do have and say little to nothing."

"I see." Mike didn't know what to say so he kept his thoughts to himself.

"However, with our subject, they know everything."

"They do? How's that?"

"With today's spy technology, satellites and all, they've got to. They're watching all the time with high-powered cameras and zoom lenses, 24/7. Since they can't handle the truth, they ignore it as if it didn't exist. You know, sweep it under the carpet, bury it, avoid the truth."

"That sounds like pretty harsh judgment, Stan."

"Well, what do you think happened to those DeBosi hair samples the speaker mentioned? A few trusting individuals trusted the government with their hair samples and the samples vanished. They're not against us; they just don't want us to know so they don't have to deal with it. They're afraid of the truth and what the public will do if the truth came out. It's fear, fear of the unknown. The government can't help us and they don't want to save DeBosi. They want it to die out, go away. That's why we have to go public. We have to get the message out to avoid extinction of the species." Stan was getting agitated as he sipped his beer.

An alarm had gone off in Mike's head. Stan was a believer in disclosure. Mike knew any information he shared with Stan would be repeated to Stan's core group in the picture, if not the public via the press. Discretion was not part of Stan's agenda. The confidentiality Mike desired to share his theories was missing here with Stan Cole. He began to plan ways to diffuse this meeting and escape gracefully.

"So, Mike, now tell me about your encounter. Then we'll figure out how to fill in one of these forms." Stan reached for a form and a pen from the end table by the sofa.

"Well, I don't know exactly how to say it, but I'm not sure if I've had an encounter or not."

"How's that, Mike?" asked Stan, puzzled.

"Well, it's this old woman I know. She lives alone out in a rural area. She claims that there's one of them buried in her backyard," said

Mike, amazed at his own ability to say nothing yet still be honest in what he said.

"She says there's one buried in her back yard?"

"Yes, that's my report..."

Stan sat back quietly on the sofa for a few minutes, reading through the form. Mike detected Stan's confusion and disappointment. He had conveyed doubt about his meeting with Sadie so effectively, that Stan had no choice but to automatically discount his story.

"Do you have any corroborating evidence? Like another person, a witness?"

"No, nothing."

Stan was quiet again. As he looked back at Mike, he spoke slowly, "This is unusual. Why do you think she's telling the truth, and not making up a story?" asked Stan. He looked back down at the blank form, still studying it carefully. As Mike answered, Stan did not look up.

"Because, I believe her," said Mike. "I thought the right thing was to come here and ask you people how to proceed." Mike was sure Stan did not believe him, which was his goal. Since he knew Stan was not the person he wanted to confide in, Mike worked hard to discredit his own story according to the criteria given in the presentation.

"Well, tell you what, Mike. This is a little beyond me. You know, I can only fill in this form if you had a first hand encounter or observation. You know, if you saw a figure walking across the road or something. I can handle that. But something buried in the back yard that you haven't seen? They designed the form for first hand observations, but what you're telling me is different. You are telling me what someone else thinks. I'm going to make a recommendation," Stan was now looking directly at Mike.

"What's that?" asked Mike.

"You need to talk to Harry," said Stan, continuing to look at Mike. "Harry will know what to do."

"Harry?" asked Mike.

"Yes, Harry Friedman, the president of the association. This one could be tricky, you know. How to draw her out? I wouldn't know how to get permission to check the story out. I don't want to do anything to mess things up. This is a delicate situation here."

"Harry Friedman?" Mike repeated the name, "Harry Friedman. That name sounds familiar. Was he the one who introduced the speaker at the meeting?"

"Oh, yes. That's the one. Here's his name and number for you." Stan offered, writing on the back of one of the blank forms.

Mike sat sipping his beer in self-satisfaction. He had succeeded in diffusing this meeting and finding a new lead. As he watched Stan write the information on the back of the form, Mike was sure he did not want to tell Stan anything. He knew Stan would not keep a word he said in confidence. Stan wanted publicity. Perhaps Harry Friedman would be different. Stan handed Mike the form with Harry's contact information on the back. Stan then picked up his phone and started dialing.

"Harry?" Stan spoke loudly into the mouthpiece. "Yes. Yes, this is Stan Cole. I'm fine, Harry. Listen, I've got a special situation with me right now where the form doesn't work. I was wondering...Yes. Yes. I'll ask."

"Mike, can you go over to Harry's this evening?" Stan asked Mike.

Instinctively, Mike refused. He did not want to take his story to another stranger with beer on his breath. "Not tonight. I'm tired and it's getting late. I'm expecting a long distance phone call at home later tonight. How about tomorrow night?"

"How's tomorrow, Harry? Yes. Ok. What time?" Stan spoke into the phone.

"What time, Mike?"

"Seven tomorrow evening is fine."

"Seven is fine," Stan spoke into the phone again. "Fine. Good. Thanks a lot, Harry," Stan hung up the phone. "You're on for seven tomorrow night with Harry. I think that's the right thing to do, Mike. Talk to Harry."

"I agree," said Mike trying not to show his relief.

"Harry knows what is best. How about another beer, Mike?"

"No, thanks. I need to be going. I wanted to get things in motion."

"I think you have put things in motion, Mike. I really think you have. Harry's your man."

Chapter Ten

A Fishy Story

The next evening Mike dialed the number Stan Cole had written on the back of the report form. "Hello, Mr. Friedman?"

"Yes, Harry Friedman speaking. How can I help you?"

Mike hesitated for a moment. He could still hang up and avoid another situation. He felt awkward and foolish. If he hung up now, he could keep his ideas to himself and not appear foolish to anyone else.

"I'm Mike Byrne. Stan Cole called you last night about my encounter. He gave me your address, but I have no idea how to get there."

"Stan didn't give you directions?"

"No. We met briefly. After he listened to part of my story, he decided he didn't know how to record the incident on the form, so he called you. I didn't think to ask for directions."

"Well, I'm not surprised. Stan has never been here, so he couldn't have given you directions. I should have asked you yesterday. Come to think of it, I'm not sure he gave me your name. We were all a bit hasty. He said you would come tonight at seven."

"I can still make it by seven if I have directions. I'm from town so it shouldn't take me too long to get there. I'm ready to leave right now."

"As I remember, you had an unusual incident that didn't fit into the standard format. Look, let's not discuss this on the phone."

"Yes, my incident is unique."

"I'm on Winding Terrace in the Great Oaks subdivision, off US41, about a mile north of town, on the east side of the highway. You shouldn't have any difficulty finding it."

"Sure, I know where that subdivision is. I don't live too far from there."

"The formal entrance is on the highway. You can't miss it. The guardhouse isn't operational. The association voted down the expense for guard services, so the guardhouse is actually empty and the gate is always open."

"Great, I'll have no trouble getting there. How do I find your house?""

"When you pass the guardhouse, take the first right. That's Winding Terrace, the perimeter road. Follow it on around. As you pass the small pond on your right, keep going. My house is the fifth one past the pond on the left side of the road. I'll turn the porch light on and the numbers are on the door."

"Thanks. I'm on my way. Stan wrote your address down for me."

"Fine. Oh, Mr. Byrne, one other thing," said Harry.

"Yes."

"Are you calling from your home phone?"

"Yes."

"Good. Be sure you always do. I don't recommend calling from any other number. To report any incidents, use the privacy of your home phone. Calling from work may be a problem. We don't want your employer or anyone else to know you called or talked to me."

"I understand," said Mike.

"Good. See you in about an hour."

Mike followed Harry's instructions and easily found the well-manicured entrance to the subdivision. As opposed to the guardhouse services, the association valued the landscaping service as the grounds were neatly trimmed and blooming flowers lined the gatehouse and lawns. As he turned right along Winding Terrace Drive, a few minutes later, Mike found Harry's house. All the houses in the subdivision consisted of one-story bungalows with pastel painted stucco over concrete block. Of the three basic models, Harry's turned out to be the smallest of the three, painted a color that Mike could only describe as pastel peach.

Great Oaks represented a typical retirement community built in Florida about fifteen years earlier. Most residents living there were middle class Americans who migrated from the North mostly to get away from the cold and snow. Great Oaks provided a community where the residents could settle down with others who thought, acted, and dressed like themselves. Mike guessed that conservative conformity described the predominant attitude in this particular community. This neighborhood differed from what he expected the president of the Almas Association to reside, so he checked his notes again for the address. Mike imagined residency here was not characteristic for someone who was the president of an organization that embraced such unorthodox beliefs. Again, doubts began to appear about his decision to meet with Harry to discuss his feelings about Sadie. He continued anyway, in hopes of finding that one person in whom he could confide safely.

The familiar, hot, humid Florida air pressed against his dark suit as soon as he stepped out of his car. A late afternoon thunderstorm had left the air heavy with a sharp increase in humidity. He removed his suit jacket to relieve the uncomfortable feeling from the remains of the rain shower. When he pushed the doorbell, he heard the Westminster chimes ring inside. He did not wait long. The door opened promptly, and he stood facing Harry Friedman, immediately recognizing the short balding man who had introduced the speaker at the Almas Association presentation.

"Mr. Byrne?"

"Yes, I'm Mike Byrne. Your directions were perfect."

"Please come in," said Harry extending his right hand towards Mike. They stood shaking hands for a moment in Harry's foyer. "Come on in. Air conditioning costs a lot these days. No advantage in cooling the outdoors."

Mike followed Harry over the white, tiled foyer into the living room where Harry directed him to a large, white leather sofa. Harry picked up a small container from the coffee table, and began feeding the fish in a large fish tank set into a built-in wall unit directly across the room.

"Please, call me Harry. I was feeding my fish when you rang the doorbell," said Harry as he opened a small lid in the back of the tank. "Excuse me a moment while I feed them."

"Angel fish…" Mike muttered, attempting to open the conversation. The enormous fish tank dominated the white washed room.

"Yes. Black lace angels. Hopefully, I have three mated pairs. This tank is my hobby. Do you keep tropical fish, Mr. Byrne?"

"Oh, no, not now. I had a small ten-gallon tank when I was a kid back in Delaware. My parents introduced me to the hobby. They gave me a tank for Christmas when I was fourteen. I kept it up until I went to college. I see you also have a lot of neons."

"This tank holds a hundred gallons of water so there's plenty of room for all of them. I recommend setting one up again when you retire, Mr. Byrne. Keeping tropical fish reduces stress and strain on your heart, besides it's not expensive. Some people around here actually collect fish and plants out of the local waterways. As you can see, I also have a couple of bottom feeders, to keep the tank clean. I plan to breed the angels."

"It's a beautiful tank," said Mike, noting the striking contrast of the jet black river gravel surrounding a large piece of white stag horn coral in the center of the tank. The constant flashes of the neons passed back and forth across the tank, circling the half a dozen angelfish and other miscellaneous species. "How do you keep the big angels from eating the little neons?"

"By balancing the tank carefully," said Harry as he turned toward Mike. "You didn't come here to talk about fish. Enough of my hobby. I noticed you were staring at me. Relax, I've grown used to your reaction. Some people don't expect a person of my background to be here in this clannish retirement community. Then, no one expects to see a retired machine-tooling operator from Michigan to be the president of the Almas Association, either. I'm used to the attention and a few comments now and again, behind my back. To tell you the truth, I spent thirty years dealing almost exclusively with people of backgrounds other than my own. When it came time to retire, I felt more comfortable here than in some subdivision made up of those from my culture."

"I apologize, I didn't realize I was staring," said Mike.

"No harm done. You and I must establish a solid foundation for open communication. We can't afford to misunderstand each other from the beginning. The issue of credibility is essential in dealing with the topic of the DeBosi."

"Yes, sir. I understand."

"Do you know why I actually like retirement here? Because everyone dresses alike, acts alike, and does the same things, often together. Do you know what that means?"

"Not really."

"That means everyone here thinks alike and is therefore totally predictable. Since I retired, I restrict my mental games of chess to the association. I don't want any distress here at home. One arena is enough for me. I may be out of my peer group here but I'm comfortable in this community."

"That way you always know what's going on."

"You didn't bring a biographical sketch or resume with you, I suppose. Did you?"

"No, I didn't know you needed one and you didn't ask. Is it necessary?"

"Well, no matter. Personally, I prefer to have a resume. Send one in a couple of days or so. No hurry, you may mail it or email it whichever is convenient. I like to gather as much information as I can about the people I interview for the database. You'll find a stack of my business cards on the small table over by the front door. Take one with you when you leave. Oh, yes, copies of the report forms we use are there also. Take a couple with you when you go, too."

"Sure, thank you," said Mike.

"Complete one of those forms at your leisure. When you finish and are happy with what you've written, send it to me, along with your resume. Be sure to fill out the section under 'Observer' so we have some personal information about you. Take your time to describe your sighting as completely as you can. Most people forget a few things and need to do some editing, so don't be fancy just do the best you can to include all the details."

"Sure," said Mike, realizing that Harry was a much different person than Stan Cole, the true believer. Harry presented a more professional approach in handling the situation than Stan. His manner worked well, making Mike feel comfortable with his laid back, casual manner. In contrast with Stan, Harry did not have an agenda. Mike filled out the observer section and placed the form down on the coffee table.

"Now, before we begin, I want you to know that I personally have never had either an observation or an encounter. I confess I'm not what they call a true believer, either."

"That surprises me. You're the president of the association. I thought everyone in the association had experienced an encounter of some kind or was, at least, a believer in the existence of the DeBosi."

"No, everyone is not there for the same reasons. Even though I'm not a believer, at the same time, I'm not a non-believer either. My approach may not be what you expected to find in a member of the Almas Association."

"Yes, already I see you're much different from what I expected. But I'm not sure what I expected either. Please, go on." Mike was beginning to be comfortable with Harry. Perhaps he had found the person he was seeking to tell his story about Sadie and his beliefs about her.

"As you know, the local branch of the association is affiliated with the Institute that sponsored the presentation at the Banyan Hotel the other night. Our guest speaker returned to the west coast for his next presentation there."

"I wanted to contact him but I didn't know how to reach him. He didn't leave any contact information. Frankly, he was the first person I thought of to contact. Now I realize you are the more appropriate person for me."

"Ken Tomlinson inspires us here, locally. We all hope he'll accept our invitation to come back next year to speak with us again. We want him to visit us annually to update the status of the Institute and the database. My office as president keeps me in contact with him for various reasons over the course of the year. My standing with the group here varies, so I'm not sure if I'll be re-elected next year. The last election was highly contested. My opponent and his followers are true believers as opposed to my more objective approach to our controversial subject."

"Your approach makes a lot of sense to me, particularly if you haven't had an encounter."

"Although the election was a victory, it was not an easy one. The majority of the membership supported my candidacy at the time. When it comes to volunteer groups, the power base of the group shifts frequently, making your standing tenuous. It's always questionable whether the overall belief system of the general membership stays static. I sense that the tenor of the belief system in the association shifts frequently, and maybe even at whim." Harry paused, watching his tropical fish as they swam silently circling in continuous motion. "I hope you don't mind if I finish feeding my fish," Harry continued as he opened the lid and tapped the container with his fingers. The flakes of fish food dropped down onto the surface of the water. In response, the fish scurried to the surface of the tank, gulping down the small bits of wafer.

"Not at all. I'm enjoying your fish."

"Most people have a television set in their living room. I put my television in the bedroom to help me get to sleep at night. The fish tank here provides my entertainment while I'm wide-awake. I find fish much more relaxing to watch than the news or sports. They're also more entertaining."

"It's a magnificent tank compared to my tiny one. Your fish are far more interesting to watch than my little tank was."

"So you told me. Even though I'm only a volunteer in the association, I take my position seriously," said Harry. "Studying the subject matter of the DeBosi and the association are fascinating. In the long run, the facts will determine who is right and who is wrong. The speaker from the other night, Ken Tomlinson was right on track in applying facts and reason in the study of phenomena. I know scientific facts fail to support our position. On the other hand, the methods applied at the Institute are crucial for developing an understanding of the reports coming in. Ken's objective approach is the only approach to counter the opposition in the scientific community."

"I didn't know what to expect meeting with you tonight. I certainly did not expect to be watching tropical fish swimming around in a big fish tank. Stan Cole only told me your name. He didn't volunteer any other information about you."

"Mr. Byrne, Stan Cole doesn't know me very well. This may seem strange to you, but we haven't talked or shared opinions, even though we both belong to the same association. For years the true believers, like Stan, ran this local organization. Their approach was provincial, strictly classifying members as either a believer, to be embraced without question, or as a non-believer to be rejected and scorned as not worthy of recognition. This cut and dried/black and white approach appalled me. When I decided to run for office, my platform espoused that such an approach on the DeBosi polarized opinion and did a disservice to the very cause we were promoting."

"I like your approach. It makes a lot of sense, whether one is a believer or not."

"I believe the DeBosi question demands serious, intelligent inquiry and should be handled scientifically. Realistically, most people don't believe in the existence of DeBosi, don't care, and will continue to avoid the organization unless we change the old approach. The general public considers the association to be a part of the lunatic fringe, a group to be avoided. People who had actual encounters or observations were also alienated by that position, and, as a result, many were likely to keep their experiences to themselves. I believe I won the election on the basis of showing the true believers that they were shooting themselves in the foot," said Harry, as he sprinkled more fish food into the tank.

"I'm beginning to understand your rationale," said Mike.

"When I moved here to Florida, somehow I believed that retirement would be a golden Garden of Eden, a place of bliss, free of the problems and conflicts of daily life. Having no interest in shuffleboard, cards or golf, I found I had little in common with my neighbors. Retirement became an empty experience, a kind of suspended living waiting for death, maybe even death before its time. At least that's what happened to me. Since my wife passed on, I found I needed something with meaning and substance to do every day. After an active life in industry, I missed being involved with people."

"I can relate to that. Everyone needs a hobby or serious activity outside of retirement. Doing nothing becomes boredom and isolation."

"You're right on that one. My wife passed when we were still back in Michigan. She didn't make it to retirement, so when I came here, I was alone. Here I am, in the Garden of Eden, and I found boredom. Several years ago, I ran across an ad for the association in the events section of the Brandon Times. The association listed their meetings, so I went to one out of curiosity to see what they were working on. When I attended the next meeting, I saw a chance to participate in something unusual. The topics discussed caught my interest, so I joined. What I like is the controversy. The whole idea stirred up my curiosity and piqued my interest. I was hooked. My experience with the association has rejuvenated my outlook on life."

"I'll bet a lot of people have the same problem with retirement. Everyone looks forward to the day they don't have to go to work. But when that day comes, day after day, they become bored because they don't have anything to do. I saw my parents and my friend's parents go through the same thing, the struggle with changing their whole life pattern. After a brief period, the husband becomes a millstone for the wife. She reacts by going out and getting a job, usually to get away from him," Mike said grinning.

For a moment, the only sound in the room was the water bubbling from the aerator in the fish tank. The fish had eaten all the food on the surface, so Harry tapped the container again. A few of the neons returned to snap at the new flakes of food on the surface. "Some of the other members began a campaign a year ago to move the association away from the status of cult or fanaticism of the true believer. Those members want to make our subject one of respectable inquiry, more scientific. They want mainstream science to join us so those who had experienced an encounter or observation have a place to tell their stories in an open, scientific arena. I always felt that many observers simply did not understand what they had seen and wanted to be taken seriously. The reason they came forward included finding someone to help understand what they had seen and reconcile the event with our current view of the world."

"Mr. Tomlinson made a lasting impression on me and opened up a new perspective for me. Do you think there are a lot of people out there who have had an observation or an encounter and won't come forward for fear of being considered attention seekers or just plain crazy?"

"Sure, that's why I like Tomlinson's organization. The Institute represents the best effort in the country to professionalize the subject and handle it scientifically. The Institute has grown to be a true credit to the cause. Our move to join the Institute provides serious credibility for us as well. As a result, our membership has grown to become more accepted by the general populace here. I research my stories to have good, solid facts if the press is called in and I make sure I don't jump too quickly to call them in."

"I see that. I'm sure the seriousness of your approach has augmented the professionalism and acceptability of the Almas Association. My impression was you had a solid group of people in attendance at the presentation."

"The Institute supported my election platform. They understood the need to keep a distance from other fringe phenomena most people associate with the DeBosi. They developed this approach to separate the Institute and the association from that fringy category. Affiliation with the Institute tipped the scale for my victory in the election."

"Mr. Tomlinson convinced me. He certainly presents himself well, both personally and professionally. His arguments appear unassailable," said Mike. "I bet most scientists have a hard time arguing with him on this subject."

"You bet. The investigators at the Institute dig deep to uncover solid scientific facts while there is still time. They believe our subject, the DeBosi, is dangerously close to extinction. The primary goal for preservation starts with knowledge and facts. They applied use of the report form not just in the States but also worldwide. Using the Institute's uniform approach to investigations and interviewing techniques helps obtain the highest quality data and fieldwork. Quality of information provides crucial data to gain understanding and acceptability."

"I think they're right. Until I heard Mr. Tomlinson, I would have dismissed the subject. In fact, had I known the topic of the presentation that evening, I probably would not have attended," Mike admitted. "I don't follow or believe in most of the fringy phenomena out there."

"You and most people. The Institute recognizes that and sees open minds as key for gaining support for the Debosi. Fraud, which is a major problem, is best approached by adoption of scientific methods. Fraud thrives in an atmosphere where something is accepted as true as long as the majority of a community supports the belief." Harry closed the lid on the fish tank. Feeding time was over.

"Well, I, for one, am glad you won the ballot."

"Mr. Byrne, I would be fooling myself if I didn't recognize there are interests that oppose an analytical approach to the subject. To get to the truth, I remain vigilant. We recently started to qualify the subject as appropriate for scientific inquiry. A handful of scientists from around the world recently acknowledged we were wrongly excluded because some saw our subject as mere fantasy. They dismissed all our observation reports as collections of fabrications made up by unreliable witnesses, making all encounters reported unreliable. They assumed many of the reports were even college pranks."

"That was my fear when I decided to find someone to tell about my encounter. I doubted anyone would take me seriously and my story would be dismissed as pure fantasy or absolute lunacy."

"You see, you are no different than any of the other observers out there. Lately, a few scientists have stuck their necks out and stated that a witness's observations may be valid evidence to be given some weight. That admission served as a giant step in the right direction because it legitimizes the work of the Institute. Perhaps, in the end, better heads will prevail, and scientists will not fear professional ridicule, loss of funding or employment simply for expressing an open mind about the subject."

"I see. I appreciate your stand to press for this approach. It is important to determine the difference between fact and truth. Many people don't realize there is a difference. With people like you heading up local associations, maybe more factual information about the subject will reduce that fear of ridicule for those reporting an encounter. There is no way of knowing how many people have not come forward due to that very issue."

"Yes, I see my job as president of the Association as similar to maintaining this fish tank. A healthy fish tank requires a delicate balancing act. Too little food and the angelfish devour the neons, and then turn on each other. If I feed them too much, then the tank develops an algae bloom and becomes clouded. Ultimately, all will be lost and I'll have to break the tank down and start over, loosing everything I struggled so hard to achieve," said Harry.

"Yes, that's the exact problem I had with my fish tank," confessed Mike. "A fish tank is an interesting model."

"Well, what all this means to you, Mr. Byrne, is that I am not going to put my arm around your shoulders and accept everything you say as true. I don't want facts; I want truth. I won't encourage you to run to the media to broadcast your observations as beliefs or truth. As a businessman, my success lies in knowing more about others than they know about me, in addition to knowing more about the subject than anyone else."

"That takes a lot of work, research and dedication."

"Yes, that's the other reason I won the election as president of this association. I know more about the subject of the DeBosi than anyone else in the membership. I made that position my cornerstone to any discussions. Now, enough about the election and the local association, I want to hear your story."

Mike told Harry about his meetings with Sadie, how Sandy had drawn him into the Sadie Sutton book project, how his beliefs had evolved from what Sadie said, and about her unusual appearance. He told Harry about the mound in back of her cabin and why he believed it was an unusual grave. He paused when he finished his story. Again, he felt foolish and embarrassed. The story sounded bizarre even to himself when he relayed the information about Sadie and the mound out loud.

"So, you met an elderly woman who you believe has mixed blood, part human and part australopithecine. In addition, you believe her husband buried a full-blooded australopithecine in a mound in this woman's backyard. Have I summarized your story accurately?" asked Harry.

"Yes. Hearing your words, it sounds bizarre, but yes, that's my encounter in a nutshell. You've summarized my thoughts accurately."

"Well, I don't know you very well yet, either. Despite this is our first meeting, to me, you do seem to be a sincere young man. That said, I'll say your story isn't strange; it's extraordinary, maybe even fantastic… But, as you see, I won't ridicule your beliefs. On the other hand, you must realize that of all the unusual tales I've heard, one of a walking, talking, half-blood with a DeBosi buried in the backyard ranks right up there at the top of my list."

"That's what I was afraid of."

"In all fairness, reports of purported half bloods exist in Siberia and China, but such tales are few and far between, and totally unsubstantiated. And, here you sit in my living room telling me you've met a half-breed not only living here in the United States of America, but around the corner here in southwestern Florida, in the slough only a few miles from home. Of course, you go on to say that, not only have you seen this half-blood, but you've sat down and talked with her over tea on a couple of occasions, and you plan to do so again this next weekend. Is this correct?" asked Harry.

"That's it, " said Mike. "When you say it back to me, it sounds crazy. But that's it."

"I admit that somehow you make the fantastic seem mundane. Thankfully you came here and not the media. I see now why Stan Cole sent you here."

"I know it sounds far fetched, but I think you would agree with me if you met Sadie."

"The first thing we need to maintain is confidentiality. I certainly would like to meet her, but I don't want to overstep my bounds right now. I'm not exaggerating when I say that your job could be at risk, to say nothing of the welfare of this woman, if you told others of your beliefs. I can't predict the consequences if such information were released to the press."

"Believe me, I've told no one, not even the young woman who introduced me to Sadie. I started to tell Stan Cole, but I was concerned his motives were contrary to my desires to keep this confidential right now. I think he dismissed me as making up a story. In any case, I didn't tell him much since I didn't feel comfortable with him. When my situation didn't fit the form, he decided to send me to you."

"You did the right thing. Neither you nor Stan could have handled the situation properly. Tell me again, exactly what happened in your meeting with Stan. I want to know exactly what you said to him."

Mike repeated his experience with Stan the previous evening.

"Good. There's nothing there for him to do anything. He was right. The form isn't designed for your situation. He did the right thing in sending you here. Your concern over confidentiality with him was well founded. Remember, he's a true believer and his group consists of those members who believe in public disclosure, often without adequate research to back it up. When they run to the media prematurely, they cause themselves and everyone else serious damage."

"As I said, I only mentioned the grave to Stan. I said nothing about Sadie," said Mike.

"Good. Often it's imperative to follow your instincts. Until we have our facts in order, don't bring anyone else in. This conversation must be kept in the strictest confidence. Don't contact Mr. Cole again. If he calls you, refer him to me. I'll handle Stan."

"No problem, thank you," said Mike, relieved. Mike was confident he had assessed each of his meetings with Harry and Stan correctly.

"I'll respect your beliefs, but I insist you tell me the truth. I also insist that you agree to keep silent until we can either discredit the stories you brought here or we can establish them as truth based on scientific facts. Dr. Tomlinson's speech took me as close as I thought I would ever get physically to the DeBosi. If you're right, then we may have to raise our expectations. Right now, we need to analyze your claims very carefully. Think for a moment. Is there anything more you would like to say?"

"I've told you everything."

"Are you sure there isn't anything you may have left out?"

"No, I've told you what I know. I can't think of anything else. I haven't left anything out."

"Well, you could be a con-artist, Mr. Byrne. If so, you certainly are a good one, because I think you are sincere in what you believe. You could also have a wild imagination, or even be deceiving yourself. Or, on the other hand, you could have found something really unique. If you have found the real thing, this discovery will be the breakthrough of the century. We run into more than our share of con-artists and people with wild imaginations in this endeavor with lots of made up encounters."

"Yes, I'm sure you do. That makes your job much more difficult to sort through all the information to get at the truth."

"The Institute recently helped ferret out a forest ranger up in Canada who finally admitted to walking around in special snow shoes he had modified for making footprints in the wilderness. Apparently, he had been carrying on his scam for years. Fame and fortune were not his goal. No one has come up with an explanation for why he did it. We have all sorts of theories and reasons for such fabrications. My job includes weeding out the hoaxes before they do any damage to the cause, bringing the zealots down to reality and fastidiously applying the scientific method to get to facts and reason. Somehow, I think you have just presented me with the biggest challenge of my career."

"I came here because I didn't know what to do. I didn't know where to go. I called your organization because I thought I could find some understanding if someone would listen to my story. Believe me, I know how crazy my story sounds."

"My first goal is to encourage you to work with us and take the needed time to find the facts. In this way, I can serve you and the association," said Harry.

"Thank you for listening. I appreciate that you have not thrown me out the door. Again, I appreciate your even handed approach."

"I'm here to keep the association on an even keel, to find the facts. I'm glad you came to me first and can only hope that you understand the need to say nothing until we have established concrete facts. I don't need reporters on my front doorstep. Frankly, I like to work in the background. However, proving your case and taking it to the public is one option we will have to explore, but much later. I hope we live up to your confidence."

"Well, where do I go from here?"

"First, don't tell anyone you've been here. Go on as you have been. This matter all rests in your hands, Mr. Byrne. If an australopithecine is buried in the lady's backyard, then we can't do anything on our own. We need her written permission to exhume the body, legally. If she allows it, the bones won't lie, they'll tell us the truth."

"Yes, I understand. That sounds reasonable."

"If her blood is mixed, as you believe, she has to consent to blood and saliva tests and submit hair samples or whatever the experts need for DNA analysis. That's how we must approach the origin issue. With your extreme beliefs, we must deal with them in a simple and straightforward manner. However, I do see another real problem," said Harry.

"Another problem? What?"

"The issue that I see is whether you will, in the end, proceed and actually confront your beliefs."

"You don't think I will? I'm dead serious about this situation. I'm not sure what you mean."

"Frankly, my experience is that your story is just theory. You may proceed to apply science and reason. If, on the other hand, you are a true believer in what you say, you will avoid taking any actions that do not reinforce your beliefs. Even if forced to face facts, which are inconsistent with your beliefs, you will undermine or attack those very facts. In short, you won't do anything to threaten your beliefs. That's my sad commentary on human nature," said Harry.

"This meeting isn't what I anticipated when I first came here. I've learned a lot from you. You're right, of course, this whole situation does fall on me. I'm the one who has to convince Sadie to consent to DNA testing so we can find the facts. I think you'll find I have an open mind."

"Good, I hope so. Oh, yes, one more thing. I'm not going to send your report form to the Institute at this time. Let's dig up some more substantial facts before we try to structure a report. Outlandish allegations require outlandish proof, Mr. Byrne. Right now, we have absolutely nothing to work with other than your beliefs. Let's wait. Sign the bottom part of the form you filled in so I have a foundation to start with. Answer all the questions about yourself, and leave the form with me."

Mike picked the unfinished form up from the coffee table, filled in the blanks, and signed it. He stood up. The meeting with Harry had ended. There was nothing more he could say or do. Harry had sized up the situation properly. The next step fell on Mike's shoulders.

"Good," said Harry, standing in response to Mike's lead. "We have addressed all the issues we can for now." He turned and led Mike to the door. "I wish you luck in your efforts, Mr. Byrne. Remember, I'll help you any way I can. I'll open an investigation file with the local association index. Call me as soon as you have something to report. I'll keep my side of the bargain. Our discussion tonight will be kept in strictest confidence. Let's see how things settle out."

Mike picked up another one of the forms by the door and one of Harry's business cards. He wanted to be sure to have Harry's address and phone number.

"Thank you," said Harry, accepting the signed form. "Remember, send me your resume as soon as you can."

"I will," promised Mike.

When Mike stepped back into the hot evening air, he felt ridiculous. He sensed that the head of the Almas Association had not believed him. After all, he thought, why should he? Mike realized if he had been in Harry's shoes and heard his own statements, he would not have believed anything about Sadie or the mound either. Harry Friedman was right, the whole issue came down to the issue of proof.

Harry turned his porch lights out almost before Mike had a chance to get into his car. As he slid into the driver's seat, Mike swore out loud to himself, "This is not the end, Harry Friedman. This is just the beginning."

Chapter Eleven

Archives

The next day Mike headed for the archives building behind the courthouse to begin his search for official documents in the county records. Paul Crawford managed the archive records and Mike was his immediate supervisor. Mike had been a key player in the department project to relocate the storage facility from the musty old basement of the courthouse to the new building. His major concern that won the support for the relocation was to protect the documents from flooding in the event of a west coast hurricane. The committee exploring the feasibility of the project decided that a new, aboveground storage facility would be safer for preservation of the records than the old leaky basement. The new structure was built according to the more strict requirements of the South Florida Building Code, the model code developed by Miami-Dade County after their experience with Hurricane Andrew. Compliance with this standard assured the safety of the official records in the event of a violent storm passing over Palmetto County. In view of the recent increase in frequency and severity of damage caused by hurricanes hitting Florida, Mike was pleased with his foresight and determination in completing the project. The records had been moved to their new, secure residence just before the onslaught of the hurricanes in the summer of '05.

As Mike approached the front door of the building, he flashed his access card across the scanner to open the door. "Hello, Paul."

"Hi, Mike. You were quick getting here. Seems like I just hung up the phone talking with you."

"I was only minutes away, across the alley when I called. Weren't we lucky to induce the powers that be to build this record center here instead of down the street? We lucked out on that one. I wanted to preserve the old records for as long as possible."

"Anyway, welcome to Palmetto County Archives. We don't see enough of you over here, even though I'm part of your department. Actually, I don't see much of anyone else either, for that matter," said Paul.

"You do such a good job, you don't need day-to-day supervision," Mike quipped.

"Ever since we moved in here, all I do is receive fax and e-mail requests for copies of records and documents. I'm the conduit for information and official records. I send the responses back the same way, fax and e-mail. Even though I'm busy most of the time, I rarely ever see anybody. Occasionally I receive a hand delivery or sometimes I have to be the messenger myself. My greatest pleasure comes from the telephone request when I actually get to talk to a human being. Most of the time, I spend my day microfilming and making back up copies."

"Well, I'm sorry. I guess I should personally check in on you more often, but you don't need me looking over your shoulder all day long."

"Yes, I'm really busy. Don't get me wrong; it's just that I'm on my own most of the time. In this age of computers, faxes and emails, I don't have many visitors, so an occasional visitor relieves the monotony. But, thanks for the compliment. This is a lonely job for the most part."

"You handle everything so well, there's no justification for additional personnel here."

"That's okay. I'm a loner and enjoy the solitude. You're welcome here anytime. I would enjoy your company, occasionally. C'mon in. You don't have to stand in front of the counter. You're not a customer."

"Well, today, I am. I thought I'd grab a cola from your machine first. Do you want one, too? I've got a couple of bucks if you have the change. I assume that machine still doesn't accept bills."

"Correct. It's still the same old-fashioned model, coins only. I've got change right here, but no thanks on the cola. I have coffee in the back room. Are you sure coffee won't do?" Paul asked, retrieving his change box from under the counter. "Remember, coffee's free." He exchanged four quarters for the dollar bill Mike offered.

"No thanks," said Mike as he put three quarters in the machine. "I can only handle one cup of coffee a day, and I already had one this morning. Is anyone using this machine now that we took out the free one?"

"Sure, the yard crew, the lot guards and messengers who have access cards use it," he hesitated. "They all use it from time to time, but me; I'm not a cola fan. The doctor says no sugar and I don't trust artificial sweeteners." Paul escorted Mike into the back room.

"I suppose if we break even in the machine we're ahead of the game. You'd probably do better if the machine took bills."

"You didn't tell me you were looking for anything in particular when you called, so I didn't prepare anything."

"No, I didn't. I thought I'd review my problem with you in person. It's an unusual request."

"If you had told me what you wanted, I would have had it ready for you when you arrived."

"Don't be so sure. You haven't heard my request yet."

"I'm sure whatever it is, I can handle it."

"Well, I do need your help," Mike began to explain his story. "The historical society decided to work on a manuscript about one of our elderly citizens. I volunteered to help. I need a birth record for her. I'll try a long shot for one on her husband as well. And, maybe a marriage record, if we have it and whatever else you can find on either one of them. I believe the husband is deceased, so I'm also looking for a death certificate for him, too," said Mike.

"That sounds simple enough to me. I don't foresee any problems. What are their names? That's all I need."

"I filled in the standard request form," said Mike, handing the form over to Paul.

"You could have faxed that over and saved yourself a trip. I see the names: S-A-D-I- E S-U-T-T-O-N and J-A-K-E J-O-H-N-S-T-O-N. The names are written clearly. Is that Jake or a shortened version of Jacob?"

"All the information I have is 'Jake,' but you might try it both ways."

"Okay, I'll do what I can."

"There's a catch," said Mike, pausing. "I'm guessing that Sadie is somewhere between one hundred eight and one hundred thirteen years old. As for Johnston, I don't have any years or dates to give you. Anything I have on him is a long shot. In addition, I don't think he's from around here originally. I'm not even sure that Johnston was his birth name. Anyway, I'm guessing his birth date to be about ten years earlier than Sadie's and I have estimated that his death was around 1912. Sadie, on the other hand, is still very much alive today."

"Wow, I see what you mean. If she's one hundred thirteen, that would make her birth year 1892. You're right, that is a problem. As you know, our records here only go back to nineteen twenty-three. We discovered this gap when we computerized the records. The consensus was that the cost-benefit ratio didn't justify going back any further than 1923."

"Also, before you ask, I don't have addresses or social security numbers for either one of them. There weren't social security numbers back then, nor did residents of the slough cooperate with the officials in registering with the county. I don't really have any numbers or dates for you to work with. You may not know this but when they started the computerization project for all the records, we realized that the original documents were created before the state was divided into counties. This meant records may have been lost, misplaced or never created."

"I guess, if I had your request, I'd bring it down in person, too. I'll start with the computer database records first, just in case we have some dumb luck. Ok, here we go, I'm putting their names into the search field now." Paul typed the two names on Mike's completed form into the computer terminal and hit enter. The database responded immediately, searching through the entries. After a brief time, the search stopped.

"Okay, what did you find?"

"Nothing. No data matches. The scan won't pick up anything before 1923. No luck. The information you want predates all of our records. I'll have to go into the archive vault," said Paul, turning to face a special steel door in the back wall. "The archive room is where we put records dating before 1923. It's dehumidified and has its own air conditioning." Paul stopped suddenly and looked directly at Mike. "I don't know why I'm telling you this," Paul apologized. "You already know all of this. You set this place up," said Paul as he opened the combination lock on the door to the archive room.

Inside the archive vault, three rows of metal shelves stood like support columns, one in the middle, and one along each side wall. Paul selected a stack of old leather bound, embossed books resting on the middle shelf.

"The biggest problem," Paul spoke slowly as he put his thoughts together out loud, "is that you're looking for records before we became a separate county. The state spun-off Palmetto County from Sarasota, as you know, and didn't start keeping its own records until around 1911. We were supposed to get a duplicate set of certain records going back to the beginning settlements in the county, but I don't think Sarasota County ever sent the copies here after the spin off. Those records are so old no one bothered to follow up on them. Our archive records date from 1911 to 1923. We started microfilming records from 1923. All the records in this special room are hand written on parchment paper with India ink pens. All the documents you need predate all of this. No one anticipated we would ever need records going back that far."

"Then, if we don't have the records, what are we looking for in here?" asked Mike.

"I can double check for copies of the records from the Sarasota County. You know, we can check out these four books. Here's another one we might try. Give me a hand and grab a couple of the volumes, if you will," said Paul.

"I've never had to look so far back into the records before," said Mike. "Since this is all new to me, I wanted your help."

"Do you want me to send an inquiry to Sarasota County to check their archive records? I could handle that for you and send a request up to Sarasota."

"I don't think that would help. The people who lived down here wouldn't have traveled all the way up there just to make official records. If they lived in the Seminole Indian River Slough, they lived their lives outside the beginnings of any official documentation system. They wouldn't have given a hoot for registering with the county so far away. It's not worth the expense to do a manual search in Sarasota. I doubt you'd find anything."

"Well, that's your decision. Only you know how desperate you are for the information. We started microfilming the records when we became a separate county. We didn't go back any earlier for the microfilming. Here's another suggestion for you. Look in the old church records the county brought in here a few years ago. They're all written in pen and ink also."

"Great suggestion. I forgot about church records. That's a good idea. Anyway, let's look through these binders first."

"These big binders are the originals. A long time ago, the county manager brought these and as many of the old church records he could find here to consolidate them in one place. Actually the early churches are good places to look for records of births through baptismal records and marriages for church members. The early churches kept the initial records before the government took over the task. The same is true for death records as churches performed funerals, too. Usually, the burials followed in the church cemeteries so the records would match the graves. Early churches kept meticulous records of life events for their members: births, deaths and marriages," said Paul. "Let's put these books out on the table and see what we can find. For records going back so far, the old church records may be all we have available."

They each carried two of the thick leather-bound volumes and placed them on the central worktable.

"I'd settle for any information on anyone with the same last name as Sutton and Johnston. That would give me a place to start," said Mike.

"Be careful. The pages in these books are extremely fragile. Remember, too, these are church records and not legal county records," warned Paul. "There's nothing official about them. We have them here for storage, that's all, for general reference. The only people who show any interest in them are individuals doing genealogical research."

"Where do I begin? This is overwhelming," said Mike. "I get the feeling this is a needle in a haystack. I doubt my subjects were ever affiliated with a church, but it's worth trying. I'll settle for finding any similar names."

"You take two volumes and I'll take two. Four major churches here served the community around the turn of the century. Look for the different sections on baptisms, marriages, and deaths. The baptism pages will have to suffice for birth records," said Paul. "Back in those times, most of the births occurred at home, so if a doctor was present, he would fill in a birth certificate and turn it in to the county for registration, but cooperation was not the best. The birth records only reflect the children who survived and were recorded as having been baptized. This doesn't mean that all births were recorded back then. The problem becomes larger when you consider that many of the settlers here may not have had a church affiliation. I'm sure there are many births that were never recorded anywhere, particularly if the parents were not affiliated with a church. So, the records in these volumes only reflect what we have from those early settlers who attended these four major churches. I don't know what we'll find. I've never had to dig into these records."

"Why are all the birth records in this volume entered in so many different handwritings?" asked Mike.

"Because there was no one person responsible for entering the names of the children and the parents in the records. Perhaps the minister, his wife or even the parents themselves wrote in the entries. See how the dates seem to be consistent? That means the minister or a clerical person from the church filled out that information. Then the parents would fill in the names of the child and their own names. Good luck reading that one," said Paul.

"These books are really heavy. Parchment and leather bound together make a substantial record book."

"At least with the two of us working the time is cut in half."

"Since Sadie is still alive, we only need to look for Johnston's name in the death records. Look for any information in either name."

"What about Sadie's parents? Should we look for similar names in the death's?"

"Sure, that's a good idea. Yes, let's check that too."

"I hate to be a nag but be careful with the pages in these books. The parchment can crack and break easily. Each of these books start around 1850 so they are really delicate."

"Sounds good to me. Let's start with births. We might have a shot there for some relevant information."

"Then check the Baptism section. Remember, back then there was no correlation between actual birth date and baptismal date."

"They should be close enough for my purpose."

"Not necessarily. Sometimes older children who were missed as infants were baptized as teens or even adults who got the faith late in life or changed churches."

"Oh, I forgot about that."

"This first volume goes up to 1930. I'm looking under funerals, for Johnston."

"Even if he wasn't a member and they didn't have a body, they might have still had a memorial service and recorded a date. Some churches also list confirmations for new converts and members."

"What does the category 'discontinued' stand for?"

"I'm not sure, but I'd guess if someone didn't pay their tithe, moved away or changed churches they would fall into that category. But they would first have to be members."

"Okay, I'll check that category, too."

Mike and Paul spent over two hours pouring through the old volumes from the four church records before they gave up.

"There's nothing here. Assuming I've been able to read all these entries correctly," said Mike. "I haven't found any entries with either name, Johnston or Sutton, in these two volumes."

"That's the same for me. We're looking into records that were kept before current standards and requirements were set for legal record keeping. So I'm not surprised we don't have any records under either name."

"I'm not surprised, either," said Mike. "I don't think either Sadie or Johnston were church goers. I think Johnston just disappeared, just like he suddenly appeared here. I'm only guessing that he was born in the New Orleans area. I don't really know if he was born there either. He could have been born just about anywhere. In addition, I don't think his death was ever reported." Mike stopped to think about his dilemma. There were no official records of any birth, or death for either Sadie or Johnston. He sighed and looked back at Paul. "Well, I've taken up too much of your time, already. I'll have to try some other direction to find any records or information about these people."

"Good luck," said Paul. "When I get a chance, I'll check into the cost of looking up records in the Sarasota county archives. So, let's put these tomes back where they belong."

"Sure, Thanks for your help. I think I'm going to need some lucky breaks," said Mike.

"I know the reason you came here is personal. I don't know what it is, but something is bothering you. Don't forget we've always been good friends. Remember, we played golf together and we used to go to the Green Frog pub on Fridays until your last promotion. Maybe I could help if I knew what's really bothering you. You're looking for information from a long time ago."

Mike pondered quietly what Paul said. He looked straight at Paul and asked, "Do you believe in Bigfoot?"

"You mean the big hairy creature out in the Pacific Northwest? No, I don't believe in those things. I think a few people made up fantastic stories to sell books. They're phony."

Mike told him about Sadie's strange appearance and suspicions about her past based on the presentation he had attended. "Look. Keep this confidential. Anyway, that's why I'm looking for records for both of them. I want to know where they came from and who they really were."

"Wow. I won't say anything to anyone. You really need to be careful about who you talk to about this. If you say too much to the wrong people, you could get into real trouble. Do you know what I mean?"

"Sure. I need someone to confide in, someone I can trust. I want to find the facts before I get in too deep."

"Look, a couple of years ago I shared an apartment with a guy from India. His name was Jamail Fahti."

"Oh, yes, I remember you talking about him."

"He told me a story about how students from all over the world used to travel to the province in northern India where he was born to study with the local gurus. There was a popular fad around twenty-five years ago about tulpas and gurus. His words made such a strong impression on me, I can't forget what he said."

"Tulpas? What are tulpas? I've never heard of them."

"Oh, tulpas are mythical beings that people see in their mind. They're friendly companions that the gurus taught their students to conjure up through meditation. From what my roommate told me, if the student was really adept, both the student and the guru could not only see the tulpa but both could talk with it. The tulpas seemed so real they actually became real for the student."

"So you think I see Sadie as a mythical being in my mind? A tulpa?"

"I don't know, Mike. The human imagination can do amazing things. I think you should consider the possibility, that's all. You know the power of suggestion is very strong for some people."

"What about the stories of the Yetis in the Himalayas? Did your roommate call them tulpas also?"

"Oh, no. He said some reports probably are, but he believed that the Asian Yeti really exists. But he also said they're not the same as Bigfoot."

"How so?"

"He told us there were actual Yeti footprints and I believe him. How can you explain the footprints if they aren't real? There may not be many Yeti left today, but they are real. They're just elusive, Mike."

"Well, I have more than footprints, Paul. I have a real being in flesh and blood."

"You may have a real person, Mike, but maybe you're subscribing tulpa characteristics to a real person. You have to consider that possibility. What you see may be something created in your own mind, not what actually exists in the real world."

"You mean I'm hallucinating? You haven't been to Indian Bend, nor have you met Sadie. She's not my imagination. If you saw her, I bet you would come to the same conclusion."

"You said others have seen this old lady?"

"Yes. Sandy has and so have the ranchers at the Circle T. Sandy is the one who brought me in to interview Sadie. She's the one from the historical society that found Sadie when she was hiking in the slough a few years ago. She's befriended her since they met."

"Has Sandy reacted the same as you?"

"No, come to think of it. She hasn't mentioned Sadie's appearance." Mike realized that Sandy had always acted if Sadie were perfectly normal.

"So, there you are. Women are very conscious of appearances, particularly in other women. Maybe when you look at this little old lady, you see a mythical being, a tulpa. Look, I want to help you, but you need to work with facts and keep your ideas to yourself until you know what you're dealing with. The world you see is a reflection of your perceptions, what you see in your mind."

"That's why I came here. I'm looking for facts."

"Well, that's good. Keep looking. All I can say is good luck with your quest."

"Thanks. I need all the help I can get."

Chapter Twelve

Suspicions

Thursday evening Mike pressed the doorbell at Harry Friedman's home. When he heard the chimes ring, Harry opened the door and greeted him pleasantly.

"Come in, Mike. Come in."

"Thank you," said Mike, as they shook hands briefly. Harry led him into his living room.

"Have a seat," said Harry sternly.

"Thank you," said Mike, wondering why Harry had unexpectedly summoned him to his home before he found more information. He was supposed to call Harry, not Harry call him. What news could Harry have that necessitated such a meeting? Could Harry have found out something important about Sadie that he hadn't found? After all, Harry had told Mike to call, but only when he was ready. Mike had found nothing more since their first meeting a few days ago.

Mike recognized the small, round container of fish food in Harry's left-hand. Harry placed it down on the table by the fish tank. The fish were vigorously snapping at wafers on the surface of the water. While Mike sat down, Harry remained standing, pacing in front of the fish tank.

"I don't suppose you have written permission to exhume a body from a back yard burial, do you?" asked Harry.

"No, I'm still working on it."

"And, I don't suppose you have anything we can use for a DNA sample, like hair or saliva, from your friend, Ms. Sadie Sutton, either?" asked Harry.

"No, I haven't given up yet. I don't know how to ask her for something like that. It's a sensitive issue. I mean, what do I say when she asks me why I need it? I've been waiting for the right opportunity to discuss it with her." He paused, looking at the floor. "But it just hasn't been appropriate to stop and make the request yet. The timing hasn't been right. I only see her for a few hours on Saturdays and I've only been out to see her twice and she tires easily," Mike blurted out defensively.

"Well, we left the responsibility for both issues with you, did we not?" Harry asked again.

"Yes. I haven't given up. We agreed I would call you when I had results. I haven't called because I don't have any more information yet." Mike was beginning to feel like a schoolboy called into the principal's office.

"But you are working on it, right? Your beliefs aren't getting in the way, are they?"

"No. I still plan to ask her for permission. I haven't forgotten."

"Ah, yes, and today I called while you were out in the field working on these issues. It's not your fault you're not ready for me. We didn't set today as a deadline. In fact, that's not why I called you here today."

"No? I came in response to your request. You called me."

"Yes, that's right, of course. I called because I have a problem. I have a feeling that you *can* tell me more than you have. You're not leveling with me."

"But I have," said Mike, stunned by the accusation, and wondering what it was that he might have left out to justify Harry's attack. What had he done wrong?

"No. I disagree." Harry was emphatic. The look on his face was chilling to Mike. "There is something you're holding back from me. I've discovered something on my own and, because it's most embarrassing, I fear there may be more that you haven't told me."

"I don't know what to say. I don't remember leaving anything out."

"Remember, we discussed the need to be totally upfront with each other?"

"Yes, yes, I remember. I've been careful to tell you every detail I remember."

"I thought you understood the need to be forthright and candid with each other, no deception. The agreement was that neither of us would hold back secrets from the other," said Harry looking directly at Mike.

"Yes, you said that and I agreed with you," said Mike firmly, meeting Harry's eyes directly. "No secrets."

"I told you I am neither a believer nor a disbeliever. As president of the association, I vowed to the membership not to be a 'yes' man to simply go along with every purported incident that comes my way. I promised the association, if they wanted a 'yes man,' then I was the wrong person for the job. My platform seeks to find the best facts we can assemble and to verify them. I promised to bring respect to our cause and attract mainstream scientists to accept DeBosi as worthy of true, unbiased inquiry."

"Yes, yes, you said all of that," said Mike, now even more confused about where Harry was headed. "You told me your position. When I first came here, I was looking for acceptance and support. You certainly turned my focus onto reality,"

"That's my job... Now, since we met, I've done some digging on my own, Mike. I started with the fact that you told me the wildest encounter story I've ever heard. You walked in here with a straight face and said that you met a woman you were convinced had mixed blood and with whom you had sipped tea. As I remember, to top things off, you insisted that she claims someone buried the body of an australopithecine in her back yard. Is this correct?" asked Harry. "Or am I overstating your position?"

"Yes. That's what I said and I still believe it's true. I think you would come to the same conclusion if you met her and heard her story. I don't care how crazy it sounds."

"Yes, you said that. So, I asked myself, is this the most bizarre encounter reported to me, ever? In fact, it's so bizarre, I didn't write up a report. I want verification to substantiate anything before I submit a formal report to the Institute. You seemed like such an honest, sincere man, so I opened a file and invested some of my personal time on it."

"I told you my honest impression of my experience," said Mike defensively.

"You're entitled to your opinions, but I don't like being played the fool," said Harry accusingly.

"No sir, no one does. And I didn't play you for a fool."

"When I first met you, I told you I would deal only with facts, no matter what they were. The Institute has developed an excellent report form, which forces the unusual into a standardized format for factual analysis. That is, except for your situation."

"Both you and Stan told me that."

"I take my job seriously, and that means more than mere words to me. While you have been on your own assignment, so, too, I have been on mine. I have treated your beliefs with the same respect as any other report made to me, whether a member or not."

"And you have," said Mike.

"That's the least we can do. So, I started my own inquiries."

"What did you find? I would like to know. So now there's something you're not telling me." Mike started to get upset.

"You, my friend, checked out. Your records bear up what you represented yourself to be. I found nothing in your past or present to suggest any motivation for greed, need for attention or fraud. When you signed our form the last time you were here, you authorized the association to make any and all personal and financial inquiries we deemed appropriate."

"I didn't read the form closely," said Mike uncomfortably. "I didn't realize I had agreed to allow that. So, what did you find to be so upset?"

"I want you to know I exercised that right. I found nothing to indicate a reason for you to fabricate such an outlandish claim. In all honesty, most of the encounters reported to us come from people who have no apparent motive for fabrication. I suppose that's what holds my interest in the subject. Your story is a bit more outlandish perhaps, but that's all. I found no basis for you to fabricate the story as you did," said Harry indignantly.

Harry paused for a moment and Mike could hear the bubbling of the aerator on the fish tank. The water in the fish tank was clear and the fish appeared to be thriving. He was so caught off guard by Harry's accusation that he didn't know how to reply, so he remained silent. He sensed that more was coming.

"When I realized that you checked out. I turned my attention to our subject, Ms. Sadie Sutton. I thought there, perhaps, I would find something, but you beat me. I contacted the records department at the courthouse and you had already been there. I know you work at the courthouse and have connections there. At first, I was elated. You were not just telling me stories of your wild beliefs. You were working to substantiate them. Most people seldom do that."

"I'm digging to find the truth, but what do you mean I beat you?"

"Very few who have observations or encounters make the effort to join our association. Most people only want to report the incident and go on about their lives. The average incident may not be forgotten, but is lost and ignored and doesn't have any impact on the lives of the observers. I have concluded your situation is different. I have a strange feeling that there is something else going on here, something I can't pinpoint. Of course, like you, I found nothing in the records about Ms. Sutton," Harry explained.

"The records in Brandon don't go back that far."

"So it seems. I agree. In a way, Sadie Sutton does not appear to exist. Officially, anyway."

"At least both of us came to the same conclusion. I didn't go back to Sarasota County because the original seat was too far away. I don't think either Sadie or Johnston would have traveled that far just to make 'official' records. People like Sadie and Johnston wouldn't have cared a hoot about official records, now or back then."

"I'm trying to remember, but didn't you tell me that Sadie had a gauze curtain blocking her from your view on your first visit?"

"Yes, there was a gauze curtain that divided the porch into two sections the first time I went there."

"Yes, and you thought it was odd, but she gave you an acceptable reason for it."

"She said she put it up to block the no-see-ums, because it was their breeding season."

"Ah, yes, the no-see-ums. What do you know about them?"

"Not much really, other than they can be really annoying."

"So you accepted her reason for the curtain and didn't see it as strange."

"Her concern seemed reasonable to me."

"Didn't you tell me this cabin is located in the swamp, out past the Interstate?"

"Yes, it's another 13 miles out off SR744."

"In my job, geography becomes important, too. I believe that would place Ms. Sutton's cabin about twenty miles from the Gulf of Mexico."

"Yes, that sounds accurate."

"I won't bother you with the technical name for no-see-ums, that's not important here. However, I did do a little research on them and what I found bothers me."

"How so, what did you find? How is that important here?"

"You see, that particular insect is found along the salt water coastline and is subject to the ebb and flow of the tides. The water in the swamp isn't tidal, is it?"

"No, I'm sure it's not."

"I didn't think so. I doubt you will find any no-see-ums there."

"So what does that mean?"

"The real issue is why would she put up that curtain for one week, or was it for your visit? It is possible she didn't know the real name of the insect that was bothering her. But it is also possible that she put that curtain up for another reason. That means the bug story was a diversion for her real reason."

"You don't really believe that, do you? What other reason could she have for going to the trouble of putting that curtain up?"

"I have no idea. The bug story doesn't check out. Because the bug story appears strange, I became suspicious. Beyond that, I have no idea what it means. Did you have any problem with bugs on your side of the curtain?"

"No, there were no bugs on the porch. Besides, the porch was screened in. I didn't see any bugs on my side. Well, I don't know what that means either. Maybe she was deliberately shielding her appearance from my view."

"Well, perhaps. Anyway, I didn't find any facts about Sadie Sutton."

"That's what I found. Sadie Sutton has no social security number, no marriage record, and no birth certificate. She appears to date back to a time where there is no evidence of her existence."

"We don't even know if the name she is using is actually her real name," said Harry. "I admit I found nothing on Sadie Sutton or any other people with that last name. That, of course, didn't stop me. I turned my attention to your friend, Ms. Stillwell."

"Sandy?" asked Mike in disbelief.

"Yes. How long have you known her?"

"I met her a few months ago, at one of the historical society meetings. She invited me to join her committee to interview Sadie. I met with her before and after each of the two trips that I made to Sadie's cabin."

"So, in effect, Ms. Stillwell was the catalyst for you to interview Ms. Sutton and the inspiration for the story you told me."

"I suppose you could say that. She's the member of the historical society most interested in writing a book about Sadie's life. In fact, she's the committee chairperson for the project. I'm just an interested member of her committee. Sandy asked me to do the interviews. That's how I became involved in the project."

"Well, I was embarrassed. What I don't understand is why you didn't tell me about Sandy. I should have been informed about her as well. I shouldn't have had to find out for myself."

"Find out what?" Mike was puzzled. "I don't understand why you're so upset. What does Sandy have to do with this?"

"First, Ms. Stillwell is the senior teller at First Bank in Brandon and has been there for five years. I also found that she lives in the Green Tree Apartments."

"Yes, I guess I knew those things when I first met you, but I didn't think those facts were relevant to my encounters with Sadie Sutton. We're not addressing Sandy. Sadie and her heritage are what I'm interested in. Why Sandy?"

"Perhaps that's not my point. You see, Mike, I'm embarrassed and upset because what I also found out, almost by accident, is that Sandy is an associate member of my organization, the Almas Association. I figured if you knew those other simpler things, certainly you would know this more relevant fact."

"The association? Sandy is a member of the association?"

"Yes, she is. I checked the membership roster."

"No, I had no idea. We never discussed anything except the interview process and what we knew about Sadie for the historical society project. I never mentioned or discussed my beliefs about Sadie with Sandy. She never said anything about herself, and she certainly didn't tell me about your association or her membership in it. I honestly did not know there was any connection between Sandy and your association."

"If you had no idea, then how is it that you attended the presentation at the hotel?"

"Sandy invited me. She told me the historical society received the tickets as a gift. She said they selected her as recipient as a reward for the work we're doing on the Sutton project. She acted as if she had no idea what the presentation was all about. I agree. It's strange that she would deliberately give me this impression if she were a member of the association. If she had told me, I would have told you."

"Strange, indeed," said Harry thoughtfully. "You see, associate members of our organization pay a smaller annual membership fee than the regular members. Associate members only receive our newsletter, which lists the schedule of events. The real issue is that associates do not sign a membership application and statement. That form is the one that gives us permission to conduct background checks. Because of this, I knew nothing about her and could not run a background check on her, legally. That may be pure coincidence, but it is a strange one."

"Now I see why you are upset. You can check me out as a total stranger but you can't check out your own associate members. Why is that? That seems like a strange policy."

"When you make a report as an observer, you sign the release form giving us permission to run a background check. As I said, she joined as an associate member, which means she paid full price for the tickets to the presentation at the hotel. Associate members don't qualify for the discounted tickets to events."

"She told me the historical society gave her the tickets."

"Really, Mr. Byrne. Don't be so naïve. Certainly you realize a member of the historical society would never be caught near an association such as this one."

"Oh, now that I think about it, you're right. Obviously, I wasn't thinking."

"I invited you to come here this evening because I thought you were involved in some diabolical plan with her. I assumed you knew about her involvement with the subject and the tie to our association. It didn't make sense that you didn't know, unless, as you infer, she withheld that information from you. I apologize for coming on so strong. I concluded that you knew her well and were deliberately holding back information from me. I smelled a rat because I thought you knew. But now, I smell a rat of quite a different nature."

"I didn't know of her membership in the association. She didn't tell me she was a member of both groups, only the historical society. I'm curious why she didn't tell me, especially since she invited me to the presentation at the hotel. Why do you think she did that?"

"That makes it even more mysterious. You know, I had a detective friend in Detroit who always told me that when he didn't understand what was going on and didn't know who was doing what to whom or why, he would stand back and trace the money, or the exceptional need for money. Money often underlies the motivation for human action. You checked out and Sadie checked out. If I am correct, Sadie has no money and has essentially lived all her life without money. I see no need to do any money tracing there."

"So, what about Sandy? I really don't know anything about her. My only involvement or knowledge about her is through the historical society."

"I think, as the detectives say, I have found the scent of the money trail. I think your friend Ms. Stillwell is planning to make a financial killing from selling Sadie's story, not the one for your historical society book, but the one for the tabloid press. To do so, she needs some one to corroborate the story, so, my guess is, she's planning to use you, and perhaps myself and the association, as well. Let's face it, your beliefs with a little polish and some back up, no matter how tenuous, would make a great tabloid story. Can't you see the headlines now? Human Marries Bigfoot, Abandoned Half-Human-Half Sasquatch

Child Found in Florida Swamp, Human Child Raised by Sasquatch Parent…Someone could make a bundle of money on this one."

"The whole thing seems a bit bizarre, a bit far fetched. Sandy seems like such a nice person to me. I don't see her manipulating Sadie's situation for personal advantage. She seems genuinely concerned about Sadie's well being."

"Think about it for a moment. Think about how you formed your beliefs. You told me it was from Sadie's appearance. Wasn't it?"

"Yes. It's Sadie. If you saw her, you would come to the same conclusion."

"Then, I ask you, when Ms. Stillwell first went to the cabin and met Sadie, what was her reaction? Was it neutral, or was it like yours? What was her impression? What did she tell you?"

"That's odd. She never mentioned anything at all about Sadie's appearance. We never discussed the topic. I had the impression that Sadie was African American. That would make sense since many run away slaves joined the Seminoles in the swamps in the 1800's."

"Yet you jumped to an extreme opinion based on her appearance. Are you now telling me that Ms. Stillwell felt nothing? And you are the only one to have reacted in such an extreme way?" posed Harry.

"Again, you've raised a good point. I repeat, Sandy never said one thing about Sadie's appearance to me or posed any theories or opinions. Now that you point that out, it does seem strange."

"Now, do you see why I jumped to my conclusions about you?" asked Harry.

"Sure, so now what do we do? There must be some specific action I can take. We need a plan."

"For the moment, do nothing. We don't know the details of her plan, at least not yet. I fear she's a step ahead of us and plans to sell the story to some rumor publisher. She needs you to play the role of an accomplice. She'll approach you soon, so we only need to wait patiently for her to influence your actions. We must stop her plans before any damage is done. You, especially, must continue as if you know nothing, as if this meeting never took place. But, be alert. I'll do what I can. The opportunity to stop her will be obvious. When she makes her move, we'll figure out how to derail her. Unfortunately, that's about all we can do right now."

"You're amazing. Once again, you've given me a reality check. You keep me from going off in the wrong direction."

"That's my job. I must do what I can to ensure that only the facts are disclosed to the public or placed in our database. My mission can be difficult. Here, you may have to act as a key player in helping our association do what it must do. I would ask you to join the association but that would be a mistake. You can't afford to tip your hand in any way right now. You'll be a valuable asset to the association later. If you joined now, you'd jeopardize all the work you're doing on the project. Stay neutral for now, but do join us later."

"I'll do what I can," said Mike. "Sandy is the one who is at risk with the historical society, so she must be planning something important. You have my full cooperation."

Chapter Thirteen

Taxes

The impromptu meeting with Harry the night before motivated Mike to continue his search for more information about Sadie and her lifetime companions. His investigation led him to the Palmetto County Property Tax Office. He found the tax office conveniently located in the courthouse building on the second floor, only one floor below his own office. He stepped downstairs for a visit during his lunch hour.

"May I help you?" asked a young woman who had been working behind the counter.

"Hi. I'm Mike Byrne. I work in the clerk's office upstairs."

"I'm Miss Terhune. Yes, I recognize you. You're lucky today, there's no one else here so you don't have to take a number," she chuckled. "Ignore that sign on the wall, you're the only customer I've had here this whole morning. What can I do for you?"

"I hope you can help me. I'm on my lunch hour so I don't have a lot of time. I want to check to see if a certain person owns her own home. I hope I'm in the right office for that."

"Yes, you've come to right place. You can even do that yourself over there on the public access terminal, as long as you have the folio number," she said, pointing to a computer terminal across the room.

"That terminal is the only way to access the system. Even I have to use it to get information."

"I'm sorry, I don't have the folio number, only her name," Mike apologized. "Can you find the folio number for me so I can look up the property?"

"Sure, to find property assessed in a certain name, I can check the assessment role for you. The search identifies all land titled in that name in this county, but there's a ten dollar fee for each search by name," she explained.

"That's exactly what I need. I only have one name so I can pay cash for the search."

"Fine. Here, fill out this form. Write the name you want me to research in the search box. Be sure to spell the name correctly and print it clearly in capital letters so I can read it. Write your name and home address in the applicant blank for our records. When you finish, I'll run it for you."

"The name is Sadie Sutton."

"That doesn't mean a thing to me. Write it in the entry blank. We'll see what the computer search finds."

"Is the assessment roll all on line?"

"Yes, I can search the database several different ways: by tax folio number, brief, legal owner, or lender. Anyone can access the database on line since it's all public records. All real estate assessed for taxes is listed in the owner's name and recorded in the database. The public access terminal is limited to folio searches only, so all other searches must be ordered through me here at the desk using this form."

"I'll need your help. I have a hunch you may not find anything. She's an elderly widow living out in the Seminole Indian River Slough at Indian Bend. I think she may own her own homestead, that's all."

"Come to think of it, that name does sound familiar. Wait while I enter it into the system. The search only takes a few seconds." Miss Terhune silently watched the computer do the search. "I thought so. I found your person."

"You did? That's good news, " said Mike, relieved that Sadie's name finally appeared somewhere in the official records. Now, at least, he could prove she really existed.

"Well, I found a lot of folio numbers listed under her name. If you want the records printed, I have to charge you $1.00 for each tax bill. Right now, of course, the receipts are from last year; this year won't be ready until October."

"You said there's a lot of folio numbers? But she only has a small cabin."

"Oh, yes. As soon as I started the search, I remembered that name. I ran these bills for someone from the State a couple of months ago, someone from the Department of Natural Resources or something like that. Your bill comes to $25.00 including the fees for the tax bill receipts, fifteen folio numbers listed in this name, plus the $10 search fee," she said, as she continued to work at the terminal behind the counter.

"That doesn't sound right," said Mike, puzzled. "The name is S-u-t-t-o-n, S-a-d-i-e. She's a little old lady living in the slough, in a small cabin out there. You must have the wrong person if you have a whole bunch of properties."

"That's the name with the spelling that you gave me. I entered it right the first time. Hold on. I'll have a print out for all of them shortly, on that printer over there, the big one," she explained as she pointed to a large printer on a table across the room. "I have to use that one to print out multiple bills."

"Are you sure? That still doesn't seem right. I'll pay for the copies, but you must have the wrong person."

"Just remember, any number of different people may have the same name. Sadie Sutton doesn't strike me as being such an unusual name. I only enter the information. The computer spits out the matches, exactly as I entered them."

"I think there's a mistake somewhere," said Mike. "I'll pay the bill for the copies, but you must have the wrong person. I looked the name up in the phone book this morning and there were no other similar names listed. I doubt there are multiple people with that name."

"Are you a homeowner?"

"No, I rent."

"Then you aren't familiar with how to read a tax printout. I'll go over these bills with you. Then you can tell me if you still think there's a mistake. You do need to pay for these first."

"Yes, please proceed. Thank you. Here's two twenty-dollar bills. Can you give me change?"

"Sure, that's not a problem. I'm the only one here during lunchtime so I have to be cashier, too. Step over to the cashier's window and I'll trade these printouts for the money," she said as she started the print run.

"Okay, I'll pay for all of them, but I still think there's some mistake. Are you sure there's only one Sadie Sutton?"

"They're coming out now. This is the tax office not the phone book, but check the addresses on the bills, you'll see if they're all going to the same place. All I did was run the name exactly as you gave it to me."

"Fine, but I'm not sure there's an address out there for her."

Mike paid the invoice and both studied the printout spread out on the counter.

"There, see the information printed in the upper left corner? That's the name of the owner of record, the property assessed, and the address where the bills are sent. Sometimes that's different than the address of the property. Not all property owners live at the address of the assessed property."

"Of course. Especially if they own more than one property."

"Now, if I'm not mistaken, all these bills show the name, Sadie Sutton, exactly as you gave it to me. Look, the address on the first one is 'C/O' which is 'in care of' the Circle T Ranch in Brandon, Florida. That means we send these tax bills to Sadie Sutton at the Circle T Ranch."

"Yes, I see that," said Mike, stunned.

"Now, look at the rest of the bills. They're all the same. The name on each bill is identical and the mailing address is the Circle T Ranch for all of them. All property assessed in her name is billed to the same address. Hold on a second," Ms. Terhune said, as she went back to her desk and began to work at her terminal again. "In addition, all the land lies in adjoining townships. Yes," she said after a minute, "The name Circle T Ranch shows up, too, with a long list of folios under that name. The Circle T and Sadie Sutton are two of the largest landowners in Palmetto County. I don't suppose you want a copy of their bills, as well, do you?"

"No, I'm only interested in property owned in Sadie Sutton's name. I don't understand why the bills are sent to the ranch."

"Any land owner on the assessment roll can send us a written request to change the billing address to anywhere they want the bills sent. If she doesn't live at the assessed property address then that's what happened in this case. She must live at the ranch so she has the bills sent there," explained Ms. Terhune.

"I see what you're saying, but the bills don't make sense to me. She lives in her cabin, not the ranch."

"There are a couple of other things that might help you. See the letters in this block over here?" she asked pointing to the first bill on the printout.

"Yes," he said, looking at the bill.

"That abbreviation is the property category. If you notice, all of the land in these bills is assessed as AU. AU is the abbreviation for agricultural use, so there's no house or residential designation on any of these bills. Weren't you looking for residential property?"

"Well, yes. I was looking for the cabin where she lives."

"If the property were her residence, the designation 'RES' would be entered there and the box next to it would be checked off as 'Homestead.' I don't see any residential or homestead designation on any of these bills."

"It's a small cabin. It can't be very valuable," said Mike weakly.

"If the property is designated as 'homestead,' the owner qualifies for a reduction in the property taxes as an exemption on the assessed value of the property. The reduction in taxes is significant. From what you've told me, she would be motivated to take advantage of the tax savings. None of these bills show any residential property, and there is no homestead exemption listed anywhere on any of them. I'm not sure I'm helping you."

"Please go on. You're helping me a lot. I don't believe her cabin would be worth much. It's a small cabin, not very valuable, I'm sure."

"Most owners are diligent about getting their exemptions for their primary residence. Of course, property owners are entitled to only one homestead exemption. Are you sure she lives there?"

"I guess I'm not finding what I was looking for."

"Well, then look here in the lower right hand corner. In this block, we show the legal description. If the bill was for a house in a subdivision, lot and block and plat book and page where the plat is recorded are entered in this block, or it would show the book and page where a condominium is filed, but all your bills are for metes and bounds."

"What does that mean? What are metes and bounds?"

"That means that the land has not been subdivided. It's still identified legally as raw section lands."

"What are raw section lands? Forgive me for all these questions, but I don't know a lot about real estate."

"You need to spend some time with a lawyer. If the property has not been subdivided, it's still classified as raw land. That coincides with the agricultural designation. The state of Florida is part of the original lands surveyed by the federal government way back. They divided the land into sections, townships, and ranges for identification purposes. If nothing has happened to the land since that original survey, it's still in the form of sections today. Look at this bill."

"Okay, I'm following you."

"This bill includes Sections 1, 2, 3, 4 and 7 in the numbered township and range. I'm not going to go over how that system works. You need a real estate course for that, but you might be interested to know that in a true section there are 640 acres. You do know what an acre is," she stated emphatically.

"Yes, I think so."

"Good, then you can see that these bills cover a lot of land. The first bill alone covers five sections of land. From all these documents, apparently your friend, Miss Sutton owns a large percentage of undeveloped property in Palmetto County. In the upper right corner, you can see the total taxes due for the year. Remember, these are last year's bills."

"Unbelievable! That's a lot of money for Sadie Sutton to be paying. These bills add up to thousands of dollars."

"Here," she said pulling a hand calculator out from a shelf under the counter. "Go ahead and add them all up if you like. You might as well calculate an exact figure."

Mike added up the tax bills. He paused, "It comes to a total of $9,987.40."

"That's because the property is still assessed as agricultural use. That designation keeps the tax bills down to a minimum. Your little old lady is pretty well off if she is paying that much money annually for all that land."

"That can't be correct," said Mike. "Sadie Sutton doesn't have any money. I only guessed that she might own her cabin."

"Well, here's another fact you might find useful. The designation of 'pt' means that the assessment is only for *part* of the section. The data field in the computer doesn't allow for a full legal description to be entered, so we use the abbreviated description. Now, look at the end of that block, there's a book and page number. That refers to the official records book and page designation for where the deed is recorded," she said.

"So, now what do I do with those numbers?"

"You can check the county records, or, I recommend you go to the Graystone Abstract Company down the street to get copies of those deeds plus any other deeds that affect the property. I suggest you talk with them because some of these bills don't have a book and page reference, so you'd have to go there anyway."

"I see. Why don't they have a reference to a deed?"

"That reference is a recently added feature in the system. I don't remember the exact year we started entering it, but we didn't always include deed references. The ones you have would have been in the same name before we started to add that reference. That's why they don't have any designation. That land must be recorded in the same name for a long time."

"You've been most helpful. I'm not sure where I need to go from here."

"I suggest you call the Circle T Ranch and talk to them. They're listed in the phone book. They'll have your answers since the bills are sent there. Oh, there is one other thing," she continued.

"Yes, go on."

"Look here, located in the middle, down near the bottom of the page, you can see the word 'paid' and a date showing whether there are prior year's taxes due. All taxes for these properties are current.

Someone pays all the taxes promptly each year. I would start at the Circle T. That's where these bills are sent. It's a valid address."

"How do you know?"

"Because the bills are current. Someone at that address is getting the bills to the right person."

"That sounds logical," said Mike, gathering up the copies of the bills. "Did you say the abstract company is just down the street?"

"Two blocks south, on the other side of the street. You can't miss it."

"Thank you so much."

"Good luck," she said as Mike went out the door.

Chapter Fourteen

The Deeds

Following Ms. Terhune's directions, Mike found the Graystone Abstract Company two blocks further down Main Street. Since the distance was only a short walk from the courthouse, his curiosity about all the land belonging to Sadie Sutton drew him to extend his lunch hour. This growing curiosity had now overtaken his better judgment, demanding answers to his questions about all the land titled in Sadie Sutton's name. The Abstract Company building stood in the middle of the block and was constructed using stones with a façade that had seen better days. Mike remembered that this was one of the buildings the historical society was considering for acquisition and restoration.

Ms. Francis Moore, as he read from her nametag, was standing ready at the order counter as he ducked out of the afternoon sun into her office. She peered at him over the top of the black-rimmed bifocals resting on the lower part of her nose. Her imposing figure gave her an air of no nonsense knowledge and years of efficiency.

"How may I help you?" she spoke briskly.

"I need copies of some deeds," Mike responded politely.

"Well, you've come to the right place. Do you have folio numbers for the properties?"

"I would like copies of the deeds referenced on these tax bills," said Mike, opening his folder on the counter for her to examine.

"Good. I'll enter the descriptions into the database for you. We charge fifteen dollars for a search which includes a copy of the last deed of record," she explained.

"I hope I can use a credit card. This sounds like it's going to be expensive. I have a whole bunch of them to do."

"Yes, that's fine. I'll enter the legal description, or as much as you have on the bill, and run the search on the database. That will pick up the last deed of record, which is probably what you want. Our database only goes back twenty years, so if you need older documents we'll have to do it another way."

"I'm looking for deeds registered to Sadie Sutton. Her name is printed on all of these bills."

"Fine. May I borrow the bills? I have to enter the data into the terminal at my desk. If I have the information in front of me, it will be easier and quicker to get your deeds."

"Sure, here they are," said Mike, handing her the stack of bills. "There are fifteen bills."

"For your information, the number of deeds may actually vary from the number of bills. For some reason, the tax collector's office separates the property into different folios based on their own arbitrary system. We suspect they only include a certain amount of land in any one folio. Let's see what I can find for you. Hmm, the property is located in only two different townships. That will make it a little easier. These bills are all in section lands."

"Is it faster that way?"

"No, not really. There's usually less activity if it's not platted. Well, I take that back. Where it's platted, there could be several deeds all in the same section. It depends on what I find. I have to run the whole section to find the deeds in those cases," she explained.

"Will that make it more expensive?"

"Sometimes. The cost depends on the activity," she said, sitting down and sliding her chair up to her terminal. She began typing on her keyboard.

"For all deeds recorded in the last twenty years, we have copies on microfilm. The database gives me the microfilm location. With the location, I can select the microfilm spool and run it to find the location of the deed. Then I can make a copy of the document from the microfilm. You might as well have a seat. It will take a few minutes for me to run all of these properties."

Mike sat down in a chair by the front door. "How long will it take? I'm on an extended lunch hour already."

"From the looks of what you have there, about twenty minutes. Everything is on the computer and these are current deeds." She answered as she continued to work at her terminal. After about ten minutes of steady typing, she stopped and printed out a list of the records Mike had requested.

"Normally Louise would be here to help me, but she took a late lunch," said Ms. Moore. "So, I'm on my own. I'll be fine if no one interrupts us."

"Okay, if I really run late, I'll call my office and tell them I'm on an errand. I can wait. This is important to me."

"Well, I hope I can find what you're looking for, Mr. - Uh, What did you say your name was?"

"Mike. Mike Byrne. Actually, I'm looking for a deed to a cabin owned by Ms. Sadie Sutton. Do you know her?"

"No, can't say that I do, but if she's on one of these deeds, I'll find her," said Ms. Moore.

"I'm puzzled by all these properties in her name and want to be sure it's not a mistake. I don't know how the records can show she owns so much property. I hope these deeds will help sort this all out," Mike said to himself.

"Now, Mr. Byrne, I have to go in the back to get these copies. There are a few deeds on this list," she said as she moved toward the back door. "I'm going to leave you here by yourself for a few moments."

"I'll wait right here."

Another twenty minutes passed before she came back with the copies. "It's not as bad as it looked. I only found eight deeds, but I have to caution you that these deeds cover only part of the properties listed on the bills you gave me. The land that's not included was last conveyed over twenty years ago. As I told you, the database doesn't go back more than twenty years. You'll have to wait until Mr. Thomas comes back later this afternoon. He can to go into the archives and find those deeds manually when he returns. Mr. Thomas takes care of all the records over twenty years old that have not been computerized."

"Is it possible to order those records? For right now, I'll settle for whatever you can give me today."

"Sure, you can. We charge extra to go into the archives because it takes us more time to locate them there. I'd wait before you order any more if you want to save some money. My advice is to look these over first to see if what you need is missing then order only what you need from the archives. It's possible you may find your answer here in these records."

"That sounds like a good idea. You've done this before…"

"Sure have. In any case, here's what I found," she said, putting the pile of deeds found on the counter. "Do you have a lawyer to go over these with you? I haven't seen you around here before."

"I work in the clerk's office. Real estate is not my expertise. I'm doing some research on this project for the historical society."

"Well, you were right. All of the deeds have your grantee, Miss Sutton listed as the owner. She's the grantee, the one who received the property. Every one of the deeds has her name there, right where it should be as the owner of record. There's a lot of land here."

"At least it's the right name. I just don't know what all this means."

"All these deeds were prepared and executed over a sixty day period, twelve years ago, as you can see from the deeds and the recording dates stamped on them. They were all recorded within ten days after they were executed, so someone was prompt to take care of business."

"What other information can you tell from the deeds?" asked Mike.

"Well, the same law firm prepared all the deeds, as you can see. That firm has been here in town for a long time. The second or third generation runs it now, I think. Actually their offices are located right around the corner. Now, that's interesting. The grantor, that's the seller, is The Circle T Ranch, Inc., a Florida corporation for all the deeds, and they're all signed by Douglas Williams, as president. The address for the ranch is given on State Road 744 here in Brandon," she added. "That's only a few miles past the interstate. That's really interesting."

"I see. Does it show how much she paid for each property on the deed?"

"No, these are all quit claim deeds. They show a consideration of ten dollars for the transaction and the documentary stamps paid were minimum on each of them. You can do that if you show on the recording form that the deed was corrective," she added.

"Corrective? What does that mean?"

"If the new deeds are issued to correct an error in prior deeds or to correct some legal defect, those deeds are usually not charged for. They are exempt because they correct a legal defect or problem," she explained. "Somewhere in the body of each deed a statement describes the purpose for making the new deed. Here the purpose of the deed corrects boundary lines between the properties of the parties. To me, these transactions seem like something more than meets the eye is going on."

"What do you mean by that?"

"I shouldn't say too much," she continued. "There's too much land involved. That's a legal issue. You should talk to the attorney who prepared the deeds or to Mr. Williams who signed the deeds for an explanation. Anyway, you need to have the lands abstracted carefully. I'm not an attorney and it looks like you need one for an explanation of what happened here."

"Please, go on. Anything you can tell me will help me to understand."

"Well, the largest part of the land covered by your tax bills is not included in these deeds. I can't draw out those descriptions. I'm not qualified to do them. Mr. Thomas has to do that, but the caption references to the sections and quarter sections do not include a lot of the property on those bills. I can tell that just by looking at them."

"What does that mean?" asked Mike

"Only that there's been no activity on the property missing from these deeds in over twenty years. The tax bills do show that all the land listed is assessed in the name of Ms. Sutton as grantee, so you are still looking for deeds recorded more than twenty years ago."

"I'm lost. What do you think these deeds are all about?"

"The notations say they are recorded to correct boundary lines. You'll have to ask the grantor, Mr. Williams or the lawyer who prepared them to find out. You can't tell much from the deeds, but I can tell you one thing."

"You can, what's that?"

"Your little old lady, Ms. Sutton, is one of the largest land holders in this county. She must be a wealthy lady."

"Well, you've been very helpful." Mike was stunned by Ms. Moore's comment about Sadie. As Mike understood Sadie's story, nothing could be farther from the truth. How could the Sadie Sutton he knew have amassed such an enormous amount of lands and live in such primitive conditions in her little cabin in the slough? "I'll contact the parties for more information. Thank you again."

"Any time, just let me know. If you need to know the history of the land, remember the abstract company has that information here. I've told you all I can from these deeds. Ask a lawyer or talk to someone at the ranch to explain what happened with all these deeds."

"Thanks for everything. I guess I'm on my own from here on," said Mike as he put all the deeds and bills back into a folder, slipped them into his briefcase, and headed back out the door into the Florida sunshine.

"Have a nice day."

"You, too."

Chapter Fifteen

The Painting

After dinner, Mike sat in his kitchen reexamining the deeds and tax bills he had spread out on the table in front of him. He searched to find any information he might have overlooked during his visit to the abstract office. Until that morning, he had not found any official records to explain who Sadie Sutton was or that she even existed. He knew that could be explained since her birth predated current official record keeping practices. Now, if she were of mixed blood, some human lineage would tell who her relatives were. Finding any relatives was of paramount importance since he now found she was one of the largest landholders in the county. Who would inherit this vast amount of property when she died? He wanted to find information to fill in the blanks of his still unanswered questions about her heritage. The question of her genetics had been the more pressing issue earlier in the morning. Now that dilemma had yielded to the new questions of how could she possibly be one of the largest landowners in the county?

Yesterday, he had simply hoped to find documentation for an acre or two as her homestead in a deed to establish real dates to work with, and a seller's name linked with hers. Instead, he found a collection of tax bills and deeds for an unexpected holding of thousands of acres. He was now painfully aware that the deeds he did have in his possession did not include documentation for all of the holdings registered in the county records in Sadie's name. The deeds that were missing could be very old. In addition, the tax bills failed to show any of the property with a homestead exemption. Each bill represented taxes for hundreds of acres, none of them including the land where her cabin was located. The lack of personal records could be due to her age and lack of protocol in the early settlement days of rural Florida for recording births, deaths and marriages, but an explanation for her enormous land holdings contradicted what he understood about her personally.

The new facts emerging in his quest did not match his assessment of the real Sadie Sutton. Her background and history remained vague and elusive. Until this morning, he had not found her name anywhere in any official record. No other person with the same name occurred in the records and her address was listed at the ranch next door, virtually eliminating the possibility that a different Sadie Sutton owned the land. This afternoon, a new picture of Sadie Sutton had emerged. The facts revealed a reverse reality; Sadie's name appeared everywhere, all over the official property records and deeds in the county. For Mike, the pieces of the puzzle were not fitting together. How could the Sadie Sutton he knew own thousands of acres of land? She was convinced that she had no assets and he had believed her. She never mentioned owning acres of property in their meetings. How did she have the money to pay the annual taxes? He had obtained excellent assistance during the day both in the tax office and the abstract company. After hours of studying the documents, he discovered nothing new in the documents on his kitchen table. As he inspected the deeds carefully, he realized the place to find his answers was obvious, the Circle T Ranch and Doug Williams. He had passed near that ranch each time he went to visit Sadie. The Circle T Ranch bordered the slough where her cabin was located. While he continued to look at the deeds and attempt to formulate an explanation, the phone rang.

"Hello," he spoke softly.

"Hi, Mike. It's Sandy. How are you?"

"I'm fine," he spoke automatically trying to decide what to tell her. He remembered Harry's words strongly urging that neither of them tell her anything. Harry was convinced she had some secret agenda and they should wait for her to disclose her plan. Should he tell her about his new findings? For the moment at least, he decided to take Harry's advice and say nothing.

"You should be proud of me. It's all set," she said.

"All set?" he asked, having no idea what she was talking about. Was Harry right? He wondered. "What's set?"

"I assume you can take off work tomorrow, as you said you could," she responded.

"Do you need me for something?"

"Of course, don't be silly. You're my main committee person."

"I do have a personal day available," he said, still at a loss to understand what she was talking about. Suddenly, he remembered that he had just used up one personal day and under county rules he could not take two personal days in a row without preapproval. He mentally reviewed his schedule for the following day. "Oh, yes, I planned to meet with a vendor about the feasibility of installing a bank ATM machine in the Court House. They canceled late this afternoon due to a software problem. So I can stop by their field office in town to pick up some materials on the equipment first thing in the morning. That will free up the rest of the morning for you."

"Good. I set up a meeting for you at ten o'clock tomorrow morning at the Circle T Ranch to meet with Doug Williams. He runs the ranch. I told him who you are and why you want to talk with him," she explained. "He's the one person at the ranch that would know the most about Sadie, as far as I know."

"Sounds fine," said Mike, trying not to show his excitement. Doug Williams was the one person he most wanted to speak to now. He had forgotten she promised to set up a meeting with him. He decided to say nothing about Sadie's land holdings to Sandy until after he talked with Doug Williams. "I can meet with Mr. Williams in the morning and be back on schedule by lunchtime. Thanks, Sandy, for setting up the meeting."

"No problem, happy to do my part. I have to run over to the hospital for a test this evening. I'll see you Saturday morning, same time, same place."

"I'll be there. Good night and thanks again." Elated, he hung up the telephone. Soon he would have answers to his questions about Sadie's land.

From the highway, the Circle T ranch house appeared to be a small, red brick, one-story house. The long driveway, lined with young live oaks, split into a circular loop outside the steps to the front door. The house was set far back from the highway on a high tract of ground in a cluster of old live oaks. A thick curtain of Spanish moss hung from the live oaks giving the homestead an air of mystery and antiquity. As he approached the house, Mike realized that the house was much larger than it appeared from the highway. In fact, it was huge, consisting of six or seven thousand square feet with an attached bunk house and a second floor with a veranda in the back. The low-lying structure was deceiving. Up close, he could see that several barns and outer buildings were clustered behind it, hidden among the over hanging Spanish moss on the live oaks.

Mike parked his car at the base of the front steps. As he walked up the stairs, he admired the massive carved oak door and pressed the doorbell. A man, of about his height opened the door and greeted him with a handshake and a smile. The man had a full head of graying brown hair with a thick matching beard and mustache. His flannel shirt opened at the collar and ended neatly tucked into his faded blue jeans and bottomed with well-worn cowboy boots. His large silver belt buckle shaped in a W attracted Mike's eyes immediately when he opened the door. Mike estimated Doug Williams to be in his late forties or early fifties.

"Byrne?" Doug Williams asked in a strong, deep voice.

"Yes, I'm Mike Byrne."

"Doug Williams, here. Come on in Mr. Byrne and get out of the heat."

"Thank you," said Mike as he followed Doug Williams into the enormous living room. Mike estimated the room to be at least eight hundred square feet in area. Darkly stained oak beams lined the high ceiling. Earth tone Mexican tiles extended across the floor into the equally large dining room. A long, dark stained wood antique table with matching carved chairs set for sixteen people was centered in the dining room. Two large custom made wrap around leather sofas, each with its own large coffee table made from local cypress knees, dominated the center of the living room. Doug led Mike over to the first sofa and motioned for him to take a seat. As he sat down, Mike faced the huge, stone fireplace filling the wall opposite the sofas.

"Have a seat, Mr. Byrne. May I get you something to drink?"

"No, thank you," said Mike as he sat down, placing his briefcase next to the coffee table in front of him. He took out a yellow notebook and pen. Doug Williams sat on a large, round matching leather hassock situated between the two sofas. "Please, call me Mike."

"Sure, Mike. I'm a casual man myself. Call me Doug."

"Fine, happy to meet with you today. I have a lot of questions to ask you for this project with the historical society."

"So, you're the representative from the historical society. Sandy told me a lot about you. I'm familiar with the group. They actually approached me recently to do an article about my family and its history, also. I'm pleased they are doing this project."

"Yes," said Mike, realizing that he had no idea what Sandy had told Doug when she set up the meeting for him. "I'm the Assistant County Clerk here in Palmetto County. I volunteered to help the society write an article or maybe a book about early life out here, through the eyes of Sadie Sutton. You do know of her?"

"Sure, we have a close relationship. She's our nearest neighbor."

"The society plans to write a history of the Circle T, with your approval. But right now, we want to focus on information about Sadie, due to her age."

"Of course. When Sandy contacted me, she had a lot of good things to say about you. I got the impression she's single, as she said you were. You'd better watch yourself there, Mike. Good looking single women can be dangerous for the single man," he said with a chuckle and a gleam in his eye.

"I'll be careful," said Mike grinning. Somehow, he had never pictured Sandy as a dangerous female. "How long has your family been here in Palmetto County?"

"My grandfather, Alvah Williams, settled here around the time of the Civil War. He started working the land as a farmer, experimenting with a number of different crops. His initial venture and basic income came from the chicken coops he set up. For a long time they were the largest coops in this area. He also started up the original Black Angus herd that parented the stock we have today. As transportation improved, and the population in the area grew, competition drove him out of the poultry business. He concentrated his attention on cattle ranching, which is what we do today."

"Yes, I noticed that you have a rather large operation here. I passed many miles of fence before I reached the drive into the ranch house."

"My grandfather started it all, passed it down to my father, and my father passed it on to me. I must have a bit of old Granddad's blood, 'cause I also like to experiment a bit. I brought in breeders for a small herd of African Brahmans and Texas Longhorns, too. We gave up chickens and basic farming back when my father was a young man. My father's efforts paid off with the Angus herd, which is what we're well known for. Dad's been gone for sixteen years. Cancer took him in his prime, Mike. He left this ranch, now fifteen thousand acres, to his four kids. I have three younger sisters."

"So, this is a family operation?"

"In name only. The four of us own and run the ranch as a corporation. I'm president and manager of operations. Before he fell ill, the old man taught me as a youngster to follow the family tradition. I took over running this place. I never said a word but just kept things going until he died. My sisters have no interest in the operation. The oldest of the three, Amy, lives in downtown Chicago. She's a spinster as the old folks called single women, but in today's terminology, she's a jet setter living the good life. She shows no interest in ranching or in settling down in any type of conventional marriage. Even though Chicago is her legal residence, she spends most of her time in private jets. She's more likely to be in Reno, Las Vegas, or Aspen than Chicago or anywhere else. Only she knows where she's going to be on a day-to-day basis. I give her credit, though, she's actually careful with her money. She's a looker, if you know what I mean. Someone else usually picks up the tab, but she's like my other sisters, Suzanne and Tiffany. They're all alike."

"How's that?"

"They're all coupon clippers. As long as the ranch succeeds financially and their share of the profits keep coming in, they leave me alone. Suzanne and Tiffany married and live in New York State, one in the City and the other upstate in Saratoga Springs. Both have kids. Tiffany has two daughters and Suzanne has a son. We get together occasionally for family reunions. Their husbands and the kids are all alike. Whatever they do with their lives, there's not a one of them willing to get their hands dirty. The kids will be lawyers or stockbrokers, or some other white-collar profession. Not a one of them has any interest in ranching. They like the income the ranch generates, but despise the work."

"You're not married, so you have no children?"

"No, and none on the way."

"That's a shame."

"Not really. It's a blessing. They all leave me alone to run the ranch. I like it that way."

"But what happens when you're gone? All will be lost. They'll probably sell the land to a developer who'll turn it all into condos."

"That's true. I thought things would be different when I started out. You know, things never turn out the way you expect. I went to one of those big land grant colleges and majored in Agriculture. Actually, we both went to the same university together. Stephanie Jensen was her name. Her family lived about ten miles from here. We both planned the whole thing together. Everyone knew we would get married one day. Both of us came from big ranches. There was no one else in our lives but each other. She majored in journalism in college. I think the break happened when she started meeting guys in her journalism classes. She found job offers available all over the world, so the travel bug bit her. I don't know if one guy swayed her, or the idea that the great, big world out there provided a more glamorous life for her than what was back here. All of a sudden, ranch life and an old stuck-in-the-mud guy like me was the last thing on her mind," said Doug sadly.

"So you lost her to the allure of adventure in the big, wide world."

"Broke my heart, Mike. Hell, there wasn't anyone else. It was too late for me. I'd put all of my time here and in college with her. I didn't know anyone else and didn't want to. She moved on to the good life and I never saw her again. Hell, we went through that fraternity-sorority exchange of pins by candlelight and all that. Then, one day in our senior year, I got the proverbial 'Dear John letter,' and that was the end. She moved to Chicago after graduation and I returned to the ranch. Well, hell, I knew where my future was. I've met a few husband hunters around from time to time, but I'm an independent sort. I adjusted to the way things are. I get up every day with both feet on the ground. I'm not going to sacrifice my life for a pretty face. I wanted to run this place since I was a kid, and that's what I've done. I think my sister Amy is a lot like me. She's independent, too. She just chose a different life style. All I know is that I couldn't live like her in a closed in box in a tall building made of many more boxes stacked up high in the sky. That's no way to live, Mike, at least not for me."

"I can see that," said Mike.

"I've lived here all my life, and I expect I'll die here. I like to hear the birds in the morning, the bellow of the bulls, the sound of a rooster at dawn, the smell of the land right here in mid-Florida on a steamy damp morning after a sudden rain shower. You can bury me right here, Mike. But, I'm concerned about what will happen to this place when I'm gone. I think the coupon clippers will sell it off so they can keep on living as they do. Tiffany's daughters will marry brokers or lawyers or, hell, they may become brokers or lawyers themselves. No, no one wants to step into my boots, Mike. Maybe one of the big farming corporations will buy this place and add it to their monster spreads. Economics has pushed the land into bigger and bigger farming conglomerates every year. The economics today have doomed the smaller places, even this size, in the long run. Little guys can't make it profitable enough to eek out a living anymore."

"You sound convinced that this place won't stay in the family. Couldn't your sisters bring in a manager to run things and keep it going?"

"You're thinking, Mike. That's what they should do. Keep the land. That's where the real wealth is, and will continue to be in the future, but I don't see that happening. My sisters like the income without doing anything to earn it. I fear they'll have a rude awakening when the next stock market crash comes. The land is the key, but no one sees it that way but me. Hell, bringing in outside management to run the place would double the cost of operations and destroy the profitability. The smaller spreads share that problem. That's why the huge operations are the ones that make it."

"Still, I think it would be a shame for your family to lose it."

"I agree. I work hard to run a tight ship here. I check the pulse daily on operating costs. They might try a manager, but I don't think it would last. Ranching is the kind of business best run hands on, if you know what I mean."

"It's been in your family so long, you must know every inch of the ranch. I would fight to keep it."

"That's sentimentality. Me? I won the luck of the draw. I never had a worry, I always knew what I was going to be doing. I'm the oldest, the only male, and the one who liked the land and the business. That was all luck. When Dad died, I was already running the place. No one was going to bust in and rock the boat."

"They were smart."

"They didn't know anything about the business, didn't want to, so they stayed out. That's why it's held together. Dad hired good lawyers. They set this place up as a corporation before Dad died so we were able to handle the estate taxes. That way they didn't kill the golden goose. That's ultimately what kills lots of farms and cattle ranches. The estate tax has destroyed more farms than the economics of running the farm. The government's power to tax is the power to destroy the people."

"Unfortunately, that's always been true."

"As you probably guessed, Granddad didn't build this house. He built the original homestead about a mile east of here. My father built this house and the modern barns out back after Granddad passed. He loved the hummock here with the oaks and Spanish moss. I'll take you around and show you the spread later. My father aggressively bought up more and more of the surrounding land as time went on, and actually doubled the original acreage. He took advantage of the failure of a number of farms on adjoining properties over time. Since the owners were desperate, he bargained for good prices and favorable terms. What he added under options and leases, the lawyers and I consolidated recently."

"Did you stumble on a gold mine to finance your growth?"

"No, actually, I found a couple of banks in New York. You see, the way cattle ranching works, it fluctuates with profitable times over an extended period of time, but on a year-to-year basis, finances may swing between big sales and long periods of drought. What I needed was good loan agreements so I could draw funds during lean periods and pay the loans back during periods of high profitability."

"A fluctuating line of credit."

"Exactly, but a secured one. I used the land as collateral." Doug paused. "I haven't discussed Sadie Sutton yet, because I wanted to fill you in about my family, first, and my background so you would understand how Sadie ties into this ranch."

"Yes, you've only told me about the history of the Circle T and your family. The big question I have on my list to ask remains, how did Sadie Sutton, who I'm sure has never had a dime to her name, become one of the largest land owners in the county, and how does she pay an annual tax obligation of thousands of dollars with no income? I picked up copies of the paid receipts for last year and I brought them with me. I did some digging into the county property records and what I found doesn't match what I see."

"I understand your confusion. Of course, you've met with her, and you can easily tell that she has no money or income, or any interest in either, so your questions are understandable."

"Precisely," said Mike. "I was shocked. When I reviewed copies of the deeds and found they didn't include all of the land, with thousands more acres more than what appears there, I was stunned. The actual tax bills showed the annual obligation of almost ten thousand dollars per year, even though the land is assessed as agricultural use. The information doesn't make any sense."

"I'm curious, what did Sadie say when you showed them to her?"

"That's just it. I haven't shown them to her. I found the records yesterday and I won't see her again until this coming Saturday, so I thought I'd ask you first," said Mike matter-of-factly.

"Well, understanding the history here will help clear this up for you. That's why I've spent the time so far telling you about our history. When I finish, I assure you it will all make sense. You see, Sadie found Granddad way back. I don't know what year it was, but I believe she was in her twenties. It was long after her male companion left her and she had been on her own for a while, after Johnston drowned."

"Yes, she told me Johnston drowned, too. But do continue. I'm anxious to hear your story about Sadie."

"Granddad met occasionally with the Indians living down in the slough to trade. They eeked out a living by hunting, fishing, and trapping, but they still needed a lot of the things the white man could provide to survive down there. Because of the clashes between the government and the Indians, the Indians had retreated into the slough to escape capture by the white man. The government wanted to move the Indians out west onto a reservation in Oklahoma and the Indians and some escaped slaves retreated into the slough to hold their ground. They used the inhospitable nature of the slough to hold off the white man with alligators, mosquitoes and the swamplands. They held their ground in the swamp until the reservations were set up. The Indians never trusted the white man's government, especially after the incidents with Osceola and Billie Bowlegs. However, through trading, they developed friendly relationships with the ranchers and other residents here in the nearby lands. Granddad was sympathetic to their cause, so he traded with them to help provide the staples they couldn't get in the slough. The Indian settlement down there thrived. They built their houses out of Sawgrass and palmetto thatching with cypress support beams. Over time, folks around here used to call their settlement Indian Bend."

"Yes, I'm familiar with some of that part of the story. The historical society has had numerous lecturers on the background and history of the Seminoles. This is where the historical society comes in today. When they found out about Indian Bend, they began to research the history of that settlement. Apparently, Sadie's parents or guardians developed a close relationship with the Indians. She told me she learned most of what she knows about plants from the Indian medicine woman."

"Well, apparently during one of Granddad's trades at Indian Bend, he met Sadie. Since she was not one of the Indians, he made the effort to get to know her. She impressed him when she showed compassion for Grandma when she became ill. Sadie made one of the Indian medicine dolls to help heal her and she spent many days with her making natural healing potions for her to drink until she recovered. Granddad was so grateful for her kindness; he offered her work on the ranch when the Indians moved to the ranches and reservations. She would have had difficulty surviving alone in the cabin since no one else was left at Indian Bend. She became an indispensable member of the family for over thirty years running the kitchen and doing housework for us. She brought us kids up, and ran the house as a nursery and preschool, not just for us but for some of the neighbor kids as well. To Granddad, she was not just part of this operation, she was a member of the family. When Granddad passed on, she continued to be an integral part of this ranch for my father and still remains so for me, too."

"I see," said Mike. "So Sadie has been part of this ranch for over three generations, more like a family member. I still don't see how she could make enough money to pay the tax bills for all the land she owns. How could she have saved enough money to have purchased that much land?"

"Well, she didn't really need any money, as much as she needed other things for survival in her cabin. She really didn't want any money either. So, we began to pay her in what evolved as a barter system that continues to work to this day. She got everything she needed right here, from us. She never had to go to town. Besides, she didn't want to go to town. We knew we had become her life and since she wasn't much of a looker, we figured she wouldn't find another husband. She didn't own a wagon or a horse, and she didn't want or need them either. She worked here and our staff did the shopping for supplies. The boys took things down to her cabin weekly as part of our operations. Since we buy most of our supplies in bulk, adding on a few things for her was never a burden. Her share was a small fraction of the total we purchased regularly."

"I can understand that. It makes sense."

"Granddad felt obligated to do more for her in exchange for all that she did for us, so he talked to our lawyers in town. They confirmed his suspicions that the cabin she lived in was built on land she didn't own. She was an out and out trespasser. He decided there was something he could do. The lawyers told him he could obtain title to a homestead of five acres with the cabin on it. Besides, he felt he owed her for giving him the sawmill. She didn't want it and wouldn't take any money for it, so he felt obligated. She turned it over to him when she moved in here. That solved a lot of problems for both of them. All she said she wanted was to be able to keep her cabin and go back there whenever she wanted."

"That was nice, but how could she pay the tax bill, even for a small piece of land with just a few acres?"

"That was easy. She worked for us. In exchange, we paid the tax bill as part of her compensation and some from the profits on the sale of the sawmill. She helped us a lot over the years. When we sold off the sawmill, another group took it over. They run the big lumberyard down by Immokalee. So, the plan was that simple. Grampa took care of the whole thing, but then somehow things got away from us. A long time ago, speculators had bought up most of the land in the slough, but repeatedly the owners would pay the taxes for a few years and then default because it was too great an expense. The lands were not profitable. No one was able to produce income from the swampland so they would eventually abandon it. Some speculators thought they would find oil or minerals but time proved that wrong. After a while, no one was interested in buying the swampland, except Granddad."

"What about the oak trees?" asked Mike. "Don't they have value as lumbar?"

"Believe it or not, even the oaks here have little value. Plenty of oak trees grew all over central Florida on high ground where the roads to haul the wood out to market were already in place. Down in the slough, there was no way to get the wood out economically. To get the trees out, they would have had to build more roads into the slough by bringing in crushed shells and coral to fill in the bogs, just like they did to build the shell road. They decided that was too costly, so the swampland simply lost value back then."

"Oh, so that's why the road to Sadie's cabin is called the shell road."

"Sure. They construct most roads here in Florida from crushed coral and shells since that's what's available. Anyway, the lawyers used to call the slough 'swamp and overflowed lands,' a term that creates a real legal problem, which I'll come back to." Doug paused and sighed. He took a deep breath and continued. "Anyway, the lawyers devised a plan. The Circle T would pay up the county back taxes for seven years. Then the lawyers would file a quiet title suit in her name under a special provision of the law, making her owner of all the land."

"That sounds like a good idea. It's something she would never have done on her own, or even know how to do."

"Exactly, but a problem emerged, no surveys existed for lands in the slough. Even the original government surveyors didn't go into the slough. No one knew the exact legal location of her cabin. As a result, they decided to deal with much more land than they planned to be sure that her cabin was included in the property conveyed to her. Then Granddad decided to include enough land to protect her privacy since the cost was nominal. In the end, they quieted title to a much larger piece of land, about six thousand acres."

"The original conveyance was six thousand acres?" Mike gasped.

"Yup. You got it. No one had kept up paying the taxes or did anything with the land in the slough, no one challenged them, and the county happily recovered back taxes. Granddad realized if the land was in friendly hands he had a buffer between developers, other ranchers and the government. Keeping the slough undeveloped fulfilled what he wanted," said Doug "The plan helped Sadie legalize her interest in the cabin and cleared the titled defects for us."

"Why didn't your Grandfather want the land for the ranch, for himself? Why didn't he just give her the five acres and keep the rest for the ranch? Why give so much away?"

"Well, originally that was the plan. He wanted to give Sadie title to a small tract she could homestead, and buy up the rest for the ranch, but it didn't work out that way. Dad and I created a bigger problem when we realized we could pick up more land in the slough cheaply. As soon as we found available tracts, we bought every parcel we could."

"Is that why the abstract company couldn't find all the original deeds? The deeds were way older than twenty years? Predating computerization?"

"Yes, in part. I probably have the abstracts here, or they're at the attorney's office. The original tract transferred to Sadie was not by deed, but by quiet title, years ago. You would have to dig way back in the old land records to find the original court order. No deed exists for that land. Later, I bought tracts of land for Circle T, or quieted the title and then deeded them over to Sadie a few years later. You can find those deeds. I'm sure you have copies of them."

"All the deeds I have, you signed. You're right. The abstract clerk told me they would have to go way back to find the title root for the main part of the land. The tax bills showed the greater portions of the land were not covered by the deeds. So what are all these deeds about? Sadie already had plenty of land. You still haven't told me everything."

"Yes, you missed the primary quiet title suit. I'm probably the only person who can explain the whole thing to you. I know you're wondering why, if she already had so much land in the beginning, why did we deed her all that additional property years later, land that was in the name of the Circle T?"

"Yes, exactly, that's my real question. Why didn't you just leave the additional land titled in the name of the ranch? Why burden someone like Sadie with all that property? She didn't understand it. What did you expect her to do with all that land?"

"I followed my father's plan to buy up as much land as possible. We purchased lands that bordered the original ranch lands and land all along the border of the slough owned by Sadie. We called her holdings the Sutton Grant. As time passed and environmental issues became political issues, concerns about the watershed arose among the ranchers and legislation was enacted to protect the watershed. I was the first one of the ranchers around here to deal with environmental issues. I modified our operations to drain all ranch effluent away from the slough. Cattle ranches are reputed to be terrible polluters, unless they handle the waste very carefully, particularly here in Southern Florida. Due to the watershed, pollution can have a tremendous impact if not controlled. The truth is, our primary interest was to keep the slough from being bought up and drained by developers or competitors, not environmental issues."

"That still doesn't explain why you gave so much land to Sadie. So, why did you give it to her? You had environmental concerns, but why use Sadie to solve that problem? The deeds show that Sadie didn't pay for the land."

"There's a straightforward answer to that, too. For many years, we had a handshake relationship with a local bank, for our financial needs. They were good people, but they were a small operation and not very sophisticated. As we expanded, we found they couldn't handle our increased needs, so I went to New York to find a larger financial institution."

"And, you found one," stated Mike, staring at Doug directly.

"Yes, but Mike, it came with a problem," Doug spoke uneasily. "When they completed the title search they found the title was not clear and turned down the loan."

"The land wasn't clear? How could that happen? Didn't your local bank do a title search?"

"The title evidence revealed that our local, small bank had ignored the problem. The New York bank found our twenty thousand acres were subject to rights of the federal government and the State of Florida so the New York bank refused the loan. They stated the value of the land, our collateral, was not sufficient to cover the loan. They found the rights of the state and the federal government impaired the ability of the land to secure the loan for their purposes. I shopped around, but the answer from everyone else came back the same. My lawyers told me the problem was the federal government had jurisdiction over all navigable water, as defined in the 1850's, and the State could claim ownership to all lands below the high water line. The old laws defined navigable waters as those on which you could float a raft. So, any water that a raft could float in was defined as legally navigable and belonged to the federal government. This fine point I knew would cover most of the slough. That was the lesser of the problems. The lawyers explained that the State could claim ownership to all lands and waterways below the high water line along the Seminole Indian River. The third problem was, over the years the river had meandered all over the slough so no one knew where the actual boundary lines were or how to determine where they rightly should be now. Without knowing where any boundary lines actually were, the entire property was shown subject to the rights of the federal and state governments, making our title to the land defective."

"So what did you do? You couldn't ignore the problem. You had to find an answer and establish firm boundaries."

"Well, that's where the lawyers earned their fees. They hired a surveyor to determine the boundary line above which no water rights could possibly exist and below which there could be claims. The lender's attorneys agreed with our setting of this line. Then I signed the deeds to all the land below that line over to Sadie. Those are the deeds you found. The remaining land, which made up our primary ranch, was free from the title defects so that they could be secured and the loan was made. So, you see, this explains the subsequent deeds and the real reason why I deeded the land to Sadie. We had to transfer the land with defective title out of the ownership of the ranch or we couldn't borrow the money. If the land had a title problem, the bank didn't want to have anything to do with it."

"That all makes sense," said Mike "but didn't you pass all the title problems over to a poor old defenseless lady who really didn't understand what was going on?" Mike was becoming visibly upset for Sadie's sake. He doubted she knew all the details of what had transpired or had any means to handle the legalities involved.

"Yes, Mike. That's true and the problems are still there. I think the state, and certainly the feds, are biding their time before they make a move for the land. We set up a small fund for legal fees for her, but we anticipate facing a real challenge in the near future. Today, they would want the land for a whole litany of reasons and the real problem is, so do a whole lot of other people. For the moment, she's okay. I don't think the government, state or federal, knows where she is or how to find her. Even the bank didn't realize she was connected with us here at the ranch. Our purpose, to secure a solid line of credit on land that is above question, succeeded. Those deeds make it look like I was crazy giving away all that land, but like I told you; I get up in the morning with both feet planted on the ground, Mike. There's a damned good reason for everything I do."

"I'm glad you told me everything. I never would have figured out what was going on by examining the deeds. Without your explanation, the purpose was not clear. But now I'm concerned about Sadie. She's not in any position to fight off all the challenges you've set up here. In covering your interests for the ranch, you've exposed Sadie to a whole raft of legal problems."

"We could never have used that land for our operations without clear title, so we used Sadie to buffer the lands from adverse interests. I sure didn't want the land in the hands of the feds with their politics and multiple agencies. They are the worst. The State, well, maybe I could live with, but the slough must be kept pristine. The land is beautiful in its natural state and we want to maintain it that way. We never expected the land to become so valuable. In a way, we've shot ourselves in the foot. Please do understand that our problems are Sadie's problems. In selfishly protecting our interests, we have created the problems we face today with a fragile old lady holding the land."

"In protecting the lands, you have set Sadie up for some rough times. That's not right. Someone needs to help her. She can't handle the legal morass you've set up here."

"She's special to us, always has been. As long as I'm here, I will continue to pay her tax bills. In my annual reports, I only show what I paid for taxes. I don't separate hers out from ours. Even my sisters don't know the details of what is going on. When it comes down to the truth, right now you and I and the lawyers are the only ones who know the whole story."

"What about Ivan? How does Ivan fit into all of this? Can he do something to help here? He's a mystery to me. Everyone talks about him but I've never seen him. He's like a phantom."

"Well, Ivan is different. Let me dispel the mystery, Mike. Unlike Sadie, we know more about him. His full name is Ivan E. Saunders. At least that's the name he's had for most of his life."

"What does that mean? Does he have any official records? A birth certificate?" Mike wrote Ivan's name in his notebook.

"According to our information, Ivan was born in Immokalee to a poor family of migrant farm workers. His parents put him up for adoption at birth. Frank Saunders owned the farm next to ours this side of Immokalee. Saunders and his wife Mabel took him in and after a time adopted him. They took Ivan in because they were older and needed a male heir to take over the farm when old man Saunders reached retirement. They didn't realize Ivan was mentally deficient until he was about nine or ten. I know it broke their hearts. When they fell on hard times and had to give up the farm, we took Ivan on as a live-in employee here at the ranch. He couldn't live on his own, so my father went to court to be appointed Ivan's legal guardian. Today, I have continued that responsibility although he's an adult. After the Saunders retired and gave up the ranch, they disappeared just like his birth parents. Word is that they moved out to Kansas. Ivan lives here, more or less, ever since. At first, we hired him and paid his income through the guardianship. Dad acquired the Saunders's property in time and most of the workers came to work for us along with Ivan."

"Sadie tells me he stays out there with her now," said Mike. "She talks about him when we have our Saturday meetings."

"Yes. They developed a close relationship over the years. Sadie developed a soft spot for him and took him under her wing. He began to spend more and more of his time with her. Frankly, he had problems from time to time getting along with the other ranch hands up here. You know how cruel young people can be. Well, he felt more comfortable with her. We dropped him as a direct employee, but he still does some menial chores that don't suit anyone else here. He walks the fence line and lets us know where repairs are needed. He chases off potential poachers and trespassers. He finds newborn calves and returns strays that get away. He's like a night watchman. So, while she stopped doing work for us a long time ago, he carries on. In return, we still take them supplies and pay her taxes in exchange. It all works out, Mike. There's no written agreement, but it works well for all of us. I could easily make a case for his value but we just take care of both of them and all of their needs. Neither one of them would blend well into regular society. So you see, I keep my feet on the ground."

"So I see," Mike echoed. "So, Ivan became the Saunders's adopted son."

"In a way yes, but it's not that simple. When I looked into it legally, Frank and Mabel never had children. They told us that Ivan was actually the son of one of their ranch hands who ran off years earlier. Neither Frank nor Mabel could remember the name of the ranch hand, so they started using Saunders as Ivan's last name when he started school. They treated him like a son and after a while everyone assumed he was."

"Did the Saunders adopt Ivan?"

"Well, no. I couldn't find any legal documents for Ivan's birth or adoption by the Saunders. No one knew his real birth name. The Saunders, as I said, added their last name to his first name and it stuck. I'm sure now both Frank and Mabel passed on. That was years ago."

"So actually, Ivan is as much of an enigma as Sadie. No past, no facts, only stories and conjecture."

"Yes, maybe that's why they feel so connected and spend time together. Like Sadie, Ivan likes the slough as much as Sadie does. Hell, if he wasn't down there with her, we would have to stop in and check up on her more often. He helps her with the chores that she can't do. If he weren't around, we'd have to move her to a nursing home, and she wouldn't last there, nor would she be happy in such a place. All she's ever known is life in the slough and at the Circle T. I'm relieved that I haven't had to face that decision because we have Ivan there to watch out for her. Anyway, now your mystery is explained. That's who Ivan is and how he fits into this whole picture."

"So when the Saunders retired and moved away, the Circle T took over their farm and Ivan came with it. Everyone here appears to be all bound up together in one big extended family, intricately tied to the ranches in one way or another."

"That's ranch life here on the Circle T, Mike, a close knit circle of people working together. Now you know the interrelationships between Sadie, Ivan and this ranch. Like you said, we're inseparable, all bound up in one package."

"Thanks for taking the time to explain it to me. That's some story. However, I'm still concerned that by being so generous and giving Sadie a home, you've left her out on a limb with a nightmare of pending legal problems with the state and federal governments."

"I'm concerned too. In fact, I'm so concerned I may need you to help me."

"Me? How could I help you with this problem? I'm not a lawyer and I don't know anything about real estate or land holdings of this magnitude."

"Everything is as I said, but let me ask you, what have you found out about Sadie?"

"Well, that's an interesting question. The real issues here, about her, we've yet to discuss. In summary, she doesn't remember much about her childhood or her parents at all. Her earliest memories are of a guy she simply calls *The Big One* and living near the Indians at Indian Bend, and then she remembers the man she calls her husband, Jake Johnston. She's vague about her youth," said Mike. "I really don't know much and there are no official records for her other than your deeds."

"If either one of us can live as long as she has and remember as much as she does, it will be a miracle. You've done your homework well, Mike. I know you have, and I might add, so did we, through our lawyers. We found the same thing, nothing in the legal records about her or where she came from. We don't even know how or when she became known as Sadie Sutton. We can't find any history for the name Sutton until after 1930 either in this county or in the parent county before Palmetto County was created. The same is true for the name Johnston, at least spelled the way she told us."

"I haven't checked the archives prior to the formation of Palmetto County, but you're right, I found nothing."

"Our best theory, Mike, is that her real parents either faced some calamity or they abandoned her. Perhaps another family brought her up, and when they, too, moved she stayed here. Maybe she stayed with one of their relatives until this man Johnston came along. All of this, of course, is pure conjecture. The theories allow us to explain the lack of any strong memory of a parent or a particular person who acted as a parent when she was young. Now, what about brothers and sisters? Did she mention any to you?"

"Nothing. She has no memory of any real family when she was young."

"This reinforces my theory. Mike, we found no parents, no brothers and sisters and, of course, no lineal descendants for Sadie Sutton."

"Lineal descendants? What do you mean?"

"Children."

"No. She refers to being married to Johnston, but that appears to be a marriage in name only. She said they didn't have any children."

"She told us the same story. There's no record of any marriage or even a Johnston registered in this county until after 1925. Oh, there are some J-o-h-a-n-n-s-o-n's, and a few other spellings, but nothing as far back as she tells us he showed up. Now in those days, Mike, my attorney's say the state recognized common law marriages. Hell, we have no evidence of anything, only her word that she ever lived with this guy. There's no record of him anywhere. According to my attorneys, Johnston could be pure fiction."

"I agree. There's nothing. I checked the records thoroughly, too."

"Look, our biggest problem now is that Sadie has no heirs and she owns all the property we transferred into her name. We need relatives now, heirs. I need help, can you help Mike?"

"What do you want me to do? I'll do what I can."

"When you leave, there's one thing about her parents you might try. She's black, so her parents might have belonged to the small, black congregation that existed around the turn of the century near here. The church catered to minority workers living in this rural part of the county. It was located on the other side of the ranch, on the way to Immokalee, but I never went there. Maybe there's a gravestone or something in the church records. The main problem is the church fell into disrepair years ago. It's physically gone. Anyway, the black population established their own church there when they were denied entry to the regular churches. The church and cemetery were on the Immokalee Road that runs into SR 744 about two miles east of here. To get there, take SR744 to Immokalee Road about four miles to the big S turn. Maybe you can find a gravestone with the Sutton name on it. I've been meaning to check it out myself, but I never found the time. If you go down there, let me know what you find. I'm curious, but, of course, that doesn't address the real problem."

"I'll check it out. That sounds like a worthwhile lead, but what do you mean by the real problem?"

"The cemetery might help with parents, but the real problem remains, no siblings and no children. No heirs, Mike. No heirs."

"Well, yes," said Mike thoughtfully, "you're right but why is that a problem now?"

"Don't you see, Mike, she's at least one hundred years old, probably older. She's not in as good a shape as she lets on. You make the call."

"You have a good point. That's why the historical society has me working with her. She's a rare treasure."

"The problem becomes that without any heirs her property will escheat into the State's general fund on her death. In which case, all we've done by putting the slough in her name is to put the property into the hands of one of our antagonists. That, Mike, is the real problem."

"Oh," said Mike as the big picture Doug had been trying to convey registered in his conscience.

"Look. A will provides an option, but the estate tax issue would still be real and create another set of problems. I don't know what she's planning to do with the land. You see, Mike, I need your help. You are the only one who can help. It's not the other way around. I need you to find what she's planning to do with the land. She's got to be under tremendous pressure from all directions. Hell, she has to be feeling it, Mike. She can't hide. Someone will find her and her holdings. The county records are public records, as you know."

"She never said a thing. Nothing. I brought the copies of the deeds I found and the tax bills here, because she said nothing to me. I did all of this on my own. I wanted to ask you because she never mentioned the land. I think she intentionally held back. I never suspected from my conversations with her that she had any kind of landholdings, let alone property holdings of this magnitude."

"I need you to find out what she's going to do with the land or just plant a seed so she knows she has to do something, soon," Doug pleaded.

"I see," said Mike "I just got the documents yesterday, and I won't see her until Saturday."

"Precisely. Look. I haven't met with her personally since Dad died. We've just helped each other. I wouldn't know where to begin. It has to be you, Mike. You have to find out what she's going to do. The title is in her name individually, free and clear. My fear is that we're going to lose her suddenly. One night, she'll die in her sleep and she'll be gone. It will be that simple. You've got to talk to her. You must have developed some rapport with her by this time. She must have some degree of trust or faith in you."

"I understand. I'll see what I can do. You feel I should approach her because I've been meeting with her on a regular basis."

"Yes." Doug hesitated as he matched Mike's gaze at the painting over the fireplace. "I see you've noticed my painting of the slough. Don't be embarrassed. That painting captivates everyone, eventually. I hung it there deliberately."

"I didn't know there were bears in the slough," said Mike, looking up at the large painting.

"Oh, yes, there still are bears in the slough, Mike, but if you look closely you'll see those aren't bears in the foreground. Those are upright creatures. Take a closer look," Doug advised.

Mike felt his pulse quicken as he stood looking up at the painting, realizing what he was seeing.

"It's an oil painting of the slough, done a number of years ago, Mike, but those aren't bears. They're Sasquatch."

"Sasquatch?" asked Mike, pretending to be unfamiliar with the subject and holding back the excitement as he spoke. His pulse continued to quicken and his heart pounded in his chest.

"Sasquatch, Mike. You've heard of them, the legendary Bigfoot. Mythical beings rumored to be living in this part of Florida, or at least, so the old stories go."

Mike's heart continued to pound heavily as he stood in front of the fireplace staring up at the painting. Excitement bubbled under his breath. He couldn't believe what he was seeing. There in the foreground of the painting an adult male DeBosi stood tall, described in paint in more detail than the wood carving at the hotel presentation. The DeBosi was looking up into a blue sky at a vulture wheeling high overhead. Two other individuals in the painting were stooped over in the shade of a large bush, grubbing with sticks around the roots. The painting presented such a stunningly realistic image that it appeared photographic in quality.

As Mike stood gaping at the painting, Doug came up and stood beside him. "When Dad was ill in the hospital up in Tampa, I brought along some of his books to read. A couple of those books left me with a lasting impression. One author researched primitive cave art. The photographic plates included pictures of European cave paintings made by our ancestors, back maybe forty thousand years ago. The pictures depicted animal drawings from early man's cave art. Oh, they had none of these beings Mike, but in nearly each cave you could see paintings of fabulous creatures, mystical beings created by the imaginings of our early ancestors. Even back then man needed magic and mystical beings. I think we still need mythical beings, even today. We need something to explain what we don't know and understand about the world, something we can't quite pin down, something mysterious. That's why I hung this painting here, over the fireplace. It's special, Mike. This is a painting of the real slough. It belongs here."

"This painting makes a real conversation piece. I don't know how it works, but it does. They look so real. I could reach out and touch them."

"That's it."

"Do you believe these beings really exist?" Mike asked, finding the opportunity to ask the question he most wanted to ask someone else.

"Well, I'll answer you this way," Doug responded hesitating. "I've told you I get up each morning with both feet firmly planted on the ground," he smiled and met Mike's gaze directly as he continued. "There's no time in my life for mythical creatures."

"Oh, yes, you did say that," said Mike, trying not to show his disappointment.

"You should have seen your eyes grow wide as saucers, Mike, as you realized what the creatures in the painting really are. Your mouth opened so wide a humming bird could have flown into it. That's what I like about the painting."

"What's that?"

"I enjoy watching how people react to it. The best reaction I've seen yet was on the faces of the bankers and their accountants here from Tampa a couple of months ago. We spent most of a day calculating the direct cost to raise a pound of beef from birth to market, a day of heavy number crunching. Slowly, one by one, they all looked up at the painting. Your reaction reminded me of theirs. Not one of them ever said a word, but they could not keep their eyes from returning to the painting. They didn't know what to say. They looked and looked, and of course, I said nothing, so they kept their thoughts to themselves. I still wonder what was going on in their minds. Hell, Mike, my motive for having this painting here was as a joke to lighten things up. But I let the mystery be. They never did ask, and I never spoke, either."

"It's so real," Mike repeated with his eyes glued to the painting. "Where did you find it?"

"Some unknown benefactor commissioned the painting by Tom Brian in 1933. His signature and the year are noted there in the lower right hand corner. Brian lived here in southern Florida specializing in local landscapes back in the late 1920's and '30's. Actually, he ran the hardware store down in Immokalee. When the depression struck, he painted to supplement his income. Well, a farmer who, for reasons unknown, had him do this painting. When the farmer died, the estate auctioned everything off. Dad picked this painting up as a novelty. No one else wanted it. Hell, the subject was really taboo in those days. Anyway, he got it for a song. Actually, I think they threw it in the deal."

"The deal?"

"The Saunders's acquisition. When Dad bought the land, he bought most of the personal property as well. He found this painting in the house before they leveled all the buildings. That whole spread is now part of the eastern end of our property."

"Well, it's captivating," said Mike.

"That it is," said Doug. "That it is."

Chapter Sixteen

Encounter At Lake Ibis

For several moments they stood in silence, looking up at the painting above the fireplace.

"C'mon, Mike. There's something special I want to show you." Doug picked up a wood cane laying on the large coffee table. He led Mike out the front door of the house and around the right side where a canopied golf cart was parked in the shade of a large live oak. Mike noticed that Doug walked with a limp, especially when he walked any distance quickly.

Doug followed Mike's gaze. "I have a bum leg, Mike. Got it from a fall. A rattlesnake startled my horse about six months ago. The snake caught us both by surprise, so I was thrown off my horse. There's a lot of them around here especially in the tall grasses. Anyway, the doctors say I'll be as good as new with a series of operations," Doug explained.

"Sounds like something you should do."

"I'm hesitant because I'll be out of commission for four months or more. Hell, I don't want to create an opportunity for my sisters to come down here and try to run this place or play nursemaid. I put it off for now. I'll get by as I am for a while 'til I can break free."

A faded green canvas canopy covered the top of the electric golf cart. The dim color matched the fiberglass body. "I use this to run around the ranch since my accident. We kept it after Dad gave it up and it's come in handy now and then. It's seen many better days but serves us fine. Climb in," said Doug. "I'll take you for a little ride down to Lake Ibis."

"Lake Ibis? Where's that?"

"That's our name for the slough up at this end when we have a wet year. The excess water forms a large shallow lake in the middle of the slough."

Mike slid into the cart on the passenger side. Within a few moments, they passed behind the house and barns on a narrow gravel trail that continued on through the live oak trees. Shortly, they approached a fence similar to the perimeter fence that ran along the highway. At right angles to the trail, the fence disappeared deep into the woods in both directions. A gate wide enough for the cart to pass through connected the fence crossing the path and, when opened, would allow them to pass through to the path down to the slough. Doug stopped the cart and opened the gate. After driving through the woody hummock for twenty minutes, Doug stopped the cart and removed the key.

"Okay, Mike, now we have to walk. We can't continue in the cart, the path is too rough." Mike swung his legs out of his side of the cart and joined Doug heading deep into the slough. They briskly followed along the path as it wound its way through the oak trees and palmettos. The surface of the path appeared similar to the shell road on the way to Sadie's cabin. The moss-covered oaks began to diminish, yielding to sable palms as the two men followed the path.

"In case you didn't figure it out, as soon as we passed through that gate we became trespassers."

"Trespassers? Why, where are we?"

"That fence marks the property line separating the ranch from the 'Sutton Grant.' You know, Sadie's property that you found in the deeds. See the ridgeline? That's where the ranch begins on the upland. The vegetation there consists mostly of palmetto scrub and live oaks. When the predominant vegetation changed to palms and the land below became boggy and floods, we entered the slough, Sadie's property. The federal government retains the rights to claim the swamp area, for the land above the water line. In the slough, whatever lies below the ordinary water line of the river, the state can claim title. By deeding off the lands below the ridgeline, we cleared our title. Like I told you back at the house, by giving land away, we improved the value of the land we kept."

"So you deeded Sadie everything below the ridgeline."

"Right. The weather dictates how our lives run out here. We adjust to times of drought when it takes longer to bring livestock to market weight," explained Doug. "Sometimes I lose an entire season. Some years are so dry lightening ignites grassland fires, and nature forces us to wait for rain to bring new grass for the cattle. If I bring in food stock for the cattle from outside, our costs jump dramatically."

"There's a lot more to running a ranch than I realized," said Mike.

"This ranching business fluctuates according to how nature plays her cards. We do well over any five-year period, but things fluctuate up and down in the short term. I'm continually borrowing then paying off, then borrowing again on a regular basis. Anyway we're now traveling though Sadie's property," Doug stated as they passed through the palm forest.

Mike could see the edge of the water ahead where the lake began. Blue sky and bright sunlight replaced the shadows of the trees where the sabal palms dotted the landscape. The natural beauty of the land and its lush vegetation spread out before them, a breathtaking vista in the sunlight as it filtered through the palm trees and Spanish moss hanging from the live oaks.

"That's Lake Ibis coming up ahead. You can see the water," said Doug. "We used to keep a dock with boats for fishing when this part of the slough belonged to us, but the attorneys told us to abandon it since the property belongs to Sadie. They advised us to remove any easements to gain access because it might harm our position if there were any challenges from the feds or the state. So, we hedge a little and keep this trail up so we can visit now and then. I just don't tell the lawyers. Hell, they'd tell us to tear it up, as well. They're protecting us from any conflict of interest."

When they reached the end of the trail, Mike could see that Lake Ibis expanded beyond what he had envisioned. The green color of the water covered an area Mike guessed to extend over a mile across. The coral and shells embedded in the path ended at the edge of the palms, only a few feet from the edge of the water. Except where the vegetation had been cleared for the dock, a thick growth of tall reeds bordered the edge of the lake. The abandoned dock had fallen into disrepair. Several boards from the section at the end of the path where the open water to the dock began were missing. The remaining support posts and planks lay half buried in the mud, rotting away in the muck. A large bull alligator lay motionless covering parts of a cluster of the boards, basking in the afternoon sun. The alligator, stretched out like a sleeping guard dog, blocked the passage to what little remained of the unserviceable dock.

Doug stopped at the edge of the path where it met the water. Small wavelets lapped gently only few feet away in response to an easterly breeze. The tall blades of Sawgrass gracefully danced in synchrony with the wavelets. Little water bugs skittered across the surface of the water. Mike could distinguish the familiar smell of warm fresh water mixed with the putrid scent of rotting vegetation characteristic of the slough. Mike recognized the smell as the same as when he visited Sadie's cabin. A flock of white ibis flew by them beyond the dock, landing in their nesting grounds hidden among the reeds. They settled down, disappearing into the tall grass about a hundred yards farther up stream. The occasional croak of the resident bullfrogs, the rhymic rustling of the blades of grass and lapping wavelets were the only sounds interrupting the quiet beauty of Lake Ibis.

"I thought you'd like the view here. In my opinion, this area is more beautiful than behind Sadie's cabin. This is my most favorite place in the world."

"This is magnificent. Nothing back in Delaware where I grew up compares with this."

"During the wet season and up through the summer months, Lake Ibis makes an impressive body of water. However, the lake is deceiving. Although it appears to be like other lakes, this one is shallow. You'd be hard pressed to find any water here over four feet deep, even out in the middle. In the dry season, the whole lake can disappear, becoming a bog. All you can see then is a few scattered puddles, a muddy marsh, and a small stream trickling through it, way over on the other side. When it's that dry, we get the lightning fires, causing the dried grass to burn. Mother Nature constantly rearranges her land here. We've experienced years when most of the palms burned up, and then other times, the floods prevent access, the whole area is flooded."

"This lake looks permanent. It's so lush. I can't imagine it any other way."

"Now, want to see something really special?"

"You mean there's more?"

"You bet. Look, over there. Don't move, be real still," he spoke softly. Mike followed the direction where Doug was pointing into the thick grassy shadows. Mike's heart skipped a beat and his pulse quickened. He could barely identify two large animals in the thick grass several yards away. Both remained half hidden as the general outline of their hairy brown bodies moved in the grass. They looked like the creatures in the painting, crouched down in the water behind the tall reeds. Had Doug brought him here to see them for real? Was this his special surprise? As they watched in silence, he heard occasional short grunts. The creatures were oblivious to the fact they were being watched. Mike was transfixed. The color of their fur nearly matched the color in the painting and on the DeBosi carving at the hotel presentation. As he watched, the animals appeared to be bent over on hands and knees grubbing in the mud. To Mike, they appeared to be groping for snails, turtles or small fish. Their full figures were obscured in the shelter of the tall grass.

"Remember that fence we passed?" Doug asked in a soft whisper. "That gate may look impressive, but it's primarily show for any inspectors. The fence only runs a couple of hundred yards in each direction. Hell, fences are expensive to install and maintain." He nodded towards the creatures still occupied in the tall reeds. "Besides, it wouldn't hold them anyway."

Mike was speechless. Doug appeared matter-of-fact about the creatures, like he had seen them many times before. "Now, I'll tell you a real secret. When the sun goes down and it gets dark, those two frequently come up behind the barn in back of the main house looking for a hand out," said Doug, smiling towards Mike.

Mike couldn't believe what he was seeing or hearing. He couldn't speak even if he had to. They remained standing quietly watching for some time until it was obvious one of the creatures had seen them and began moving directly toward them. Mike felt his pulse quicken again.

Doug fumbled with a paper bag he had brought with him from the cart. As the closest creature broke through the tall grass, Mike could see that it was not what he had imagined. A young male buffalo strode confidently towards them. While the animal was far from what he had imagined a moment before, the vision in front of him was unexpected. The young bison moved directly out of the water towards Doug.

Doug withdrew a handful of sugar cubes from the bag and stretched out his arm toward the animal with his palm full of sweet morsels. The buffalo gingerly nibbled them out of his open palm. From the bold behavior of the animal, Mike realized that this event had occurred many times before. Doug had trained the animals to welcome his gift of sweet morsels as he offered them in his open hand.

Mike tempered his disappointment by the fact he had never seen a live buffalo so close, let alone meet a buffalo in a Florida swamp. His only exposure to buffalo was limited to the movie screen where they appeared in great herds chased by either cowboys or Indians on the open plains.

"There's nothing to be afraid of, Mike. Buffalo are merely another type of cattle. A few imaginative people created those old tales of ferocious beasts. Picture some homesteader out in the old west, writing home about his exploits. Is he going to tell his friends and relatives back in Philadelphia that he shot a cow? That's not romantic. Oh, you look a little stunned, Mike. I was too when we first brought buffalo here. The young ones head down here into the slough to eat the new grass shoots and to stay cool by the water. The older ones have more trouble in the soft mud, so they stay up on the hummock. These two were both born right here on the Circle T. Hell, I may be experimenting, but I was not the first to bring bison to Florida. Now ranchers boast a few thousand head in Florida. The real pioneers beat us. I suppose my old man would roll over in his grave, but I think buffalo may be our future."

"You're kidding," said Mike, stunned. "I never heard of buffalo in Florida. This is a new one for me."

"Yeah, I think we're going to find that buffalo cost less to bring to market than cattle, less maintenance. North America is their natural grazing range. This subtropical climate doesn't bother them either. Although there are many advantages to raising buffalo over cattle, the major drawback is our culture. Most people limit their diet to pork, chicken and beef and maybe an occasional fish. They're not willing to try new things to eat. The market for buffalo as a food source just hasn't developed, but when it does, I want to be in it. All the new water control and pollution regulations could help do it. Environmental regulations could make cattle ranching so expensive that buffalo could replace beef in the American marketplace in our lifetimes. We've got fifteen buffalo at the Circle T right now. We're learning how best to raise them. A year ago, I came down to the edge of the lake before I knew these two had developed their affection for the slough. They were grazing like we found them today. I wasn't really expecting anything but the usual birds and frogs. When I first saw the blotches of brown fur out in the grass, well, I'll tell you, for a minute it damned well scared me half to death. Hell, I didn't know what I was looking at," he said, smiling over at Mike.

"I know what you must have felt."

"Now don't you go telling anyone I said that. You know I live by keeping both my boots on solid ground." Doug was grinning.

"I was just thinking about your painting,"

"Ha," scoffed Doug. "Maybe my ranch hands get their stories from that old painting. It's just a conversation piece, Mike. I'm not trying to perpetuate any myths or start anything else. Anyway, I've been working on creating a market for buffalo. I've got four places up in Tampa offering buffalo burgers along with regular hamburgers on their menu. One western style restaurant north of Tampa offers buffalo steak on their menu. In the meantime, I let these two come down here to eat the young grass shoots. They're safe here. They're too big for that bull alligator to attack them for his meals," he said, pointing to the big bull alligator still basking in the sun near the remnants of the dock. "If I thought that guy was dangerous, I'd have moved these two back up to the ranch and made sure they couldn't get back down here."

"Did you ever see one of those creatures in your painting?" asked Mike, knowing he was treading into dangerous territory by pressing the issue.

"Oh, those creatures in the painting? A Sasquatch or Bigfoot or whatever they call them these days? Me? Personally? No. I've never had the pleasure, but hell, most of my help claims to have seen one or two. This whole part of the state is full of reported sightings. Me, I keep an open mind. I mean, what the hell? Who knows what other creatures live in this world? All I know is, if we don't stop having more and more babies, there'll be nothing *but* humans on this earth. In a few years this whole county will be one never-ending subdivision. It's a shame because a place like this should be preserved for its natural beauty."

Doug reached into the bag and produced a few more sugar cubes. The second buffalo stopped grazing and headed out of the water towards them.

"That's enough for you, feller," said Doug, addressing the first buffalo. "You leave some sugar for Sadie."

"Sadie?"

"Oh, I call this one Ted and the female, Sadie. Don't you dare tell Sadie I've named a buffalo after her. To me, Sadie and the buffalo are both creatures of the swamp. Anyway, in this part of Florida, you'll hear lots of stories and sightings of swamp creatures. I don't give them much heed myself. I tell my staff I don't care what they see or tell anyone, I just don't want them to mention the ranch. What they see off the property is not any of my business. The last thing I want is some crazy character out here shooting a buffalo, because he thought it was something he saw in a movie or dreamed up in his mind. We have enough trouble with trespassers and young kids breaking in here for fun."

Mike kept his thoughts about Sadie to himself.

"Here," said Doug, handing the bag of sugar cubes to Mike. "Go ahead, give her a couple of cubes. She's too shy to come by us. Besides, Ted blocks her out because he wants all the sugar for himself."

Mike took the bag of sugar cubes from Doug and cautiously approached the smaller buffalo, standing a few feet away. She approached cautiously when he held out his hand with the sugar cubes visible.

"It's a shame."

"What is?" asked Mike, as the young buffalo greedily nibbled the sugar cubes out of his hand, drooling heavily. When the cubes were gone, Mike pulled his handkerchief out of his pant's pocket and wiped the grassy smelling saliva off of his hands.

"I'd like to stay down here all day but we both have work to do."

"Well, I'm out of sugar cubes," said Mike. "I'm ready to go if you are."

"Let's go then. I've babbled on long enough. Time to get you back to your car. I've taken up your whole morning. I wanted you to see the lake and the beauty of the slough here. This area is different from what you've seen by Sadie. The view is nicer here, upstream. This place is special to me. It's one of my favorite escape destinations. With our population expanding out of control, few natural ecosystems are left anymore with abundant wildlife. The slough should be preserved for future generations."

"Thanks for showing me Lake Ibis. I agree this place is special."

"No problem. I believe in treating everyone like they're family. You never know when you're going to need a friend. I think that's why we take care of Sadie the way we do. She's one of us, Mike."

"Yes, well, you've done a lot for her," said Mike as they turned back towards the cart.

"It's time to get out of here. We've been lucky so far, but I'm worried about them." Doug's gaze was focused off in the distance.

"The buffalo?"

"No. Mosquitoes," said Doug, as they started back up the path.

Chapter Seventeen

The Cemetery

Doug Williams is an enigma, Mike protested as he drove down the driveway of the Circle T Ranch. Mike could not stop mulling over his meeting with Doug Williams as he drove back toward town. Doug had repeatedly told him how he got up each day with both feet on the ground, meaning he only dealt with reality. Doug had thoroughly explained how and why Sadie owned the wetlands in the slough. Everything Doug did had a purpose and everything made sense. Although Doug appeared to be the person he said he claimed to be, Mike sensed that something was amiss. Mike focused on the inconsistency between the contrasting reality of the painting and Doug's continued reference to the creatures in the painting as "mythical" figures. Doug professed to be a non-believer, yet that painting hung prominently over his fireplace. Mike could not dismiss the grin on Doug's face when he spoke about the painting. During the tour of the slough and Lake Ibis, Doug had admitted that the first time he had seen the buffalo there he had imagined they might be something else.

Doug admitted that all of his staff claimed to have had observations or encounters, yet he expressly instructed them *not* to mention the ranch in relation to their sightings. The strongest memory for Mike was the way Doug spoke, the way he grinned when he talked about the painting, as if it were all a joke. Mike wondered if Doug was really a believer with the painting as a sign to other believers that he was one of them. Of course, Doug would not admit to his beliefs due to his stature in the community. That would make sense if he were using the painting to express his beliefs. For Mike, the William's family represented the conservative elite of the southern Florida cattle ranchers. Why would Doug flaunt such an unorthodox painting of a taboo subject at the type of visitors he entertained? Mike did not know how to react to Doug Williams. Perhaps Doug was implying more than he was saying when he claimed to keep both feet on the ground. Perhaps he knew from personal experience that the DeBosi was real and was protecting Sadie from curiosity seekers and the insensitivity of the media and paparazzi. Mike sensed that Doug knew more about Sadie and Ivan than he was willing to discuss. Mike had no answers, only more questions now that he had met with Doug Williams. His interest piqued at Doug's casual reference to the old church and cemetery down the Immokalee Road. Even though the suggestion seemed to be a casual remark, the facts about the church and cemetery gnawed at his curiosity and still unsated thirst for facts about Sadie's heritage.

If the old church and cemetery held some as yet unrevealed secret, he had to check them out. So, when he turned onto SR 744, he drove east, away from Brandon. He decided to follow Doug's suggestion to find the old church and cemetery. If he could find some clue about Sadie's parents, who they were and where they were from, then it was worth the effort of looking into what may be there. At least one side of her family had to be human and this could be traced.

The Immokalee Road intersected SR 744 and ran south towards its namesake, the small town of Immokalee. Mike found the road roughly two miles from the ranch, exactly where Doug said it would be. He followed the road for a little under four miles to where it started to make a sharp turn. As Doug had surmised, the church was no longer there. Empty grasslands filled the open area across each side of the road. The east side of the berm was wide, wide enough for the remains of an abandoned parking lot. Mike pulled off the road onto this open area and parked his car. The presence of black gravel visible between the scattered weeds, palmettos and grasses confirmed his theory that the area had once been a parking lot.

This, he thought, had to be the right place, even if the church was gone. On both sides of the road, the fields had recently been plowed. On the side where he pulled over, the farmer had clearly avoided the area bordering the edge of the parking lot over to the field along the boundary road. The unplowed area consisted of two to three acres overgrown with weeds and shrubs. Once past the unplowed tract, the farmer had resumed plowing his original line, avoiding the overgrown area intentionally. Mike guessed the unplowed area was likely to be where the foundation of the church remained and the farmer knew to avoid the hidden stones buried there.

Mike stepped out of his air-conditioned car into the oppressive heat. The midday sun filled the zenith above in a cloudless sky. The humid air hung so heavy Mike found it difficult to breathe once he left his car. There wasn't even a hint of a breeze. A thick cloud of dragonflies filled the air as he approached the dense weeds and buzzed over his head as he entered the center of the unplowed area. The remains of the foundation stones lay scattered randomly in the grass. Occasional indentations in the earth formed stagnant puddles of water and the remains of rotting support timbers crisscrossed over the surface of the puddles. The size and location of the foundation stones suggested to Mike he had found where the small church once stood.

As he continued to survey the area, he found the crumbled remains of a stonewall that had surrounded the front of the church and parking area. The rubble continued to run toward the back of the tract where another pile of rotting timbers and stones lay, solidifying his convictions that he had found the remains of the church foundation. As he walked through the weeds, he could see the distinct depressions of many graves, identifying the location of the cemetery. The remains of the cemetery was encircled by the crumbled remains of another stonewall. The stone rubble surrounding the area ran from the road to the back of the tract, then northerly for about fifty yards before turning back to the road. A few of the graves had collapsed and left concave depressions in the distinct regular shapes of sagging graves. Clearly, the cemetery and church had been abandoned many years ago. Judging from the condition of the cemetery and lack of marble or granite markers, Mike presumed the original graves had been marked with boards or wooden crosses long lost to the intense subtropical elements.

In the tall grass in front of him, he caught the shimmer of a long, black snake as it slithered across the gravel and disappeared into a pile of crumbling rocks. He counted fifty-seven identifiable gravesites when he saw the snake and decided that there was little here to help him. With the lack of legible grave markers, he would not be able to identify anyone who had been buried there. He had reached another dead end. Remembering Doug's warnings, "Mid-Florida is rattlesnake territory," Mike knew it was time to leave. Wandering here in the tall grass was dangerous. He returned to the open parking area and the safety of his car.

Mike admitted to himself this excursion had ended up being a wild goose chase. Why had Doug sent me here? He wondered as he drove back past the ranch. Doug had been friendly enough and appeared to be forthright. Everything he had said about the cemetery had been correct, except that the grave markers had weathered away. Had the suggestion been a random thought or had Doug been trying to tell him something? If so, what was Doug trying to tell him? Doug had explained the deeds and the tax bills and all the legalities. Everything checked out, nothing seemed to be out of place. The ring of truth ran through all of what Doug had told him. Still, Mike felt something did not seem right. He sensed that Doug had not told him everything.

Mike's thoughts remained fixed on analyzing his encounter with Doug Williams. The painting bothered him the most. The subject of that painting seemed strange for Doug to select as a prominent decoration in the Circle T Ranch living room. Doug openly flaunted his opinion on the subject, in spite of his verbal denial. Perhaps Doug had some knowledge that the creatures were actually real, creatures that few people, at least publicly, would admit to having seen. The topic was taboo. So why would he hang that picture as the centerpiece in his living room? Was Doug making a non-verbal statement that the creatures were real? Doug admitted the subject was controversial and he used the painting merely as a conversation piece. The painting would be more appropriate in Harry's house, but then, even Harry was not a believer. No, Mike thought, the painting was not appropriate there either. Finally he decided, the painting would have been more appropriate on the stage during the presentation at the hotel. That would have been the proper place for it. The painting did not belong where it was, in the living room of the Circle T Ranch.

As he thought more about the morning's meeting and Doug's behavior, even the trip to Lake Ibis had been strained. Why had Doug taken him into the slough to see two young buffalo? Was Doug implying that the creatures were real? Mike was not sure why Doug had insisted on making the excursion to Lake Ibis. The more he thought about it, the more he became convinced that Doug was not telling him everything. Something important was missing and Doug was holding back information. Doug, he thought, was playing a game and had left out an important piece to the puzzle. Mike concluded that Doug knew a lot more about Sadie than he was willing to tell.

As he drove back under the interstate overpass, he realized he had not been alert. Doug, he thought, had in fact given him a lead and it was not the cemetery. Mike had discovered a lot of information over last few days, but was not applying it. He had simply not put all of the pieces together. He pulled into the parking lot for the Mango Inn. Entering the lobby where the public phones were located, he found the number he wanted and dialed it as quickly as he could.

"Hello, Palmetto County Tax Office, Miss Terhune speaking."

"Miss Terhune, this is Mike Byrne. Remember me? I needed copies of the tax bills for properties owned by Sadie Sutton."

"Oh, yes, Mr. Byrne. I remember you. I hope you found what you were looking for."

"Yes, I did. Thank you for helping."

"Is there something else I can help you with today?"

"Yes, I do need a favor. Do you have the assessor's maps handy on the back tables?"

"Yes, of course. They're right where I left them the other day."

"Can you check another property for me? I don't have the folio number or property description, but I can tell you exactly where it's located on the map. If you take SR 744 out about seventeen miles to the Immokalee Road, then go south about four miles to what may be a section corner, you'll find a small church parcel taxed differently than the surrounding land. The road turns there, so the intersection is unusual. I think the church tract runs along the section line. At least, that's my guess from what you told me the other day."

"Well, it's all rural land out there. I'll find it. I bet it's a correction corner. I'm not supposed to do this over the phone. You're supposed to come in and place an order and pay up before I do anything."

"Wait, I'm a county employee, does that make a difference?"

"Of course, you should have told me that the other day. All I need is your employee number, and department. We can bill your department directly."

"I'll come in and pay in cash tomorrow noon, on my lunch hour. My number is PC 45329, and I'm in General Administration Department."

"Good. I can work with that. I didn't know you were a county employee. That makes a big difference."

"The other day was personal. Do you think you can find the tract?"

"Sure, I can find anything on the overlay map. I know the tract you're talking about." She stopped speaking suddenly, then resumed, "Hold on. Here it is. I have the section. Let me find it in the book." Then she was gone for a few moments. "Alright, I have the folio number for you."

"Can you run it and find the owner of record?"

"Hold on," she paused and left the phone off the hook. When she came back, she continued, "It's registered to the Emanuel Baptist Church. Do you need the folio number?"

"No, what address do you have in the records for the church?"

"A rural route number in town."

"That won't help. Can you see if there's another property and address listed under the same name?"

"Hold on," she said. There was another pause before she returned. "Here it is. The same name appears on another parcel. The address has the same route number, but under the address, 121 Station Street. That's in town, too."

"Thank you. You're an angel. I'll find what I need from there. I have a county map in my car. The street's on the map, I'll find it. Hold those bills and the printouts for me, I'll pick them up tomorrow noon time."

"I'll save them for you. If you don't come in tomorrow, I'll bill your office by the end of the day. By the way, there's another thing you should know."

"What is that?"

"These are church parcels. We send out tax bills, but they don't show anything due as long as they're active churches."

"The one out on Immokalee Road obviously hasn't been used for years. The church building is gone and the cemetery was abandoned eons ago."

"You're forgetting one thing."

"What's that?"

"The dead are still buried there, aren't they?"

"Yes," said Mike. "I'm sure they are."

"Then it's still considered active church property," she said. "A church owned cemetery is considered an active church even when the church isn't there anymore. No taxes, Mr. Byrne. You know, separation of church and state."

"Oh, you're right. I forgot. I'll be at your office at noon tomorrow and I'll pay the bill then."

Mike was feeling better now. He had applied what he had learned, something that he knew, something that even Doug would be familiar with. There was a new lead, and Mike felt this was where Doug wanted him to go. Beaming with self-confidence, he checked his map for the street address Miss Terhune had given him. He was familiar with the area, but it was not a part of town he would frequent. The area was a poor, black section on the edge of town. An hour after he left the cemetery, he found the neighborhood. A liquor store was located just down the street from the small church at the address she had given him. Across the street from the church, he noticed two small shanty houses set back under the live oaks. All of the buildings on the street were snuggled under enormous old live oaks with heavy burdens of Spanish moss hanging from the expansive limbs. Once he parked in front of the church, he noticed a group of men were gathered in an unimproved lot playing cards, gossiping, and drinking out of bottles wrapped in brown paper bags. Mike eyed them carefully. The half dozen men seemed not to notice his presence and continued their activities, ignoring him. As he stepped onto the sidewalk, he saw an older man dressed in well-worn coveralls and a tattered white tee shirt, sitting on the front steps of the church. His curly white hair, bordering a central balding area, contrasted with his dark skin. As Mike drew near, the old man peered up at him over the top of the newspaper he was reading.

"Afternoon," said the elderly black man. "You seem to be a long way from home." Mike detected a strong southern accent and became uncomfortable with the awareness that he was a stranger here.

"I'm looking for someone; hopefully the secretary or pastor for the church," said Mike glancing behind the man toward the church.

"You're in the right place," said the black man, "but there's no secretary around. You'll have to do with me. I know most of what's happening around here, which I might add isn't much these days."

"Well then, you'll do. Actually I'm trying to trace some people who may have been buried out in the cemetery on Immokalee Road, the abandoned cemetery owned by this church."

"You do want to go back some. We haven't been out there in a long time."

"That property is registered with the county in the name of this church. Do you know anything about it back when it was active? The buildings are gone but the cemetery is still there."

"It's a shame we couldn't support that church. We're a poor community here as you can see. We barely have enough funds to keep this church open and the cemetery clean. I do the work but I don't get paid all the time, like I should. I keep up the grounds as best I can," said the old man. He extended his right hand towards Mike, "My name is Jeremiah Hooten."

"Glad to meet you, Jeremiah. I'm Mike Byrne. I'm trying to find relatives of people who may be buried out there. Do you know if there are any records or lists of the people buried in that cemetery? There aren't any markers out there. They're all gone."

"Nope. No one's maintained that place in a long time, Mr. Byrne. It's a shame, but it's a long way out there and there's no funds, but you got the right person. No one else around here but me is old enough to remember much about that church. Yes, suh, I'm old enough to remember."

"Do you remember the names of any of the people buried there?"

"Oh, the dead? You're interested in the dead? No. I don't have that kind of memory, but I do know what happened to the records. There used to be a book. We called it 'the book of the dead.' The problem was it was all in pen and ink on old paper. The minister listed all those buried in the cemetery out there when he finished with a funeral."

"Do you still have it?"

"Well, that book is gone now. See, they built this church here after the hurricane in 1926 demolished the original church here and out there. We couldn't fix up both churches. Not enough money. Since this one here had a larger attendance, they rebuilt this one. As I recall, the tail end of that hurricane, one that crossed The Keys and came up the Gulf was what did it. The storm was big and slow and skittered along the coast. As a result, we got a wallop. That storm knocked down everything. Most buildings back then weren't built like they are now, so we rebuilt what we could. The rain ruined the book. When it dried out there was nothing left 'cause the ink ran, so they burned it with the rest of the debris from the storm."

"Oh," said Mike, unable to hide his disappointment. "Can I run a couple of names by you? Would you remember anyone?"

"You kin try. I don't think I can remember much from back that far. I was a young 'un then. You can check the cemetery here, too. We keep a 'book of the dead' for this cemetery here. This one's in good shape."

"Well," Mike hesitated, "the names I'm looking for are Sutton and Johnston. That's all I have, no first names, only last names."

"Can't say as I remember those names. And, I kin tell you for sure there's none of those folks buried here either. Not in this church's cemetery."

Mike felt his hopes sag. Had Doug intentionally run him on a wild goose chase, playing an empty shell game? Or, maybe Mike was mistaken and Doug had only mentioned the cemetery in passing.

"Has anyone else ever come here asking silly questions like me?"

"Naw, not that I remember. White folks don't come here much. Say you from the lottery commission or anything like that?"

"I'm afraid not," said Mike, smiling. "No such luck."

Mike took a few bills out of his wallet and handed them to Jeremiah. "Here's something for your trouble."

"No thanks, the history lesson's free, so's my time."

"Then consider it a donation to the church welfare fund, and the cemetery."

"Now that's something we can use," said Jeremiah, accepting the bills. "You come back here on Sunday anytime afore noon. This place may be dead now, but the old ladies here, they can make this place jump on Sunday. You'd be surprised how they get the spirit rolling."

"Thanks for the invitation. I'll come by here sometime."

Mike drove away dejected. He thought he had a serious lead from Doug. Instead, he hit another dead end. Was Doug's comment an off-the-cuff random thought? Or did Doug have some hidden agenda in sending him out to the abandoned church and cemetery? If so, he had no idea what it was.

Chapter Eighteen

Vultures

Saturday morning marked his third trip to Sadie's cabin. Because she said she was not feeling well, Sandy called and cancelled meeting him for both breakfast and their follow up luncheon. Mike was on his own. This meeting with Sadie began the same as the first two. Sadie was expecting him, inviting him in before he knocked on the screen door. His table and chair were sitting in the same place as before, the small table was set with a glass of tea on a coaster in the middle of a clean, white linen tablecloth.

As before, Sadie relaxed down in her chair and began rocking gently back and forth in a steady rhythm. Today, Sadie was wearing a dark blue, floral print dress. For the first time, her lap blanket was missing and he could see the crisscrossing laces of her old-fashioned boots below the hem of her dress. Once again, her glowing red eyes held his attention, triggering the rush of his original beliefs about her heritage.

"Did you see 'em?" she asked, starting the conversation as he settled down in his chair.

"See them? Who?" he asked unsure of what she was talking about.

"Yep. They were still out there when you came in," she said, looking out toward the porch opening, into the sky above. "I saw them when I opened the screen door for you."

"They were? I didn't see anyone."

"The vultures, big, black turkey vultures, circling overhead."

"Oh, I didn't see them, but I wasn't looking up either."

"They were up there, way up there, circling overhead. They're easy to see. If you're going to learn the ways of the slough, then you've gotta watch what's going on around you, or you'll never learn the ways of the slough."

"I never was interested in birds, let alone vultures, but I'll look for them now that I know."

"When you leave today, step out onto the shell road and look up. You'll see 'em from there, high up, circling right over this cabin, Mike. You'll see 'em. Mark my words. They're there. What do you know 'bout vultures, Mike?"

"Not much. I've only seen the human ones, hanging around the courthouse. Everyone jokes about them, comparing them to the real vultures sitting on the peak of the courthouse roof."

"Turkey vultures, the ones up there are more common than black ones. Turkey vultures are different from the black vulture. Black ones don't have that silver stripe on the bottom of their wings when they're in flight. You can tell the turkey vultures by their red beaks and feet. Plus they have special powers, a kind of intuition. They just know. There are those who say vultures only eat dead flesh, so those folks think they're safe, but they just don't know. Like so many other creatures in nature, vultures live off dead meat. The difference is vultures have to be there first to survive. When they're around, they're around for a reason and they're real quiet. Watch out for the turkey vulture. The black ones are okay. They're the noisy ones so you'll hear 'em. It's the quiet ones you gotta worry about."

"I've heard they have exceptional eyesight. What are these special powers you say they have? I've never heard anything about that. Sounds like superstition to me."

"Others say it's their sense of smell, but I say it's their special powers. They sense death coming, Mike, before it happens, like a sixth sense.

That's when they start to circle. That's how they're first on the scene; they sense it before it happens."

"I never heard that before."

"That's one of the secrets of the slough. That's why it's important to look up. When you leave here, you'll see 'em. They're a sign for me, Mike. A warning."

"What? What are you talking about…a sign for you?"

"There's so much you don't know about the slough," she continued. "Things are not always what they seem to be. You have to look real careful to see what's really going on."

"Well, you've lived here all your life. I'm not surprised you know so much about the slough. I'm learning. You're my teacher, you have a better sense of the ways here." Mike put the folder with the tax bills and deeds down on the table and took a sip from the glass of tea.

"Yes, and I think you learned something this week. I see it in your eyes. Is that some work you brought with you today?" Sadie's eyes were directed towards the folders Mike had placed on the table beside his glass of tea.

"Well, yes. I went to the county tax office Monday. I thought perhaps, just perhaps, under some of the old homestead laws you might own this cabin. I wasn't sure. I checked the official records for birth certificates and marriage licenses in the early part of the century. I wanted to find dates for your birth and marriage."

"And what did you find there?" she asked.

"Nothing. The county records don't go back that far. Then I checked the current tax records. That's where I got my first shock. The clerk printed out this long sheet of folios. I brought copies with me. At first, I thought there was some mistake. There are thousands of acres assessed in your name under a whole group of different folio numbers, and the taxes for all of them are paid up to date."

"Yes, that's true. You're very smart. I knew you were smart enough to find that out. That's what I told Sandy. What else did you find?"

"Well, then I went down the street to the abstract company. They gave me deeds to the last eight property conveyances in your name. Yesterday I met with Doug Williams at the Circle T and I showed him what I found. He told me the story of why all the land is in your name."

"Seems like I can't keep any secrets from you, Mike"

"You never told me you owned all this land. I had no idea. I thought you had nothing, only this cabin and a small plot around it. I told the tax office they had the wrong person. I thought there had to be someone else with the same name. Of course, they showed me that the tax bills are all sent to you in care of the Circle T Ranch. Doug Williams filled me in on the rest."

"So you've caught up to me. Yup, I see I can't keep any secrets from you. You'll find me out. I didn't tell you because I didn't think we were ready to go into that yet."

"How can you say we weren't ready? You should have told me. The information would have helped me and saved me a lot of time and trouble. This is not the kind of information I should be learning from the tax office."

"I figure the tax office is as good as anybody else. Truth is I didn't tell you because I thought there still was plenty of time and I had someone else. You probably still think this coming out here was to chat about your history book and drink tea. You think you have been interviewing me."

"Yes, That's what I was asked to do."

"That's what got you out here. You think your friend Sandy sent you out here for the book. I told you to look careful so you see what's really going on, but you didn't listen. It's all the opposite."

"The opposite, opposite of what?" he asked. Mike was confused.

"Don't you see, your friend Sandy could have interviewed me for that book. She could have done this project all by herself. She didn't need you. She sent you here so that I could interview you."

"You interview me?" he asked trying not to sound confused.

"Yes, Mike. Things aren't always what they appear to be. Sandy thought you were the perfect one to replace her."

"To replace her to write the book?"

"No, Mike. You still don't see it. I'm a little surprised. This is not about the book, Mike. It's about the slough. Take away the land and you have nothing to write about. Your book won't mean much unless it tells the story of the land, just like I been telling you. You have the all the facts in front of you. Doug Williams told you the whole story."

"Doug told me about the deeds. But that puts you in a bad spot."

"What do you mean by a bad spot? I love the land and this isn't the end. I'm not in a bad spot. I'm holding the land to protect it."

"But you could have a lot of problems with the state and federal governments over the land. That's what I understand from what Doug told me. You can't handle that legally or financially. Aren't you upset about that? Why have you put yourself in that position? And Sandy knows all about this, too?"

"Of course. I suppose Sandy didn't tell you about herself."

"No, Sandy didn't talk about herself. You said replace Sandy, what do you mean? She told me nothing about herself. She's been meeting with me each week after I met with you. She asked me questions about information for the book but that's all."

"Well, that's over now. You know how old I am and you know I have no one to leave this land to. I have no relatives. I want the land preserved for future generations, so does Doug Williams. Sandy also shared that concern. Doug asked me to serve and I did, but now I'm getting too old. That's all. I need someone to represent this place, someone to take title as trustee and replace me in the records."

"Well, that makes sense. Doug said he was concerned about what would happen to the land when you were gone. He's afraid the government would take over. He suggested that I bring up the subject with you today."

"So you are catching on after all. You need to know that my first choice was Sandy. I wanted her to take over while I was still here."

"I agree, she's perfect. You should turn the land over to Sandy."

"Well, that's not going to happen. At first there was no rush, Mike, but now things have changed and there's no time left. I can see she didn't tell you her secret."

"Sandy had a secret? She didn't tell me any secrets. We talked about you and Indian Bend. She didn't tell me anything about herself. She only talked about the historical society and the book, working on this project with you."

"Sandy had a secret. You must never tell her I told you. I suppose those are things you and I can talk about now. A secret isn't a secret anymore once it's told. I figure she didn't want you to know. Of course if she did tell you, it wouldn't be a secret anymore, would it?"

"You have my word. I won't tell anyone, so we will have a secret. I promise."

"I believe you, Mike. What she didn't tell you is that she's dying. She has no time left."

"Dying? She's a young woman, she's younger than me. How can she be dying? She didn't look ill."

"Yes, she is. She's very ill. She has a rare disease I don't pretend to understand. She told me it's the cancer. There's no treatment and they can't operate. She said all known cases have been fatal. Seems the patient can live a fairly normal life for a time then suddenly there's only a few weeks left to live. Sandy's at that last stage. Mike, she's gone home to her family to die. She left while she could still travel on her own. She wanted to be here to see things through but time ran out on her. She flew out early this morning to go back north with her family. I'll miss her. I've gotten real attached to her. Sandy's gone, Mike. We'll never see her again. Seems some can live to be a hundred, like me, and some die young. Age don't matter none when it comes to be your time."

"Gone home to die?" Mike was stunned. "Now I understand why she didn't meet me today. She cancelled and didn't tell me why. She called me last night and told me not to wait for her today. She excused herself saying she wasn't feeling well."

"For a while now, I've been worried that one night I'd go to sleep and never wake up. Before she left, Sandy made me promise to take care of the land this week while I still had time. I did. I took care of the land. As part of that promise, I agreed to ask you this week."

"Ask me what?"

"Ask you to take title to the land and act as trustee, to replace me in the deeds. Someone has to step in and preserve the land and all the wildlife living here. Sandy trusted you. She knew you could be that person and now I believe it, too."

"I don't know what to say. I'm flattered. I don't know what to say or where to begin such a responsibility."

"Don't be worried. Hear me out. Sandy was sure of you, but I wasn't convinced at first. I didn't know how you would react so I had two deeds prepared by the lawyers. They brought both of them out here the day before yesterday. The notary and a witness came so I could sign them right here without going anywhere. We did that. Both deeds are now executed and back with the lawyers. One makes you the new owner as trustee and the other makes Doug Williams the owner."

"Oh," was all Mike could say.

"I wanted to sign one deed and leave the new owner blank. I thought it would be easier to type that in later, but the lawyer said it wasn't legal that way. Now hear me out." She continued, responding to Mike's obvious nervousness. "Doug said he would serve only as a courtesy to me because we're friends, but we both know he's not the right person. He's a rancher, an interested party, but his interests are not the same as mine. He wouldn't be the best one to negotiate with the courthouse vultures who will be knocking at the door. Of course, if there's no one else, he agreed to take care of the land."

"Doug never said anything about all this. He gave me the impression he didn't know what you were going to do. He asked me to press you to talk about your intentions today."

"Of course he wouldn't say anything. That discussion wouldn't have been proper. He doesn't own the land. I own the land until this Wednesday. Now, as I said, the lawyers hold two deeds for all of my land. Since only one of them can be recorded, the other one will be destroyed."

"I never thought about helping this way, but for you, I would help if that is what you want me to do."

"I never asked you before, but you are the one. You live in the outside world; you'd deal well with the legal vultures, Mike. If you need legal advice, Doug can provide his law office. They're familiar with all the details of the land. I can see you're not greedy, and you have no need for media attention. Of most importance, you respect and appreciate the natural world here and why this place is so special."

"Yes, the slough is special. I'm honored at your request. If you want me to serve as trustee, I'm willing to do it. Yes, I'll do it for you if that's what you see best."

"But there's more to it than that. Hear me out. Don't make your decision too lightly or quickly. This is only your third visit here. I couldn't make up my mind before. I wasn't sure what to do. Time has run out for Sandy and the vultures circling over my head are warning me as well. As I said, I signed two deeds and they're in the hands of the lawyers in town."

"Yes, I know Doug's firm. Their offices are located down the street from the courthouse where I work."

"Hold on, hear me out Mike, before you speak. I'm not finished yet."

"Yes, Sadie, I'm listening."

"I gave the attorneys instructions to record the deed to Doug Williams this coming Wednesday."

"Then you made up your mind, and you don't need me."

"I told you to hear me out. You're jumping ahead. Let me finish. They've been told to record that deed unless they receive a certain paper from you by noon this coming Tuesday."

"Tuesday, by noon?" he asked realizing he was again jumping ahead.

"Yes. Look under the tablecloth. You'll see a form in duplicate prepared by the lawyers," she said pausing while he pulled the papers out from under the tablecloth and read the document slowly. "Read the prepared statement for you to sign, accepting delivery of the deeds in your name. The brief agreement with me states you will hold title as trustee, agreeing that the land shall be preserved in its natural state to the best of your abilities."

"Yes, that's basically what it says," Mike responded as he reviewed the documents.

"Good. The deeds allow you to make decisions and act freely as you see fit. No one can challenge your actions. This agreement is just between us. You will do what you think is best for the land. That's all."

"Okay. I read it. It's simple, but I have a lot of questions."

"I know you do. So do I. You see Mike, I decided to do this because I know you have those questions about me and the slough. You cannot ask these questions. Again, hear me out. Do not ask your questions now." Sadie paused, then continued. "In fact, you can *never* ask these questions. I insist you think about my conditions for becoming trustee before you make your decision."

"You said I have until Tuesday noon?"

"To become trustee, you must sign both copies of the agreement. Take them home to think it over. If you sign the agreement, you must deliver it to the lawyers by noon this Tuesday. If you deliver the signed agreement, they will record the deeds with your name and destroy the ones with Doug William's name. If you decide not to go forward and act as trustee then they will record the other deeds for Doug. The deeds that are not recorded will be destroyed. Do you understand?"

"Yes, I understand." Mike responded.

"Well then, I believe you are ready. The decision is up to you."

Chapter Nineteen

Secrets Preserved

"So, remember, if you decide to accept the agreement, take your signed copy to the law office by noon on Tuesday. Be sure the secretary stamps it as received on that date and time. Have them make two copies, one for their office and one for you. If you make that delivery on time, you will be trustee for all the land deeded in my name," said Sadie. "Do you understand?"

"Yes," said Mike. "I'll make the delivery on time. I'm honored to be trustee for the slough."

"Wait, Mike. Don't make your commitment yet. You must take the time to think it over for two reasons. The lawyers do not want anyone to claim that I pressured you, so they insisted you have time to make the decision about acting as trustee, away from my presence. Also, there's another issue, a second reason. Personally, I don't want you to make a mistake."

"But I've already made up my mind."

"Mike, I'll be as delicate as I can," she continued, ignoring his response. "I see it in your eyes, and on your face. I see things you don't think I can see. You have questions, ones that you cannot ask, about me, about this place. I know your beliefs."

"I think I have..." stammered Mike.

"Please. Hold your tongue, Mike. Say nothing. I see strong beliefs in you. Your beliefs will serve you well, but I also see a flicker of doubt. That makes you want to question your beliefs and that makes you dangerous. Your questions are normal. Stop. Don't apologize. What do you really know about me? I've watched you write down notes on our visits, very carefully. What do you know about my past? How do you know who I am?" she asked, staring at him with her eyes blazing.

"I, I have only what you say. I researched the records for information about you in the courthouse, but the records don't go back that far. There was no doctor to witness a birth certificate; you weren't born in a hospital. Your parents weren't a part of a church when you were born. Your birth was never registered in the official county records," said Mike. "I do have the tax bills and the deeds that are recorded in your name, but no legal records documenting your birth or that you actually exist, outside of the deeds. Other than that, I only have my belief in you and that what you have told me is the truth."

"Did Doug Williams tell you his theory about where my mother is buried?" she asked. "He has his own ideas about my mother."

"Well, sort of, but not directly,...So I went to the church cemetery and ruins out on Immokalee Road the same morning after I met with him. I found the location near the ranch where there once was a church and adjoining cemetery but there was really nothing of any substance remaining there."

"Tell me, what did you find?"

"I'm sure I found the remains of the church and cemetery he was referring to. I could tell there had been a cemetery there, but all the grave markers were gone, and what was left of any gravestones was not legible. I could tell where the graves were as some of them had fallen in. No one will ever know who was buried there."

"Umm. So you see, in your world, I was never born and only exist because of the land deeds. You can't even be sure who I really am or where I came from."

"I know your name is Sadie Sutton."

"Only because that's the name I told you was mine. How do you know that's my real name? When I'm gone, there will only be the tax records and the deeds to document my ever having existed in your world. Did you know a notary can simply say they have personal knowledge of a person to officially certify the record? They don't need to see any documents to verify who the person is if they know of them personally. I've been a friend of the law firm for over two generations. That's how they know me. They don't know me any other way. No one has been able to discover anything else about me. That bothers you, doesn't it, Mike?"

"Yes, I've tried every source I could find to disclose some hard facts in the records about you. In the end, you're correct. I found nothing except the deeds."

"You may write that history book you talked about, but the role as trustee is far more important. Your history book will be just words about a dubious person you really know nothing about, only what that person has told you. On the other hand, the slough must be protected. The land is forever. There are only a few places like this one remaining in the world. Once they're gone and the wildlife leaves, no one can bring them back."

"You said there is a second reason to wait before I made my decision," said Mike, wondering what other issue could exist.

"Yes, I didn't forget it. Remember, I spend most of my time here in this cabin. I don't go anywhere, but I read a lot and think about how people act. One thing stands out for me is how folks can't distinguish fact from fancy imaginations. Some things, they can sit down and reason out. They use reason more than fact to prove what they accept as truth. Then there are other things they accept as true no matter what, and with no hard proof at all, and totally without reason. I call those things beliefs…" Sadie stopped speaking and looked hard at Mike.

"I'm not sure I agree, but you're entitled to your opinions. You're very observant about people and the slough."

"You're not drinking your tea," Sadie changed the subject.

"You're right." Mike picked up his glass and took a sip at her suggestion. He had forgotten about the tea. Suddenly he realized he was very thirsty.

"Do you know what belief is?"

"Well…" Mike stammered, swallowing a sip of tea.

"Belief is like the vultures," Sadie interrupted, "They know about death before it happens. There are things a body just knows. Belief is something you accept as reality, as truth, without any proof, without any reason or even without any facts to support it. A belief is accepted on its face for what it is and there is no way to prove it. It's true because we believe it's true," she said. "Like me, I believe the vultures have magical powers to see death before anyone else. I know it's true, I can't prove it, but I know it in my mind and heart. I accept it, but I can't prove it. My belief doesn't mean anything to anyone else, it's only important to me. In fact, it doesn't even matter if you don't believe it. It's true for me and that's the end of it."

"Yes, I guess you're right, I never thought about it like that."

"You're not a scientist, are you?"

"No, I'm a clerk, an administrator who works in the County Clerk's office. I'm a supervisor, too."

"Sandy told me that, before I met you. Science is the exact opposite of belief. For a thing to be accepted as fact, scientists must prove it beyond a doubt, using the analytical method of reason and examination of the facts. Science and belief are opposite ideas, don't you think?"

"What you say makes a lot of sense."

"There's a funny thing about belief, Mike. Have you noticed, once someone has a belief, they stick to it, no matter what? When someone else comes along and challenges that belief, most people get their dander up, becoming extremely emotional in defending that belief. The greatest danger is that they become unmovable the more they are challenged and the more heated the issue becomes."

"Yes, I've seen and done that, too. That's common human behavior. People behave that way a lot."

"So I'm concerned that if you want to be trustee for the land, you can't do what you are thinking about doing. To prove your belief to be true, is to venture down a path I don't think you want to take. My observations of human nature have shown me that you will suffer personally when you try to prove a belief is true."

"You're asking me forget my questions?"

"Yes, but you have to decide for yourself. I can't tell you what to do, but if you want to be trustee for the land, leave belief alone, Mike. Everyone needs to have beliefs. Beliefs enrich the experience of life and give things meaning. Beliefs are the things that are beyond science that cannot be addressed when you try to reason facts. Don't destroy your beliefs, Mike. Leave them as they are," said Sadie. "You'll be better off if you do. If you don't, you can't act as trustee."

"Okay, I think I understand what you're asking of me."

"Think of it this way, Mike. What if I were to cooperate with you and help you find the answers to your questions. You might promise me that you would keep the answers to yourself, that you're just curious and want answers to your questions. You would even claim that you *can* keep a secret. To find the answers to those questions, you need the help of outsiders. Let me clarify this for you. What do you think would happen if you are correct in your beliefs? Would these other people keep the answers to these things secret? Would they respect me, you, the land? What would happen if they also knew the answers to your questions? What then? What would happen to this place? What would happen to me? And all that would happen, for what purpose? Would these people be concerned about the consequences of their actions?"

"Oh, I see your point. The knowledge would potentially open everything up to the whole world. They wouldn't leave you, me or the land alone."

"Fortunately, greed and publicity are not options in your make up. What is your purpose here? Merely personal curiosity? Curiosity, because doubt is gnawing at your beliefs? Then I ask, who would be hurt by such a frivolous search? You? Me? The slough? What would happen to us who live here in the slough? What would happen to me, to Ivan, the birds, the alligators and frogs and the other residents here?"

"Things would happen that we don't want. So, I guess it's not important to look for things we don't need to know. I wasn't thinking things through very well," said Mike, fumbling with the buttons on his shirtsleeves. "That knowledge might bring many people here to the slough and they would trample it down to nothing. The birds and frogs and vegetation would be destroyed."

"What if science shows you to be wrong? If you are a true believer, Mike, you'll be doomed to spend your days denying the facts, questioning their results and methods, always seeking reinforcement for your beliefs. The story of belief is the story of rejection of rational, empirical proof. Such a direction would ruin you, Mike. You are better than that. Even if your better senses prevailed, and you accepted the facts, could you do the job as trustee with the same enthusiasm if the facts destroyed your beliefs? I think not," she said.

"I - I'm not sure," stammered Mike.

"I am. I'm sure. So, for these reasons, I have insisted on giving you time to make your decision to accept the responsibility to be trustee of the land. You must give up any and all of those questions concerning your beliefs. Cherish your beliefs; protect them as you would this land and all that's in it," she continued. "To undertake the responsibility as trustee in this agreement will not be easy. The decision is yours and yours alone." She stopped and the seriousness in her face and eyes lifted. She continued, "but enough of my bantering and babbling. I'm getting carried away again like a wild old hen who's lost her head. There's nothing more I can say. I think our visits having tea together on my porch have come to an end."

Mike said nothing. She was right. He picked up the glass of tea and drank the rest down, all in one gulp. He put the empty glass down on the table. He needed to think about what she had said, even though he was sure what his answer was going to be. Standing up to go he glanced over at her. "Did I ever tell you that you make a great glass of tea?" he said smiling.

"Yes, you have, each time you came to visit. 'Course you should thank the sun, not me."

"Well, I thank you again for your hospitality and words of wisdom. I do understand what you have told me. Rest assured, I will not disappoint you."

"Save your words for now. Let your actions speak for you. Remember the vultures circling overhead. Don't forget to look up and see them. They're still there. Be aware of what is happening here in the slough."

"Oh, yes, the vultures. I had forgotten about them." Sadie followed him to the screen door.

"Don't you worry none about them, their presence here at the cabin has nothing to do with you. You have nothing to fear."

"But you said they see death before it happens."

"Yes, I believe they can, but they're here for me, Mike, not you. That's why you only have until noon Tuesday."

Chapter Twenty

Fire

Mike opened his eyes in response to the ringing phone. When he looked at his watch, the LED read 11:45 PM. His television was still on. He had fallen asleep on the sofa watching the late night news. Annoyed at the late hour, he slowly stretched across the end table to reach the phone.

"Hello," Mike spoke as soon as he picked up the receiver.

"Mike?" responded a male voice.

"This is Mike. I can't hear you. Hold on a second. Let me turn down the TV so I can hear you." Without sitting up, he pressed the TV off button on the remote. "Okay, go ahead."

"No problem. Sorry to disturb you so late. This is Doug, Doug Williams at the Circle T."

"Yes, Doug, I recognize your voice. What's up?" Mike wondered why Doug Williams was calling him so late.

"Not so good, actually. Sorry to call so late but I needed to reach you right away."

"What's wrong?" Mike detected the strained urgency in Doug's voice.

"Look, there's a fire in the slough."

"A fire? Where?"

"We saw the glow from the flames and smoke coming up over the tree line. I just sent a few hands down to the slough to investigate. It could be a brush fire but it's coming from the direction of Sadie's cabin, Mike. I'm not sure yet, so I'm headed over there now. What's strange is this is the wet season so there shouldn't be any fires down there this time of year. The flames appear to be coming from one section judging from the direction of the smoke. It's intense. I don't think I've ever seen a fire like this in the slough. Such a strong fire needs a lot of dry wood to burn that brightly. The only thing I can think of that would have enough fuel for such a bright fire is Sadie's cabin."

"Sadie's cabin…" was all Mike could say. A dark feeling of dread began to rise from his subconscious gnawing at his conscience, telling him that something terrible had happened. His mind was numb and still groggy from waking up suddenly.

"I told the guys to go directly to the cabin to help Sadie and to be sure she's safe. The ground and the trees down there are saturated from the rain. Her cabin is the only thing down there that could provide the prime source for such an intense fire now. There's nothing else that could burn so bright, it's too wet. Besides, even if it's not her cabin we need to be sure she's safe. I want to get her out of there as fast as I can."

"Oh," was all Mike could muster.

"Hell, Mike, I don't know what it is. The cabin is the only thing down there dry enough to fuel a fire…" Doug was obviously upset. Mike could hear the raw emotion in his voice and the repetition of his fears chilled Mike to the bone. "Anyway, I wanted to warn you. My foreman will be calling me back any time now. I'm headed there as fast as I can."

"You're convinced it's her cabin, otherwise you wouldn't have called me so late." Mike finally found some words.

"I wanted you to know right away. I don't think I'm wrong. My guys aren't equipped to do much more than get her out of there. They don't have any fire fighting equipment. I called the volunteer fire department and the sheriff. Damn, I'm sure it's her place, but until I hear from them, I can't confirm anything."

"I understand. I'm on my way."

"I called you first," said Doug. "You'll have to call anyone else, including your friend Miss Stillwell. Right now, she's the only other person I can think of we should notify."

"She's gone," said Mike. "Sandy left the state Saturday morning. She had to go back home for a family emergency."

"Oh, I'm sorry to hear that. I hope everything works out for her. Well, look. I'll meet you at Sadie's place."

"I'm on my way, too. I hope this is a mistake."

"I'm sure it's not. I hope I'm wrong. Hell, I don't know what else it could be. Look." He stopped and the phone was silent for a few seconds. "Of course I could be wrong. I hope I'm wrong. When you come out, just follow the glow. You can't miss it. If I'm wrong, come up here to the house for a stiff drink for getting up at this hour."

"I'm on my way. See you at Sadie's." Mike hung up the phone. He was wide-awake now. He scrambled off the sofa, grabbing his shoes and a light jacket. As he started dressing, he noticed that his hands were shaking and he was having difficulty with the buttons on his jacket. He didn't know what to bring. After finding a flashlight, a first aid kit and an old blanket in his front hall closet, he had a sense he was doing something constructive to help. Even though he superficially thought these things might help, deep in his gut, he knew they wouldn't. He ran through his mind who else to call. He didn't know who or how to reach anyone at the county aid office at this hour. It was too late to call. Then he realized that it was better to say nothing until he knew more.

He drove quickly, almost recklessly through town, out SR 744, past the Red Star Diner, past the Banyan Inn, under the Interstate, then out along the fences between the cattle ranches towards the turn for the shell road. Driving at night was different than his trips on Saturday mornings. With the memories of his meetings with Sandy and Sadie replaying vividly in his mind, perhaps, he thought, just perhaps Doug Williams is wrong. Perhaps, just perhaps, it's all a mistake, and Sadie is fine, but something instinctively told him differently.

After driving about ten miles past the interstate, he could see the orange glow in the night sky coming from the slough. Like Doug warned, he couldn't miss it. The discomforting glow lit up the sky like a morning sunrise in the direction of Sadie's cabin, again just as Doug Williams had warned him. When the white fence line started on his right, he slowed down. He did not want to miss the turn for the shell road. That turn would be easy to miss in the dark. The closer he got to the shell road, the greater his discomfort became. Once there, missing the turn into the shell road was not a problem. A sheriff's car parked near the entrance nearly blocked the narrow opening in the vegetation. As he turned into the opening, he could smell the aroma of burning wood and creosote. The flashing emergency light on the top of the sheriff's car added to the eerie light reflecting back from the low lying scrub palmettos as the red beam circled in place. The flashes of light mirrored the skips of his heartbeat as he stopped behind the sheriff's car. There was no longer any question of where the flames originated. The glow in the sky was much brighter here, and the source was a short distance down the shell road. He could see the flames leaping over the low-lying vegetation. If it wasn't Sadie's cabin, the fire was certainly very near it. The scent of burning timbers was unmistakable and could only come from one source. As the scent grew stronger, the smell played on his growing sense of disaster.

Mike leaned out of the window of his car to greet the occupant in the sheriff's car. The deputy stepped out of the squad car. As he approached Mike's car, he turned the beam of his flashlight directly into Mike's face, temporarily blinding him.

"I'm Mike Byrne. I'm a relative of the woman who lives down there." Mike shadowed his eyes with the back of his hand and forearm.

"I'm not supposed to let anyone down there, but let me check. Wait here in your car while I call in," said the officer, moving back toward his car to call on the radio. Mike waited for what seemed like an eternity, even though the deputy was actually gone only a couple of minutes.

"You're okay. I told them you knew the people in the cabin. They're expecting you," said the deputy. "Be careful, the road is narrow, only one lane with marshes on both sides. If you miss the road, you'll be in trouble fast."

"I know the way. Did they find her?"

"I don't know who or what they found," said the officer. "All I know is there's a cabin fire down there. I don't know if anyone was in it. Just a fire, that's all. Someone said it was an old abandoned hunting cabin. Just in case, we sent an emergency ambulance down there, but it hasn't come back up here yet. That's all I know..." his voice trailed off.

"Thanks," said Mike as he eased his car onto the shell road. He didn't have to drive far to see the officer was right. For sure, the fire had engulfed Sadie's cabin. Mike took a deep breath and swallowed hard, his throat had tightened up against the thick smoke and smell permeating the air. The whole area was lit up as bright as daylight. He pulled up behind the emergency rescue ambulance blocking the road ahead. Parking behind it, he walked quickly past the ambulance and a district fire truck. The emergency medical personnel and the firemen were standing together on the road in front of what was left of Sadie's cabin. Mike hesitated, upset. They were all standing quietly in the road, watching the blaze, doing nothing.

"You from the press?" asked a fireman as Mike approached.

"No," said Mike. "I'm Mike Byrne. I know Sadie Sutton, the old lady who lives in this cabin."

"Who did you say you are?" said the fireman, as a second man came over to greet him. "Did you say someone actually lives out here?"

"I'm Mike, Mike Byrne. I know the elderly woman who lives in the cabin," Mike repeated. "Have you seen her?"

"You mean the woman who *used to* live in the cabin," said the first fireman as they stood watching the blaze. "There won't be anything left when these flames die down."

"We're just making sure the fire doesn't spread," said the second man. "It was too far gone when we got here. All we can do here is wait for it to burn out. There's nothing we could have done to save it. There's no one alive inside, now. The logs were really dry. They must have been really old. All we can do is keep an eye on it so the fire doesn't spread."

"What about Sadie?" asked Mike. "And there was a young man, too, who lived here with her."

"We haven't seen anybody here. That fire was so hot we couldn't get near the place. As you can see, there's not much left. In another hour, the fire will burn itself out. If there was anyone inside, they were burned to a crisp long before we got here."

"It's a good thing you're here. We may need you to identify the remains. How many people did you say were in there?" the fireman asked.

"One for sure, maybe two," said Mike. "With any warning at all, they both could have gotten out. If they had a few minutes, they would both have made it out, in my opinion. Ivan would have pulled Sadie out of the fire if he was here."

A third fireman approached them, "Are you Mike Byrne?"

"Yes. I'm Mike Byrne."

"Greetings, I'm Lieutenant Travis Goins. Doug Williams called our fire captain. He put me in charge. He called us to check this out. Doug told me to expect you. He said I was to tell you to wait here while he took his ranch crew out into the swamp to look for the perps. He thinks they may have set the fire and then took off."

"Who set it?" asked Mike.

"It's just a theory. He thinks maybe your friends who live here; some guy named Ivan and the old lady may be out in the swamp. Let's hope Doug's right. If they didn't get out, they've burned up. He was right, in a way, though. This fire's too hot and burned too fast. He's suspicious. Those are characteristics of arson. Doug thought the perps set the fire then took off into the swamp. If anyone can find them in the swamp tonight, it's Doug and his workers. They know the swamp. Let's hope he's right about them getting out. C'mon over to the fire truck and have a seat. You look a little shaky. A cup of coffee will do you good," said Travis.

"You can see it for yourself," said the first fireman. "Anyone in there didn't stand a chance."

At that moment, what was left of the logs in the north wall of the cabin collapsed into the flames and a huge cloud of sparks burst into the night sky. The sparks danced brightly on the updraft heat of the flames.

"Thanks, a cup of coffee sounds good. I need to settle my nerves," said Mike weakly. His knees were suddenly shaky and about to buckle. Only the running board of the fire truck saved him from collapsing as he sat down on the side of the nearest truck. Mike could not picture Sadie and Ivan walking or running into the slough for safety. Maybe Ivan had pulled her out and carried her to safety. He had helped her all his life, there was no reason he would not have been around when the fire started. Maybe Ivan had started it by accident in the shed that used to be next to the cabin. Mike knew Ivan would have pulled Sadie to safety. He was supposed to be big and strong as a bull in spite of his mental limitations.

Travis draped a blanket over Mike's shoulders and handed him a Styrofoam cup filled with warm coffee. Mike sipped the coffee slowly marking the heat of the liquid as it spread into his body, soothing his nerves and warming his hands.

"Rest a bit. You look like you have a touch of shock. Take it easy and sip your coffee slowly. Doug and his boys have been out there for at least half an hour. I have no idea how long before they come back. I doubt it will be much longer. Don't worry. If anyone was in there, no one will be going through the ashes until they cool down and have daylight to work on it. We won't do anything tonight. I asked the emergency guys to hang around a little longer in case Doug finds somebody out in the swamp," said Travis. "If they don't come back soon I'm going to send these guys home. If Doug needs help, he'll call."

"Good. I'm not sure I would be any help identifying remains," said Mike.

"That takes a thorough sifting in daylight to find anything. They won't need you to do that. The medical examiners will handle this. No matter what they find, you won't be much help. Doug and his guys took off with flashlights. Better he than me. I wouldn't go out in that swamp in the dark for anything," said Travis. "There's no telling what you'd run into at night. There's too many 'gators and snakes for my peace of mind."

"I'm with you," said Mike, watching the fire burn. He remembered Sadie mentioned she wanted to either be buried in the slough or have her ashes scattered here. With this turn of events, he sensed her wish might have come true. "Who do you think would do this? Set an old lady's cabin on fire?"

"Maybe an old lady and her friend," one of the emergency responders answered.

"Why would she do that? She's a nice person," Mike defended his friend.

"Are you kidding? It happens a lot. They set the place on fire, trying to make it look like an accident."

"Why? Why do that? It was their home."

"Insurance, fire insurance, for the money. People do a lot of crazy things for the money. When they don't have the money to pay the bills or make the repairs, they'll burn the place down to collect the money to go somewhere else. It happens more often than you'd think."

"Oh," Mike stopped. He didn't know what to say. He couldn't picture Sadie setting her own cabin on fire or inducing Ivan or anyone else to do it for her, not the way she had spoken about the cabin and the slough.

"Are you going to be alright?" asked Travis. Both firemen were watching the cup of coffee shake in Mike's hand.

"I'll be fine," said Mike. "Give me a few minutes to let this whole affair sink in. My nerves need to settle down." Sadie's words from the last conversation only days ago played in his head like a movie. Did she plan this? He remembered her warnings about the vultures. Time seemed to pass slowly as he sat watching the flames devour what remained of Sadie's cabin, leaving only glowing embers and a pile of gray ashes and cinders. He waited for Doug to return while he sipped his coffee. In an hour, the flames began to lose their intensity. Having burned the cabin to the ground, the fire had finally run out of fuel. In two hours, the fire had reduced the cabin down to glowing coals. After another half an hour, with no word from Doug, the emergency crew left, driving the empty ambulance out of the slough, down the shell road. Travis walked back from the remains of the cabin and glowing embers to where Mike was sitting. Nothing recognizable as the cabin, the shed, or any vegetation around it remained. Mike was still sitting on the running board of the fire truck, staring with his eyes fixed on the glowing embers that had once been Sadie's cabin remembering his conversations there and sipping tea.

"How you doing, Mr. Byrne?" he asked.

"Thanks, I'm doing better. This is so sudden," said Mike.

"We're pulling up stakes and going home. There's nothing more for us to do here. The situation is under control and the fire is dying. We're all volunteers with regular jobs to go to in the morning. I don't know what happened to Doug and his guys, but this fire is as good as dead. We'll throw some more buckets of water on it to be sure it won't flare up again and spread. That was our major concern, after checking for survivors."

"I guess the fireworks are over and it's time to go home," said Mike, in a daze.

"I called the coroner so his crew and the sheriff's men can come out here sometime in the morning when things have cooled down. I don't know what time they'll be here. If I were you, I'd go on home. There's nothing left to do here. Besides, it's not safe to stay out here alone at night. I recommend you check in with the sheriff and the coroner's office in the morning. I gave them your name when I called in. Call them for information. I'm sure they'll want to talk to you. You need a good night's sleep. Doug will call you when he gets in to let you know what he found," said Travis. "If you're not up to driving home tonight, the deputy can give you a lift home."

"Thanks for the offer but I'm fine, really. I won't stay out here by myself tonight. I'll be fine driving home."

"Good. I'll be in touch with Doug. I'll tell him you were here," said Travis.

"Sure, thanks for everything," said Mike, standing for the first time in a couple of hours.

Travis went over to the remains of the cabin and poked the glowing embers with a stick. A small cloud of glowing sparks drifted up into the night, flickering out before they rose above the trees. "Put another couple of buckets of water on this then let's go boys. We're done here tonight."

Doug's vehicles were still parked along the edge of the shell road, so no one would be up at the ranch. Mike knew the best thing he could do was to go home and get some rest. He knew staying here any longer was futile. When Doug did come back, Mike was sure he would return without either Sadie or Ivan. He sensed that one way or another, beginning tonight, Sadie was gone forever.

Chapter Twenty-one

The Trustee

As he reviewed the series of events that had occurred over the past week, Mike reflected on the depth of Sadie's wisdom. Remembering her warnings, he had to admit Sadie appeared to be clairvoyant. The vultures had circled overhead and now she was gone. Remembering the courthouse vultures, Mike had followed her instructions and signed the agreement, turning it over to the attorneys in time to become trustee of what Doug had called the Sutton Grant. The deeds were not recorded yet, but would be within three days, according to the attorneys. The black vultures resting on the peak of the courthouse roof reminded him to look up, as Sadie had warned. He did not have to look out of his office window to know that the legal vultures were already beginning to circle the courthouse.

Three days after Sadie's cabin burned down, Mike sat at his desk jotting down a list of all those claiming an interest in, or seeking to buy rights to the slough. He listed three state agencies, four federal departments, a bottled water company, a lumber company, two environmental groups, an adjoining farm to the north, two land developers, the County Commissioners, and a drainage district. He conjectured there would be even more once the news spread. Most of the claimants had inquired through secondary sources who passed the names on to him. Mike anticipated that once the deeds were recorded, more interested parties would emerge to contend with. Someone in the recording office had leaked information to the local newspaper and the information was included in the brief news article about the fire in the Brandon Times. As soon as the actual deed returned from the recording office, anyone researching the deeds could pick up the change in the County Clerk's database. Even though the information was not entered in the database yet, the change in ownership already seemed to be public knowledge.

One call received late in the afternoon unsettled him more than any of the others that came into his office. When the phone rang, he answered as he usually did, "County Clerk's Office, Mike Byrne speaking."

"Mike. Harry Friedman here."

Mike's heart sank. He could hear the excitement and pressure in Harry's voice. So much had happened so quickly, Mike had completely forgotten about Harry Friedman. Now it seemed as though he had met Harry in the distant past, almost as if the man had never existed. Even though he had sought out Harry for support to help him find information about Sadie's heritage, Mike now did not want to speak to him. Harry had become a man with the determination of a bull terrier seeking the truth about Sadie. As a result, Mike now saw Harry as dangerous and regretted telling him about Sadie and his theories about her heritage. Mike had lit a flame of intense desire in Harry to find the truth about Sadie. Harry desperately wanted facts and Mike desperately wanted to avoid discussing Sadie with Harry. Mike remembered his promises to Sadie about his beliefs.

"Yes. Harry. How are you?" said Mike lamely, surprised that he was able to keep his voice calm, stuffing down the emotions he was feeling.

"I hadn't heard from you, Mike. I saw the article in the paper about Sadie Sutton's cabin burning to the ground and that she perished in the fire. I want to express my sympathy."

"Thank you for your thoughts, Harry. I'm sorry I didn't call you. I'm still in shock. I haven't talked with anyone. I can hardly believe she's gone."

"Understandably. You must be very upset."

"She must have died in the fire. No one knows how it started. I went out there the night of the fire and stayed most of the night watching it burn. The cabin is totally gone. Everything is gone, Harry. There's nothing left, not a trace."

"There's *always* something, Mike, something that can be checked out. Teeth can survive a fire. I'm no expert in formal inquests, but I think they can do a lot with teeth, or even pieces of bone can be tested for DNA."

"They found nothing," Mike repeated. "I went back the next day and I watched the coroner's officers sift through all the ashes. They treated the area like a crime scene. Both of them are gone. Ivan and Sadie are both missing." Mike paused for a few moments. "They worked all day, digging and sifting after the area had cooled down. I was amazed at how thorough they were. I've never seen anything like it. Of course, they didn't dig up the whole slough. The cabin was resting on rock supports above the bog, so all the ashes and any remains dropped down into the bog, out of sight. I can vouch for the investigation team; they did their job. There was nothing, Harry. No teeth, no bones, only ashes remain."

"I called the Coroner and requested a copy of the autopsy report. There wasn't any report made. When I asked for a copy of the death certificate for my files, their response was interesting."

"What did they say?"

"The coroner said he could not issue a death certificate and there was no autopsy, because there was no body, no remains..." Harry sounded frustrated "I didn't know Ivan was missing, too."

"That's what they told me. The folks at the Circle T haven't seen Ivan either. The coroner's position is that she must be listed as missing in the sheriff's office because they found no body. Ivan, too. They could issue a report if they had found teeth or bones. But with nothing, there's no death certificate, no report."

"That's why I called. I wanted your input on whether they found anything. Frankly, I was worried there may be a cover up. You had some strong beliefs, Mike, and this whole fire business seems suspicious to me, especially after what you told me. I have to question everything in view of what you suspected about Sadie."

"Relax, Harry. I was there, at the cabin, the night of the fire. The people at the ranch next door called me when they saw the smoke and flames. I stayed all night watching the flames and felt the heat. As I said before, I went back the next day and watched while they sifted through the ashes. They don't know how the fire started and they didn't recover a thing. The fire was just too hot."

"Well, as I understand, they can recover DNA from bones and teeth. That would have helped, but if they didn't recover any. I'm sorry, I'm not helping you," said Harry, his voice drifting lower. "What about your friend, Miss Stilwell? Does she know anything? What was her reaction when she found out the cabin burned and Sadie disappeared?"

"She doesn't know anything. Harry, we were wrong about her. Apparently, she has a serious medical condition and left the state Saturday morning, days before the fire. She probably doesn't even know about the fire. She returned to somewhere in New England for treatment for her medical condition. From what Sadie told me Saturday, she won't be coming back. Her condition is terminal."

"Oh, sorry. I had no idea she was ill."

"Neither did I. Sadie told me Saturday. Apparently, she didn't want anyone to know. I appreciate what you're trying to do, but I've accepted the fact that Sadie's gone. We both have to accept it. It seems we will never be able to find the answers to our questions."

"That must bother you a lot, not knowing the answers. Here you were so conscientious in searching for the facts, only to have the whole investigation end abruptly. If Sadie is gone, then there's nothing available to check her background. No one will ever know without a body or DNA. Interesting, intriguing, unsolvable."

"What is?"

"We found no record of her birth. In a way, she appeared out of nowhere, and now she's gone, with no record of her death either. There's no official record of her life. Seems as if she never really existed, like she's a phantom spirit…"

Mike said nothing about the deeds or the tax records. He was anxious to change the subject, away from Sadie. "I figure she must have had a stroke or heart attack and knocked over a kerosene lamp. I don't want to think she suffered. I've accepted her death because I know there's nothing I can do," said Mike, thinking he had handled the situation with Harry well and had successfully diffused the subject of Sadie.

Mike was wrong about Harry.

"Well, all is not lost, Mike. Remember, we have the mound. I assume the mound in back of her cabin is intact, undisturbed," said Harry. Mike had forgotten about the mound. "The fire would not have disturbed the mound."

Mike's heart skipped a beat. Here he was, congratulating himself for sidetracking Harry so the secrets of the slough would be preserved, but Harry opened the door again in his search for truth. Harry reminded Mike about a truth that Mike now wanted to avoid, and a truth he needed to avoid to protect the slough.

"Yes," said Mike slowly. "Yes, I'm sure it's still there." He could not deny the truth, although he wished there was some way he could.

"So you see, Mike. All is not lost. We still have the remains of *The Big One* in the mound. Oh, and that's not all. I have some other good news."

"Good news?" asked Mike, knowing any news from Harry at this point was not going to be good.

"Yes. Although it's a rumor right now, I heard from the recorder's office that you might have been successful in winning Sadie over. What can you tell me about this?"

"What is this about? I haven't heard any rumors."

"The rumor is that Sadie deeded the cabin over to you. I'm sure there's not much land, but I'll bet if she did, the deed will include the mound. If you're named in the deed to the land, then as owner, you'll be in control of excavating it." Mike could tell that Harry was excited about the prospect of digging up the mound. Harry's hopes for continuing the investigation into the secret of Sadie's heritage were burning strong.

"Oh," said Mike, remaining non-committal. Knowing that all Harry had at the moment was a rumor, Mike realized the real danger would arise when the official deeds were recorded and available as public knowledge. The fear that Harry would be at the head of the line to check on the official deeds and would find out how much land was involved seeped into Mike's consciousness.

"You got lucky. If she died without heirs, her property would have gone to the state. With that scenario, we'd never be able to break through the red tape to get permission to excavate the mound. The land would be tied up for years. You may have lucked out. But, I'm speculating. We'll be able to check out the rumor in a day or two."

"Yes, I guess we'll find out," Mike mirrored Harry, saying as little as possible. How was he going to keep Harry out of the slough now?

"Well, congratulations, anyway. I admit I had my doubts about you. True believers rarely confront their beliefs. They usually run for cover to protect what they believe is true. When we met, I saw that you were committed to dig for the truth, no matter what the price to your beliefs. You passed the level of a true believer. Keep your spirits up. We have not lost yet. We may have lost Sadie, but we still have the mound," said Harry. Mike could hear the excitement in Harry's voice. "If she had lived, we might have eventually gained her cooperation to test for DNA, but we still have the remains of *The Big One* in the mound."

"Yes, it looks like we might." There was no emotion in his voice. How was he going to keep Harry from excavating the mound and protect the slough? Harry's declaration, "We still have the mound," echoed in his head like a warrior's battle cry. Harry was not going to let go of the mound. He had sunk his teeth into the mound like a bull terrier grabbing onto a piece of rawhide.

"I've been doing some serious thinking about the way to handle this. There is only one approach for us to take. We'll apply to have the mound classified as an Indian burial site and bring it to the attention of the archaeological association. After all, everyone knows the history of Indian Bend. The early Indian settlements in the area before the reservations were organized will give credence to our application. They'll salivate at the idea of excavating an Indian burial mound. Besides, I trust the science of the archaeological association better than calling in the coroner or a government agency. I don't trust government agencies; they usually have a hidden agenda. I like the idea of a private group, like the archaeological association. Their objectives promote discovering the facts in support of true science. If the mound contains what we think it does, we must avoid involving any political group or government agency."

"I agree," said Mike, feeling trapped. He had to find a way to diffuse Harry from pursuing the excavation of the mound. He could not allow the excavation of the mound. He had promised Sadie. The chain of events revolving around his association with Sadie and the slough was bizarre. Harry, who had initially been his friend and ally, was now his adversary. It was not Harry's fault. Mike was the one who had changed, not Harry. Harry was still doggedly pursuing the truth, which Mike wanted to avoid.

"Well, look, this is all premature. Let's see what shows up in the records. We can't go forward on the basis of innuendos and rumors. As soon as I can, I'll get a copy of the deed for you."

"Yes, we have to wait and see." Harry was making his points. Mike wondered what Harry was going to do when he found out how much land was involved. Mike's fears became real; Harry's dogged determination to excavate the mound would drive him to be the first one in line to get a copy of the new deeds. Soon, Harry would know that he was in control of the land and the mound and would be back expecting him to cooperate.

"Don't forget, I'm still here to help you. I don't want you to lose hope. I'll do as much as I can to help. Fortunately, the future may be in your hands. Call anytime. You have my numbers. I'm here to help you, " Harry reminded Mike.

"Thanks, Harry. Thanks for the call. I appreciate it."

Once they hung up, Mike thought about the strange position he now found himself in. The situation was almost funny. With this phone call, Mike realized how much he had changed in a matter of a few days. Sadie had been right again. With her disappearance, the protection of the slough was completely in his control. He was sure she had died, but not in the fire. The more he reviewed the series of events, the more he was convinced that somehow she had orchestrated her own disappearance, and possibly even her own death. From the discussion at their last meeting, he knew she would never have agreed to provide samples for DNA testing and she would never have wanted an autopsy conducted on her remains. He knew she had found another way, a way that ensured the protection of her secret. She would not have done this unless she was protecting what she knew as true from being discovered. He remembered her statement about the old people from the early days. She had solved the problem of her own past. He did not have to worry about preserving her secret. Sadie had protected her own secret. As a creature of the slough, Sadie lived and died according to the ways of the slough. Her words echoed in his thoughts, "The slough takes care of it's own."

The mound was a different matter. After this conversation with Harry, the importance of his role clearly emerged; no one could be allowed to discover what was buried there. His ability to protect the slough depended on protecting the integrity of the mound. To protect the slough, he had to protect its secrets. Sadie had done her part, now it was his turn. His ability to protect the slough and keep curiosity seekers and developers from discovering the contents of the mound with possibly the greatest discovery in the history of mankind, the remains of a DeBosi, would be worth millions.

Mike's task would be difficult, his greatest challenge. If Harry called in the coroner, claiming a recent burial, the coroner could overrule Mike's denial of access to the property. Harry, at the moment, did not want the coroner in, but what would he do if Mike refused to allow access to the mound by the archaeological association? Harry was a believer in finding the facts. How far would Harry push in his search for the truth? Harry was now Mike's biggest problem.

Mike also believed that Doug Williams knew much, much more about Sadie than he had volunteered, but Mike was also sure that Doug would never reveal anything more about Sadie. Whatever Doug knew, out of loyalty to Sadie, he would keep to himself. Mike thought, one of his first acts, as trustee would be to close the shell road. Closing the shell road would block access to the slough and keep the public and curious out so no one else would ever discover the mound. That would be easy, but how was he going to diffuse Harry?

Chapter Twenty-two

Apology

Four days later, Mike received the answer to his question of how to diffuse Harry. A small parcel had arrived for him at his apartment building when he picked up his mail. At first glance, the hand printing on the package was not familiar. Looking closer, he recognized Sandy's name at a post office box address in Boston, printed in the return address box.

An envelope was attached to the outside of the package. He hurried up the stairs to his apartment, anxious to read Sandy's letter. The letter was typed on standard printer paper with an incomprehensible erratic scribble in ink at the bottom. Sandy's name had been carefully typed beneath the signature, with the word "dictated" and the letters "erc" following. Mike concluded another person whose initials were "erc" had actually typed the letter for Sandy, who had then signed her name below. Strangely, the dates on the letter matched the postmark on the envelope and the body of the letter was centered under the heading: 'APOLOGY,' typed in bold letters.

APOLOGY

Dear Mike,

I hope this letter finds you well and installed as trustee for Sadie's land. I write this letter to apologize and explain our actions in our enthusiasm to protect the land. I am compelled to confess that Sadie and I conspired to entice you into being Sadie's replacement trustee. This letter is my personal apology for my part in this conspiracy. Sadie will have to speak for herself. In considering what we did, I apologize for any harm or embarrassment we may have caused you if we succeeded.

I asked Sadie to explain why I had to leave Florida so suddenly. My time ran out faster than the doctors anticipated. I was diagnosed with a rare pancreatic cancer almost a year ago. Individuals with this disease may lead a normal life for a while, but near the end, the most unpleasant death comes on quickly. When you receive this letter, you will not be able to reach me and I ask that you do not try. I have accepted my fate and ask you to do the same.

Hopefully, you will already be trustee for Sadie's land. I really wanted to be there to see it happen, but my failing strength prevented me from staying any longer. I knew when I first met you that we could count on you to do what was right. Sadie grew to share that opinion and, at the end, quickly acted to put our plans into motion. Sadie and I sensed you were the best suited to protect the land. Doug will continue to help with funding and legal advice as he did with Sadie.

As you know, I met Sadie when the historical society sent me looking for the original settlement at Indian Bend. Over time, Sadie and I became good friends. Although I had agreed to act as trustee for her, my illness and her age, forced us to change our plans. When I met you at the historical society meetings, I could not simply ask you to be the trustee, to act as fiduciary for thousands of acres with all their complicated legal problems. You would have quickly run for the hills. In all honesty, why should you undertake such an obligation?

Sadie and I planned our conspiracy to entice you into becoming the trustee in one of our weekly chats. I can't say who thought of it first. We used Sadie's appearance to capture your curiosity. Once we agreed, I joined the local Almas Association and all the pieces fell into place. From the association, I learned about the presentation we attended. Your exposure to that lecture was a lucky coincidence. After that, we planned all of your meetings with Sadie and, especially the one with Doug Williams at the Circle T Ranch. We didn't want you to be overwhelmed all at once. We wanted you to know exactly what was involved with the lands.

Our plan was simple, to create the opportunity for you to become a believer. Sadie understood how human behavior quickly causes individuals to adopt a belief, often without thought and then defended with great emotion. She was sure that once you became a believer, you would accept the role of trustee, willingly and enthusiastically to protect the lands. I knew you were the one when we came out of that presentation at the hotel. Sadie, I'm sure was very good at her job. We were careful to let you use your own judgment to adopt your own beliefs. We may have taken advantage of you, but we let you draw your own conclusions and make your own decision.

I apologize for both of us in that we used you then we went away, leaving you to stand alone. As you know, Sadie practiced the ancient art of doll making she learned from the Indian medicine woman when the Miccosukees and Seminoles lived near Indian Bend. Before I became ill, Sadie made one of her spiritual dolls to guide my spirit as trustee for the slough. When we met during the time she created the doll, we meditated, holding ancient rituals to enlist guidance from the Indian spirits for its creation. I was surprised as the doll took on a persona of its own. When she blessed and gave me the doll, I experienced something I never knew possible. Somehow the doll conveyed an acceptance of my role and a feeling of connection with the universe and nature. I experienced a peace I could not explain. The doll has fulfilled its purpose with me and I will not need it now, so I pass my gift to you. May the blessings of the spirits Sadie conjured up for this doll guide you in your new role as trustee for the lands. I wanted to pass it to you personally, but my medical condition prevailed. Take special care of this totem, Sadie conveyed special spiritual powers to this doll. As I found, these special creations serve important needs for adults, far different than what we are used to when they are a child's toy.

Sadie would not approve of this letter. However, I ask the spirits for guidance for you in handling the future of the slough. I warn you to be careful with your beliefs. I'm concerned about the consequences of the beliefs you have adopted.

In the beginning, for us, the ends justified the means, but now I feel we owe you an apology and a warning. Did Sadie ever tell you who or what she was or where she came from? Did she ever tell you who or what was buried in her back yard? I know she would not. What you now believe is based on what you saw, or wanted to see and hear. Your conclusions are your own. I have known Sadie for some time and met with her on many occasions, but I do not know what it is she calls her "secret." I have never asked about her past or what she may have in her backyard. I was concerned only with helping her find a replacement trustee. I never asked her about those things because those issues were not important to me. I was simply there to help her in our mission of inducing you to become trustee for the land. In light of her concern, I doubt she will ever tell anyone the truth of her "secret." So you see, I have left you with your beliefs. I can only urge that you examine them carefully before you act in reliance on them. That is the real purpose of my letter.

I hope you will not think too badly of us, and will forgive both of us for our conspiracy. We created the opportunity for you to take on an important task and have passed a spiritual guide to assist you. I write to apologize for the conspiracy and warn you to be careful.

Sincerely,
Sandy

Mike read the letter a second time and carefully opened the small parcel. As he lifted the flaps on the box, he removed the figure from the plain tissue paper surrounding it. The image in front of him stopped him short. In his hands, a male doll crafted from clay, palmetto fronds and dressed in dark brown pants gazed back at him with an expression of pride and affection. He gasped as he recognized the familiar face of his grandfather. Memories of the many hours spent in the outdoors with this kind, gentle old man washed over his mind. Sadie had resurrected the one person Mike had most loved and respected as a child, bringing his life from the woodlands of Delaware full circle to the swamplands in Florida. What better guide to assist him in overseeing the protection of Sadie's cherished treasure, the slough?

Mike placed the doll on his dining room table. He would find an appropriate place for it later. Right now, he knew what to do. He made a copy of the letter, then wrote on the top of the first page: "Harry: for your information, Mike." Folding the letter, he placed it in an envelope addressed to Harry Friedman and the return address as his own. He added a stamp and put the letter in the mail. Mike was sure he would never hear from Harry Friedman again. Now the mound would remain intact and Sadie's "Secret" was one that went with her to the grave.

Chapter Twenty-three

The Gift

Mike called Doug Williams as soon as he received the recorded deeds from the attorney's office. All the required recording information was stamped on the top of the first page of the deeds. His phone call was merely a courtesy. Two weeks had elapsed since the deeds were recorded, so now anyone could obtain the information from the county database. The general counsel at the Circle T's law firm had handled the transfer to him and the ranch had paid the legal fees. Mike was sure Doug was advised as soon as he had delivered the agreement with Sadie to the law firm. Nevertheless, he still felt obligated to personally acknowledge to Doug he had received the recorded deeds. From now on, he would be working closely with Doug on matters about the slough and he knew Doug was going to be his best advisor when the legal vultures started their tactics. In all likelihood, Doug would be the only person he could trust.

"Doug?" he spoke into the receiver.

"Mike, good to hear from you. Congratulations on becoming trustee," said Doug enthusiastically.

"Thank you. I just received the recorded deeds in the mail."

"Good. Come on over to the ranch this evening. Let's celebrate. We have a lot to talk about."

"Okay," said Mike, surprised at Doug's enthusiasm. Mike had believed Doug actually wanted to be trustee and felt defensive in making the call.

"Why don't you come after dinner, after seven? I need to feed my crew first. How's that time for you?"

"Sounds fine. I'll be at the ranch by seven or seven thirty."

"Bring the deeds with you. We'll sit down and check the legal descriptions against my files to make sure all of the tracts of land are listed."

"Sure, I'm experienced at reading legal descriptions, so I can help check them, too."

"Great. We can compare the lots against the county map. I have one here. Again, thanks for stepping in as trustee. You have no idea how relieved I am."

"Relieved? I thought you wanted the job yourself."

"No. Not really. Can you imagine it? If you hadn't stepped up to the plate, Sadie and the lawyers were going to name me as trustee. Hell, what a nightmare that would have created. What were they thinking?"

"I'm not sure. Why would that have been a problem? You looked like the best fit to me."

"Not really. We spent years keeping the ranch and members of the family separate from ownership of the slough. The family has always taken the position that ownership of the slough was a conflict of interest for the ranch. Becoming trustee for Sadie's land would have put me right back in the middle of the morass. My feeling is that we would serve as a deep pocket for both the state and the feds to bleed us dry with their requirements for the land. The problems of the slough have to be kept separate from the ranch operations."

"Where is the conflict of interest?" I don't understand how it would be a conflict of interest for you. To me, it seems to be a natural role for you as owner of the Circle T."

"If I took title to the slough, I would have been in control of a pristine clear watershed. Control of the slough by a rancher would have caused strife with the government agencies. In addition, the environmentalists would not have looked kindly at that, either."

"What's wrong with a rancher being trustee for the slough?"

"The Circle T is a cattle ranch, Mike. The feds and the environmental lobbyists consider cattle ranchers one of the worst polluters of water in the country. Some of the more radical environmental groups go so far as to put us on a par with toxic waste dumps. Putting the president of a cattle ranch in as trustee of the slough would reduce any positive leverage we currently have with those people. They would have roasted me so I would never get any cooperation. Hell, do you know who you are, Mike?"

"I thought I did until you asked."

"You're Mr. Clean, that's who you are."

"Mr. Clean?"

"From the perspective of the environmentalists and government agencies. They'll bend over backwards to give you concessions I could never get as a rancher. Look. I couldn't talk to you about it before now, because the attorneys didn't want anyone to influence you. You had to make the decision on your own. That's why I was so abrupt when we talked the other day. Anyway, I'll see you this evening. We can talk more then."

"I'll be there. I know I'll need your help and knowledge of the land." He hung up feeling relieved of a giant burden. For some reason, he had convinced himself that Doug wanted to be the trustee, if for no other reason than to get the land back under control of the ranch once Sadie was gone. After all, the Circle T money purchased the land, supported Sadie's title to the slough and continued to provide the funds to pay the annual taxes. Mike was convinced that Doug had not contacted him about the deeds because he had wanted the job for himself. Contrary to his beliefs, he found Doug was elated that he had stepped in, and with good reason. Doug's rationale made sense.

When Mike arrived at the ranch that evening, Doug met him at the door.

"C'mon in, Mike," he said, ushering Mike into the living room. "Have a seat."

As he settled into the leather couch, Mike noted there was a bottle of champagne on the coffee table in front of him and two glasses beside it. When he looked up over the fireplace mantle, he noticed a striking difference. The painting of the slough was missing. Looking around the room, he saw the painting resting against the arm of the sofa farthest away from him. Files and surveys were spread out across one of the coffee tables and the county map on the other.

"I got a head start this afternoon. I asked the attorneys to fax over a copy of the deeds. They were glad you called. They directed me to avoid being involved in the transfer process and communicating with you before the deeds were recorded. They're glad you called to tell me you had received them."

"I see."

"Do you remember the last time we spoke?"

"The day after the fire. You called to tell me Sadie died in the flames. You said you had gone out looking for her, but never found her."

"Yes, I remember now. Are you sure we never talked about ownership of the land in that conversation?"

"Our conversation was brief. We only talked about the fire. The only time we discussed Sadie and the slough was in our first meeting. You answered a lot of my questions about the land during that conversation."

"I'm sorry I had to be so brief in our last phone conversation. Government agencies tap phone lines at any time, and you'll never know it. I was brief because I didn't dare say anything over the phone."

Doug poured the champagne into the two glasses and handed one to Mike. "Here's to your new role as trustee. You're one of the largest land owners in the county."

"The reality hasn't sunk in yet," said Mike, accepting the glass.

"You know, I knew instantly you would be the best one for the job when I met you. Oh, I wasn't sure you'd accept the responsibility to step in, but you were the one person who could do it without stirring up the government. Writing history books is not your destiny. Besides, I knew my job, too. Both Sadie and Ms. Stillwell highly recommended you."

"Your job? You were in on this conspiracy with Sandy and Sadie?"

"Of course, I had to stir up your interest in the land any way I could."

"Well, you did your job. In fact, you did it very well. I'll never forget our trip down to Lake Ibis."

Doug smiled and raised his glass. "Well, let's celebrate this evening before the proverbial stuff starts to hit the fan." When they both had emptied their glasses, Doug poured refills. "I know this isn't fair," said Doug, when he finished filling the glasses.

"What isn't fair?"

"Your role," said Doug, as he took a sip of champagne. "Here we are, celebrating your new position, when the reality is that you'll soon be cursing me along with everyone else."

"Are you alluding to the legal vultures?"

Doug nodded affirmatively and raised his glass again. They both took a sip of champagne.

"Sadie warned me about the vultures."

"Maybe I should offer you condolences. Hell, I don't mean that, Mike. You've taken on an important task, and I appreciate you stepping in for us. Don't forget, I'm here to back you up and support you as best I can."

"Thanks again for that," said Mike, taking another sip of champagne. "Frankly, I have no one else to turn to for help."

"You must have a lot of questions on your mind, not the least of which is how we are going to finance your new responsibility."

"That problem had crossed my mind. I'm not rich and I certainly don't have the kind of money to support this large tract of land and pay the taxes."

"Don't worry about that, we'll continue to pick up the taxes as long as necessary, and we'll cover your legal expenses. Our issues are common ones. You are really our surrogate, so we have an obligation to back you up, like we did for Sadie."

"You're really telling me to anticipate problems right away."

"Believe me, the feds and the state will be on you like flies on fly paper."

"Well, I'm glad to have assistance."

"I invited you here this evening to assure you we will support you. Please consider the ranch your home, Mike. There are no wiretaps here. You can ask any questions you have on your mind. You and I are going to have to work together very closely. We need to be on the same page at all times. Our adversaries will try to divide us any way they can."

"Well," said Mike, hesitating momentarily. "I have a thousand questions. I've been curious ever since the night of the fire. How did you know Sadie wasn't home that night, when you finally got to her cabin? You took off looking for her before they searched for any remains in the ashes. I wondered whether you were looking for her, or whether you actually found her? Did you know where she was all the time? I have a lot of questions spinning around in my head. None of the firemen thought the fire was an accident."

"Whoa," said Doug, smiling, then pausing to take another sip of champagne. "I see we have to set some boundaries here in our conversations."

"You mean rules?"

"Everyone has private places where they keep special secrets. The slough has secrets, and only Sadie knew all of them."

"Yes, I know. Sadie knew and loved the slough."

"She was so good at keeping those secrets, Mike. She took them with her. You must understand, I will never do anything or say anything to undermine those secrets. Most likely we have different beliefs about Sadie and the history of the slough. Because we're going to work together, we need to agree to avoid any discussion of certain topics. Some of these are issues that include questions about Sadie, Ivan and, of course, mythical beings," he added, smiling. "That is the one important understanding that you and I must have."

"Okay, I understand. I stepped over the line."

"Yup. I'm glad you recognize it. I should have anticipated your questions. We must avoid discussing anything about topics where we might have different beliefs. If we can do that, we'll get along just fine," said Doug, smiling again.

"I understand."

"Enough then. I have a gift for you, one you will appreciate," said Doug as he moved around the coffee table to the other side of the sofa.

"A gift? For me? Haven't I gotten enough with the land? That was gift enough."

Doug said nothing as he retrieved the painting resting against the arm of the sofa, the painting that had hung over the fireplace mantle. "This is yours, Mike. I have a new painting coming next week to hang over the fireplace. It's an exciting new work done by a young, up and coming artist."

"Is it abstract art?"

"No, I selected a painting of the slough, but there are no mythical creatures in it. This one belongs to you. I saw the impact it had on you. If there's one person who should own it, it's the trustee of the slough," said Doug, presenting the painting to Mike. "Oh, I have one bit of advice for you about this painting. Since it has special effects on certain people, be careful where you hang it."

"Thank you. I don't know what to say," said Mike. "I'm overwhelmed."

"Then say nothing," said Doug. "Isn't that the lesson Sadie taught us? If you don't know what to say, then it's best your thoughts remain unsaid?"

Mike said nothing.

Chapter Twenty-four

A Glitch

When Saturday morning arrived, Mike sadly realized there would be no more breakfast and lunch visits with Sandy at the diner and no more meetings with Sadie. Both Sandy and Sadie were gone. Mike could only go forward, so he spent the morning rewriting and assembling the notes he had taken during his interviews with Sadie. He included only those things he thought were historically appropriate. Tomorrow afternoon, Sunday at two o'clock, he had scheduled a meeting with Ms. Abernathy to begin working on the book about Indian Bend for the society. As he excluded his beliefs about Sadie, the exercise made him think about what might have happened.

There were, he thought, too many loose ends. He remembered how sure he felt that he would never see Sadie again when leaving the smoldering remains of her cabin. He began to write his thoughts down on an extra page in his notebook, a page that he would not share with Ms. Abernathy. Why had he been so sure he would never see her again? What knowledge was buried deep in his subconscious?

If the fire were an accident, then the event began when Sadie had a heart attack or had fallen asleep and knocked over a kerosene lamp. In that scenario, she either died in the fire or Ivan saved her and took her into the slough. In a second scenario, it was possible both Sadie and Ivan died in the fire, but, as he thought about it, that alternative seemed remote. The coroner had reported, even though they searched the bog under the cabin thoroughly, they found no bones or teeth. Mike posed Sadie's age may account for her having no teeth left to discover, and her bones too brittle to survive the intense fire.

Ivan, on the other hand, was another matter. Something of his teeth and bones should have survived. Since he slept in the shed, he could have easily escaped, or run off when he realized he could not save her. Maybe it was Ivan that Doug sought that evening.

Still dissatisfied with his theories, Mike continued to hypothesize alternatives. Hadn't the firemen said the fire was too hot and looked like arson? If so, Mike doubted that Sadie had set it. He concluded only two suspects; either Ivan or someone acting on Doug's instructions set the fire. Ivan's dedication to Sadie diminished the possibility of a motive for him to have set the fire. Ivan's limited mental abilities and dedication to Sadie would direct him to help Sadie, not burn the cabin down. If the fire were the result of arson, both Sadie and Ivan would have escaped.

Why, he wondered, would Doug have had the cabin burned to the ground? Had Doug waited until the fire had destroyed the cabin before he called Mike or reported the fire? If this were the case, as Mike now believed, why did Doug have the fire set? Wasn't Doug also concerned with Sadie's welfare? Why burn her cabin down? It made no sense. Mike was missing something. Sadie advised him to be observant, or he would miss what was really going on. What had he missed?

According to the firemen, Doug had gone out into the slough to look for Sadie and Ivan, but he had done so before the ashes had been sifted for remains. Mike believed that Doug took off without waiting because he already knew there were no remains in the fire. This theory made sense if Doug was responsible for setting it. He would have arranged to get Sadie and Ivan out before the fire was started, but again why destroy their home?

What if Doug wanted people to think Sadie died in the fire? He had reported Sadie missing and filed a missing person's report with the police. The county refused to issue a death certificate because the coroner had found no remains. In the end, Doug succeeded because everyone now believed Sadie died in the fire even though there was no evidence to substantiate the facts. No one was looking for her now.

Still, what was the objective in burning down the cabin to make it look like she died in the fire? Mike did not like loose ends and for a moment he was stymied.

Suddenly he realized that he had been close when he had considered the alternative of an accident. What if Sadie had actually had a fatal heart attack before the fire? If she had died before the fire started, what would have happened? What if Ivan had found her and had run to Doug and told him Sadie was dead? Ivan would not have known what to do and would need help. In that scenario, Ivan would turn to Doug for help. What if Doug was a believer or even knew the facts of Sadie's past? The one thing Doug would do was ensure her secret was preserved. To do that he would have burned down the cabin, but only after the body was removed and taken out into the slough to be secretly buried someplace else. Was that why Doug was gone so long the evening of the fire? Did he go out into the slough to bury her, not to find her?

With this theory in mind, everything seemed to fit neatly into place, until he remembered the mound. Was the mound in the back of the cabin because the DeBosi buried there was Sadie's father? Or was her story correct that the site was merely the place where the death occurred? Was there really a body buried in the mound or was that merely Sadie's contribution to the conspiracy she and Sandy had constructed? He was convinced Sadie's mother, a full-blooded human, was buried in the cemetery on Immokalee Road. Even if there had been grave markers, what name should he have been looking for? Since women usually take the name of their husband, could it be that Sadie knew her father was not human, and Sutton was just a name she made up? Her mother would probably be buried using her maiden name, a totally unknown name in all the information he had collected. Even if he had found legible grave markers, Sadie had never mentioned her mother's name. He would never have found her.

Now, the mound was a problem. Mike picked up his phone and dialed the Circle T. "Doug?"

"Yes. Mike?"

"I thought I'd give you a ring. There's something we need to take care of right away."

"Of course, there are a lot of things we need to address if we're going to allow access to the slough as a private park."

"We should limit access to a picnic area up by the highway," said Mike.

"Why? The public won't see much up there. Don't forget, the real beauty of the slough is down along the water, near Lake Ibis. I've got a couple of other ideas on how to design an access road for you to consider."

"I'm anxious to hear them, but right now, we have to protect the mound. We need to close access to the old shell road up near the highway so no one can enter the slough there. Neither one of us wants anyone digging up the mound. Can you put up a locked gate?"

"Hell, Mike, I'm way ahead of you. You've seen all our fences."

"Yes."

"One thing we have around the ranch is a tractor mounted with a post hole digger for installing fences. We've already put in a fence to block the entrance to the shell road. I concur; the shell road can't be used for public access. We already did a little landscaping while we were there, too."

"Landscaping? What do you mean by that?"

"We planted a half dozen young oak trees and a bunch of shrubs and palmettos along the roadbed. Give nature a year or two, and you'll never know that road existed. I should have told you. Somehow, I thought you'd know. Only those who know exactly what they're looking for would ever go down there now."

"As usual, you're way ahead of me."

"The timing of your call is uncanny."

"Why?"

"I was just about to call you."

"You were?"

"Look. There's a glitch."

"A glitch? In what?"

"Did I tell you about my sister, Amy?"

"Sure, the jetsetter."

"Well, it seems she's decided to settle down."

"Settle down? You mean she's getting married?"

"Oh, no. She has no interest in being a housewife or raising babies. She's much too independent for that. No, she's coming back to the ranch. She's tired of jet setting and that whole scene. She says she misses the ranch."

"The ranch? With you?"

"You got it. When I told her my foreman decided to retire, Amy said she wanted his job. The way she figures it, she'll carry her own weight and our overhead would remain the same. She's a lot like me. She really keeps both feet on the ground. If you ask me, the guys who were picking up her tabs realized she had no intention of settling down with any one of them."

"Their loss is your gain. You won't have to handle the ranch by yourself anymore."

"Unfortunately, that's the glitch."

"You lost me."

"Did I tell you Amy has a degree in accounting?"

"No. You didn't tell me that. You just said she was a jetsetter."

"She's a damn bean counter, Mike. I love her to death, but that's her training."

"I see."

"You do realize what that means to us?"

"I'm not sure. You'd best explain it."

"Hell, Mike. The ranch has been paying the taxes for the slough properties for years, but the taxes are not assessed in the name of the ranch. On top of that I've paid the legal fees for Sadie and I've promised to cover you, again out of the ranch's general funds."

"I know, and I appreciate it."

"What I'm saying is that if she comes down here, it's only a matter of time before she gets into the books. When that happens, it won't take long for her to discover what I've been doing."

"You have a valid reason for picking up those expenses. Certainly she'll understand that."

"Obviously, you're not familiar with bean counter mentality. We haven't been close for years. Common sense is not the usual characteristic of a bean counter; dollars and sense on the bottom line are what count. I'm afraid she may not agree with the rationale for what I've been doing."

"Do you think we have to change our plans?"

"No, not our plans, just our timetable, that's all. Hell, I don't have any specific ideas yet. I wanted to alert you to the problem. The dreamer in me wants to believe she'll fit in and understand what we're doing. Unfortunately, I'm a realist. We don't have to do anything drastic today, but we'll have to think about timing for the future."

Chapter Twenty-five

Mythical Beings

The soft evening moonlight streaked into the master bedroom through the sliding glass door on the veranda. From out in the slough, Doug could hear the sound of the myriad tree toads and the occasional deep-throated bellows of the bullfrogs. The view out of the second floor of the house through the drapes appeared like a fairyland. The moonlight filtered irregularly through the Spanish moss draped thickly from the limbs of the great oak tree leaving irregular patterns of light scattered over the tops of the sabal palms bordering the edge of the slough. Off in the distance, the moonlight danced lightly in the mist rising from the surface of Lake Ibis. Doug heard a soft tap on his bedroom door.

"C'mon in," Doug responded from his station at the large oak carved antique desk where he was working on papers spread out in front of him.

"It's only me, Doctor Mom, with your medicine," said Amy as she pushed open the door. She was carrying a small silver tray with a bottle of wine and two wine glasses. She put the tray down on the edge of his desk and poured wine into each of the glasses.

"You know, I envy you your view from this room," she continued after handing him one of the filled glasses. She gazed out into the moonlight and slowly moved out onto the small veranda to take in the expanded view. "This view is stunning. I had forgotten how beautiful this land is, all these years I've been away."

Doug stood and followed her out onto the veranda. He could smell the rich odor of the slough in the moonlight. "I have an idea. Since you enjoy this room so much, why don't you use it while I'm in the hospital getting my knee worked over again? After all, this place belongs to all of us."

"No thanks. You don't know what a treat it is to be away for years and then come home to my own childhood room."

"I never changed a thing in it. I'm sure you noticed."

"Don't tell me you knew I would come back."

"I admit I never dreamed you'd be coming back for good. Frankly, I was even more surprised that you agreed to our plan to protect the slough by using Sadie and Mike Byrne. What a relief to have finally struck a settlement with the State."

"You know, I've never met him."

"Who?"

"Mike Byrne, your new trustee."

"I'll set up a luncheon date for the three of us so you can meet him. You'll like him. He's an interesting person and now he's an author, you know."

"He is? I didn't know. What did he write about?"

"He co-authored the book about Sadie and the historical background of the slough at Indian Bend. I've got a few complementary copies downstairs in the den. I'll give you one."

"I'd like that. I bet he learned more about Sadie than I ever knew. She was just one of the family to me. I never asked her much about her past or her life in the cabin."

"Be careful, though."

"Careful, about what?"

"He's single. You know how dangerous single men can be."

Amy laughed lightly. "Oh, now you're being funny. Don't worry; if there's one thing I've learned since I've been away, it's how to handle men. Besides, I know you. You say that about single women, too."

"Yes, I guess I'll have to warn Mike about you, too."

"Don't bother. If I know you as well as I do, you already warned him about single women."

Doug laughed. "You know, when you came back here, I was surprised," Doug changed the subject avoiding a topic he knew they need not discuss.

"How so? I always thought I was an open book."

"An open book? You? Hardly. I had no idea how you would react when I told you about the plot with Sadie and Sandy to put Mike in charge to save the slough and protect our interests here at the ranch. I didn't know you were a member of the High Mountain Conservation Club and actively interested in the pet projects of a wildlife preservation group. I pictured you as a highflying jet setter comfortable with your extravagant life style, thoughtless about saving our natural habitats. I never thought you would understand our motives."

"Never judge a book by its cover. But that's not fair either. I admit I was surprised when you told me the story of how you, Sadie and Sandy put your plan together. I pictured you as a cold, insensitive land baron, a tough guy who would never take care of Sadie like you did. She wouldn't have survived all these years if you hadn't looked out for her."

"Well, I guess there's a lesson in there for both of us. You never really do know someone until the chips are down."

"Sure, if you're going to judge that book, you'd best read every page before you make up your mind or express an opinion. I did understand your motive and agree with what you did, but I shudder that Sadie burned up in her cabin. I can't stop thinking about it."

"That's not what happened. Sadie didn't die in the fire."

"What? She didn't? What happened?"

"Sadie died quietly in her sleep. She just didn't wake up one day. Unfortunately, Ivan found her. He was upset and came to me right away. He didn't know she was gone, but I knew, so I sent a couple of guys down there to help him move her body out of the cabin. We buried her in the slough. I told them to burn down the cabin so everyone would think she died in the fire. I didn't want them to find her body. Hell, Amy, I couldn't bear to think about having an autopsy and a burial in a cemetery. You know what would have happened if we had turned her body over to the coroner. That would have created a sensation."

"You're right about that. You couldn't let them get their hands on her body."

"Besides, I knew she wanted to be buried in the slough. Just like *The Big One*."

"How could you do that? It's all wet out there and the water table would cause a body to float to the surface, like bayou country."

"We used a shallow grave and then built a mound over it and covered the mound with rocks. We found a shaded spot in the slough on a small, elevated hummock. It looks like an island. We buried her next to a sabal palm. You'd never find it unless you knew what you were looking for and knew the exact location."

"She was like a mother to me. Will you take me there sometime? I'd like to go."

"Sure. You and I and Ivan will go."

"It looks like Ivan has already turned in for the night. I thought he stayed up late reading." Amy was looking down at the rooms toward the end of the horse barn where they had set up his home at the ranch. "His light is out."

Doug already had noticed the missing light. He knew on a moonlit night like this, Ivan would be down in the slough. Doug turned his gaze to the new flower garden Amy had planted along the side of the house soon after her return to the ranch. The last of all the flowers had been rooted up.

"You're going to be mad at me," Doug confessed.

"Mad? Why?"

"Your new flowers are all gone."

"Yes, I noticed," Amy said as she looked down at the ruined garden. "I'm not mad. What do you suppose got to my plants?"

"Hell, I don't know. Some creature from the slough, an armadillo, a wild pig, raccoons, who knows. Probably some night animal."

Suddenly, a long, low wailing cry came from the direction of the slough and seemed to echo across the lake.

"Did you hear that?" she asked.

"How could I miss it?"

"What do you think that was? You know the slough. If anyone would know that sound, you would. I've been away too long. I don't remember hearing anything like that."

"I can't say for sure, but it might be a Florida panther," he said, hoping she would accept his explanation.

"A Florida panther? There are panthers here?"

"Sure."

"I didn't know the panther was found north of the Everglades."

"Trust me. I've seen them here."

"We should tell the park people. They may want to spread the word. More people may want to visit the park to see the panther."

"I don't think so. There are some things best kept secret."

"Why? Spreading the knowledge that the panther is here would help draw attention to the park."

"That's exactly the problem. You don't want everyone to know everything about the slough."

"Why not?"

"Well, hunters for one reason. There are always those singular hunters that want to bag a special, rare trophy to hang out by the fireplace as an ego builder, especially when they know it's not legal."

"Oh, yes. I see your point. You're wise, Doug. You know all the good secrets about this place and how to protect them."

"No, I only know a few of its secrets, only Sadie knew them all."

Again, a long sad cry came from far out in the slough.

"Do you remember when we were kids you used to tell us about how fabulous creatures lived in the slough? Sometimes they were giants, or dwarfs or elves, other times you told us they were the only living dinosaurs and occasionally little green men from Mars who crashed in the slough. The only similarity in the stories was that all of the creatures were hiding from us in special secret places."

Doug chuckled. "Yes, I remember my stories," Doug said, smiling.

"Maybe that's what we're hearing, one of your mythical creatures. It sure doesn't sound human."

"A toast then," said Doug, raising his glass in the air.

She touched her glass to his.

"To mythical beings," he said with a grin and a twinkle in his eye.

"To mythical beings," she said as they emptied their glasses. "I don't know about you, but I'm exhausted. I've had a long tiring day and I'm turning in for the night. Do you know there was one good thing about your childhood creatures?"

"And what was that, my dear sister?"

"They were always gone when I woke up in the morning," she said as she put her empty glass down on the tray next to the wine bottle. "Good night, dear brother." She turned and left the room, closing the door behind her.

****

Doug heard the cry again. This time it was longer, a long, low piercing wail. He turned his reading lamp off, crossed the room and opened the sliding glass door to the veranda. The moon had risen higher in the night sky and its size had shrunk down to about the circumference of a quarter. For some time, he stood in the doorway, staring out towards the slough.

He was not the only one to hear the cry from the slough. On the patio across the way, the shadow of a man stood at the edge of the thick vegetation. The moonlight danced over his shadowy figure as the gentle breeze caused the leaves and Spanish moss to flutter across the light. Doug always noticed this shadow when he heard the cry. The man stood faintly visible in the flickering moonlight that filtered down through the Spanish moss hanging from the branches of the ancient live oak trees. The cry had disturbed the sleep of that man as well, so much so that he, too, was drawn to the patio as it had done so many times before. This time he did not hide in the shadows of the slough, but was caught in the light of the full moon. The man stared back in the direction of the veranda where Doug was standing.

****

Did the man know? Did the man understand? Even though this man was much younger, he was like a father. The man had unselfishly provided work, shelter and food, yet he was sure the man expected him to live his life in the man's world. He had tried and he had lived there because it was important to take care of his mother. But now she was gone and for the first time, he was free to live his life as he chose.

How could he tell the man about his feelings? How could he explain the difficult decision he now had made? All he knew was that he could not continue to live his life in two worlds. He knew he had protected the slough and that made his decision now possible. Would this kind man who had been like a father to him understand his decision? He only hoped that this decision would not hurt the man he loved and admired. Slowly he stripped his clothing from his body so that he stood naked before the light of the moon. The gentle caress of the wind across the hair on his chest and back ran exciting sensations up and down his spine, awakening his mind to his new life. With the light of the full moon, the man standing on the veranda could not miss seeing his actions.

Everything had always been done to make him feel like he was one of them while he knew in his heart that he never could be. The man had protected him when he was younger from the ridicule of the other children. He had tried so hard to make him feel comfortable, to fit in. But it really didn't work. Did the man understand that he did not belong here? He had controlled these feelings out of respect and love for his mother, but now she was gone.

Again there was the call from the slough, lower, more quiet now, but the same call. It was time for him to go. There were tears in his eyes as he looked up at the man standing on the veranda in the moonlight.

As he watched, the man nodded. Was it true that this surrogate father, this man who had befriended him for so long and helped him bury his mother and stayed with him to comfort him at her graveside understood what he was about to do? To erase any question, the man nodded again and raised a glass in what he knew was a salute. His heart jumped. The man understood. He was free. He could now follow his inner urgings without doubts, without second thoughts. He no longer had to worry about his mother or the feelings of the man. He could be who he was.

As if to reassure him, the man raised his glass again. There was another muffled cry from behind the trees. He looked again at the man on the veranda. Wiping the tears from his eyes, he turned toward the comforting shadows of the trees and dense undergrowth of the slough. He would never look back. He would miss the man, but that world was now gone from him forever.

****

"Good night, dear brother," Doug raised his glass in a final toast. "Be well. Be free."

Chapter Twenty-six

Epilogue

A year had elapsed since the recording of the deeds from Sadie Sutton to Mike Byrne as trustee for Sadie's land holdings in the slough.

Ms. Abigail Abernathy opened her front door in response to the doorbell. "Why Ms. Samantha Eggerton, you're right on time. Please, do come in. I've set us up out back on the porch."

"I picked up your Tampa paper, Abby. I found it on the walk."

Abigail led her guest out to the screened porch and motioned for Samantha to select a chair at the circular table. "Thanks for bringing in my paper. Please have a seat. I've set out peach tea and sweet cakes," said Ms. Abernathy, accepting the newspaper.

"My, my, my, we do have a lot to prepare for next week's meeting of the society, Abby."

"Yes, I know. We're starting early today, so we should have plenty of time."

"Now that the funding has finally come through for the restoration of the abstract building, we have a lot of things to add to the agenda."

"Yes, ma'm. I have the committee notes right here."

"Oh, wait. Before we start, I brought three copies of the Palmetto County Gazette and the Brandon Times that contain articles I thought might be of interest to you," said Samantha, sliding a thick manila folder across the table.

"Why, thank you so much for thinking of me," said Abigail, as she poured them each a cup of tea. The gentle aroma of peach filled the air. "There was some confusion over my renewal subscription for the Gazette so I've missed almost three weeks. Frankly, I miss the local paper. It's my eyes and ears. I love the local paper; I find so many things going on around here that don't appear anywhere else. Unfortunately, I'm going to be out of touch on the local scene for a few more days. I'm told everything should be straightened out by next week."

"Yes. You told me over the phone," said Samantha, taking a sip of tea. "Oh this tea is lovely. Peach, my favorite." After pausing to take a bite out of one of the sweet cakes, she continued, "Well, Abby, a person in your position needs to know everything that's going on."

Abigail opened the folder and picked up the top newspaper. "Yes, yes. I thought you'd like the peach."

"Why yes, I do. Oh, I highlighted the articles I thought were important by circling them with a yellow felt tip pen. That should save you a little time."

"So I see. I appreciate your thoughtfulness."

The first highlighted item on the back page circled an advertisement in the current edition of the Gazette dated two days earlier. The article filled half the page. The advertisement announced the book: *A Personal History of Palmetto County*, published by the Palmetto County Historical Society. Pictures of the co-authors, Abigail Abernathy and Mike Byrne, were prominently displayed in the ad. The article referenced the fact that the authors owed much of their material to the late Sadie Sutton and to Doug Williams of the Circle T Ranch.

"I personally approved the proof, Abby. I hope the format's all right."

"It looks fine to me. In fact, it's perfect. I could not have done a better job myself. It should help sell a few copies of the book and help fund the society."

As much as she enjoyed seeing her name in print, Abigail turned to the second newspaper article from the Brandon Times, dated several days earlier. The article appearing on the front page marked for her attention described the settlement of a lawsuit, which had been filed by the federal government against the state. The plaintiff claimed that a large part of the Seminole Indian River Slough was navigable. The federal government sought to gain control over the area. According to Doug Williams, the paper's source for the article, and material witness for the state, the case had been settled out of court, and the federal government had executed a disclaimer of any interest in the property. Abigail nodded approvingly as she read it.

The second article, also on page one of the same edition, described a second lawsuit. This action was filed by the State of Florida against Mike Byrne, as trustee of the Seminole Indian River Slough. According to the article, the state claimed title to a large part of the slough on the basis that the land was swamp and overflow lands, and thus belonged to the state. According to the defendant, Mike Byrne, the parties had reached a settlement. Mr. Byrne was quoted as saying that he had executed a quitclaim deed conveying title to the State Department of Natural Resources on the condition that the land would be used for a state park. The deed, he was quoted as saying, included restrictions that prohibited the use of the land for hunting, fishing, logging, mining or any other commercial venture. In addition, the deed clearly stated the land was to be preserved in its natural condition and become a wildlife refuge. According to a representative of the state, the grant would make up the largest state park in Florida, and one of the largest non-federal parks in the country.

"Mike really did the right thing," said Abigail, looking over at Samantha. "I'm proud of him."

"Yes, everyone seems to agree. The word around town is that the state would eventually have won the lawsuit. All of us are so proud of what he did. Now the public can enjoy that land as a state park and the birds and fish will be protected."

"Oh look, the article continues, Billie Fleetfoot was appointed unanimously by both the Seminole Tribes of Florida and the Miccosukee Tribes as the Seminole Commissioner on the Park Preservation Committee for the new Indian Bend State Park."

"Yes, isn't that nice. He did give such an informative talk at our meeting last year. I think it's wonderful that the Indians are working so hard to help restore the swampland and the natural watershed throughout Southern Florida and the Everglades. Such an important project."

"I agree. Maybe they can fix the mistakes the government made years ago when they started to drain the swamps."

The final article that appeared in a week old edition of the Gazette included a quotation from Mr. Harry Friedman, the newly installed president of the Palmetto County Archaeological Association, a not-for-profit corporation of both professionals and amateurs interested in archaeology. According to Mr. Friedman, the local association abandoned its excavation in the Seminole Indian River Slough where it had been digging at what was reputed to be a small Indian burial mound. According to Harry Friedman, the local association had abandoned its efforts at Indian Bend after three months of meticulous digging. His crew failed to find any bones or artifacts. He went on to explain that the results were not totally unexpected due to the extremely acidic nature of the soil. Acidic soil generally makes the discovery of bone and other organic material extremely unlikely.

Ms. Abernathy smiled briefly after reading the articles and placed the papers back into the folder. "That's a shame," she said, looking up at Samantha.

"What's a shame, Abby?"

"To find out what was in that mound, they needed to find something tangible. They found nothing. Now we'll never know anything about it. It appears the acidity of the swamp dissolved anything of value."

"If they didn't find anything in the ground, there's nothing of record, Abby. I guess the true history of the mound will remain a secret forever."

"Well, that just shows that Mother Nature wins over time. There's a lesson there for us all, over time, everything is reduced to the basic elements so they can be recycled back into nature. Whatever was there, if anything, has been reduced and recycled." She paused and then continued with a new thought, "I'd like to bring all these articles to the next meeting of the historical society, since most of our members know Mike."

"I don't see why not."

"I wanted to run the idea by you before I went ahead. As the new chairperson of the election committee supporting Mike's bid to run for Clerk of the Court, I would like to take advantage of the opportunity to put in a good word for him."

"Go ahead. I see no harm in that. We're proud to have him as one of our outstanding citizens and a member of the historical society. Besides, I think the articles are all of historical interest. The advertisement for the book is, of course, our own and totally appropriate to inform the attendees at the general meeting. I think this book will be a good fund raiser for the society, too."

"Mike had to deal with some very powerful people in those lawsuits, and he handled himself remarkably well. I think he'll make a good County Clerk," said Abigail, as she paused to take a sip of tea.

"Yes, I agree," said Samantha. "I believe he will."

About The Authors

Jon C. Hall graduated from Purdue University, Lafayette, Indiana, and Indiana University School of Law-Indianapolis. He was admitted to the Bar in Indiana, Illinois, and Florida.

He specialized in real estate law, practicing in Indiana, Illinois and Florida. Due to health reasons, he retired from the active practice of law in 2000, teaching law courses to paralegals at Essex County Community College in New Jersey where he lived with his sister until his death in 2004. He maintained an active interest in nature, environmental issues, and archaeology, formerly a member of the South Florida Archaeological Association, the Florida Anthropological Society, the Roebling Chapter of the National Society for Industrial Archaeology, and The Write Group in Montclair, New Jersey.

Barbara D. Hall graduated from Wittenberg University, Springfield, Ohio and obtained a Master's degree from The Ohio State University, Columbus, Ohio.

She was a consultant in the pharmaceutical industry, specializing in Food and Drug Law, and maintained a New Jersey Real Estate License; investing and managing real estate properties. In retirement, she assisted her brother during the last few years of his life writing and editing books, sharing interests in photography, sailing, nature, and archaeology.

Barbara is a member of The Write Group in Montclair, New Jersey and the International Woman's Writing Guild.

Other Publications

BOKURU, by Jon C. Hall, edited by Barbara D. Hall, AuthorHouse, Bloomington, Indiana, published June 2005.

ADAM'S EVE -A Handbook for the Social Revolution; ECOA and the Story of Adam and Eve; by Jon C. Hall, J. D., and Barbara D. Hall. AuthorHouse, Bloomington, Indiana, May 2006. Barbara was awarded 1st in the state of New Jersey at NJ Federation of Women's Clubs Achievement Day for the cover design; and Foreword Magazine's Silver Award for Book of the Year 2006 for Independently Published work in Family and Relationships.

visit our website: www.ournaturematters.net

Printed in the United States
201558BV00003B/55-72/A

9 781434 338532